# Reign or Shine

## The Forged Flower Saga
### Book 1

Coriana Hope

Reign or Shine: The Forged Flower Saga, Book 1 by Coriana Hope

Cover Art: Rebecca Frank

ISBN: 979-8986181110

*My first book is for my first sibling, my first reader, and my first supporter. Thank you, Connor.*

# Part 1

*"You are the light of the world. A city set on a mountain cannot be hidden." Matthew 5:14*

*"He who plots evil doing—men call him an intriguer." Proverbs 24:8*

# Chapter 1. Party Crashing

*Once upon a time . . .*

That's how my story was supposed to start. That's how SnowWhite (my mother), and all the other royals in every kingdom, everywhere in Clystopia, thought it would start. Everyone except me. I always figured it would start with someone screaming.

"Aaaaaaahhhhhhhh!!!!"

I twitched, looking up from my hands resting idly on my lap. The maid at my door looked the same as she had the time she walked in on me climbing the canopy on my bed—horrified, scandalized, and repulsed. A black, leggy dot dangled in the doorway in front of her.

"Relax," I said, getting off the futon and walking over. "It's just a spider."

*'Tis naught but a spider.*

My last tutor's nasally turkey gobble of a voice resonated in my head, even though she had finally given up on me and quit three weeks ago. She'd stayed longer than most, though, and since it was summer, my parents hadn't hired another one. As if I didn't have enough annoying voices constantly rebuking me out loud. I didn't need hers popping into my head too.

I scooped up the little spider, who was hardly more than a speck, and took him across the room to my balcony, releasing him over the railing's edge. He floated away, free of the confines of the stone castle. It was raining, and I hoped the little guy didn't drown. Could spiders drown? I didn't know.

I returned indoors but left the balcony doors open. I wasn't supposed to keep them open when it rained, but I liked rain and the fresh breeze that came with it, especially today.

"I beg your pardon, Your Highness," the maid, Brenna, said. "I am terribly frightened of spiders."

No kidding. "Don't worry about it. Do you have a message for me?" I asked, even though I already knew she did, and what it was.

"The King and Queen have asked me to escort you to the carriage that awaits in the courtyard. They are preparing to depart for SeaCrest, and wish to arrive well before the parade."

I swallowed. I'd been ready to leave for an hour, but I hadn't wanted to drag myself into the carriage sooner than I had to. I'd begged my parents, Queen SnowWhite and King Orrluxe, to let me skip the birthday parade and garden party that were being held for the neighboring princess. They would represent our kingdom of Agaedith better without me. I would likely end up doing something to embarrass them in front of all the other reigning monarchs and heirs. But my mother insisted I participate because practically every royal family would be attending, and it would reflect poorly on us if the only Clystopian heir that didn't show up was the one who lived only two miles away.

"I'll be down in a few minutes. You can go," I said. I didn't need to be *escorted*. I could find my own way out of the castle, thank you very much.

"If it is all the same to you, Your Highness, perhaps I can accompany you anyway? The Queen was particularly adamant that I should stay with you."

"Fine, I'm coming." Rolling my eyes, I returned to the balcony and latched the glass doors. Grabbing the pair of pristine white gloves on my cherrywood nightstand, I opened my shoe closet and shoved my feet into a pair of silk slippers. Today was definitely not a high heel day. No day, in fact, was a high heel day. Sticking a random crown from the crown cabinet onto my head, I spared a longing glance toward my bed—and the entrance to the secret passageway hidden beneath it—then strode from the room as Brenna bowed me out.

I led the way across halls and down staircases of cold gray stone that no amount of lush red carpet, richly colored tapestries, or sparkling gem statues could disguise. The walls seemed to press closer around me every minute. I preferred to travel *within* the walls, through the multitude of hidden passages that twined through the castle and grounds. My mother didn't know about them. She was too concerned about dirtying her dresses to scoot through dust and cobwebs. When my dad was a young prince, he'd gone exploring as I did, but he was too regal and kingish to do that anymore.

Surprisingly, the servants didn't know about many of the passages either. Or if they did, they rarely used them. I filched snacks from the kitchen or a book from the library anytime I wanted. I escaped the castle when I was grounded or spied on my parents' royal conferences. The conferences were usually boring, though. I overheard lots of news and gossip from the servants, much of which was about me, my parents, or other royal families in neighboring kingdoms. They complained about us a lot. Technically, I could have them beheaded for that, but the way I saw it, that wouldn't make them like us more.

My mother eyed me as I descended the main staircase to the entrance hall. She languished on a gilded bench along the edge of the wall, but her fingers tapped the elbow rest impatiently.

I looked nothing like her with her hair "as black as ebony," skin "as white as snow," lips "as red as blood," and a facial expression as pathetic as a hurt puppy. I'd inherited my father's stormy eyes as well as his brown hair and golden skin. Neither of them had passed their personality to me, which was a puzzle I'd yet to solve.

When our eyes met, SnowWhite rose and called to me by my full name, Chrisithia. I clenched my jaw. She knew I disliked being called that. She did it just to irritate me, since I'd irritated her by arriving ten seconds late. To everyone else, I was Chris.

As soon as my toes hit the bottom step, SnowWhite commented on my poor choice of footwear. Slippers made of silk should not be worn on rainy days, which I should know by my age. My crown did not match my dress—had I not noticed? And I should have picked out a necklace, because my neck looked ever so bare.

My jaw stayed clenched. In all other ways, though, I tried to look repentant. If my eyes glazed over or my mouth turned rebelliously downward, she'd notice and be all over me for that next.

Apparently, my mother had endured a rough childhood. Both her parents died when she was young, so she was left alone with her sister

RoseRed and her grandmother. When she grew older and married, she also lost her first husband, and then had to deal with her evil mother-in-law, who was out to kill her. Luckily, my dad, who happened to be a handsome prince, rescued her from a magical slumber by awakening her with a kiss.

I couldn't help but think that if I had been her, I would have stolen the stupid mother-in-law's magic mirror, started a revolution with the dwarves, overthrown the evil queen, and left the prince out of the equation. But maybe that was just me.

After finishing her rant, SnowWhite floated out the door, her swishing skirts barely fitting through. My father sent me a stern look before trailing after her.

Already frustrated, I took a deep breath before stepping outside. It looked like the weather would be gray and drizzly for hours. If I didn't have a stupid parade float to ride around in, I would have gone for a walk in the orchard. Sloshing through puddles of muddy water until my dress was waterlogged and my skin more wrinkly than a dried apricot was fun, and it was an excellent way to aggravate my parents. I hoped the parade would be canceled due to everyone complaining about ruining their hair.

I turned my face up to the crystalline droplets, but a black umbrella popped up over my head, blocking them. I frowned, turning to see who was preventing my small mutiny: the butler. He was far too proactive for my liking.

Huffing, I walked briskly toward the waiting carriage so that he had to hurry after with the umbrella to keep me from being soaked. Instead of following the path, I cut across the grass. My silk slippers felt like sponges on my feet, squishing through the greenery.

One of the carriage horses snorted as I came up.

"Hi, Stormy!" I greeted the black horse with a friendly scratch on the mane before the butler could advise me against it. Stormy's stall was next to the stall of my own horse, Snowy. My white gloves turned wet and hairy, but my perfectly pristine mother would be irritated, so I didn't mind.

Ignoring the butler's arm held out to assist me into the carriage, I leaped inside nimbly. My father followed, leading my mother by the arm. They'd fallen behind me when I took the grassy shortcut. The two of them seated themselves across from me, still holding each other's hands.

SnowWhite brushed her voluminous amounts of clothing out of her way. Unfortunately, that meant they were now in my way. Flailing underneath a sea of my mother's skirt train, ribbons, and cloak, I gasped for air.

"Help!" I squeaked. They ignored me. I doubted they would even care if I met my end through skirt suffocation.

Disentangling myself with some difficulty, I hung halfway out the window to get some space and escape the heavy scent of my mother's apple cinnamon perfume.

The ride was over quickly, but unfortunately the rain finished even faster. By the time we reached Castle SeaCrest, sleepy sunlight streamed over the sandy beaches and made the sea sparkle like freshly cut diamonds from Agaedith's dwarf mines. I scented a salty tang in the air much nicer than any perfume. Even the smell of rotting seaweed was an improvement.

Though I was used to living surrounded by thick deciduous trees, I liked the openness of the ocean. I enjoyed the expansive view and feel of the wind, and I wondered what would happen if I stowed away on a ship and set out on an adventure, leaving all royal foolishness behind. The sea was a place for dreaming. It amazed me that only two miles away, the sandy soil gave way to rich loam that allowed the familiar woods and apple trees to grow around Castle Agaedith. Some folks believed that a powerful but benevolent sorcerer had cast a climate spell over the beachside kingdom because he wanted somewhere warm to retire, but no one knew for sure how or why the environment changed so suddenly.

Along the coastline, servants prepared parade floats, making last minute adjustments and helping royals with costume details. Our carriage stopped beside a float decorated with realistic-looking apple trees heavy with ripe red fruit. The driver opened the door, and my parents stepped out. When I tried to follow them, the driver slammed the door in my face. Okay, then. I would stay there.

The carriage lurched again, taking me to a separate float. It had apple trees as well, but the boughs were covered in pink and white flowers. The driver finally let me get out, but as soon as I did, I was attacked.

The float designers and their assistants dragged me behind a screen and grappled with my hair until I felt as if I had none left. One maid peeled my waterlogged slippers off my feet and held them between one finger and a thumb, her lips curling in disgust. Another maid shoved a pair of pastel pink kitten heels on me. Then they undressed me to my corset and petticoats and tossed a pink, floor-length dress stitched with real, freshly picked flowers over my head.

Even the flowers were pink! That worst of colors stalked me everywhere. Since I was a princess, it was a difficult hue to escape. I would have drowned in pink gowns, decorations, and accessories by that point if I hadn't thrown a fit when I was four and trashed all my possessions of that color. Since then, any new pink items given to me were immediately regifted or shoved into the recesses of my closet.

But what could I do—insist I be allowed to wear the dress I'd arrived in? Even though I was a royal, I had very little control when it came to my wardrobe—or my diet, hobbies, lessons, responsibilities, or schedule, for that matter.

A bell sounded, and the servants ushered me onto the float and then abandoned me. It was too late to take drastic measures. I would have to settle for the thin pink garment and hope the flowers didn't decide to wilt off me, leaving my clothing full of holes. Who had designed such a dress anyway?

A band started up, playing an unfamiliar romantic tune with violins and a harp. It created a questionable ambiance for a parade. Presumably, there would be lots of people shouting and clapping. A more spirited song would have set the atmosphere better.

Though the floats ahead of me had already moved away, following a path along the coast, I wasn't prepared when the ground beneath my feet took off without me. After nearly falling over and flashing a crowd of onlookers in the process, I managed to grab a tree branch above my head. It cracked, but held long enough for me to regain my balance.

Whoops! I considered what to do with the broken branch. Taking a quick glance around to make sure no one was watching, I tossed it to the side. Unfortunately, I hadn't seen the assistant who was still standing there.

"Sorry!" I called as it bonked him on the head. Oh yes—the parade was off to a great start.

After the brief excitement was over, though, it became monotonous. I turned to the left. Hey, people! I waved and smiled. I turned to the right.

More people! I smiled and waved. I refrained from picking my wedgie because everyone was watching. And so on. But that was okay with me. I didn't mind boring. I could entertain myself quite easily.

Being in a parade was great for people-watching. Since everyone was in a crowd, no one thought anyone could be watching them. Most commoners wore darker colors that didn't stain easily, like green, brown, gray, or black. The shopkeepers stood out because of their blue and purple attire. They had more money to spend on clothes than the fishermen and fruit gatherers, and more reason to look nice. But overall, the SeaCrest economy seemed like it was adequately supporting its citizens, since very few people looked murderously at the parade participants or stroked their hoes and harpoons with longing.

Poverty wasn't unheard of, though. I saw a child dressed in a white sack with *flour* printed on the front. His sister had one that said *potato*. Three women wore hats decorated with dyed seagull feathers in an attempt to look exotic, and their jewelry was made of shells and sea glass. Instead of a toy, a toddler sucked on a piece of seaweed. Sandals woven from palm fronds weren't an uncommon replacement for shoes, and many people's skin looked withered like raisins from years of exposure to constant sunlight.

I kicked off my heels. Three rubies formed a glistening cluster at each of the toes. Were they real? I didn't know. I tore all six off anyway and tossed them toward the children in food-sack clothing. Then I threw the shoes, too, because I wanted to be rid of them. They were heels, and they were pink.

Deciding that I couldn't see enough beneath the fake trees, I climbed to the top of the artificial canopy and looked out over the line in front of me. Most princes and princesses stood on the same float as their parents, but not all. Princess Coralla, the birthday girl, led the parade. She waved from the bow of a magnificent ship, complete with a mast, sails, and rowers. Laomi, one of Coralla's close friends, stood high in an open tower, her long jet-black braid tumbling down and coiling at the base. Her black and gold dress was a stark contrast to the pastel colors most other princesses wore, but she thrust her chin upward with utter confidence.

Smiling and waving a few floats down were my twin cousins, SunGold and StarSilver. If my aunt had given birth to only one child, I would have been named StarSilver. Instead, while sulking about having the name for her baby "stolen" from her, SnowWhite named me after the first random plant she saw after I was born—forsythia. That's how I ended up bearing such a flowery, monstrous mouthful of a name.

One of the coolest floats was a green and gold dragon spouting orange flames. The prince who rode it sat proudly in front of the wings. It was difficult to recognize him from the back, but I thought it might be Lanovan, Laomi's twin brother.

I wouldn't have minded a float like that, but princesses were supposed to get captured and be held hostage by dragons, not befriend them. In fact, the idea that anyone, even a knight, could ride or be on good terms with a dragon was absurd. Maybe Lanovan or his parents were trying to send some sort of political message.

I sighed, swishing a fly away from my face. The little bugs were getting annoying—they kept buzzing by my eyes, blocking my vision. One landed on my sleeve, but as I was about to swat it away, I froze. What kind of fly had black and yellow stripes? Uh-oh.

When another bee landed on one of the flowers in my dress, I swiped at it without thinking.

"OW!"

Sliding down my perch in the tree, I hit the base of the float with a dull thud. For a few seconds, the bees were distracted and landed on the fake flowers of the apple trees. But before long, they buzzed away, disappointed in the lack of nectar, and came to annoy me again.

Scowling, I gritted my teeth as the poison from the sting pounded through my veins, making my hand throb and burn. Worse, I could do nothing to stop other bees from swarming me. It would only be a matter of time until I was stung again, unless I got rid of them somehow. I scanned my surroundings for helpful items. My only tools were what was on the float: fake trees, fake grass, and fake flowers. Nothing useful for anything except float-making.

On the bright side, there wasn't a stinger stuck in my finger.

"OW!" The situation was getting ridiculous. I strode to the front of my woodland habitat, where two white horses from our castle's stable, Hail and Blizzard, pulled the float. I didn't recognize the driver, but there was no time to waste on a formal introduction.

"I need to get off the float," I told him. "Please pull up, just for a second, and I'll jump down."

"Yes, Your Highness. Of course." The driver nodded, keeping his eyes on the line of floats ahead.

A bee landed on his neck.

"Um, don't—" I tried to warn him, but it was too late. He slapped at his neck, and then jolted to attention as the little beast stung him.

"Ah, ah!" Jerking his head, he dropped the reins. "Tell me, Your Highness, what was it that just bit me? Did you see?"

"It was a bee. I'm sorry. They're all around me because I'm in this dress made of flowers. That's why I need to get off." I grit my teeth as I spoke, not because I was angry, but because the venom stung worse with every passing second.

"A bee. . . a bee! I'm 'llergic to bees, ya know, Your 'ighness." His words slurred together. His hand slumped away from his neck, revealing a red swollen patch, already far bigger than the bee itself and growing larger by the second.

"Do you have an antidote?"

I prayed that he did. I knew one existed, but if it wasn't administered quickly, the man could die.

He patted his pockets with a trembling hand. For a second, he looked confused. The bump on his neck was now the size of a plum. The sucking sound of his breathing told me that his windpipe was closing.

"M' wife. M' wife's got the anniedote."

Before I interpreted what he way saying, he lurched sideways, rolling off the driver's seat to the ground. The drop was taller than I was.

"Sir! Are you okay?" Dumb question—of course he wasn't okay, he was suffocating.

He didn't answer, but picked himself up and careened back toward where the parade originated.

"Help him!" I shouted to no one in particular. Then I climbed into the driver's seat and sat there, stumped. Where had the reins gone? I didn't know how to drive a team, but I knew I needed reins. And fast, because the horses were headed off course toward some crisp, dewy grass. I leaned forward, looking at the path below. Yep, there were the reins, trailing uselessly on the ground.

I brushed at a tickling on my arm unconsciously and yelped when I received another sting. I took a deep breath. No need to panic. The pain from the stings was just making my mind fuzzy. I couldn't stop the horses or steer them, but I could jump off the side of the float and let someone else worry about stopping it. Someone would surely step up and take hold of the horses once they realized the float had no driver and its resident royal had bailed.

I stood, clambering back over the driver's seat. The audience was shouting, "Oh!" "Look out!" "Get out of the way!" and "There's no driver!" No one felt the need to grab the horses' harness and stop them, though.

I prepared to jump. It was a long way down for someone in a dress and bare feet on a moving parade float. I told myself I probably wouldn't get hurt—any more hurt than I already was, anyway. The buzzing from the insects prompted me to hurry. Six fuzzy legs crawled up the back of my neck.

One of the horses suddenly snorted, then shrieked in surprise. I looked back and saw both horses lay their ears back and prance around. A bee had stung one of them, and the other was nervous about what was bothering his friend.

I knew horses. Parade horses didn't spook easily, but all horses usually responded to pain the same way.

I braced myself against the only thing available: a fake tree. But when the horses took off, the tree toppled over, and me with it. I tumbled across the float, desperately trying to grab something before I fell off the back, but everything I grasped was falling too. Crashing to the sand, I rolled to a stop at the ocean's edge. I looked up and watched helplessly as the two horses careened through the parade, jostling floats and making the other horses restless, or in the worst cases, rear and buck frantically. Finally, they swerved too sharply, and the float tipped over onto the beach. A curious wave drifted forward, and then drew back out to sea with lots of new tree-shaped trash to play with. Luckily, it left poor Blizzard and Hail, who were having a hard enough time as it was.

The previously cheering crowd began to murmur excitedly, gossiping, and all the royals in view turned to glare at the person who dared wreck Coralla's birthday parade. Gulping, I glanced back toward my parents' float. Their murderous stares matched those of the others and then some. My mother's white-as-snow cheeks were stained pink with mortification, and I could see the storms brewing in my father's eyes from across the beach. I was in for it.

# Chapter 2. An Experience

Since my room was too far away to send me to, my parents banished me to the carriage. I strode there, bare feet burning on the sand, and whipped off the flower dress before entering. I didn't care who saw me in my undergarments—I was not going to wear that object of torment any longer.

Shut in the dark stuffiness of the carriage, I clenched my jaw, trying to master the pain of five beestings. The burning of the red puffy spots had dimmed to a dull ache, but the constant discomfort made my stomach queasy. I still felt phantom creepy crawlies making their way up my back and neck. The loud buzzing of insects feasting on the flower nectar in the discarded dress just outside didn't help either.

Before lecturing me, my parents had a servant bring me the green dress I had arrived in. Slipping it over my head, I tied all the sashes and ribbons without assistance. Learning how to lace myself backward without looking a mirror was something I'd mastered at age seven. I would never have been able to sneak out of my room at night otherwise.

Once dressed, there was nothing left to do but sit, twiddling my swollen thumbs, and brace myself for the lecture. My mother sat next to me, and my father opposite. Between her vast dress and his broad shoulders, I felt puny.

SnowWhite started the tirade, already in tears. What on earth had I been doing? She and my father had been watching the entire time, mortified, as I ripped apart my shoes and threw them off the float. Then I had engaged in even more destructive behavior as I climbed the faux trees and caused them to bend at unnatural angles. Shameless! As if that foolish behavior were not enough, I had to shove the driver onto the ground, causing him to sprain a wrist! Sometimes princesses had to participate in activities they did not wish to so that they remained in good standing in society. It was time I understood that.

I was relieved to hear that the driver hadn't suffocated from his allergic reaction, at least. Otherwise, she would have accused me of murdering him.

"Mother, I promise I didn't sh—"

My father interrupted me to say that I should not interrupt my mother when she was speaking with me. It was useless to point out that she wasn't speaking *with* me, she was speaking *at* me, so I scowled and stayed quiet. Being quiet was something I knew I couldn't do for long, though.

My father continued where my mother left off. My selfish, immature behavior had to stop. In less than two years, I would have my inauguration ball, when I would begin courting. The year after that, he and my mother expected me to be married. However, a hooligan dressed in finery would acquire no suitors. Something had to change *immediately*. He was tired of waiting for me to become mature and stop disgracing the family.

Their words hurt worse than my beestings. It felt like they were trying to squash me into a tiny bowl too small for a goldfish. No swimming, no jumping, no nibbling allowed—I had to float in stasis, a perfect, live ornament, until they wearied of me or I died.

The parade had been halted for twenty minutes while horses were calmed down and floats repaired, but it wasn't a catastrophe. Why should I be disgraced when I was only trying to protect myself? If that was what repulsed suitors, I didn't want anything to do with them, either.

Defiance of my life's fate lit my anger, and injustice fueled the flames. I let my burning rage get the better of me.

"I didn't shove the driver! Why won't you let me explain what happened? Do you think I go around asking myself, 'Huh, how should I disgrace the family name today?' Things happen. Like today, when I was swarmed by bees. Honestly, the dressmakers must have been drunk when they—"

My father interrupted me again. That was enough, he scolded me. Why had I not informed them of the bees before?

"Maybe because you were too busy *speaking with me* to hear what I had to say."

My father's eyes became dangerous, stormy slits.

I had better curb my sarcastic tongue, he instructed, or I would find it cut out of my mouth.

Not washed with soap, but cut out. Punishments escalated quickly with monarchs for parents.

At SnowWhite's prompting, I showed them the swollen spots on my arm, neck, ankle, and shoulder. The fifth sting was in a place I didn't normally display to the public, so I didn't mention it. My father called out the window for a servant to fetch a cup of ice.

SnowWhite sighed. Once the ice came, she said, we would leave.

"Fine." I wasn't afraid of embarrassment, but I was tired of being around so many people.

No, my father clarified, I did not understand. He and my mother would be leaving. It would be some time before they could show their faces in good society again. I would remain behind to apologize in person to Princess Coralla. The carriage would return for me later in the evening.

I stomped out of the carriage. "Good luck making me apologize when you aren't even here," I snarled, and then slammed the door.

My father opened the door to come after me and have the last word, but I ran. He would have had to run as well to catch up, and that he would never do—it would be unseemly.

Fuming, I ducked around a stone wall and pressed myself against it until the carriage wheels rolled away and I stopped feeling steam coming out my ears. Then I stalked toward the magnificent garden party Coralla was hosting in her family's royal gardens. Without the threat of my parents' condescending eyes watching me, maybe I could relax.

Tea lights hung from the palm trees, and under an expansive sand-colored canopy, several long tables held little heart-shaped hors d'oeuvres, dozens of cookies, mouth-watering fudge, and a ten-layer cake. Frothy soups and fresh crunchy-looking salads waited enticingly at another table, and seafood samplers were at the next. The kings, queens, princes, princesses, lords, and ladies from the various kingdoms of Clystopia milled around, socializing and sipping punch or wine.

Breathing in the sweet smell of food, I headed over to grab something to eat. Nothing cheered me up like stuffing my face. I grabbed dessert first since no one was there to stop me. I could always try some soup or something later if I was still hungry.

Munching on a melty brownie and holding a glass of ice to my neck to sooth one of my stings, I wandered among the guests to blend in, but didn't try to find someone I knew. I wanted to eat, not talk. Besides, everyone I knew either didn't like me or thought I was strange but tried unsuccessfully to hide their opinion by being polite. I didn't mind, because that was the way I felt about them, too. We weren't compatible.

"Hello, Chris! Tell me what you think of my new dress! It's a custom Leather Diamonds, made expressly for this occasion."

I dragged my feet across the sand to my cousins. StarSilver twirled before me, her long blonde hair spiraling outward to smack me in the face. Her dress was too frilly and pink. But all I mumbled was "It's quite nice."

"But mine is better, is it not, cousin?" SunGold said, striking a pose. StarSilver's fraternal twin was the taller and curvier of the two, with golden hair instead of platinum.

Her dress wasn't pink, at least. But the orange hue contrasted poorly with her skin tone, which was the same shade as the inside of an almond. It made her look sickly.

"The silks it was made from were imported from across the sea in Anduralon," she bragged.

I could have told her that Anduralon didn't exist and whatever dressmaker she employed had scammed her, but I just shrugged my shoulders. "That one's nice too."

Neither of them seemed to hear me. "Oh my, look at that prince!"

StarSilver nudged her sister and tilted her head in the direction of a boy about our age, who was sipping punch.

"Oooooh, I see him! That is Arcturus, correct?"

"I believe so. It is difficult to tell in this light. But he has gotten much cuter since the party at Towers back in the spring, has he not?"

"Yes, he has a really fine nose."

"You know who else has a fine nose?"

"Who?"

"Laomi's brother, Lanovan. Is he here tonight? I saw him riding a dragon float in the parade."

"No. I do not suppose you know the reason?"

"What happened?"

"He gave up his entire birthright to his sister!"

"You cannot be serious! What a scandal!"

"I hardly believed it either at first, but it is true. Laomi mentioned it to Ashella, who told Coralla, who I just spoke with five minutes ago. What she said was . . ."

While they were distracted with fine noses and scandals, I managed to sneak away—well, almost.

"Chrisithia! Might I have a word?"

Raising my eyebrows, I slowly turned on my heels to see the original reason I hadn't wanted to come to the party marching over, looking as mad as the bees that had stung me. I sighed. Why certain people insisted on using my full name when they had witnessed my violent reaction before, I would never know.

"Don't call me Chrisithia," I said.

"I will call you what I like," Princess Coralla snapped. A sneer contorted what would have been a pretty face, with tanned skin, sea-glass eyes, and rose-petal lips. Her dress was so froofy that she was in danger of disappearing in it. Though we were close to the same age and our kingdoms were at peace, I couldn't remember a time when we hadn't despised each other.

"This is *my* party, in *my* kingdom, and I cannot *believe* how you have insulted me with your shameless behavior."

I stiffened.

"I graciously invited you, even though you have managed to ruin every other event I have ever held, and this is how you repay me? I stubbed my toe when the parade float had to jolt to a stop to let your runaway horses by. You made me look like an incompetent child in front of my entire kingdom, and that is something I will not forgive easily."

My jaw clenched. I didn't appreciate the lecture from a spoiled teenage princess. "Oh, go rub some sand on it."

She huffed. "How dare you! You are my guest, still here only because I have not requested that the guards remove you. In fact, I am not sure why

I let you remain, when you bring nothing desirable to any social event. You know your personality is the reason no one likes you, right?"

Sparks lit in my eyes.

"And *look* at yourself! Your dress is far too casual for a formal party such as this. Your sense of style is nonexistent."

Criticizing what I wore? Really? The sparks caught, burning up the kindling of my patience.

"Your mother is an inspiring example for you to follow, and yet you never have. My parents and I both agree that it is of no fault of theirs that you are . . . the way you are. All the blame lies with you. You have the potential for great beauty, but you're always playing in the dirt like a commoner."

SnowWhite, a great example? That girl had something stuck in her eyes. The kindling was engulfed, and the flames devoured all that was left. I twitched, trying to contain my emotions.

"And now the incidents today. How selfish can you *possibly* be? You ruined my birthday, and for what? Spite? I have never done anything to deserve the humiliation you forced me to endure today."

My endurance reached its limit. "Hold my brownie," I said to a passing waiter.

"Never, ever again, Chrisithia, will I—"

*WHAM!*

The red that had been building behind my vision exploded. I lost the inner battle with my control and decked her.

"*Now* your birthday is ruined." I smirked at her lying on the ground, watery-eyed and shocked. I enjoyed the sight for five delicious seconds. Then, lifting my skirts, I stepped over her splayed figure.

Retrieving my dessert from the gaping waiter, I crammed it into my mouth and strode off. I was too angry to feel pain anymore, so I tossed my cup of ice to the side. Pulling myself up a secluded tree, I eased onto the garden wall. The party was dull, and I wanted to remove myself from the situation before I did anything else that would be deemed improper. I pictured myself lighting the tablecloth on fire with one of the lanterns, or bumping the cake onto someone standing beneath. I might even somehow manage to break a wine barrel and make a drunken slip-and-slide on the sandy walkway. That would never do. I'd just walk around and explore for a bit by myself until someone came to find me. I'd likely be banished from the kingdom once Coralla blubbered to her parents. King Alaric and Queen Aquanetta doted on their daughter. I had to cool my temper before I could handle another lecture.

Standing atop the wall, I glanced around. No one was watching. I lowered myself on the other side until only my fingertips hung onto the stone, then dropped. I landed in a crouch, then swiftly stood to survey my surroundings. Twenty yards away the sea began, sparkling in the sunset. Palm trees and seagrass dotted the area sporadically, and the breeze carried the free scent of salty ocean to me. I breathed in, enjoying how the flow of the ocean and the cry of the seagulls drowned out the sounds of stilted laughter and clinking glasses from the party.

Off to the left was a wide river, merging with the sea along the coast, and to my right were dense woods. Choosing my path randomly, I headed into the forest.

I hiked along quietly, the life of the greenery pulsing around me, leeching my anger. It was vibrant, with tropical birds singing, ants marching, trees swaying, and the peaceful murmur of the sea in the background. The toucans didn't care what my dress looked like. The howler monkeys didn't care if I was rude. The mosquitoes were quite fond of me, even though I slapped at them harder than I had hit Coralla.

As I made my way through the undergrowth, an unnatural, piercing tune caught my attention. Someone was whistling. Curious, I followed the sound. Who would be out here when all the activity was going on inside the garden walls? Maybe it was a townsperson working late, or a servant escaping the toils required of them at the party.

The noise led me to a tree with a trunk thick enough for a bear to hide behind. Following it upward with my gaze, I spotted a boy. He was about my age, lanky, and he held himself with casual confidence. Old muddy pants and an overlarge, once-white tunic were his only clothes. He didn't even have shoes. The thing that struck me most, though, was that he was so *pale*. His hair was silvery white, and his skin looked almost bloodless. That threw me off for a second. Was he a pixie or an elf or something? I'd never met any humans, royal or otherwise, who looked like him. Curious, I took another step forward, only for my foot to land on an old, rotted branch.

*CRACK!*

I refrained from wincing as the elf-boy stopped whistling and turned his gaze to me. I supposed I would have to introduce myself. But my throat stayed stuck as he continued looking at me, and me at him. I'd never been great at first impressions, and if he decided to put a spell on me because I said something he thought was mean, well, that wouldn't be ideal.

Finally, I cleared my throat. Instead of introducing myself, however, what came out of my mouth was "How did you get up there?" The lowest branch was a good nine feet off the ground.

"I flew."

I wasn't sure whether to believe him or not. The silence stretched on for a few more moments, and then the boy stood and jumped off the branch. At that height, it wasn't a dangerous leap, but a twig caught his tunic and threw him off balance. He tumbled to the ground, landing heavily.

I hesitated a moment, then stepped forward and offered him my hand. "Couldn't you have just flown down?" I smiled.

"Nah, that would have been too easy." He smiled too—a quirky half-smile that revealed a dimple in one cheek. It made his face appear more human and less mythical. "I'm Kedrik," he said, looking up at me.

My heart lodged itself in my throat. His irises were blood red. I started thinking he might be a vampire. They flew, right? I'd never met a vampire, so I didn't know exactly what they were supposed to look like. But I knew they drank blood—human blood.

"I'm Chris," I replied without skipping a beat. If I was going to get eaten, better I faced it and fought, and maybe get a good kick in, than run away screaming and be taken out from behind. Balancing on the balls of my feet, I braced myself for an attack.

"Nice to meet you, Chris. I have a quick question." His tone was pleasant and conversational as he took my outstretched hand and hauled himself to his feet. "Why aren't you running away screaming like everyone else does when I meet them for the first time?"

His comment took me by surprise. Could he tell I was frightened? "It's not like you're attacking me," I pointed out. "In fact, meeting you is the most interesting thing that's happened to me all day. Even if you killed me and drank my blood, it would almost be worth it."

"Your life must be incredibly dull."

"You've no idea. Also, if you were a vampire and wanted to eat me, running wouldn't help. Vampires are faster than humans." I'd read about vampires in a book on mythical creatures I stole from the castle's library. I had to steal it, because my parents thought it included concepts too violent for my tender, feminine mind.

"So you would stand there and let the vampire eat you instead?"

"Of course not. I am prepared to gouge out your eyeballs if you try to attack me."

The boy nodded thoughtfully. "Except you just told me what you were preparing to do, so I can defend myself and then kill you."

I kept my gaze trained on his. "But maybe I just told you that so you would be busy defending your eyes and would leave my actual target exposed."

He folded his arms and lounged against the tree, regarding me quizzically. "That's . . . an interesting way to think."

"Thank you." I wasn't sure if it had been a compliment, but I decided to take it as one.

"Well, you'll be happy to know that I'm not a vampire, and I won't eat you—just in case you were wondering."

"Thanks. That's a relief." I didn't know if I trusted him or not, but ultimately it didn't matter. I was too curious to leave.

"No problem."

"Since you won't eat me, I won't gouge out your eyeballs."

"Likewise relieved." He tilted his head. "Aren't you one of the party guests? What are you doing way out here?"

"I got bored—nothing fun to do after I finished stuffing my face. Plus, I overstayed my welcome. I'll probably be kicked out of the kingdom after what I did." A grin worked its way onto my face. I didn't know why I felt like laughing—what I'd done wasn't funny. I should have been scuffing the ground with my shoe, overwhelmed by guilt. But the light, bubbly sensation wouldn't go away. And my fist still hurt pleasantly.

"You mean wrecking the parade? Yeah, I heard about that. My sister wouldn't stop whining about it. I could hear her from the castle. You'd think she'd relax for once, on her birthday, at—"

"Wait, what? Who's your sister?" I must have heard wrong.

"Coralla. I wouldn't expect you to know me—my family never makes me go to royal gatherings. You can see why." There was no bitterness in his voice; it was just a statement.

I, on the other hand, was flabbergasted. There was no resemblance between Kedrik and the rest of his family. Even so, I couldn't believe that I had never met him before. How could I know Corolla almost my whole life and not realize she had a brother?

"But I've never heard of you, even though you're a *royal*. And you weren't in her parade today, or at the party this evening . . . That's just wrong. It's like . . ." Like they were ashamed of him, so they hid him away. For once, I tried to be tactful and didn't finish the sentence out loud.

"You think? Suits me just fine. They get to pretend I don't exist, and I get to do pretty much whatever I want."

Doing whatever one wanted sounded fun. I would have liked to do that more often, though not at the expense of my existence being acknowledged.

"What is it that you do?" I asked.

"Hike around, climb trees, sword fight, invent stuff—and I play pranks on my sister." He looked like an imp when he smirked, eyes flashing.

I was caught between pity and jealousy. I wasn't allowed weapons. When I was six, I'd chased the servants around with a knife, pretending to be a knight, and since then, my parents had banned me from owning anything deadlier than an embroidery needle. And a sword was, in my mind, the ultimate weapon. Because of the safety hazard, I wasn't allowed to "hike around" either, and climbing trees in a dress was frowned upon.

"Do you do anything interesting for fun?" he asked.

Before I could reply, there was a sudden crashing noise as someone stomped toward us in the woods. I tensed. It was probably a servant, sent to find me. Oh well. I'd had my fun. The worst they could do was issue a royal decree in front of the whole party that I was hereafter banished from the kingdom for the rest of my life or until I was a hundred years old, whichever came last. Nothing to worry about.

It was indeed a servant who emerged from the underbrush. A short, stocky man with beads of perspiration on his forehead shook a dead leaf from his uniform shoe. His black and white clothing matched that of the waiters at the party.

"Ah!" He bowed low upon seeing Kedrik. "Prince Kedrik! Fancy meeting you here!"

Kedrik frowned, aggravated. "Is the whole party coming out to find me, or are my hiding places getting too predictable?"

"Terribly sorry, Your Highness. You see, there's been some trouble at the party. One of the guests attacked your sister and then ran off. We've been searching for her for over an hour, but we can't find her anywhere in the gardens! Meanwhile," he said, lowering his voice, "your sister is having a fit while the nurse tries to bring down the swelling, the guests are beginning to leave, the Queen is either going to behead someone or drop dead of a stroke, and the King couldn't take the stress any longer and has escaped to the kitchens for a hot fudge sundae."

So much drama over one punch. If it were two princes who'd gotten into an argument, everyone would consider it a stroke of fortune that the fight stopped after the first hit. As it was, I'd caused a ruckus—*another* ruckus, that is. If I were smart, I would be getting nervous about the consequences of what I'd done. But I still didn't regret hitting her. I felt quite accomplished. That probably meant I was a horrible person with no conscience or empathy, but at least I was honest with myself. The situation being the way it was, I felt no shame in admitting what I'd done.

"That was me."

Kedrik raised his eyebrows at me.

The man looked too, and an expression of shock alighted on his face. "YOU!" Jumping forward, he grabbed my arm.

"Relax, I'm not going anywhere." I wouldn't run away, but neither would I apologize. I wasn't sorry, so I wasn't going to lie and say I was.

"Let her go, Tom. She's a royal, remember. You can't just drag her wherever you want." Tom immediately dropped my arm and leaped back, as if I was suddenly infested with fleas. "Let me guess," Kedrik went on, "Coralla had it coming to her, didn't she?"

"Only for about five years."

"Thought as much." He blinked. "I'm a horrible brother. I should feel protective of Coralla and despise you, but instead I'm going to shake your hand."

He held his hand out, and I shook it. It didn't feel like a royal hand. It was callused, from sword fighting and climbing trees, probably. My gloves had disappeared sometime over the course of the day, and I felt self-conscious of the soft weakness of my skin.

"Just a head's up, you will probably be banished," he said, "and you might have to pay a tithe for damages."

"I figured as much." One last scene to get through before I returned to my life of confinement. I sniffed indifferently, but inside I almost welcomed the excitement. Coralla had been right about one thing: I was shameless.

Kedrik watched my reaction. "If you like, Tom can arrange for a carriage to wait for you outside the back entrance, and I'll lead you over there. You can leave and no one will know."

Tom did not look too thrilled about that idea. "But the Queen requested that the Princess be brought to her," he fretted.

I was actually in agreement with Tom. "You want to help me *run away*?" I said to Kedrik. "I can't do that—it would be cowardly. Thanks for your offer, but no thanks. If the Queen wants me, she'll get what she asked for."

Kedrik sighed. "I didn't mean to imply you were a coward. I was just thinking of avoiding another confrontation. My mother is mad—she just wants someone to vent her anger on. She can banish you and request compensation perfectly well through a letter."

"She can vent her anger on me all she likes. There are a couple things I need to tell her, too."

Kedrik watched me steadily with a slight crease between his brows, as if I was a puzzle he was trying to figure out.

Clearing his throat, Tom spoke up. "Your Highness, she's a stubborn one, I can tell. I don't think you'll be able to persuade her to like your idea."

"Oh, be quiet," Kedrik snapped, irritated. "You just want the bonus my parents will give you when you turn her in. Fine," he said to me, "do what you want—I can't stop you. My family can get pretty vicious when they're mad at someone, though."

"They can't hurt me." I sounded confident, even to myself.

"I hope so. Well, good luck. Meeting you was . . . an experience."

Like I was supposed to know what that meant. "Uh, same with you." I paused. Then I thought, why not? "You're the only person I've enjoyed talking to all day," I added.

Whirling around, I strode back through the woods the way I had come with Tom rushing to keep up with me. Even before I entered the courtyard, servants swarmed us.

"Keep your hands off me," I warned. "I'm not going to run off."

I heard Tom mumble, "Just remember that *I* was the one who found her."

Soon I and a whole caravan of followers arrived at the gardens, where the Queen, red in the face, was still issuing commands at a shrieking pitch.

"You there! Have you found the little witch that struck my daughter yet? No? Well, hop to it then! And YOU!" The servant under her gaze flinched. "That butter over there is completely melted! A disgrace! Replace it immediately!"

The Queen spouted several other orders before she spotted me.

"AHA! There you are!" She marched over, taking what she undoubtedly believed was a threatening stance. She resembled a ruffled peacock.

"If your parents were here, they'd certainly get an earful from me about how to raise their insubordinate daughter! As it is, I will have a talk with you instead! Now, what do you have to say for yourself?"

"SeaCrest parties are lame, and their hosts are insufferable." One of these days, my bluntness was going to get me killed.

"How dare you!"

"You asked what I had to say for myself, so here it is: your daughter is a conceited brat. I'm not sorry I hit her, and I'll do it again if she keeps running her mouth. That's the only way I can get it through that hollow head of hears that I want her to leave me alone."

The Queen's lip curled. "Impudent chit! You emulate the commoner children, running around like a filthy heathen, and you think to criticize *her*?"

I laughed. "At least I don't believe that the entire realm is graced because of my existence. Just because Coralla is your special, favored child doesn't mean anyone else cares half a sand dollar about her."

I hadn't planned on putting the part about the "favored child" into my rant—it just slipped in. In the back of my mind, I was still indignant on behalf of Kedrik.

The Queen spluttered, trying but failing to think of something to say. My brash rudeness caught her off guard. She'd been expecting me to be cowed.

Taking the opportunity, I leaned in closer. "No matter what you say or do, you can't hurt me, and you can't make me feel sorry. So give up. I'm leaving."

"You are no longer welcome here, girl. I will see to it that my husband banishes you."

I blinked at her. "You can't banish me yourself?"

I hadn't meant for it to sound mocking—I was honestly surprised. But the Queen's carefully made-up face folded in an ugly way, like an old cabbage head.

Before she could respond, I did as I promised and left. My parent's carriage had returned to fetch me, though they weren't in it. Clicking to Stormy and Thunder, the driver guided us out of the courtyard and onto the path home. Cloistered in the darkened cab, I drew my legs close and squeezed my eyes shut, concentrating on breathing evenly.

# Chapter 3. Pranks and Promises

The butler bowed as the carriage drove up to the front door. "Good evening, Your Highness. Their Majesties the King and Queen decided to take a holiday with your aunt, Queen RoseRed."

I knew without asking that my parents' holiday was just that—a holiday away from me and the burden of being my parents. Well, good. I wouldn't have to deal with them for a while.

"They plan to remain abroad until the end of the summer," the butler continued. "So you should stay with Grandmother Rose."

Even better! My outlook on the evening brightened. "Great. I'll go see her now."

"Ah, Your Highness—" the driver spoke up.

"I don't need to be driven, Sam. I can walk." I jumped down from the carriage. "Thanks!" I called over my shoulder as I left, practically skipping.

Dusk had fallen, and the lightning bugs danced to the song of the crickets. They didn't provide much light, so I stepped with care to keep from falling on my face. Wandering down the path, I passed the stables, where my horse Snowy rested in her stall. Poor girl; I hadn't visited her all day—the party had prevented it. Ben, the stable boy, had undoubtably already taken care of her in my place.

I continued to the outskirts of the grounds, just past the castle wall, where a stone cottage surrounded by a haphazard yet loved herb garden sat. Before I even reached the door, warm lamplight streamed over the threshold as it opened.

"There you are, Chris," Grandmother Rose said, enfolding me in a hug. She smelled like basil. Her rosy face crinkled at the corners of her eyes and mouth when she smiled at me.

"My parents will be gone the rest of the summer."

"I know. That means you get to stay with me." She drew me inside, then brushed the flyaway strands from her messy gray bun out of her face and busied herself with some medicinal concoction on the counter.

I entered the cozy home and stood by the plant box in the window, which was filled with more herbs. "Looks like your echinacea is blooming nicely," I commented.

"Thanks. Can you water it?"

She handed me a watering can without looking and let go. I almost dropped it, sloshing water all over the floor. I gave the remainder of the water to the purple flowers, and then knelt to clean the puddle I'd spilled.

"Don't use the hem of your dress," Grandmother said, still facing away. "There's a towel on the hook near the stove."

I reached for the towel, suppressing a smile.

Technically speaking, Grandmother Rose wasn't my grandmother at all. She wasn't anyone's grandmother, but everyone called her that ever since I could remember. When my mother was in labor with me, the midwife was nowhere to be found. Eager to get into the world, I'd started coming a month and a half earlier than expected, and no one was ready. The castle doctor hadn't expected to help with the birth at all and was dancing with the cook in the kitchen, too drunk to walk through a doorway, let alone deliver a baby. My father panicked while my mother, terrified to madness, shrieked with pain. A servant who knew Grandmother for her herbal remedies and calming bedside manner suggested she be called. Grandmother came to the castle, and within a few hours I was born, healthy and screaming. Mother was perfectly fine as well. Both my parents were so grateful, they told her they would grant any favor she wished.

Grandmother had looked fondly at me and smiled. "I'd like to see this little one grow up."

So my parents had ordered a little stone cottage be built on the edge of the woods, just outside the castle grounds, and granted her a small plot of land next to it for a garden. She'd lived there ever since.

As I stood from wiping the floor, Grandmother held out a jar of yellowish salve she'd just finished making. "This is for you. I heard you got stung today."

"They don't feel so bad now, just—"

"Sore and itchy?"

"Yeah."

"This will help."

Taking the soggy towel from me, she tossed it on the counter and tended my stings. She murmured a prayer as she gently smeared the ointment over the swollen red spots.

"May my action and Your power work together to nourish and heal."

She always said that prayer, or one like it, over her herbal concoctions before distributing or administering them.

While she worked, I told her about the dress made of apple blossoms and the disaster it caused.

Grandmother rolled her eyes. "Your dressmakers must never have been out of Agaedith before. I don't think those were apple blossoms. From the sound of it, they were cyreniums, which look a lot like apple blossoms, but only grow in SeaCrest during the summer. Since apple blossoms aren't in season, they would have had to find a substitute. If they had any sense, they would have kept away from a plant they weren't familiar with, especially one that grows in the tropics. There's a certain type of bee that only pollinates cyrenium flowers. The bugs were probably having a field day with so many of their favorite snacks in one spot."

"Field day is one way to describe it."

After she finished daubing salve onto the last swollen spot on my arm, she returned the jar to the counter. Then she planted a gentle, dry kiss on my forehead. "So how did the garden party go? Did anyone bother you about the parade?"

I swallowed. "Coralla did."

She raised an eyebrow, but waited for me to finish the story.

"She kept ranting about how she was so much better than I was, and how I embarrassed her and ruined her whole birthday. She wouldn't let me explain, so . . . I hit her."

A muscle twitched in Grandmother's jaw. She closed her eyes, suddenly looking very tired. We'd talked about this before—about getting into fights and controlling my temper.

"And so, by hitting her, you proved what?"

"I wasn't trying to prove anything. I just lost control. I'm sorry, it won't happen again."

Grandmother snorted. I didn't blame her. It wasn't the first time I'd made the same promise.

"She wanted a reaction from you, Chris, so she could continue saying how inferior and uncivilized you are." She left the implication dangling in the air: *and you gave her that reaction.*

Returning to the counter, she wrung out the soaked towel like she was strangling someone, and then got to work on the dishes in the sink like she was trying to flay the metal off the pots. Unlike most commoners, Grandmother's cottage had indoor plumbing.

"I can't let her talk to me like that," I defended myself. "Then all of them would take advantage of me."

Them. The stuck-up royal heirs who would rule their kingdoms while I ruled mine. This realm was going to plummet downhill fast.

"Not caring what someone thinks of you isn't the same as letting them take advantage of you," Grandmother explained. "Do you know what annoys people? When they're mad at you, and you're unfazed. You just say 'okay, whatever,' and move on. They won't understand why they can no longer affect you, and it will frustrate them more than violence."

I shrugged. "I don't know if I can make that work."

She shot me a weary smile. "You don't have to. If you are truly independent, it will work on its own."

"What's that supposed to mean?"

"Once you build enough self-esteem, you won't care if people hate you, and it will be easier to put up with them."

"Oh." I paused, watching Grandmother continue to scrub the shine right off her dishes. "I really am sorry," I said again. I wasn't lying. There was something about Grandmother that made me want to be better than I was.

Grandmother stopped pumping water and dried her hands. "I know," she said. "To be honest, I'm madder at them than you."

"Them? You mean Coralla and . . ."

"Not Coralla, her parents. Someone needs to teach those idiots how to raise a child."

I stifled a snicker. Grandmother was the only commoner I knew who wasn't afraid to call the reigning monarchs of the neighboring kingdom idiots.

"One more question," she said, putting her hands on her hips. "Are you okay?"

"I'm okay." I said it because it was the truth, not because that's what I thought she wanted to hear.

"Good. I love you, Chris, always. Know that, all right? I love you no matter what."

That word, *love*, warmed me. Her voice offered the safety of acceptance that I received nowhere else. "I know. I love you, too."

Later, after dinner, I remembered something else. "Grandmother, is there a condition that makes people's skin very white, and their eyes red?"

"That sounds like albinism," she answered. "It's when an animal is born without color, making their fur white and their eyes pink or red. No one knows what causes it. Why?"

"Because I met someone today who was like that—Kedrik, Coralla's brother."

I waited for her surprised reaction, but her eyes didn't even widen.

"Not many people have met the prince of the seaside kingdom. Was he actually at the party?"

"What? You know about him?"

"I met him once, many years ago, but I was sworn to secrecy. His parents are self-conscious about their image and like to keep their son and his ailment quiet. I was summoned to find a cure, but nothing is wrong. The boy is perfectly healthy; his appearance is just unusual. But appearance, to many royals, is the most important part of ruling."

It did seem that way. There was so much more to a person, though, than what they looked like. Kedrik seemed like a decent guy, despite his startling looks, but Coralla was both as pretty and as nasty as they came.

I was surprised to realize that I wouldn't mind seeing Kedrik again, and even get to know him better. I wasn't close with many people. Grandmother Rose was the person I cared for most, and sometimes I was sure Snowy could read my thoughts. But Ben the stable boy was the only person my age I saw regularly, and he and I mostly raced horses against each other and argued about which animal was better. It wasn't a friendship. It was a rivalry.

I'd probably never run into Kedrik again, though, since I was banished from SeaCrest.

"I haven't seen him in years—not since his parents gave up on my help," Grandmother went on. "Are they hiding him away?"

"Sort of," I admitted. "He didn't seem to mind, though. I don't think he cares what people think of him."

"I bet you two would get along." Grandmother's eyes watched me steadily.

"Maybe." I shrugged dismissively.

Is that what drew me to him—his independent spirit? Wait, what? I wasn't drawn to him. Not me. Caring about people was dangerous. It inevitably led to rejection, which was why I mostly refrained from the habit.

We talked for a while longer, and then I set up the cot Grandmother kept in the closet for my visits. She tucked me in, and I fell asleep gazing out the window as the full, shining moon bathed me in its soothing light.

An amazing fragrance drifting through the air woke me. I sniffed—oatmeal, with heaps of brown sugar.

Rolling over, I fell off the cot. Luckily, it was close to the ground.

"Gotta take care o' Snowy," I murmured, my mouth still not awake.

"Don't worry about your horse," Grandmother said. "Ben will have already fed her. It's his job, you know. Stick around and have some breakfast, then you can go riding."

I turned around to peer out the window and almost blinded myself. Grandmother was right. It was way past horse-feeding time. There was no point in going to the stables immediately, and I couldn't refuse Grandmother's oatmeal. My stomach was already protesting loudly for its favorite food of all time, so I stayed.

After eating, I helped Grandmother with the dishes, then changed into the riding clothes I kept stashed in the closet. Pulling my hair into a snarly ponytail, I walked out the door. Then I walked back in.

"Grandmother, do you have—"

"In the vegetable bin." She jerked her head toward the crate in the corner.

I pried the lid open, fishing around for the carrot I had been about to ask for. The orange roots were on the shriveled side, so I took two.

"Have a good ride," Grandmother called as I left again. "Come back for lunch, okay?"

I waved a hand to show that I'd heard.

The wind gusted around my skirts as I ambled over the grounds, blowing them around like ship sails, but otherwise the weather was perfect for riding. The ground was slightly sodden from the rain the previous day, though, so I'd have to take that into account and adjust Snowy's stride.

The stables smelled like sweat, hay, feed, and manure. The scent was comforting in its familiar earthiness. As I walked down the aisle to Snowy's stall, the stable hands ignored me. When my parents entered the stable, everyone stopped work to stand respectfully erect as they walked by, but I was there so often that no one would get anything done if they did that for me.

"Have you seen Ben?" I asked a man mucking out a stall.

"Morning, Your Highness. Ben took Big Red out for exercise about ten minutes ago, I think."

"Thanks."

Ben probably hoped to have Red warmed up and ready to race by the time Snowy and I arrived. Then he'd try to pressure me to run her cold.

"Not going to happen," I muttered to myself.

Before I even reached her stall, Snowy sensed me coming and stuck her head over the door. She nickered loudly when I entered her stall as if to say *where on earth have you been?*

"Sorry girl," I said, hugging her. "I would have come sooner if I could. Stupid Coralla and her party kept me away."

Snowy nibbled on my hair, accepting my apology. I kissed her nose. Even though I hadn't brushed her yesterday, her coat still shone a luminescent white. Her mane hung down her neck in soft waves, and she kept all her messes in one remote corner of the stall. I was pretty sure God had mixed up which of us was supposed to be the horse and which the princess.

I held out the carrots I brought for her on the palm of my hand. She sniffed them airily, and then gave me a dry look, as if they were hardly compensation for a whole day of ignoring her.

"Fine then, if you don't want them, *I'll* eat them." I took a bite out of one to tease her.

Flicking her ears indignantly, she reached her head forward to lip the remaining treats off of my hand.

I couldn't imagine a life without Snowy. I came to her stall every time I was upset, and she comforted me with her steady presence. And if she was anxious, frisky, or irritated because of a pebble caught in her hoof or a fly bite, I'd know about it within a minute. We were tuned to each other. This morning she was healthy and pleasant, though bored from being cooped up the previous day.

"C'mon," I said, slipping a halter over her head. "Let's get you ready to race!"

Once fully tacked, I rode her to the racing field. It was more of a dirt path, since Ben and I had used it so many times. The dark brown swath stretched between two copses of trees and extended a few hundred yards. Above, the sky radiated summer brilliance. Besides a few birds soaring high above, the rustling trees were the only audience.

As the wind blew, Snowy listed away from my lead, nostrils flaring as she smelled the fruit from the nearby apple orchard.

"They aren't ripe yet, girl, you have to wait. If I give you one now, you would spit it back into my hand."

Snowy shook out her mane as if to tell me that I was speaking nonsense.

"You know, if you didn't exercise, like, every day, you would be round."

She did not deign to reply.

"What took you so long?" Ben called from the racing meadow, already astride the big red horse. Big Red was not one of the horses I had named.

"Somehow, my bridle ended up in the feed bin, even though I know I put it back on the hook last time I rode."

Ben shrugged innocently. "Probably mice."

"Uh-huh." I didn't pursue the subject. When Ben returned to the barn, he would find his favorite brush dangling from the rafters, easily retrieved unless you had a fear of heights like he did. I'd tell him I saw the mice do it.

That was how our relationship operated. He stole the stirrups off my saddle, and the next day, his boots had no laces. I poured pine tree sap in his hair when he was dozing in the barn, then he placed a dead snake on the lid of the special feed only Snowy ate, and I made a fool of myself screaming and chopping it to pieces with a shovel. We constantly tried to outsmart each other, playing new pranks that were always more cunning than the last ones. It kept us on our toes and prevented us from ever becoming friends. The only unspoken rules of the game were that we never harmed the horses, and I never used my royal authority.

Like I'd predicted, Ben tried to get me to race Snowy cold.

"Red and I have waited forever for you two to show up. Let's go already, or I'm going to have to get back to my shift."

"If you leave, you forfeit the race," I said. "It's not my fault you got here early."

I took the time to warm up Snowy properly, ignoring Ben looking down his nose at us the whole time. I took comfort in the knowledge that he could only do that when he was on a large warhorse—on the ground, I was half an inch taller than him.

Once her muscles were warmed up, I leaned forward to pat Snowy's neck.

"Are you ready, girl?" I whispered. "Ben thinks Big Red can beat you—what do you say to that?"

Snowy snorted indignantly, flicking her tail.

"That's right," I continued, "he's delusional. You're ten times the horse Red is. We've just got to prove it, right here, right now."

My competitive energy flowed into her, and she tossed her head, nostrils flaring. She was ready.

We trotted to the starting line. In absence of a referee to tell us "ready, set, go," I'd fashioned a crude slide with a metal ball at the top and gong at the bottom. I would pull a string, releasing the ball. When it hit the gong, we would start. Ben used to cheat, but then I remarked how he didn't believe he could beat me fairly and he stopped.

"*Finally*," Ben said, trying to get under my skin. He was aware of my temper and how he could use it to distract me from the race. It was the only way he ever won.

I ignored him, yanking the starting string.

*GONG!*

I hardly needed to squeeze Snowy's sides to get her to take off. She leaped forward in a smooth, fluid motion, gaining speed. We flew down the track, two bodies melding into one movement to achieve our goal. Speed, focus, desire, passion. The closer we came to the finish, the stronger our bond. I never felt more alive, more sense of belonging, than when she and I ran together. The air parted to let us through. The wind brought moisture to my eyes, but I didn't wipe it away. The stable boy and red horse melted into the background. They were irrelevant.

Breaking free of the finish line, we slowed and turned together to see Ben and Red finish over three lengths behind us. I raised my fist. We hadn't pulled off a win that huge in a while. Leaning down, I stroked Snowy's neck and promised to somehow obtain a ripe apple for her. She snorted happily.

When I sat up to thank Ben for the race, though, his face was smug.

"You don't have to get so excited. I let you win."

Happiness shattered, my temper went up a notch, like lava rising inside an active volcano.

"Liar! You never 'let' us win. Just because we're better than you and any other horse in the world isn't an excuse to . . . to be like that!"

"I'm not lying. The King and Queen told me to let you win most of the races so you wouldn't feel bad about having a useless horse like her." Curling his lip, he gestured at Snowy.

Even though I knew angering me was Ben's aim, I was incensed. I gripped the reins with trembling hands. Snowy, sensing my agitation, pawed the ground.

"I guess you don't remember that she was the reject foal of a second-rate mare, do you?" he continued. "You wouldn't—you were only a toddler. But I've heard the story from the stable master. He would have dispatched of her if you hadn't shown up at the last minute to see the new foal and fallen in love like a stupid little girl."

The lava in me boiled, rising at a rapid rate. It was one thing to have a bad racing day, but spouting brutal lies about my beloved Snowy was intolerable.

"Of course, everything would be different if you were a boy, but since you're the princess, I have to go easy."

Snowy reared. It was a good thing, too, because it made me concentrate on something that didn't involve images of smashing Ben's head beneath a carriage wheel and feeding his eyeballs to crows. I'd been ready to scream at him that I wanted a rematch—and if he didn't win, I'd have him hanged. Motivation like that would be sure to get him moving, but I had promised Grandmother Rose just last night that I would try to rein in my temper and not let people get under my skin.

I regained my seat and settled Snowy. "Shhh, girl, I'm sorry, I'm sorry. I'm okay now," I whispered, too quiet for Ben to hear.

I kept my eyes on her ears, which kept flipping up and down—a sign she was wary. I couldn't lose it again, not after the incident with Coralla only yesterday. I didn't want to give Ben the satisfaction of knowing he made me lash out in a tantrum. I didn't want to give him that control.

What I wanted was for him to eat his words. I wanted to win—not just the race, but also the battle of insults and cunning we never stopped playing. I was smarter. I was stronger. He needed to acknowledge that.

So, for once, I didn't act first; I thought. If I could trick him into thinking that I was doing what he wanted to do, trap him with his own words to make him look like a fool, or both, that would put me on top.

I looked up at him. Whatever he saw in my eyes made the smug look melt off his face like ice cream off a cone in the burning sun. Big Red skittered beneath him like a flighty yearling.

"I have an idea," I said.

The trees shuddered, and the sun chose that moment to dramatically disappear behind a cloud. It was like I had timed it purposefully.

"I want a rematch," I said, "but let's raise the stakes, because obviously you need something to motivate you." I paused to let the suspense gather.

I practically saw it coalescing in a fog above Ben's head. He was more apprehensive than excited, though. That needed adjusting. I wanted him to want to win.

"If you win, I will owe you a favor. If I win, you will owe me one. You can ask for anything—higher pay, an artifact of the royal family that you covet, a better job, a horse of your own—anything I can grant as Princess Heir of Agaedith, I will give you."

Running a hand through his stringy brown hair, Ben considered my offer. "How do I know you'll follow through? You could deny your promise. I'm a commoner, I have no way to make you pay up."

I squeezed my tongue between my teeth to keep from spitting out the first words that popped into my head. Provoking me wouldn't work today. "I'll keep my promise. And if you lose, you can be sure I *will* make you pay up, so there's another reason to not let me win."

"If I can't gain anything, then maybe I don't want to race." The beginnings of a smirk tugged at the corners of his mouth.

"If you refuse to race, then you're a coward who's afraid that a girl—a *princess*—might be a better rider than you."

He was trapped. Satisfied that he wouldn't leave, I let Snowy canter back to the starting line, not giving the stable boy a chance to reply. My blood pounded in rhythm with Snowy's hooves. My intensity burned, and Snowy could sense it. She was still irritated, flicking her ears back, then forward, and tossing her head. Rage coursed through us both, and soon we were equally high strung and fidgety. That was good. We'd move fast if we were on the same page.

At last, Ben drew Big Red beside us. I focused my thoughts. Destroy. Pulverize. Annihilate.

As soon as the gong sounded, we shot forward. Our reputations were at stake, and we would not lose. There was no feeling of freedom this time. Snowy's thudding hooves and my beating heart sounded in my ears. Our sweat formed streams, and our harsh breath cut the air. Everywhere I looked was red.

The race was much closer than before, but we could still win easily. Ben and Red ran behind us skittishly, hanging on to our tailwind and fluttering like frightened butterflies. Pathetic. There was no mercy in me. My heart was diamond-shard hard. Leaning forward, I urged Snowy to give it all she had, and she responded, speeding up.

What happened next was the wind's fault. My gnarled hair streamed off to the densely wooded side of the meadow and caught on some twigs. Suddenly, my hair was ripping from my head, branches were ripping from trees, and trees ripped me from Snowy's back. The world went upside down. Then, like most things that get thrown, I plummeted to the ground.

I hit the dirt and curled into a protective ball as debris and a squirrel rained over me. Too close to stop in time, Ben and Red thundered past, inches away. To my relief, no hooves cleaved my skull open. When the danger passed, I looked up, and Snowy was already there, nosing me worriedly. She had come back to see if I was all right. Absently, I reached up and put my fingertips on her cheek. The red horse and his rider were victorious.

I stood, using the saddle as support. Nothing appeared to be broken; the ground was damp and soft. I almost wished something had been broken, so my resentment would be drowned in pain.

As soon as Ben saw I wasn't injured, the smug expression took over his countenance again. "I told you girls couldn't race. Typical—your hair *would* get caught in a tree."

As I turned toward him, he must have caught the murderous look in my eyes, because he turned Big Red and trotted away rapidly.

As soon as he disappeared around the bend, I sagged against Snowy. I had been insulted, injured, and then insulted again. My head hurt where my hair was nearly yanked out, and I'd landed on my arm awkwardly.

Grandmother was wrong. I didn't have low self-esteem. I liked me. I suffered because I refused to be the princess everyone wanted me to be. I didn't like her. Unfortunately, being myself made me a pariah.

"Let's go, Snowy," I said, running my hand through her wavy mane. "Somewhere we'll be left alone."

She breathed over my face, fixing her dark pool of an eye on me worriedly.

I couldn't stay there and feel sorry for myself any longer. I had to distract myself by *doing* something. After leaning my head on Snowy's shoulder for a moment, I remounted her. Immediately in front of us was a winding trail leading into the forest. My parents had forbidden me to enter Wild Thyme Woods, and Grandmother's rule was to stay on castle grounds. Because of that, I tried to limit my woodland explorations to once a month. It had been three weeks since I'd been in the forest. That was close enough to a month if I rounded up.

# Chapter 4. Birds of a Flaming Feather

The forest made reality seem less real. I relaxed. Warm and drowsy, the green leaves swayed lazily. Sun streaming through the canopy dappled the ferns covering the ground. Squirrels scampered over fallen logs, and the birds sang overlapping songs. In patches of sunlight, exotic flowers like pink daisies, silver roses, and blue-eyed Susans stretched skyward.

I'd never explored the current path before. It was deer-made, rather than one that servants had cleared for the fox hunting trips my father took occasionally. We followed the thin, twisted route, allowing the forest to envelop us.

The deeper we delved, the more magical it became. Human civilization tended to smother the land's natural magic, but it remained dense in the wilderness—a haven for mystical creatures.

My eyes wandered off the path after a disappearing foxtail, and my breath caught. A tree with glowing golden leaves stood alone in a circle of immaculate grass. Flitting around it were hundreds of tiny multicolored glows—fairies. Their wingbeats were as quiet as a gathering of butterflies, though their movements were more agile. The tree was their home. As I peered closer, I spotted little rooms and a staircase through a hole in the bark.

Mesmerized, I directed Snowy from the trail toward the sparkling miniature kingdom. She stepped quietly, avoiding crunchy leaves and sticks. Tilting her head to the side, she tried to get a better look at them too.

When we drew close, a few of the lacy-winged figures fluttered around my face, allowing me to see them in detail. They were as diverse as humans—some pale, some dark, some thin, some quite a bit thicker, some with long hair, and others as bald as mushrooms. A different colored aura pulsed from each of them, reflecting either mood or personality. None of them was larger than a finger.

The fairies' clothes were woven of natural materials. I spotted flower petal skirts, leaf boots, and berry headdresses. Guard fairies with bark armor flew toward us, brandishing thorn weapons.

I didn't want a thorn nose ring, so I steered Snowy back to the trail. She stepped daintily on the unfamiliar ground, holding her neck and tail high. When we came to a fork, I always chose the left-hand path so I'd know how to come back. Holly, thorns, and fallen logs sprang up more often the farther we went. Bushes tangled with each other and tried to blend Snowy's tail into the mix, but she flicked it out of reach.

A yellow-and-brown-spotted furball darted across the path to a patch of toadstools and began munching on them. Snowy tossed her head in apprehension, but I assured her that the brownie wasn't going to eat her next. As we passed it, suspicious green eyes stared at us, and its pointed ears twitched. Seeing that we weren't going to steal its lunch, the tiny black nose burrowed back into the mushrooms contentedly.

Thirsty, we stopped by a stream to drink. I heard galloping hooves, and a streak of pure white mane and a golden horn glinted in the sun on the ridge above us. Then the unicorn vanished into the brush. Snowy stiffened, but I knew she was more awestruck than afraid. I was dazzled too, even though I wasn't convinced that what we'd just glimpsed was real.

Dismounting, I took a sip of stream water. It was cool, but not icy, and no dead things or mine runoff had spoiled it. It had a hint of peppermint.

I let Snowy drink too, and then we continued. I felt like we were headed *somewhere*, instead of just meandering. Wherever the path ended, it would be an important spot.

A breeze shifted the tree branches. The rustling hiss of leaves was mesmerizing, and I let my eyelids droop. I wasn't paying attention when the air became saturated with hot moisture, bright pink and yellow splashes covered the green foliage, and the undergrowth transitioned to mossy vines. Snowy's hooves thumped over sandy soil.

I jerked my head up when, through the birdsong, I heard a familiar whistling tune. Steering Snowy around a sand elf mound, I turned her toward the music.

As Snowy pushed past a palm frond, I spotted Kedrik once more hanging out in a tree. The previous night, I'd assumed I would never see him again, yet there he was. Next to him sat an eagle-sized bird with feathers shimmering like flames.

Kedrik stopped whistling, and the bird picked up the tune. From the moment it began, I understood that the song belonged to it, not Kedrik. The music drifted over me like flower petals, and I wanted to cry—the good kind of crying. It made me remember watching the sun rise over the apple orchard with Snowy, and finding my first secret passage when I was five, and all the times Grandmother let me play outside in the pouring rain. The memories glowed, reminding me that life could be fun once in a while, and the bright spots were worth striving for.

The bird turned his head, looking directly at me, and stopped singing. I desperately tried to remember the tune, but it slipped away like a dream after the first few waking moments. Only the glowing feeling remained.

I couldn't look away from the creature. I felt like it was searching my soul for something. My eyes began to water because I couldn't blink.

"What's there, Fyre?" Kedrik followed the flaming bird's gaze.

Fyre turned away, and I rubbed my eyes.

"Hey!" Kedrik called, recognizing me. "Chris, right? Good to see you! Um, do you have something in your eye?"

I stopped blinking. "Nope, I'm fine. You do like to sit in trees, don't you?" I said, changing the subject.

"Yeah. They don't mind, though. In case you were wondering, you're officially banished. My parents sent a proclamation to Agaedith this morning." He stroked Fyre's flickering feathers. To my surprise, he didn't get burned.

"I know—I just lost my way. Do you want me to leave?"

It hadn't even registered that I was in SeaCrest until that moment. I'd been careless. If nothing else, the iguanas hanging from the tree boughs should have tipped me off. Would Kedrik turn me in? I didn't get the impression he was that kind of guy, but then again, I didn't know him. At any rate, he would have to catch me first, and that wasn't going to happen when I had Snowy with me.

"No! That's not what I meant. I don't mind you being here—just don't let anyone else catch you. I think the whole issue is kind of funny, actually."

"Yeah?" I'd always felt that everyone took royal protocol too seriously. Only Grandmother had ever agreed with me, though.

He patted the branch beside him. "Do you want to talk for a bit? Fyre can lift you up."

"Sure." Hopefully, since Kedrik didn't appear burned, I wouldn't be either. I doubted that being incinerated by a flaming bird would be a pleasant death.

Kedrik said something to Fyre I couldn't hear. Then the bird swooped down and plucked me off Snowy. I stifled a yelp before realizing it was fun to rise through the air. My feet dangled. A free feeling expanding in my chest made me grin. It was similar to the thrill of racing. Meanwhile, Snowy watched me, unconcerned, while I floated away. Then she walked to a bush to nibble some leaves. Either she sensed I was in safe claws, or she didn't care whether I lived or died. Hopefully the former.

Fyre set me on the branch and surveyed me. If he had eyebrows, they would have been raised. But I suspected that as a bird of fire, eyebrows were a commodity that could never last.

"Thank you," I said, running my eyes over his red and gold plumage. Phoenixes were rarer than finding an ant baked into a chocolate cake. I didn't know much about them. No one did. There were only rumors about them bursting into flame and resurrecting from their own ashes, healing with tears, and surviving off dewdrops for sustenance. I didn't know if any of it was true. They were magical creatures that did magical things and kept to themselves.

Fyre nodded. *No problem.*

It didn't surprise me that he could talk, though it was unnerving how his voice penetrated my mind instead of using sound.

"There's quite a view up here," I said, attempting conversation.

"Yeah. I spend a lot of time here in the woods with Fyre. It's peaceful. Not like in the castle, where there's always something going on and I'm in the way."

"Really? It's the opposite at my kingdom. My parents are gone a lot, so the place is empty except for servants. Even when they're around, nothing ever seems to happen."

"Must be nice." He leaned back against the trunk, clasping his hands behind his head.

"Not really. It's creepy. I don't like to be inside unless I'm spying on people in one of the secret passages."

"You have passages? That's cool. There aren't any at Castle SeaCrest, and believe me, I've looked."

"So what is there to do out here?"

He bit his lip, considering something. Then he nodded. "Well, I could tell you, but . . ." He stood, balancing on the branch. "It would be more fun to show you. If you don't mind hanging out in a kingdom you're banished from for a while."

"Okay!" I didn't have anything else planned for the day.

*Hold on*, Fyre said, spreading his flaming wings.

I managed to grab a claw before he took off, dangling Kedrik and me beneath him. I wasn't sure how a raptor-size bird could fly with both of us, but his strength was impressive. Flapping only a few times, he rose above the treetops effortlessly. I decided I loved flying even more than racing on horseback. It was as if when I raced, I loved it because it was as close to flying as I could get. But riding the air was smoother and faster—rocks, troughs in the ground, and shrubs couldn't impede me. And the risk was heightened. The long drop made me giddy with excitement. It gave me a sense of power I never had when I overlooked the kingdom from a tower. I was a voyager in the best part of the world.

We didn't go far. A snaking silver river slithered beneath, and without warning, Fyre dipped, then dropped us.

Stifling a shriek, I looked at Kedrik, who plunged alongside me with a look of electrifying delight on his face. My stomach lodged in my throat as I fell toward the water.

While Kedrik did a perfect swan dive, I held my nose and hit the water in an ungainly cannonball. The river rumbled around me, swirling possessively as I sank. My dress was light and didn't drag me down much, but it wrapped around my waist. Not good! Kicking, I headed toward the surface. I breached the water and opened my eyes to see Kedrik already bobbing along, doing a back float.

"I forgot to ask," he said, "but can you swim?"

I splashed him in the face, making him splutter.

"Hey!" he protested. "I'm sorry!"

"It's all right. You win—that was way more fun than sneaking around a castle."

"That was just the grand entrance. Come on, I'll show you what's *really* fun."

He struck out for the shore using a powerful crawl, while I ducked under the water to swim after him. My riding skirts swept around me, slowing me down and making me feel like a jellyfish. He reached the shore before I did and proceeded to retrieve a canvas knapsack from Fyre, pulling a long, thick rope out of it. He tied the rope firmly to an oak tree overhanging the river. I hauled my dripping self to shore just in time to see him jump from a lower branch while holding on to the rope and swing over the river until he was completely horizontal. Then he let go, hitting the water with a roaring splash.

I snatched the rope as it swung back. Mounting the low branch, I jumped onto the knot at the bottom of the rope and swung out.

"Aaaaahhh!" Kedrik gave a shout as I let go and almost landed on top of him.

I dunked beneath the water for a few seconds before popping back up to apologize. "I didn't know you were still there!"

"Uh-huh. Sure. You just wanted to get back at me for almost drowning you."

I grinned. "Maybe."

We swam and swung like monkey-fish while Fyre observed from the shore.

"Hey Fyre!" I called. "What happens if you get wet?" Did his feathers just *look* like fire, or would his wings sizzle out if dampened?

*Have you ever seen salt on a slug?*

Yikes.

"So, is it not true that you only eat dewdrops to survive?"

Fyre rolled his eyes. *I'd never seen a bird do that before. Dewdrops are just water. If I ate them, I wouldn't survive at all.*

My brow furrowed. "So what—"

*Fire. I absorb energy from the heat of flames.*

That made a lot more sense than dewdrops.

*You ask a lot of stupid questions.*

"Fyre!" Kedrik scolded. "Sorry about him," Kedrik said, treading water next to me. "He doesn't mean any harm, he's just rude and sarcastic. We don't usually hang out with other people." His white hair was plastered to his pale head, making him look almost skeletal.

I shrugged. "It's okay. I've never met a phoenix before, so I don't know much about them. My questions probably are stupid." I tilted my head. "Can you teach me how to dive?"

His shoulders relaxed in relief. "Sure."

When we were tired of swimming—and I was tired of belly flopping off a tree branch over and over—we sat on the sandy bank and tried to dry out. After a while, we realized we weren't getting any drier because the air was too humid. So we climbed trees, racing. We were evenly matched. Kedrik liked to spend time in trees, and I climbed in and out of my room using the tree next to my balcony almost every day. Not once did he claim that he was going easy on me because I was a girl.

I lost track of time until my stomach rumbled. Grandmother Rose told me to be back for lunch. Judging by the sun, it was way past that time. Whoops.

From my perch in the boughs of a birch, I surveyed the area for Snowy. I knew she wouldn't wander off, and it didn't take long to spot her shining coat among the underbrush.

"I think I should head back," I called to Kedrik in the branches above me.

He clambered down to my level, shaking the leaves. "Already? I thought you said your parents were gone."

"They are, but I'm staying with my Grandmother. She's probably worried since I said I'd be back for lunch. And technically, I'm not allowed in these woods."

"Oh. Well then, yeah, you should go." I was surprised to hear disappointment in his voice. I was even more surprised to find that I was disappointed too. I'd been having fun. With a person.

"So I'm guessing you won't come back, since you aren't allowed?"

I waved my hand like I was brushing a bug away. "I'll be back, as long as I can find the place again." Not being allowed had never stopped me from doing anything before.

"Cool."

We climbed down together and I retrieved Snowy, who was munching on some bushes that were hopefully not poisonous.

"Enjoying your snack break?" I asked her.

Nickering softly, she breathed in my face. I led her out of a burr patch before plucking out the single sticky seed that caught in her mane. She snorted, nosing my dress. The entire front and side of it was covered with burrs. Of course. I ignored them, mounting up.

"See you later, Kedrik."

"See you."

"Bye, Fyre!" I peered into the canopy, trying to catch a last glimpse of him.

*Something is wrong*, he said.

Underneath me, Snowy stiffened, ears laying back. Despite the heat, her pelt suddenly shivered.

"Whoa, come on now. What's bothering you?" I knew better than to ignore her superior animal senses. If something was scaring her, it scared me too. What was it? Bear? Wolves? Woodland dragon???

"Everything is quiet," Kedrik whispered.

There were no more monkeys chattering or birds singing. Even the sloth that had been hanging out on the same branch the entire time we'd been there had skedaddled.

"When there's a tsunami, all the animals move to higher ground," he murmured. "But that can't be it, we're too far inland . . ."

Snowy's shrill whinny pierced the unnaturally silent forest, and the earth unraveled, lashing out at us.

The stoic birch tree we'd been climbing lunged for us, using its branches as bludgeons. Smaller saplings uprooted themselves, spraying earth, and crawled toward us like giant stick spiders. All around, other trees were doing the same, whipping their branches and vines and using their boughs as clubs.

Panicking, Snowy reared, dancing on her hind legs. I held on, but couldn't do much else. I didn't understand what was happening. Trees were trees, not monsters. They grew from seeds to sprouts to massive pillars of wood and stayed put for hundreds of years and then died. At least, that's what they had done until ten seconds ago. Now even the smallest trees were jostling for position to attack.

I used all my strength to bring Snowy under control without falling off. She landed heavily, and I managed to get her turned toward the river. Trees didn't grow in rivers. Maybe if we went swimming, the deranged forest wouldn't follow us.

A mossy, green vine shot out, twining itself around my neck. It forced my head back as it tightened, choking me. Releasing the reins, I clutched at the thick coils. Snowy pranced, not realizing that she was making it worse. I had no weapon, and my fingernails were as useful against the ropey vine as a banana for starting a fire. I opened my mouth to scream, but no sound came out. I was gripping Snowy too hard with my legs. She would run soon, hanging me. No air . . . had to breathe . . .

Spots broke over my vision before the pressure abruptly slackened. Tearing away the loosened plant, I gasped for air. A glint of silver caught my eye, and I looked left to see Kedrik chopping away at the oncoming trees with a sword. Fyre was there too, incinerating branches that got too close. Grasping the reins once more, I forced Snowy toward them.

"GRAB ON!" I yelled to Kedrik, offering a hand.

Immediately he took my arm, swinging up behind me. My decision left us trapped. The trees swayed closer, heedless of the sword and flames nipping at them. Branches whipped about while leaves fell like rain. Completely encircled, I pointed and yelled.

"FYRE!"

The phoenix swooped up, wings crackling with sparks. He knew what to do. A jet of golden fire erupted from his beak, scorching a thrashing tree. So starving were the flames that they raced up the trunk instantaneously, consuming branches, leaves, and vines within seconds. The tree blackened and toppled, sending a shower of hissing sparks airborne. The other trees shied away, terrified of receiving the same treatment. In doing so, they left a small opening. All I had to do was convince Snowy to jump over the smoldering wreck of a tree to escape.

I might as well have asked her to sidle up to the monster plants surrounding us and teach them to ballroom dance. She fought my direction, tossing her head and whinnying shrilly as if to say, *YOU'RE CRAZY! I'm not going near that fire if it's the last thing I do! And it probably would be!*

"Come on, Snowy! I promise you we'll make it! You can do it!" Kedrik and I did our best to usher her forward, but pressure from the reins and kicking didn't work. The gap began to close.

Then Fyre sang. It was only a few notes, but it was enough. The whipping trees slowed, and the dying golden flames brightened, quickening. Despite our dire situation, calm washed over me. Snowy stopped prancing and stood paralyzed, breathing evenly. Feeling like I was in a fuzzy dream, I guided her one more time to face the fallen tree. In a trance, she cantered forward and leaped over the smoldering pile, landing smoothly on the other side. Fyre soared through behind us.

Outside the entrapment, the earth roiled and crumbled as the trees lifted their entrenched roots and swung their branches haphazardly. Noticing our escape, some pulled themselves from Fyre's song-spell and pursued us.

Letting Fyre take the lead, I urged Snowy onward, hoping that we would reach the river before the trees fully regained their awareness. Snowy dodged as a branch cudgel swung past and pivoted away when a thick oak lurched to block her. Footing was horrible because of the shifting dirt, but even though she stumbled, she never fell.

Some saplings lunged at us like hounds, swatting at Snowy's flank. Kedrik hacked at them and tried not to fall off while I sat there, useless. I would have done anything for a weapon—be Coralla's best friend, kiss Ben on the lips—anything. Gripping the reins so tightly I half expected them to disintegrate, I concentrated on guiding Snowy to the river.

It was barely thirty yards away, but Snowy was fighting against the collapsing ground for every step, sides heaving and foam frothing from her mouth.

"Come on Snowy, you can do this! Keep working, keep racing! Just make it to the river, then you'll be done!"

I couldn't hear myself shouting over the groaning and cracking of hundreds of years' worth of timber. A sapling wrapped its pliable twigs around my wrist and tried to unseat me. Kedrik chopped it in half, leaving me with a dangling vegetation bracelet. Another tree tripped Snowy, who plunged headlong before catching herself. Kedrik and I slid forward, and I jarred myself against her neck. With a grunt, she raised herself and plowed onward.

Kedrik pitched sideways while attacking a tree. Grabbing his shirt, I hauled him upright. He steadied himself against the saddle as well as he could. It was obvious he wasn't used to riding. Instead of moving with Snowy's stride, he was tense and resistant, making it harder for them both.

Suddenly, a great creaking sound came from behind us. A tall cypress that ended in a spear-like point hurled itself toward Snowy while another tree blocked our way forward in an attempt to shish-kabob us.

Fyre intervened in a swathe of brilliant light. He hurled a blinding orange ball of flame at the oncoming tree. It caught fire at once, but that didn't stop the angry, dying tree from spearing a charred stick through Fyre's chest. The blazing cypress kept coming, engulfing us in the orange fire as it fell.

Kedrik, Snowy, and I screamed as the flames rushed over us, licking up our arms and legs. I waited for the pain, but it didn't come. The only sensation was that of being tickled by a warm feather. Groaning, the murderous tree died by fire while we didn't suffer a sneeze.

"Fyre, no!" Kedrik dove off Snowy, racing to his friend.

The phoenix floated, paralyzed, while blood poured from his wound, mingling with his feathers. Drops of scarlet liquid dripped onto the ground, then became a constant stream.

With a shrill cry that almost cleaved my skull open, Fyre burst into ruby red flame, falling into Kedrik's outstretched arms. Dropping to his knees,

Kedrik bowed his head as his best friend turned to ash. His shoulders shook.

Fighting emotion, I turned away, hyperaware of the danger closing in. One last tree stood between us and the river. It loomed on the edge of the burning coals, waiting for us to make our move. More encroached, but slowly, as if Fyre's dying note held them at bay.

While Kedrik poured Fyre's ashes into his knapsack, I dismounted and grabbed a handful of coals. They felt like warm, flaky cookies. Walking to the very edge of the protective ember field, I flung the cinders at the last tree. As soon as they hit the bark, they exploded into an inferno. The force of it blew my hair back, but like before, I didn't get burned. As the tree blackened and died, it let out a hissing scream. Then it collapsed, its crumbling body finishing the glowing ember path to the river.

But the coals we stood on were nearly dead already.

"Kedrik, come on. We have to go." He was still dumping handfuls of ash into his knapsack. The trees were closing in again.

"Just a minute."

We didn't have a minute, or even a fraction of one. The coals were fading to black, and the trees were coming. Making a decision, I dropped Snowy's reins and slapped her flank, sending her running for the river. She was smart and stayed on the ember path. I stumbled back toward Kedrik and scooped up his sword. He'd dropped it when Fyre fell into his arms.

A thorn web descended toward him. Lunging, I swatted it away with the flat of the blade. I'd never wielded a sword before. It was cumbersome, but it got the job done.

"Kedrik, now!"

He jumped up, swinging the knapsack over his shoulder. Grabbing my non-sword bearing arm, he raced across the embers. I batted back a few more plants and ran after him, trying not to trip and impale myself. We leaped over a trunk that tried to kneecap us. Sparks splashed into the air when we landed, and the trees flinched away again. Reaching the river, we jumped off the bank.

# Chapter 5. Accidental Slaughter

I struck out toward Snowy, who was swimming in the middle of the river. The water moved sluggishly, and I couldn't touch the bottom. My waterlogged dress felt like someone riding on my shoulders. It hadn't felt heavy when I was swimming before, but now that I was exhausted, I barely stayed afloat. Carrying Kedrik's sword certainly didn't help.

Gasping, I swiveled to survey the shore. Trees clustered at the edge, but none touched the water. I almost cried with relief.

"I guess they don't want to get wet any more than they want to get incinerated," Kedrik commented.

"Yeah," I agreed, but I lacked the lung capacity to say more.

"Here, I can take my sword back," Kedrik said, relieving me of its weight. He shoved the entire thing in his knapsack. I was surprised that it fit, but I didn't have the energy to comment.

"Thanks."

Even without the sword, I struggled to keep my head above water. Unlacing my boots, I offered them to the river. Then, loosening the ties on my dress, I slipped it over my head. I'd rather be seen in my underskirt and corset than drown. I was about to let the dress sink, but then I had an idea. I tied the sleeves and neck together to block the holes, then swept the skirt over my head to capture a bubble of air. Voila. Instant flotation device. Using it to support my weight, I continued toward my horse.

Reaching Snowy, I fished around for her reins. Her ears were flipping back and forth again, and she was showing the whites of her eyes. I murmured to her softly, laying a hand on her neck. She was scared, and maybe hurt, but not panicky. I'd never asked her to swim much, so I didn't know how long she could.

"We need to get back to land," Kedrik said, voicing my thoughts. "Let's see if the trees on the opposite side of the river are possessed too."

I nodded and swam after him, leading Snowy with one hand and holding my dress floaty with the other.

"You think the trees are possessed?" I asked.

"That's what Fyre told me." His lip trembled at the mention of his friend. "He didn't know what was doing the possessing, though. Just said it was something powerful that shouldn't exist. We probably weren't the targets of the attack either—just in the way." Swallowing emotion, he faced away.

"If that's the case, they didn't need to try so hard to kill us," I grumbled.

We reached the opposite shore to find that the trees there were possessed as well. The ground was cut up from roots tearing themselves free, and branches swayed in warning when we got close. I bit back a shout of frustration. I couldn't afford to waste the energy. My shoulders, arms, and thighs burned with fatigue. Swimming wasn't something I did often.

"Okay, so we have to find somewhere without trees," Kedrik said, staying practical. "You want to try upstream or downstream?"

"Downstream. There's no way I'm swimming against the current."

"Good idea." He looked as tired as I felt. Or maybe he was mourning Fyre. His eyes weren't as piercing as usual, and his mouth was set in a straight line.

We swam for what seemed like a few more years. After a while, my dress floaty deflated and sank.

The river curved back into Agaedith, but the trees didn't thin. I was about to let the river have me so I could take a nap when something bumped against my leg. Praying it was a log and not a river monster trying to tenderize its next meal, I picked up the pace. Snowy and I had started to lag behind Kedrik.

"What lives in this river?" I asked when I caught up.

I'd been swimming in it for fun for the past two hours, but the question hadn't occurred to me then. That part of the river had been clearer, and Fyre had been watching over us. Now we were exhausted and struggling to keep our heads above swirling brown murk.

"Um . . ." He mumbled something unintelligible. "Fish, turtles, some harmless water snakes—that's about it."

"You're a really bad liar."

"I know. Just . . . don't worry about it, all right?" He glanced back, and I saw fear twisting his face.

With every kick, I expected to hit a crocodile, piranha, anaconda, or some other horrible monster that would bite my feet off.

Finally, we found a spot.

"There." Kedrik pointed to a place where the rock-covered bank sloped steeply. A dark hole marked the mouth of a natural cave, eroded from the constant passing water.

"Let's go."

Sodden and exhausted, we dragged ourselves to the cave. The entrance was sandy and flooded with several inches of water. The sun only penetrated a few feet inside.

"You don't think anything lives here, do you?" I asked. I watched Snowy for any sign that she scented danger, but her head hung low, and she favored her left foreleg.

"I doubt it. It's too wet. But I'll go first with my sword, just in case." Drawing the weapon from his knapsack, he stepped into the cave.

For a second, I remained in the knee-deep water, apprehensive. Then something brushed my bare ankle, and I jumped onto a rock, hauling Snowy with me.

"It's okay, girl," I said, more to myself than her. "We'll be able to rest soon, and I'll check out that leg."

Snowy flicked her ears to show that she'd heard. We plunged into the darkness after Kedrik. Near the entrance, water still swirled around our feet in a shallow pool, but there wasn't enough to hide some creature that might want to eat us. After half a dozen steps, the cave sloped upward, allowing us to walk on dry sand.

"Kedrik, are you there?" My voice cracked with fear.

"Yeah. The place looks clear. There's a dry ledge over here big enough for Snowy to stand with us, if you want to come over."

I led her toward the sound of Kedrik's voice. Something lumpy and soft gave way under my foot with a cracking noise. I jumped into the air in surprise, hit my head on the ceiling, shouted, landed on the same lumpy stuff, and then ran three steps until Snowy's reins ended and soft sand cushioned my feet again. I choked, gasping in the dark and trying not to hyperventilate. Snowy stomped her feet, snorting. Then she let out a shrill whinny that echoed around the cave. She was as spooked as I was.

"What? What happened?" Kedrik demanded from somewhere up ahead.

"I'm fine. We're fine. I just thought—nothing." I gathered my terror and shoved it away.

Calming myself with a deep breath, I let my trembling muscles relax even as Snowy screeched again. I knew that her panic was a warning, but I couldn't figure out what was wrong until I stopped panicking myself.

The reins jerked out of my hands as Snowy bolted. Her hooves pounded over the sand, then splashed through the shallow water at the cave's edge. She was gone. I was too surprised to even shout after her, let alone chase her down. And I didn't want to step on soft things that squished and cracked under my stockings again.

For a second, I stood alone in the dark. "Kedrik?" I called.

"Yeah?" His voice trembled as much as mine.

"We can't stay here. Snowy sensed it was dangerous and ran."

"But where else can we go?"

Good question. If I returned to the water, I'd sink, and if we went up the side of the slope, we'd be in the trees again. I squeezed my eyes shut, trying to control the despair suffocating my thoughts. "Let me think."

I had to find Snowy before she became even more injured. And to do that, I had to not die. The trees wanted to kill me, so I had to stay away from them. But were all the trees possessed? I doubted it. That would have to be one powerful magic spirit. Fyre told Kedrik we weren't the targets, either. We'd just been in the way. So maybe we were far enough out of the way now. Was it worth the risk to check?

Feeling my way along the cavern wall, I headed back toward the entrance, checking every step to make sure nothing but sand was underfoot.

I felt better once light illuminated my steps again, but I didn't leave, still feeling indecisive.

I started when something touched my arm.

"It's just me," Kedrik said. He stood beside me and stuck his sword in the sand. His damp white hair stuck up all over his head because he'd tried to push it out of his eyes.

Hissing a breath through my teeth, I tried to compose myself, but I couldn't get rid of the feeling that something else dangerous was about to happen. Snowy wouldn't have taken off if it was safe. I wished Kedrik would pick up his sword again.

I had just enough time to catch my breath before the wolves came home.

A pair of gleaming yellow eyes met mine at the cave entrance. Transfixed, I stared as a rough muzzle, shaggy legs, and grayish black pelt seemingly materialized from the rock. The massive wolf was the size of a pony. Riding it would be a bad idea, though, since it looked like it would consider me a snack instead of a passenger.

Seven other wolves followed behind the black one. They were of average size, and didn't carry themselves with the same intelligent ferocity the black one did. Clearly, the big one was the alpha. The others glanced between him and Kedrik and me as if they wanted to eat us but weren't sure if they were allowed. The alpha glared at us, licking his lips.

"Why do I bother hunting when I could order delivery?" a gravelly voice snarled.

Did the alpha just talk? My skin felt like centipedes were crawling over it. I backed away from the wolves slowly. I glanced at Kedrik for confirmation that I wasn't going insane.

"A Speaking Wolf," he breathed. Drawing his sword out of the sand, Kedrik retreated with me into the cave's impenetrable dark.

"Not only can I speak, I can hear you too. And I can smell your fear. So you can quit trying to hide it."

The alpha bared his teeth at me in a feral grin. I clenched my jaw, glaring back at him. He couldn't tell me what to do.

"I thought only cats played with their food," I snapped. "If you're going to eat us, then do it already."

Anger helped me bury fear.

The alpha tilted his head, considering me. "You're in a hurry to die," he commented. "But maybe I'm full. Maybe I like watching you squirm like newborn rats. Maybe I want to catch my breath after almost getting killed by the forest." The alpha flicked his tail, brushing a twig off his flank.

"Before you eat us, you should know that we're royals," Kedrik spoke up. "I'm prince of SeaCrest, and she's Princess Heir of Agaedith. We'll be missed. Once they find out you killed us, you won't live."

The wolf twitched his whiskers dismissively. "Best not leave any evidence, then."

A skinny gray wolf suddenly yipped, running in a circle in excitement. It darted toward us. Kedrik raised his sword. I stood there stupidly because I didn't have a sword to raise.

A growling bark by the alpha sent the gray wolf slinking back to the entrance, tail between its legs. The alpha bared its teeth at it, and the gray wolf cowered, nosing the underside of the alpha's jaw in apology.

*Not yet*, was the obvious message. The alpha wanted to play with us. We could stall, then. But for what? No one was looking for us. The alpha could probably smell the truth if we tried to lie and say a rescue party was on its way.

The alpha sniffed the air. "The smell of the horse excites the pack more than your human scent. It's too bad it didn't stick around for a few more minutes. Now I'll have to get the betas to chase it down and haul it back to the cave."

Flicking his ears, he gave a low growl and tilted his head toward the river. Three wolves stalked off, panting in anticipation. The remainder of the pack clustered around the alpha, giving him fawning looks and wiggling their haunches in excitement. The alpha stood with all four paws planted, ignoring the attention, and fixed his gaze on Kedrik and me, his prey.

I bit my lip, regretting ever venturing into the woods. I knew I wouldn't live past the next hour, but if I thought there was a chance of survival, I would have promised myself to never set foot in a forest again.

The alpha opened his mouth slightly, tasting the air. "Wolf blood. Why do I smell it? Did you kill the omega to hide in the cave? He was supposed to be watching the newborn pups . . ."

I shuddered when a grotesque thought crept into my head. Newborn pups. Things squelching under my feet. I looked down and saw red and brown streaks across my white stockings. Clapping both hands over my mouth, I tried to stifle my scream, bending almost double with the effort. Despite my dire situation, guilt pierced me—that, and disgust.

"Chris?" Kedrik didn't take his eyes off the wolves, but there was concern in his voice.

I raised my head enough to look at the alpha again as a deep earthquake of a growl rumbled toward me. His hackles spiked, making him look as big as a grizzly. As I met his eyes, he drew his lips back in a snarl. His teeth were as long as my fingers. He wasn't a wolf playing with his food anymore. He was a parent who wanted vengeance on the creatures that murdered his young.

One of the other wolves howled into the sky. The alpha snapped his jaws, creeping forward.

"Run." I whispered the word hoarsely before grabbing Kedrik's arm and taking off into the cave.

The sand sucked at my feet, slowing me down. I felt like I was sprinting in place. The sound of splashing water reverberated off the cave walls as our pursuers jumped through the flooded entrance after us.

My only thought was that the wolves had to have an emergency exit in case the place flooded. The trick would be finding it. In the dark. With wolves chasing us. And no weapon to defend myself.

Kedrik's arm slipped from my grasp, but I heard him panting beside me. I closed my eyes to run, because seeing was useless. Reaching out an arm, I felt against the wall as I ran so that I wouldn't slam into it.

But even with that precaution, running in a cave in the dark was bound to end badly. I didn't feel the jagged strip of rock jutting out of the ceiling in time. I slammed into it headlong, bounced off, and fell on my back.

Dazed, I tried to get up, but only managed to flail around like a beetle stuck on its back. Then a paw the size of a plow horse's hoof pressed against my chest. Claws dug into my corset. They weren't sharp, but I knew that dull knives hurt the worst.

I smelled the alpha's breath. Rancid meat, puke, and heat combined to form an odor that almost killed me by itself. I couldn't see his dark pelt against the black of the cave, but I knew his jaw was inches from my face, readying itself for the kill. He could see me, though, so I clenched my fists and stared straight ahead defiantly, even as my heart threatened to dance right out of my chest.

I wasn't brave—my mind just couldn't grasp that this was real. So I used that to my advantage in my last moments and made no sound, no effort at all. I waited.

A shout rang out. "Let there be light!"

Suddenly, the whole cave lit up, and every whisker, hair, and bit of plaque on every tooth of the wolf in front of me became stark. I almost peed myself. Almost.

The alpha blinked against the light, but didn't flinch. Barking once, he bent forward and closed his jaws over my neck. Before he could clench his teeth together and rip my throat out, a stream of golden stuff, like a liquid sparkler, zapped against his face. Yelping, the alpha leaped away from me. Another liquid sparkler hit him in the side, and he danced sideways. Other wolves were leaping around like they were part of a ballet as lights hit them in the face, burrowed themselves into their fur, or stung their paws.

"Don't stop!" a woman's familiar voice urged. Silhouetted at the entryway, she waved a glowing wand, directing the light that attacked the predators.

I scrambled to my feet and ran once again. Kedrik's feet thudded close behind. We reached the back of the cave. The flashes of light were too intermittent to help with visibility, but a fresh breeze tickled my skin, so I followed the direction it came from.

"This way!" I tugged Kedrik's shirt, guiding him.

I dodged around a boulder, and suddenly spotted light filtering through thick, leafy undergrowth that blocked a back exit. Without slowing, I threw myself against the vines, determined to break through.

Rough wood scraped against my skin, but I pressed on. What were a few more scratches after the day I'd had?

The brush gave way, and I tumbled into a mossy glade. Landing on my hands and knees, I fought to catch my breath. Rushing through after me, Kedrik brandished his sword, preparing to fight if the trees lining the clearing encroached.

But aside from leaves rustling as the summer wind blew through the branches, the forest remained quiet, the roots of its giants firmly planted.

"Are you okay?" Kedrik asked, sinking to his knees.

But he'd let his guard down too soon. A snuffling growl came from the cave's exit, and the skinny gray wolf leaped through.

"Look out!" I shouted.

Standing, Kedrik managed to half raise his sword before the wolf tackled him. Both of them thudded to the mossy ground.

Swaying, I got to my feet and ran to help. All I could see of Kedrik was a single sock sticking out from beneath the beast's pelt.

The wolf on top of him lay unmoving, and its yellow eyes were glazed over. I had to dig my hands into its matted fur and shove with all my strength to get it off him.

I gasped, horrified, when I saw Kedrik's body. His entire shirtfront was soaked with scarlet blood. His eyes were closed, and no movement came from his chest. I felt his bloodstained wrist for a pulse, but I'd never felt someone for a pulse before, and I wasn't sure how to do it. At least, that's what I told myself when I couldn't feel anything.

Suddenly, he took a huge breath, blinking open eyes that matched the blood pooling around him.

"Thanks for getting that thing off me. I thought I was going to suffocate. Wet dog smells terrible!" He wrinkled his nose. Then he noticed the look on my face. "What?"

"Look at you! You have blood all over you! How are you still alive?"

He glanced down at his shirt, grimacing. "I think I'd feel a slight twinge somewhere if it was my blood."

"Oh." Relieved, I gazed a moment at the inverted wolf corpse. A gaping sword wound split open its chest, and blood and innards oozed out sluggishly like a river of death. I didn't feel sad about this wolf's death like

I did about the pups'. This one wanted to kill us, while the pups had been innocent babies.

My head felt itchy. I reached up to scratch my scalp, and my hand came away bloody.

"Looks like you got a nasty knock on the head," Kedrik said, standing. "You all right?"

I opened my mouth to say I was fine, but something in my stomach suddenly twisted. "Um . . ." I said instead. My eyesight blurred, and I couldn't hear anything except my own breathing, which sounded loud in my ears.

I knew what was about to happen, but I was powerless to prevent it. One of the few things I hated about myself, the thing that turned me into a helpless bunny rabbit, was the sight of my own blood. Nauseated and humiliated, I was helpless against my body's extreme reaction.

Somehow, I ended up on the ground while two people stood over me. One was Kedrik. The other was an older lady with blue, sparkly hair shaped like cotton candy and a dress to match. I relaxed, thinking that even if I was eaten by a wolf in my helpless state, at least they would be able to get to safety. Then I stopped thinking at all.

# Chapter 6. Men Call Him an Intriguer

Someone was wheezing. *In . . . out . . . in . . . out.* I listened to it for a while, until I realized it was me. That meant I wasn't dead. Hooray! When I opened my eyes, I couldn't see much besides a purple ceiling and light filtering in through a window nearby.

How did I escape from the cave? And where was I now? Did Kedrik and Snowy get away, too?

The thought of them sparked my adrenaline, and I bolted upright. Immediately, I felt as if someone were stabbing a pitchfork into my head. My insides convulsed, and I squeezed my eyes shut. Acid boiled up from my stomach, and I puked. A pot materialized in my lap, catching it. Then I dry heaved a few times.

Limbs shaking, I lay back down. All the different words for puke danced around in my head. Throw up, hurl, upchuck, heave, blow chunks, vomit, sick, regurgitate, toss your cookies, pray to the porcelain god . . . The recitation didn't help my storm-tossed stomach.

Once the pounding in my head eased, I tried moving again, slowly. My surroundings were unfamiliar. I was in a poufy bed with soft purple sheets. The rest of the room—the walls, the plush rug, the furniture—was obnoxiously purple. It felt like I was inside an orchid. The afternoon sun poured through the sheer, petallike draperies, lighting the space.

I twisted toward the door when the knob rattled. As my head began to ache again, I winced, closing my eyes.

"It's okay, honey. You're safe now."

I groaned.

"Poor darling. Not feeling better yet? Maybe a sip of water will help."

I opened my eyes just in time to see the woman with blue hair pull a thin rod of light from her sleeve and give it a wave.

"Beside still waters!"

The puke-pot disappeared, replaced by a glass of water. Propping myself on a fuzzy purple pillow, I peered at it suspiciously. Did she just turn my vomit into water and ask me to drink it? After sniffing the cup and determining that it was as watery as any water I'd ever had, I sipped it, rinsing away the taste of puke and mud.

After my queasy quivering subsided, I stared at the person who'd saved me. She didn't look like the type who could take on a wolf pack single-handedly. With her sweeping purple dress adorned with silver stars, a pouf of blue hair, and a heartwarming smile that crinkled the corners of her eyes, she looked like a dotty aunt. At least, she would look like an aunt, if it wasn't for the wings. Shimmering with iridescence, they fluttered behind her, making her hover several inches off the floor.

"Fairy Godmother," I rasped. "You saved us."

Every young royal had a Fairy Godmother—a magical guardian who watched over and comforted young princes and princesses as they made their way through life's trials from birth until they reached their happily ever after. My own was eccentric, but we got along. I hadn't seen her in several months, though, and it hadn't occurred to me that she might have magic powerful enough to escape the wolves.

"I'm glad I made it in time." She patted my hand.

"Thank you. How—how did you know we needed help? I thought you only came when I cried."

"You're not my only charge, honey. There are other royal children I look after too."

"Kedrik?"

She nodded.

I let out a long breath. Kedrik had cried, summoning Fairy Godmother. His practicality and presence of mind had saved us both.

"Are you ready for some food now?" With a flick of her wand, she cast, "Loaves and fishes," and a steaming meal arrived.

Now that my stomach had settled, the scent of grilled salmon and garlic bread intoxicated me. I'd worked up an appetite fighting for my life against possessed trees and angry wolves. But I hesitated. "Where is Kedrik? And what about my horse, Snowy? She ran away a few minutes before the wolves came. I need to find her before they do." If they hadn't already found her. How long had I been out?

"No worries. I transported them to safety, too," she said as she poured me a cup of tea without adding sugar or milk, just the way I liked it. She'd spent enough time comforting me to know. "They're resting and healing, like you. Feel free to go see Kedrik when you've finished eating. He's in the Green Room."

Giving my hand a squeeze, she left. Reassured, I wasted no more time digging into my food. I inhaled the fish, bread, mashed potatoes, roasted carrots, and tossed salad in almost one breath. Even though three different pies showed up on the tray, I skipped dessert in favor of going to find the Green Room. I hoped Fairy Godmother was right and Kedrik wasn't hurt.

A fresh set of clothing appeared when I got out of bed, so I changed out of my slimy, mud-streaked undergarments. Then I departed the overly purple room to search for an overly green room.

The hallway was like a solidified rainbow, with sparkly, multicolored stone walls and a different color decorating each doorway. Fairy Godmother was either very rich or very magical. No commoner had such a lavish living space.

I knocked on a forest green door before entering. I hoped it was the right one, because there were also mint green and lime green doors available. When no one answered, I barged in and spotted Kedrik sitting on a couch eating his salmon dinner. Fairy Godmother wasn't there. The room was furnished like the Purple Room, except—what a shocker—it was all green. Rather than a flower, I felt enfolded in a jungle.

"The food here is good, isn't it?" I commented, plopping into an easy chair near him.

Kedrik nodded, helping himself to the garlic bread.

"I'm glad you aren't hurt." I felt like I'd known him longer than one day. Sharing a near-death experience did that, I guessed.

He swallowed. "Yeah, me too. You. I mean—I'm glad you're okay too. I'm sorry about Snowy, though."

"Fairy Godmother said she's alright." My gaze dropped to the floor when I remembered that while Snowy was safe, Fyre was dead. I swallowed, not sure what to say. Kedrik seemed to be taking the blow all right. If it was me, I would be inconsolable.

Poor Fyre. If it hadn't been for him, the trees would have killed us. He must have loved Kedrik a lot to sacrifice himself for our escape.

"I heard what you did. Crying was a brilliant idea—I wish I'd thought of it."

Kedrik's fork clattered to his plate. "It wasn't exactly a strategy," he admitted. "When Fyre died . . . I couldn't help it. I was overwhelmed." His shoulders hunched, his wispy white hair shading his face from view.

I understood. Just as princesses had certain expectations to fulfill, there were unfair burdens that fell on princes' shoulders too. To be seen crying was social death for a prince. It was considered weak and unmanly. Seeking comfort was okay for princesses and crybabies, but princes had to be stoic.

"Besides," he continued, "it almost didn't work. Fairy Godmother said it took a while to track us once we went into the river. She barely made it in time."

I folded my arms. "Mourning your friend is understandable. I'm not going to complain that it saved my life either."

He looked up at me, lips slightly parted, as if I'd surprised him with my response.

The intensity of his gaze made me fidget. "What?" I mumbled, looking down at myself. "Is my dress on inside out?"

"No. Um . . ." Ears red, Kedrik picked up his fork and resumed stuffing his face.

When finished, he, like me, skipped the pie. "I wish I knew what possessed the trees. I've practically lived in the woods my whole life, and nothing like that has ever happened. Trees are incredibly powerful. It would have to be some strong magic to take control of them."

"It doesn't make sense. That's the scariest part. We can't just live the rest of our lives without encountering another tree, but if we get too close to one, it might try to kill us!" I wondered what the goal of the attack had been, and if it was successful. If the impressive power we'd faced was just a side effect, what kind of force had the trees unleashed against the actual target? And who, or what, was using the trees to attack?

"Oh, good, you're both here!" Fairy Godmother flitted into the room, startling us. Her dress had changed to dark, dappled green. The skirts rippled around her like liquid when she moved.

She alighted in an overstuffed loveseat. "So, how are we feeling, toots?" She directed her question at Kedrik, who looked slightly uncomfortable at being called *toots*.

I stifled a smile.

"Fine, thanks," Kedrik said. "You aren't going to get into any trouble for saving us, are you?"

"I am free to aid you against a mortal threat if it is not your fate to die at that time. It's written in the fine print on page 3,386 of my guidebook, *Rules Regulating Refined Fairy Godmothers.*"

Kedrik snorted laughter that he quickly turned into a cough, but then he started choking for real.

"Goodness me, are you quite all right?" Concerned, Fairy Godmother patted him on the back while I looked away, trying not to crack up.

"Do you know what was controlling the trees?" I asked once Kedrik was able to breathe again. "Or why?" Maybe her magic could give us some insight.

"It's complicated," Fairy Godmother said, wringing her hands.

In adult-speak, that meant she either didn't know, or didn't want to tell us.

"Was it a demon?" Kedrik asked.

"Nooo . . ."

"A sorcerer?" I guessed.

"No."

"An ancient evil rising from past defeat to wreak vengeance on those who thwarted it before?"

Fairy Godmother blinked at Kedrik with owl eyes. "You've been reading too many fairy tales."

"At least *try* to tell us! I'd like to know why I almost died!" I crossed my arms in a huff.

"Well, dearies, the problem is I don't really know. I've been all over Clystopia in my line of work, and oftentimes outside of the realm as well. I've lived longer than I care to admit. I know the energy of all the magical creatures, from halcyons to dragons to hippocampi, but I've never sensed something like that. It's new to me. And new threats are sometimes the worst, because nobody knows what to expect from them." Her forehead wrinkled in distress.

All three of us became quiet. The ticking pendulum of a grandfather clock swung back and forth somewhere, and the wind whooshed against the windowpane.

Trying to reassure her, Kedrik returned Fairy Godmother's pat on the back.

Frustrated, I clenched my fists. "So, it doesn't have a name? It's a nameless evil terrorizing the forest for an unknown reason?"

"I'm sorry, honey. It will take time to track it down and figure out what it is and what it wants. But I promise I will be on the lookout for any information on it."

It wasn't encouraging, but I knew she was offering to do all she could.

"I do have a nice surprise for you two, though!" Like someone lighting a match, Fairy Godmother brightened as soon as the topic was changed. "Rule number 512 of my guidebook allows me to grant each of you a wish due to extenuating circumstances!"

"Cool." Kedrik half smiled.

"A wish?" I'd studied wishes in history before. They tended to cause more trouble than good.

Fairy Godmother misunderstood the tone of my voice. "Yes, just one wish. I'm not a djinn."

I'd no idea what a djinn was, so I decided to stop talking before I offended her.

"There are a few stipulations," she went on. "Your wish must be something for yourself, not a friend or someone you'd like to help, and whatever you wish for must be a physical object. So, for example, you can't wish for someone to fall in love with you."

As if I would ever wish for that.

"But you can wish for pretty clothes, or jewelry, or weapons, or candy, or a pet squirrel."

"Oh." Kedrik looked as glum as a bloodhound. I felt the same way. We were royals—we had all the stuff we could ever want. What we lacked couldn't be held, bought, or, apparently, wished for.

I could wish for a sword, or a bow and arrow, or a spear, or something else to defend myself with. But if I marched into the castle with anything bigger than nail clippers, my parents would hear about it and have it confiscated. Princesses were supposed to hold on to the arm of their father or husband, not the grip of a sword. But . . . if I got caught in a desperate situation, like running from wolves, the wish could be useful.

"Can we save the wish for later?"

Fairy Godmother looked taken aback. "I—I've never done anything of the sort before." She paused. The twinkling smile grew over her face like a plant stretching toward the sun. "I do believe I can manage it. If you'll excuse me, I shall go prepare the wish. I'll be back in a few minutes."

"Hey, wait! Could you do mine that way too?" Kedrik asked.

"Certainly, honey." She flew out of the room, her wings humming like a bee's.

"Good idea, Chris. If something tries to kill us again, it will be good to have a secret weapon. We might even have more than one."

Grabbing his knapsack, he cradled it gingerly before opening the flap and reaching inside. At first, I thought it was speckled gray dirt that he was cupping in his hand. But among the pile of ashes, a tiny flame-colored chick head popped out. Fyre! The little bird cooed, fluffing his shimmering red, orange, and gold down.

"He's all right!" I gasped, surprised.

Kedrik smiled secretively. "Phoenixes are reborn from their ashes."

So that part of phoenix lore was true. Luckily Kedrik knew that, or poor baby Fyre might still be out there among the fighting trees.

"Does he remember us?" I asked.

"Not yet, since he's a baby. As he gets older, he'll start to remember his past lives—I think."

I gazed at the chick. His feathers were slicked to his knobby body as if damp, but they still glowed like lit coals. I stroked my pinkie finger over his head, and he closed his eyes, enjoying the attention.

Fairy Godmother zipped back into the room. Swiftly, Kedrik slipped Fyre back into his satchel. The hatchling was our secret.

"I've done it, dearies! Here's one wish for each of you."

Procuring two pendants, she strung a bit of twine through them and hung them around our necks. Normally I avoided jewelry because it got caught in things and jangled, but that little trinket might save my life one day, so I accepted it gratefully.

As I examined the transparent, tear-shaped pendant, coppery orange color filled it, swirling and flickering like wildfire. When I touched a fingertip to it, it glowed brighter. I tucked the wish into the neckline of my dress. The pendant warmed against my skin.

Kedrik's teardrop wishing gem turned glistening blue-green, like the ocean on a sunny day.

We thanked Fairy Godmother for her generosity and acted suitably awed.

"No problem, dearies. Your pendants are invisible to everyone but each other, so no one will ask awkward questions." Clapping her hands, Fairy Godmother announced, "Now! You should both return home before your parents send out their royal armadas to search for you. Just tell me where specifically you want to go, and I'll transport you."

Pulling her wand from the sleeve of her gown, she began waving it in complex patterns.

"Wings of dawn," she murmured.

A loop appeared and slowly expanded to display a series of places in rapid succession: a turreted stone castle, a mountain range shaped like a bowl, a pine forest, a misty swamp, an underwater coral reef, and a meadow with grass swaying in the breeze. The images were like liquid paints swiftly swirling in midair, and they almost gave me vertigo.

"Well," Kedrik began with a sigh, "I doubt anyone's even noticed I'm gone yet, but I guess I'll go—"

I cut him off. "We'll *both* go to Grandmother Rose's cottage, just outside Castle Agaedith's walls."

Kedrik nodded. "Yeah. There."

Grandmother's stone cottage came into sharp focus within the loop. The wooden door was propped open to welcome visitors and keep the place cool. I took a step forward, but then hesitated.

"Wait, what about Snowy?"

"She will be waiting for you in the barn," Fairy Godmother promised.

"All right, then. Let's go." Snatching his knapsack, Kedrik took my arm and pulled me through. He didn't seem to mind my forceful invitation to my kingdom. In fact, he seemed more excited to go to Agaedith than he had his own home. "Thanks again for the wishes, Fairy Godmother!" he tossed back, but we were already gone.

By blinking quickly against the piercing sunset, my eyes slowly adjusted to the surroundings. There was the cottage, door propped open, just like we'd seen in the portal. An enticing mixture of spicy and earthy scents wafted from the herb garden, and a furious Grandmother was storming over to Kedrik and me with her hands on her hips. I gulped.

"Where have you been?" she asked sternly. Grandmother never yelled, but when she gave me that furious, I-expect-more-of-you look, it was just as bad.

"You always pick the worst times to disappear. I told you to be back for lunch. Then Ben said you went trail riding, which you know isn't allowed. When a tornado touched down over the forest, I thought you were a goner. You're always involved in whatever trouble is nearby."

"I'm sorry." I felt like I said those two words more often than anything else. "I did go into the forest, but I didn't see a tornado."

Kedrik shuffled his feet, no doubt trying to look invisible. Grandmother was intimidating when she wanted to be, and he was part of the reason I hadn't made it back in time.

"Uh-huh," Grandmother said, not believing me. "So, I suppose you got all torn up by falling into a mud hole lined with thorns."

Kedrik spoke up. "It's kind of my fault Chris didn't make it back when she was supposed to. We were hanging out."

Grandmother's worried face softened a bit when she faced him. "Hello again, Kedrik. I don't suppose you remember me?"

Kedrik shook his head.

"I didn't think so. You were very young when your parents hired me. My name is Grandmother Rose. I'm a healer, not anyone's grandmother, but that's what everyone calls me, so feel free to do the same."

"You're *everyone's* grandmother," I corrected.

"That too. Come on inside. You can tell me what really happened while you rest. You both seem worn out."

Kedrik and I exchanged a look, confused. At Fairy Godmother's castle, we had put on clean clothes and ate a huge meal. But now we were back in our torn, dirt-stained outfits we'd been wearing in the forest, our hair was matted and strewn with leaves, and numerous cuts and scratches covered any unprotected skin. My damp petticoats clung to me. We did look suspiciously like a tornado had picked us up, whirled us around, and then deposited us at the forest's edge. My stomach rumbled. I felt like a starving bear just coming out of hibernation.

Grandmother Rose ushered Kedrik through the doorway, but enfolded me in a hug before I could follow. "You'll never know how scared I was. When you didn't come home, and the tornado was sighted . . ."

Releasing me, she said, "Your cousins, Jameson and Philip, were hunting with a few friends from SeaCrest. All the royals in the hunting party disappeared. The pages who returned said a tornado touched down right over their group and swept them up."

I stepped back. The cousins on my father's side were older than me, and we weren't close, but the idea of them being torn apart by a twister was still alarming.

Grandmother peered into my face. "You really didn't see a tornado, did you?"

I shook my head. Despite my many faults, I wasn't a liar. I was terrible at it, so it was easiest just to be honest.

"Where were they hunting?" I asked.

"The forest in SeaCrest, near our border."

The same place Kedrik and I had been. Mutant trees attacking us at the same time my cousins got sucked up into a tornado wasn't a coincidence.

Considered separately, the events might not seem connected, but I felt that they were. Perhaps my cousins and their royal friends had been the objective of the attack that Kedrik and I got too close to.

"You have an idea about something," Grandmother commented.

I was startled at how easily she read my face.

She moved to the side to let me in the cottage. "You can come in now, and tell me about it later." Patting my shoulder, she followed me inside.

I went straight to the closet to grab one of the dresses I kept stashed there and slipped it over my head. I was about to take a seat on the couch when I remembered Snowy. Excusing myself to check on her, I raced back outside.

Opening the squeaky barn door, I entered her stall. Unlike Kedrik and me, she barely looked like she went into the woods at all. I felt along her legs for inflammation and checked her hooves. Overexertion had caused one foreleg to swell, but it was nothing that cold therapy and a few days of rest wouldn't fix. Unperturbed, she nibbled at my hair like usual. When I blew gently into her face, teasing her, she nickered, tossing her head.

"What a day, huh, girl?" I wrapped my arm around her withers, resting my cheek against her neck. "I'm so sorry, and I'm so glad you're okay. No more forest rides until it's safe, I promise. We'll stick to the meadow."

Apart from her gentle breathing, she stood completely still. If she had died, I would have broken. And if it had been my fault, I might never have healed.

Upon reentering the cottage, I almost staggered under the mouthwatering smell of beef vegetable stew. My stomach complained loudly while I reached for the bowl Grandmother poured me. Kedrik set his knapsack close to the stove, and then came to stand by my chair.

"Can your grandmother be trusted?" he whispered. "Because Fyre *really* wants out . . ."

Peeking at the woodstove, I spotted his knapsack hopping around the floor.

"Yes." I smirked. "I think she already knows something's up anyway. Your bag is trying to fly up her skirt."

I grinned as Kedrik whirled around to face a baffled Grandmother.

"Sorry!" Diving, he grabbed the strap before it vanished beneath the folds of Grandmother's apron.

Gathering his precious bundle close, he undid the clasp. The baby Fyre couldn't fly yet, so he rolled out of the bag like a flaming polo ball, sparks flying. Finally able to stretch his little wings, Fyre gave a contented chirp.

Grandmother observed the phoenix with a practiced eye, unperturbed at the luminous orange eyes blinking up at her. "I haven't seen a phoenix in ages," she said. "Come here, little one, I know just what you want."

Popping open the woodstove door, she allowed Fyre to snuggle in among the flames.

Since when had Grandmother been acquainted with phoenix care?

"There you go," she cooed. "I made that fire nice and hot, didn't I?"

The flames caressed and nourished Fyre's twiggy body, becoming brighter and livelier the closer they were to him. Fyre closed his eyes, relaxing.

While we ate our steaming stew, I told Grandmother what happened. As I spoke, her shoulders drooped, her eyes faded, and her wrinkles became more pronounced, like an ancient boulder being eroded by the wind. I didn't twist the story to make it sound less dangerous, though. I didn't need to protect Grandmother—she was the one who protected me. Yes, she was older than most commoners would ever get, but that meant she knew a lot of stuff. I had no doubt she would believe us. She'd just accepted a phoenix, after all.

I left out the part about Fairy Godmother rescuing us, though. One of the rules of having a Fairy Godmother was that we weren't allowed to talk about her with anyone who didn't also have a Fairy Godmother, or we would lose her forever. So I just said we managed to escape the cave, and the wolves retreated after Kedrik killed one of them.

"Before he died," I finished, "Fyre told us that the trees were possessed, and that whatever controlled them wasn't after us. We were just in the way. Maybe my cousins and the SeaCrest Lords were the targets, and the trees were just keeping Kedrik and me away from the real action."

Grandmother's brow furrowed. "It's as good a theory as any. The twister I saw definitely wasn't natural."

"Do you know what creature has that kind of power?" Kedrik asked.

"No."

"So it's a new threat," I said, recalling Fairy Godmother's words.

"Probably. It's safer to assume it's a threat and be surprised if it's not rather than the other way around." Grandmother mumbled something else that I didn't hear.

"What?"

"I was thinking of a quote from the Bible, 'He who plots evil doing—men call him an intriguer.'"

I scowled. "Great, so we've given it a name. Any idea how to stop it before it decides to kidnap more people?"

"Don't use that tone with me. Naming a foe is the first step to defeating it. If something has a name, it is real. And everything real is beatable."

"So, how do we fight it?" Kedrik asked.

"We? An old lady and two royal kids? We can't fight it."

It did sound absurd when she put it like that. But I doubted either my or Kedrik's parents would believe us if we told them that there was an Intriguer running around kidnapping people with tornadoes and using shrubbery to whomp innocent passersby.

"So, what do we do, then? No one will believe our story," Kedrik said.

Grandmother, as always, was practical. "Nobody needs to believe what actually happened. Five royals just went missing. The rulers of SeaCrest and Agaedith won't ignore that. They can strengthen their border patrols, train more recruits, and place more guards on the wall. They might even send out hunting parties or hire extra help from the Knight Orders."

"If it comes after us again, though, shouldn't we know how to fight back?" It only made sense. I'd gotten caught in a battle for my life without a weapon. But even if I had a sword, I wouldn't have fared much better since I didn't know how to wield one. When I briefly held Kedrik's during the fight, I could barely lift it.

"If it comes to fighting one on one with the Intriguer, you're already dead," Grandmother said unhelpfully. "And tomorrow, just in case it comes looking for you, you are staying inside the cottage."

My mouth fell open. "You're grounding me? All day?" I couldn't say it wasn't fair, but that didn't mean I had to like it.

"For your safety, yes."

"Uh, not to be rude, but how safe is a cottage against mutant trees and twisters?" Kedrik pointed out.

Instead of being offended, Grandmother smiled. "You'd make a very good point, Kedrik, if this were a regular cottage. However, I am friends with a sorcerer who put a great many magical wards around the place for me when it was first built."

Kedrik raised his eyebrows, impressed. I caught him giving a sidelong glance out the window to see if he could spot the invisible magic shields.

I hated Grandmother Rose's punishments—that's really what it was, of course. Keeping me safe was only part of her motivation. If she'd assigned me chores, like mucking out a dozen horse stalls, weeding the garden, or fixing the leak on the castle roof, I wouldn't have minded. But Grandmother was smarter than that, so instead I would be stuck in her miniscule cottage, bored and miserable.

At least Grandmother persuaded Kedrik to spend the night. He couldn't trek back home in the dark forest without protection, and it was too late to ask the guards to send a patrol with him.

I set him up in the spare bedroom that I never used before collapsing into my cot.

# Chapter 7. Thuh Sped uv Lite

The next morning, I found myself with nothing to do but stare out the window, willing the seconds of the day to pass faster. I'd made breakfast, eaten, and cleaned up. Morning wasn't even over yet, and I was starting to go stir-crazy. The stone walls were closing in on me. Soon it would be hard to breathe, then I would start to hallucinate, and then probably scream at the phantoms about to eat my soul . . .

I nearly leaped through the roof when Fyre hopped over and nipped my fingers. I almost wished I had, because at least then there would be some fresh air. Instead, I gazed wildly around for a second before settling down and stroking Fyre's warm feathered head.

A floorboard creaked behind us, and I looked up glumly, expecting to see Grandmother Rose with another boring suggestion about what to do to entertain myself. Instead, Kedrik's pale features greeted me. He offered me a hand up, but I ignored it.

"I can stand on my own, thanks," I grumbled, giving a flawless demonstration.

My irritation slipped off him like a raindrop rolling off a leaf. "Don't be mad for the rest of the day," he entreated. "We'll find something to do."

"We? I thought you were leaving this morning."

"Nope. Look outside."

I looked through the window again, actually seeing what was out there for the first time. The sky was an ominous gray, angry clouds churned, threatening to spill, and wind whipped the trees around.

"I can't take Fyre into a storm, so I'm stuck here."

"If you really want to leave, you could take a carriage," I suggested hesitantly. I didn't want him to abandon me to a boring death, but I was in enough trouble with SeaCrest as it was without accusations of holding him hostage added to my list of transgressions.

"The horses might get scared of the thunder and bolt into the woods, or get stuck in mud. I'll just wait it out and go home later, or tomorrow. My parents won't notice I'm gone."

"All right." That was an unexpected perk to my day of imprisonment. "So . . . whatwegonnado?"

It wasn't easy to come up with something. Grandmother only had four rooms in her cottage: bathroom, bedroom, spare bedroom, and the kitchen and living area. There were no passages to explore. Kedrik couldn't teach me to swordfight because there wasn't enough room. We played with Fyre for a little bit while were thinking, but soon the little guy got tired and fell asleep on Kedrik's lap.

I stared out the window again, watching lightning flashes. They looked like huge cracks opening in the sky, and I half expected a different world to dump into ours, *plop*, like an egg yolk. Then came the thunder, sounding like God had eaten marbles and they were rumbling around in his stomach. The noise vibrated the little cottage, but the magical wards protected it from storm damage.

Even when I was little, I had never been afraid of storms. They kept me awake, but only because I loved to watch and listen to their raw power. Now, though, even the strength of the storm couldn't keep me from fidgeting. Maybe because I'd recently experienced something more mysterious and deadly than the crashes of light and noise.

My eyes wandered to Grandmother Rose, knitting comfortably in her rocking chair. I'd sooner gouge my eyes out with the needles than sit hunched over for hours just to make a mitten that I'd lose as soon as I walked out the door.

Kedrik sat with his back to me, rummaging through his knapsack for something interesting. He had his whole arm up to his shoulder submerged, and echoing clangs and smashes came from the depths.

"What are you looking for?" I asked.

Instead of answering, he threw Fyre onto my lap, who woke with an indignant squawk. I watched, amazed, as Kedrik's whole torso disappeared into a bag that looked like it could barely fit one of my pink poufy dresses (the kind my mother ordered for me that I always mysteriously "misplaced," i.e., sliced into bite-size pieces and fed to the fire).

"Here, hold these for a second," Kedrik instructed. He dumped an assortment of random items from his bag on my lap, burying Fyre. Quickly I dug the phoenix out of the charcoal briquettes, grappling hook, ornate but cracked hand mirror, book titled *So You Want to Be a Sword Smith?*, and a vial of eye drops. Fyre's flames looked a bit ruffled, but the bird energetically hopped up and promptly swallowed a briquette. I didn't have time to see if he was choking, because Kedrik began tossing more things from his knapsack, which I finally realized was a magical space-enhancing bag. There was half a loaf of bread (stale, but not moldy); a rusted bronze shield; a pocketknife with a saw blade, screwdriver, lock pick, and other weirder tools; a watering can; a fedora; and a high-heeled shoe. I assumed that the last item belonged to his sister. At last, Kedrik emerged with a triumphant look. He clutched two quills, a bottle of ink, a roll of parchment, and another book with a blurred title.

"What's that?"

"It's a code book. We can use it to create our own personal code, so when I return to SeaCrest, we can communicate without my parents finding out. I-if you want to." He swallowed, suddenly looking very vulnerable.

"That sounds like a great idea." Once he left, we might not see each other for a long time. The thought left me dispirited. With this strategy, at least we could communicate.

Kedrik's ears tinged pink, and he busied himself with flipping through the book.

"A combo of steganography and cryptography is a must," he mumbled to himself. "Systematic transposition is too boring, and scytale isn't good for short messages. A substitution cipher would work well for our purposes, not too complicated or time consuming, but should it be monoalphabetic or polyalphabetic? Or maybe homophonic?" He looked up at me. "What do you think?"

"I don't know what you're talking about."

"Oh, all right. Let's stick with mono then. We can make it harder to decipher by mixing up or misspelling the words before encryption."

"Fine by me."

Scribbling something down on a piece of paper, he handed it to me. "Can you read this?"

Dgrnoas phly fetsar than thuh sped uv lite.

Staring at each word intently, I soon made out the meaning. "'Dragons fly faster than the speed of light,'" I announced. "Do they really?"

"I've no idea. But I'm glad you can read it, because not everyone can. And we would have a serious security problem if we had to spell all the words right, because cryptanalysts could use frequency analysis much easier."

"Do you really think anyone is going to be that determined to decode our letters?"

"You can never be too sure."

I bit back a smile, privately thinking that Kedrik was just having fun by purposely taking this way too seriously.

He handed me a quill and piece of parchment. "Do you want to help create symbols for each letter? We'll need personal symbols, too. That way we don't have to sign our names."

"Sure—I know what my symbol will be." Taking a quill, I doodled a flame at the top of the parchment roll.

"And here's mine." He drew a water droplet with a few waves around it.

Fyre wanted to have a signature too, but he got too excited and burned up the quill, making a hole in the parchment. We decided the hole would be just as good a signature as anything else and put Fyre's name beside it.

"I have a pot of tea here, you two, if you would like some," Grandmother Rose said, pouring herself a cup.

Kedrik passed on the offer, but I poured myself a large cup and breathed in the aroma of chamomile. Grandmother had taught me that it was an herb used to soothe anxiety. Either she was trying to make me quit fidgeting, or she herself was worried about something, like the kidnappings. I wished I could comfort her, but I didn't know what to say.

As I drank my tea, I helped Kedrik form our code while trying not to think about impending doom. We developed simple symbols for letters, times, days of the week, and words we thought we might use often, and then translated our scribbles and notes on fresh pieces of parchment, one for each of us.

"Let's practice!" I suggested when we finished.

I came up with a message: *Fyre wants out of the stove.* I could tell Fyre really *did* want out of the stove because he was pecking on the window and flapping his downy wings. The last time I took him out, though, he burned me, so I decided it was Kedrik's turn.

First, I changed the message to: *Fyre wnats out uv svote.* Then I used our code to finish the encryption.

I exchanged encrypted notes with Kedrik. His read:

Which decoded was: *Grandmother Rose mkeas gud kukyz.*

Translated, it read: *Grandmother Rose makes good cookies.*

She certainly did—but when had he tried her baking? I pivoted to see him snatch another cookie from the tea tray on his way to the woodstove, where Fyre awaited him with an expectant look. Codes were fun! Grabbing a melty chocolate chip cookie, I munched contentedly.

---

The next morning, a suffocating gray blanket of clouds blocked the sun. The sky matched my mood after Grandmother insisted that Kedrik return home with her and a company of soldiers for protection. She forbade me from coming along.

"Does the word 'banishment' mean anything to you?" Grandmother demanded after I wouldn't stop pestering her to let me accompany them.

"Not really. Besides, my parents specifically asked you to keep an eye on me. That will be difficult if you're visiting another kingdom," I pointed out.

"Nice try, but you're still not coming. Just stay in the castle until I return. I'll only be a few hours."

Normally, it wouldn't take so long to ride to Castle SeaCrest and back, but Grandmother planned to take the long route around the forest. She thought it best to avoid the trees until she knew for sure that the Intriguer no longer controlled them.

"Fine," I huffed.

I pet the top of Fyre's head with a single finger. "Bye, Fyre. Maybe next time I see you, you'll remember me."

The baby phoenix cooed like a dove. Nestling him in his knapsack, Kedrik buckled the strap securely.

"Your parents won't be mad at you for staying away so long, will they?" I asked.

"Nah. I told you—they probably haven't even realized I'm not around. Either that or they're having a party celebrating my absence."

I fisted my hands in my skirts. "Well, stay safe. See you later."

"See you."

Once the carriage pulled away, I didn't stay to watch it roll down the road. I didn't go the castle like I was supposed to, either. Instead, I went to the stables to see Snowy. When I opened her door, a bucket of water dumped over my shoulders.

"Gah!"

Wiping droplets from my face, I glared up at the rafters, where Ben had rigged the bucket with a piece of string. It wasn't the worst prank he'd ever pulled. He could have filled it with manure instead of muddy water. I decided to overlook his shenanigan since I didn't have any motivation to think of and execute a trick of my own. More important thoughts consumed my focus. After checking the rest of the pathway for traps, I stepped into the stall.

Snowy blinked at me sympathetically, and then nosed my pockets for the carrots I'd brought her.

"Yeah, yeah, I know—you don't care if I'm soggy as long as your snack isn't."

She crunched her treat merrily, as if to say *my thoughts exactly*. Since I was already wet, I figured I might as well bathe her, so I got more buckets of water, made them sudsy with soap, and washed the dust out of her coat. I curry combed her, brushed her, and picked out her hooves. She enjoyed the attention. I washed and conditioned her mane, combing all the knots out until it fell in cascading waves like a unicorn's.

"There—now you're a real princess's horse."

Too bad she didn't have a real princess to ride her. She would have to make do with me. Saddling her, I led her out of the stable and mounted up.

"Just walking today, girl. We both need a rest."

Taking a calculated risk, I walked her through the apple orchard, where she lost no time in grabbing an unripe apple in her teeth, taking a bite, and spitting it out. She let the rest of the apples hang after that. Up and down each row, we kept a leisurely pace. None of the trees moved without the wind to stir them, and Snowy's ears stayed relaxed and upright.

*Chris!*

"What?" I swiveled in the saddle, but there was no one there. The nearest servant was half a dozen rows away adding fertilizer to the base of a tree, not paying me the least attention.

The unfamiliar voice came again. *We're sorry, Chris.*

"Sorry for what?"

*Chris . . .* The voice didn't sound human. It was whispery, like a ghost.

Snowy was still at ease, but a shiver crawled down my spine. I led her out of the orchard, and the voice stopped trying to speak to me. We walked through the meadow instead, sticking to the middle, away from the forest's edge. The trees seemed unfazed by our presence. They didn't lift a single root.

Next, I let Snowy parade around the castle a few times. She stepped high, lifting her head and tail, as if all the guards and gardeners were privileged to witness the momentous occasion of her walking in a circle.

"Show off."

She tossed her head and pranced a little.

After we'd covered the castle perimeter enough times for it to get boring, I returned her to the stables, brushed her out again, and got her fresh water.

"Okay, your royal horseness, I will see you later."

She nuzzled me, not wanting me to go.

"You're right. It's just us now, so we've got to stick together." I gave her mane a scratch.

Snowy responded by nibbling my hair.

"Hey!" Smiling, I shied away as her moist breath tickled my neck. "I don't need a haircut!"

I stopped messing around as the door at the other end of the barn creaked. If it was Ben, I didn't want to see him. He'd know I'd fallen into his trap and would act all smug about it. I didn't want to deal with the favor I owed him yet either. Peeping out of Snowy's stall, I spotted Ben, another stable hand, and the head horse trainer, John.

"Your Highness? Princess Chris?" John called.

Kissing Snowy on the nose, I whispered a goodbye and slipped out of her stall, walking quickly to the back exit, away from the three servants.

"Wait! Princess! We're here to take you—"

I broke into a sprint, not listening to the end of John's plea. I was tired of being taken places I didn't want to go. That's all my life was as a princess, and it was too much to handle right then. Bursting through the exit, I ran across the paddocks toward the lawn, climbing fences, while my pursuers called for me to stop. Instead, I raced around the castle, welcoming the cool shadow it draped over me. For a moment, I was out of their sight. Running my hands along a stone that jutted from the wall slightly, I shoved it. Three stones at the bottom of the wall moved back, revealing a passage. I jumped into the dark space just as the chasers rounded the corner, letting myself be swallowed whole.

They ran past, and I closed the passage. Leisurely, I wandered through my castle prison in the dark. I might not have known anything about codes, but when it came to sneaking around my home unseen, I was an expert. But I was also in trouble—that much was clear, since someone sent three servants to fetch me. Were my parents back? They'd only been gone a few days, but perhaps they'd decided I needed more punishment and turned around.

For now, I wouldn't let them find me. I'd reign over the passageways a while longer. No one could take me anywhere or make me do anything when I was threading through the outside of the inside of my home. My parents would wait, like cats outside a mousehole, for me to return to the real part of the castle, and then I'd get a lecture and be sent to my room.

As I came to the end of the passage, voices reached me from the library just outside. A maid was sobbing her snot out about being dumped by her boyfriend. Her friend tried to comfort her.

"You can cry, Cara, it's okay. I'm here. Robert was a jerk, and you deserve better."

*Sob*— "I thought—" *sniffle sniffle sob*— "h-he—" *sobsobsobsob*— "*LOVED* me!"

"I know, I know. Just let it out. No one's here but us."

Gagging, I backed away. I'd use the exit behind the unused fireplace in the kitchen instead, and filch some food while I was there.

Shouting echoed from the kitchen long before I reached the exit. Peeping through the crack in the panel, I frowned. Edna, the chief chef, was hollering at a servant girl for burning the ham glaze. The vine whip of a girl, who couldn't be older than eight, cowered against the wall. Behind Edna, on the stove, a pot of stew threatened to boil over, but Edna was too busy waving her ladle and shouting to notice. Then she smacked the ladle against the child's cheek with a sharp *crack* before yelling some more. The girl didn't make any noise, but tears trickled down her cheeks like liquid crystals, running over her chin and into her curly golden hair.

Sneaking out of the fireplace, I slunk over and tapped Edna on the shoulder. The portly, red-faced woman wheeled around, brandishing her cooking utensil like a mace.

"WHO—" She cut her bellow short when she realized who she was facing.

I raised an eyebrow.

"Oh—Your Highness! Please forgive me. I did not know you were here."

"Obviously." I surveyed the kitchen disinterestedly, and then plucked a bread roll and a ripe pear from some baskets. "I'm not pleased with the way you treat your workers when you think no one's watching. I'll come back soon to see how everyone's putting up with you. If I hear a *rumor* that you've been mistreating anyone again, I'll fire you on the spot. Got it?" I was being generous. She didn't deserve a second chance after hitting a child, but I didn't actually have the authority to fire her without consulting my parents. She may or may not have known that. I did, however, have the power to make her wish she had been fired. And that she was definitely aware of.

The head cook spluttered and babbled incoherently.

Just before leaving, I turned back. "By the way, your stew's burning. And don't use the ladle you've been slapping people with to stir it."

The kitchen girl favored me with a desolate little smile, but it never reached her eyes.

When I retreated back up the passage, I noticed the crying maid and her friend no longer blocked the alternate exit. I crept out of the library wall behind a flowery, overstuffed futon.

Striding past shelves, I snatched a colorful tome with a writhing dragon on the spine that caught my eye. Hefting the bulky coffee-table book under my arm, I continued toward the opening of the next passage. I wasn't an avid reader, but I enjoyed flipping through books on magical creatures. The illustrations would give me something to look at as I enjoyed my snack.

As I swept out the door, I almost got squashed by a waiter who was nodding off against the door. He caught himself before falling on me just in time.

"Excuse me, Your Highness," he murmured sleepily, bowing. As he yawned and stretched, I recognized him.

"Oh! Your Highness!" He bowed again, this time more alert. "Everyone has been searching the castle for you—"

"I hear you, Robert," I said. Then I held up a hand, forestalling further comments. "Why did you ditch Cara? It broke her heart."

Robert gasped and stammered as I ducked around him.

I sighed. "I seem to be having that effect on a lot of people today." I was around the corner before he recovered his composure.

Shifting the sword of an old suit of armor to open another passage, I climbed into it. This one was less dank and dusty than the others, since I traveled it regularly and kept it clean. Steep stone steps led upward in the pitch darkness. I felt my way along the cool walls, moving by feel rather than sight. A few times the stairs branched off, but I held the middle path until the very top, where the steps ended at the ceiling. Only experience kept me from slamming my head against the rock. It seemed like a dead end, but I knew better. Pushing hard on the ceiling, I moved the stone block up and over, revealing the underside of my bed.

I clambered out of the hole, but paused before inching my way out from beneath the bed skirt. If my parents were still searching for me, the first place they'd check was my room. Even if they'd already sent servants by, it was only a matter of time before someone stopped in again. However, no one who popped their head around the door would think to check beneath the bed before declaring the room empty.

With that in mind, I gathered a few pillows and blankets, and then stuffed them under the bed before crawling after them. Settling myself in my cozy makeshift fort, I munched on my snacks while flipping through *Fantastical Creatures and Their Natural Habitats, Version IV*. I was careful not to get crumbs in the pages. I didn't like books that smelled like mold any more than the next person. Besides, that would be wasting perfectly good bread.

There was only one page about phoenixes in the book. They were said to be exceptionally rare. Their songs were spells and their tears had healing powers. Other than that, there wasn't anything I didn't already know. Fyre had shown me more than any book ever could.

The next few pages were boring—fairies, gnomes, brownies . . . Ooh, a dragon! A full-page illustration of a jet-black mountain dragon stared me down. The painting had such precise detail that the individual ridges on each scale and the cornea fibers in the challenging orange eyes were visible. The dragon's claws, horns, and spine looked like they were made of diamond. Whipping to the side was its tail, the tip of it probably sharp enough to slice through armor like an overripe peach. I sighed involuntarily and traced my fingers over the scaly hide. I wondered what the scales would feel like in real life. There wasn't a sizing chart on the poster, so I was clueless about how big the dragon was supposed to be.

I gobbled up page after page after that, enjoying the artwork and descriptions of various dragon species. Many of them, much to my chagrin, loved to snack on fair maidens, and princesses in particular. I wondered why they were so picky. Maybe princesses looked cleaner than the average villager to them? And the way they made their kills made me shudder. Some squeezed them, some drowned them, some barbequed them, and some just said, "Down the hatch," and swallowed their prey alive.

I was staring at a depiction of a dragon with one ruby-heeled foot sticking out of its maw when I heard my bedroom door open.

"Princess Chris?" a tentative voice called.

Instead of withdrawing when I didn't answer, the door creaked open wider, and multiple sets of footsteps shuffled over the threshold.

How dare they! Servants milled about *my* room, rubbing their shoes all over the carpet and sitting in the lounge chairs without permission. I ground my teeth. They had no right to barge in and hang out, and I was going to make sure they were all fired!

"Are you sure we won't get fired for barging in here and hanging out?" a nervous male voice piped up. "We don't have any right to be here."

"Grandmother Rose told us to wait for her here. As long as nothing goes missing, she won't let us be punished," an older woman reassured.

"Where could the princess have gone? It's not like her to avoid Grandmother," a third person huffed. "I need to get back to my washing. If I get behind on my quota because I was sent to play hide-and-seek with the princess . . ."

I stopped listening. Did they say *Grandmother* was the one looking for me, not my parents? Uh-oh. I'd been avoiding her for hours. Heedless of the indignity of a princess skulking under her bed, I rolled out from my hiding place, much to the astonishment of everyone.

I held up my hand before anyone could speak. "Don't even say it. I'm heading down to Grandmother's cottage right now."

Ignoring more stuttering and gaping faces, I strode through my room and out the door. I heard the receding voices as I jogged away.

"She was beneath the bed the whole time? I thought you checked the room hours ago!"

"I didn't think I had to look there!"

"Well, obviously, you do."

"Yay! We didn't get fired!"

# Chapter 8. Tree Friend

Hair tangled and streaming behind me like scraggly ivy vines, I burst through the cottage door.

Grandmother, who had been lacing up hiking boots when I walked in, started unlacing them. "Chris! Where have you been? I was starting to think the trees had gotten you."

She surveyed the cobwebs in my hair and dirt smeared on my hands and dress. "Wait, don't tell me—you were in the passages."

I nodded. "I thought my parents had returned and sent for me, and I didn't want to see them. No one told me until just now that it was you asking for me."

"I told you I'd be back in a few hours."

"I know—I just kind of panicked and forgot when people started running after me and shouting. What did you need me for?"

"Oh, that." She waved her hand dismissively. "I just wanted to let you know I was back and ask if you'd eaten dinner yet. Then no one knew where you were, so I called on the servants to search. I was about to go into the forest when you came back."

"If I was taken by the forest, you would have never found my body."

"You're probably right. I still had to look, though."

Pulling off her boots, she went to the woodstove and stirred the coals. Then she put a pot of water on to boil for tea. Once it was ready, she steeped licorice root—my favorite—and, after murmuring her prayer for healing and nourishment, handed me a mug. It was aromatic with a tingly sweet aftertaste.

"How did the drop off go?" I asked as we sipped.

"The King and Queen were in the middle of a costume party when we rolled up," she replied, buttering a roll. "The guests thought Kedrik was dressed as a vampire, and the Queen had the butler usher him upstairs before anyone could figure out the truth."

She bit into her roll, chewing ferociously.

"What did Alaric do?" I asked. The King of SeaCrest had been noticeably absent when I'd caused a scene by hitting Coralla.

"Nothing, really—it was the Queen who got all indignant and puffed up like a pigeon. I think she told the butler to lock Kedrik in his room."

"Oh." I sipped my tea. "So I probably won't hear from him for a while, then." Kedrik was grounded, and I was alone again.

"Most likely," Grandmother agreed. "Between your banishment, the mad trees, tornadoes plucking people up, and the wolves that are out for revenge, your traveling options are severely limited."

In other words, because I'd ventured into the woods when I wasn't supposed to, I'd effectively trapped myself from now until gray hair started growing out of my ears.

Early the next morning, before the sunrise dissolved the fog shrouding the grounds, I left the cottage. I visited and fed Snowy, but I released her into the pasture instead of saddling her.

Kissing her nose, I slipped her halter off and closed the gate. Then I retraced the route I took the day before to the passage in the castle's protective wall. Instead of going underground all the way into the castle, I took another exit and ended up popping up in the middle of the stone path in the courtyard. No one was around to witness me emerge from the earth like an undead corpse, luckily.

I walked around the castle to the cherry tree underneath my balcony window. Keeping my distance, I stared the tree down. It didn't stare back. Or, if it did, I couldn't tell.

I took one step closer, paused, and then shuffled forward again. I was being overly cautious—like the trees in the orchard, this tree had never acted out of the ordinary. Only the ones deep in the forest had uprooted themselves and tried to kill me. Still, I wanted to give it the chance to try to take me out when no one was watching. I wanted answers, and I was sure the trees had some. Baiting them into attacking me was currently the only idea I had.

I kept my eyes peeled like potatoes for any twitching or leaf-shivering that wasn't accompanied by a breeze, but there was nothing.

"I'm right here, and no one's watching," I told the tree. "Now is your chance."

I felt stupid talking to a plant, especially when it didn't respond.

One foot at a time, I eventually came close enough to smell the tree's unripe fruit. But even though I was within range, it didn't strike.

"I guess you're not being possessed right now," I said.

A leaf fluttered, bobbing up and down. My eyes bugged, and I took three hasty steps back. I waited, heart pounding, for something else to happen, but nothing did. I started to wonder if I imagined the leaf moving on its own, or if I'd overreacted to a bug landing on it.

Folding my arms, I stood for fifteen unfruitful minutes before turning around and marching away. I wasn't done with my investigation, but the cherry tree and I were getting nowhere. I'd try the orchard next. After all, that was where I'd heard the voice calling my name and apologizing.

I wandered up and down the rows of gnarly apple trees, waiting for one of them to trip me with a root or chuck a piece of worm-eaten fruit at me.

"Hello?" I called out.

"Good morning, Your Highness!"

I jumped, whirling around and landing in what I hoped was a stance similar to that of a ninja. A gardener in a floppy hat blinked at me.

"I'm sorry, I thought you were talking to me. Did I frighten you?"

"No, it's all right. Carry on."

I backed away, letting the servant return to picking up fallen fruit and putting it in his bucket. Blowing a piece of hair out of my eyes, I gazed skyward. The sun was up, chasing the mist away. A heat bug started up its chirruping buzz.

*Chris.*

I stood rigid as I heard my name.

*I'm sorry.*

"Sorry for what? Where are you?" I kept my voice down so the gardener didn't think I was talking to him again. When I glanced back, he was still busy with his work. The voice didn't seem to reach his ears, only mine.

*We're all sorry.*

I turned my head to either side, then scanned the treetops, searching for whoever might be talking to me, but no one was there. Sweat trickled down the back of my neck as it occurred to me—maybe it was the trees themselves.

---

⟨symbols⟩ Ͳ  ⸗  ⊙∙✳!⸜  ∙ΘⳘ⁂ ✳ ∴)  ~⟨!  !!⊙✳ ,  ⊙ᴏ∙⁓!⸜

I worked to decode the secret message Fyre had delivered. In the week since I'd seen him, the phoenix had gone from a hatchling to a fledgling. He had enough flight feathers to make it the short distance between SeaCrest and Agaedith, but needed to rest in the stove between trips.

*meet on fresot rhode Wednesday night. itz safe, pmrisoe*

*Meet on forest road Wednesday night. It's safe, promise.*

Decoding the message made me stupidly pleased with myself. And the message itself made me almost giddy with excitement. Since realizing the trees were communicating with me, I hadn't made much progress. When I told Grandmother the trees were trying to apologize, she said they couldn't be trusted. I spent most of the next week inside, under guard, or helping Grandmother work in her garden. I weeded that patch of dirt so well that the weeds practically pleaded for mercy every time I walked by. I could only ride Snowy in the ring or paddock—no meadow racing. The result was that I was barely out of sight long enough to use the bathroom, let alone sneak off to the orchard again.

It sounded like Kedrik had been more successful than me—so much so that he thought it was safe to meet. I doubted Grandmother would agree, though. I debated keeping the message a secret and sneaking out, but just thinking about that made my insides crumple with guilt. I wasn't that bad of a person yet.

"Grandmother, Kedrik discovered something about the trees. He says it's safe to meet on the forest path. Can I go?"

Without looking up from her knitting, she reached out a hand for the decoded message. My mouth gumming up with nerves, I gave it to her.

"You got all that from this bit of gibberish?" she demanded after reading it. "I would need a book of explanation to convince me to let you take such a stupid risk."

"I don't want to be on house arrest for the rest of my life!" I complained.

"I know. You're right, it's not fair. There will be plenty of that when you get older. You shouldn't have to put up with it now." Grandmother put down her knitting and looked me in the eye. "You realize that I would be the most horrible grandmother in the history of grandmothers if I let you go in the woods, by yourself, at night, where wolves, trees, and Intriguers are waiting to kill you, just to meet a boy."

No decent rebuttal came to mind. Eyes dropping to the floorboards, I sighed. "I'll tell him I can't go, then."

"Oh, you can go. I just have to come with you." Grandmother smiled playfully. "I want to figure out what's wrong as much as you do."

A laugh burst from me. I had the coolest grandmother ever.

On Wednesday evening, I laced up my boots, Grandmother grabbed her walking stick, and we headed toward SeaCrest. The sinking sun streamed over the path, making it look like we were traveling across liquid gold. The breeze whispered enticingly from the trees, and when the road forked, we took the path that snaked into the woods.

Kedrik met us at the SeaCrest border just after the sun dipped below the horizon and the shadows awakened. He held my reply message, and Fyre was perched on his shoulder like a feathery torch.

"Kedrik! You're alive!"

"Is that surprising? Mother locked me in my room and said I'd be there until she decided otherwise, but she forgot there was more than one door." He shook his head at the unbelievable incompetence of his captor.

"So much for your parents not noticing you were gone." He wasn't as scary looking as I remembered him. In fact, I felt the urge to hug him, but I didn't know how he'd respond, so I didn't.

"I don't think they did, actually. When I arrived, I had to walk through a party they were throwing, and they didn't like that. But I got some party food, and they didn't yell at me because it would have looked bad in front of the guests."

"Both of us are glad that you didn't die in the week you were at home," Grandmother spoke up. I didn't miss the sarcasm in her words. "I don't mean to rush things, but being in the forest after dark is not something I'm looking forward to. In the letter you sent to Chris, you mentioned that you thought the trees were safe again. How do you know?"

Grandmother leaned on her stick, looking at Kedrik evenly. In my reply letter, I'd told Kedrik that Grandmother insisted on coming, so he wasn't surprised to see her with me.

"I took a risk and let the trees show me what happened from their perspective. There was enough proof for me to decide that I could trust them. I've been hanging out in the woods for the past few days, and nothing's happened to me."

"What did they tell you?" I asked. All I'd heard from them was my name and *sorry* over and over.

"I'll let Burlaku tell you the same thing he told me."

Before I could ask who Burlaku was, an old man with gnarly limbs and shaggy hair materialized from the forest. His skin looked like wrinkled leather. I couldn't help but stare. Instead of regular clothes, he wore a covering of moss, bark, and vines. He looked strangely familiar, but in an abstract way, as if I had dreamed about him.

"Hello, again," Burlaku rumbled in a deep voice that reminded me of wind blowing through a tunnel. "You recognize me, I believe."

"Yes," I hesitated, trying to pinpoint where exactly I had seen a jungle man with a bird's nest hairstyle before. Then the blindingly obvious hit me. Burlaku wasn't a *man* at all—he was a tree spirit. Somehow, I recognized him as the oak tree Kedrik had tied the rope swing to when we were playing in the river. He must have moved around a lot during the fight and re-rooted himself near the road.

My eyes hardened, suspicious. "Yes, I do recognize you. You're one of the trees that tried to kill us." I put my hands on my hips, wishing I had a sword to draw.

Burlaku nodded in understanding. His neck made a creaking sound. "An act the forest can never undo, though we hope to offer recompense. Come, I will show you what happened, and maybe we can understand each other."

He reached a twiggy hand toward me.

*Understand. Understand. Understand.* The word reverberated in my mind. Instinctively, I knew what Burlaku was asking me to do. I reached my own arm out until our hands met, palm to palm. His skin was rough like bark. My eyes blurred. I felt like I was spinning, and then my senses shifted. It wasn't dark, because I felt light without seeing it. I breathed without lungs through thousands of tiny holes in my leaves. The sweetest taste was earth and rain, and the dearest sounds were the millions of creatures living their lives around and on me.

The breeze tickled my branches as I swayed with it. My roots stretched into the cool earth, making me aware of everything that was happening, above and below ground, for over a hundred yards. I even felt vibrations from other trees in the root network miles away. Many insects and animals crawled on or around me, most unaware that I was cognizant of them. Three of these lives played under my limbs and in the river nearby: two human children and a phoenix.

Like me, the other trees stretched their arms up toward the sun. Like me, they were gentle giants, more powerful than the walking creatures of the earth, but unmoving. We let time go by while we watched and listened. That was the way we lived. I was a symbol of peace—always had been, and thought I always would be until I died, giving up my life as sustenance to the forest.

There was no warning before it happened. As if killed, the vibrations from my brothers and sisters stilled. All signs of life vanished—I didn't know if the creatures were gone, or if my senses had failed. A blast of icy fire shot from my roots to my leaf tips. I was frozen and burned all at once, and I withdrew from my body to a corner of my mind as I waited for it to stop. When the shock and pain boiled away, I found I couldn't return.

Something *else* occupied my bark. Slowly, my spirit grew exhausted in the darkness and withered. My thoughts died before they bloomed.

With a gasp, my eyes shot open. I blinked, adjusting to my returned sight. I was lying on the road, drenched in sweat, with dirt stuck all over me. Kedrik's cool hand brushed a piece of hair from my face. I sat up shakily.

"Wow."

"That was pretty much my reaction too," Kedrik said.

The trees *had* been controlled. They were victims as much as we were. The Intriguer was one powerful . . . whatever it was. If it could control so many of the forest's trees, how would anyone ever stop it?

"Hmm," Grandmother said.

Sitting up, I saw that her eyes were glassy, as if she'd just come out of a vision too. But, unlike me, she still stood stoically, leaning on her stick for support.

"How come you didn't fall over and get covered in sweat?" I complained.

"This wasn't my first vision. I have to admit, though, I wasn't expecting it to be so painful." Arching her back, she rolled her shoulders. Tilting her head to either side, she popped her neck.

"Seriously." I got to my knees, and when I didn't feel like I was going to fall over, stood all the way up.

"You good?" Kedrik asked, watching to make sure I didn't collapse.

"Yeah."

He left my side to check on Grandmother.

"I'm fine, thank you," she said, waving him away.

"Do you have understanding for us now?" Burlaku asked. A gust of wind swept over the path, making his arms sway and hair and beard rustle like leaves.

I nodded. "I know you never wanted to kill us. The Intriguer hurt you, too. But what if it takes over you again? You were helpless before."

"That's what I was wondering," Grandmother said.

"It cannot happen again," Burlaku said firmly. "We can now recognize the Intriguer's magic and band our spirits together to drive it out. Never again will it use our bodies to harm the forest or its creatures." His words were garbled because of trying to speak through a mossy mustache, but

I understood. Alone, the tree spirits had been taken by surprise and overpowered, but through their root network, they could respond to an attack together almost instantaneously, forming an impenetrable shield.

"Trees have a covenant with all living creatures. The one with humans is the most sacred, for they have been given dominion over all. Because of the Intriguer, as you call it, we trees broke that covenant of peace and killed many creatures. We tried to kill you too. To atone for the crime, the forest will offer you a gift." He walked, swaying, over to Kedrik, and placed a fingertip on his forehead. Then he did the same to me.

"You are marked as tree friends. We hope you will use the gift to defeat the Intriguer."

A shadow of concern swept over Grandmother's face. She tightened her grip on her staff.

I touched the spot on my forehead where he'd tapped, but didn't feel anything except skin. "Thank you," I said. Though I didn't know what a tree friend was, it was nice that they were trying to make up for almost killing us.

Another gust of wind blew, going right through Burlaku. His shape broke apart, sticks and leaves and brush flying every direction. A pinecone hit me in the eyeball.

"Ow."

When the air calmed, Grandmother pressed her lips together. "The forest is safer than anywhere now, with the trees watching out for you." she said. For some reason, though, she didn't look happy about it.

"What's wrong?" I asked. "Now I can stop driving you crazy because I'm bored all the time."

"That's the good part. I don't have to worry as much when you're traipsing all over the woods. But just because you have this special relationship with the forest doesn't mean you can take on the Intriguer. You know that, right?"

"Of course."

Being buddies with trees didn't change my powerlessness. Sometimes, Grandmother was a worrywart. I couldn't hold it against her, though; she loved me and wanted to keep me safe.

Even though I'd reassured her, I still caught her watching me seriously as we trudged home.

The stick whipped through the air, heading for my shoulder. Raising my own weapon, I barely managed to block the blow. Spinning out of the deflection, my attacker slashed at my shins. I jumped just in time, then sidestepped to take advantage of my opponent's awkward position. I aimed a powerful thrust at his middle, but he ducked and rolled away. My momentum carried me forward, and I plummeted to the leafy ground.

"Oof!"

"You lost your center of balance," Kedrik said, holding his stick over me.

"No kidding." If it had been a real battle, I'd have died. Actually, I'd have died a long time ago, this being the umpteenth time Kedrik had beaten me.

"You're too impulsive with your moves. Wait for me to make a mistake before moving in. Otherwise, you did pretty well this time."

"Pretty well" wasn't good enough, though. In a battle against a huge wolf, "pretty well" still meant dead. I nodded absentmindedly.

"Oh no!" I exclaimed. "There's your mother!"

If Kedrik could have gotten any paler, he would have. "Where?" He whirled around.

Having successfully distracted him, I grabbed my weapon and leaped up to begin the battle again.

For several days, we'd met at our new spot, which we called "the Grove" because the trees had spaced themselves evenly when they settled after the attack. Burlaku stood sentinel nearby, and we used a knot in a paradise tree named Struckan to leave messages for each other. Grandmother allowed me to venture into the forest almost anytime I wanted now, if I let her know beforehand. No longer fearing for Snowy's safety, I usually rode her on my excursions.

Kedrik's family, however, had no idea what their prince was up to. Aquanetta was suspicious of him for being escorted home by someone from

Agaedith, even though he didn't reveal that he'd been anywhere near the castle or me. We worried about being discovered, but didn't see what we could do about it other than continue to be careful.

Disarming me, Kedrik pointed his stick at me again.

"What did you do wrong this time?" he panted. At least I was making him work.

"Uhhh . . ."

"Exactly—you lost concentration."

I gave a sheepish grin, wiping my sweaty face on my sleeve.

"Let's take a break," Kedrik suggested.

Thinking he was suggesting it for my sake, I bristled. "Why? Are you tired?"

"Yes. You should be, too. If you're not tired, then you're not working hard enough."

Since he'd admitted he was tired as well, I consented. Wandering to the riverside at the edge of the Grove, we removed our shoes to wade. Kedrik never told me what dangerous things lived in the river, but the trees along the shore assured us that nothing that lived there currently wanted to eat us. That was enough for me.

The riverbed was mucky and clouded with silt, which was why I didn't see the sinkhole until my leg vanished under the water. Off balance, my head dunked beneath the surface. While underwater, I heard the river swishing, laughing at me. When I disengaged my leg, the tunic and breeches that Kedrik lent me were dripping and muddy, and Kedrik was grinning.

"Smooth. Leave it to you to find the only sand pit in the river," he said with a laugh.

Smiling in spite of myself, I drew my clenched fists across the water, splattering shimmering droplets at his face.

"Hey!"

He spun in a circle, holding his arms on the water so a wave splashed over me. After that, it was a water war. We kicked and punched so many crystalline droplets into the air, we probably looked like a pair of fountains. From the shore, the trees watched us, confused about why we were playing in their drinking water. All the fish nearby sensed our battle and stayed away, and little water bugs skittered to calmer areas that they could stand on.

When we were more waterlogged than rainclouds, we dragged ourselves to shore to dry out in the sun.

We were idly skipping stones when Fyre came soaring down from a thermal, landing neatly at Kedrik's feet. He gripped a piece of rolled parchment proudly in his talons.

"Hello, Fyre," I cooed, stroking his silky plumage. "Nice to see you. Your flying skills are getting better every day." It was astounding how quickly he grew. Fyre nuzzled my hand while Kedrik disentangled the message from his claws.

"Fyre, you can let go of the—ow!" Kedrik snatched his hand back, putting his finger in his mouth where a trickle of blood had appeared.

Chirping an apology, Fyre cocked his head to see if his friend was all right.

"It's okay, it wasn't your fault. I just scraped myself on your sharp claws," Kedrik reassured him.

"Let me see it," I said, reaching for his hand.

"It's just a scratch," he protested, holding his injury close.

"Maybe it is now, but if it gets infected, you won't be able to sword fight."

"Fine." He held out his hand, and I took it in mine. Blue capillaries traced beneath the thin skin like tree roots. I'd gotten a deep tan from being outside so much, but his skin was as white as ever. If anything, it was a little pink from sunburn—he burned so easily. We tried to train in the shade as much as possible, but patches of sunlight were scattered here and there.

The scratch wasn't deep, but it stretched all the way down the inside of his thumb. A trickle of blood dripped from the tip, but most of the outer layers of skin hadn't been broken.

"See?" Kedrik said. "It's not a big deal."

"Fine, but make sure you keep it clean. If you ever do get a bad cut, come to the cottage and Grandmother or I can treat it." I knew a lot about herbal first aid from being around Grandmother Rose so often. That kind of stuff interested me and was useful in situations like this.

"Yes, ma'am." Kedrik saluted, teasing me.

Fyre at last relinquished the parchment to Kedrik, who read it intently.

I was curious about who else knew Fyre. I'd been under the impression that Kedrik kept him secret from others to prevent people from using his powers for their own gain.

"Is the letter important?" I asked.

"Yep—it's a surprise. We're going to have to ride Snowy to get there. Make sure she has lots of energy next time we meet."

"Get where? What are you talking about?"

"You'll see." He looked at me out of the corner of his eyes and smiled mysteriously.

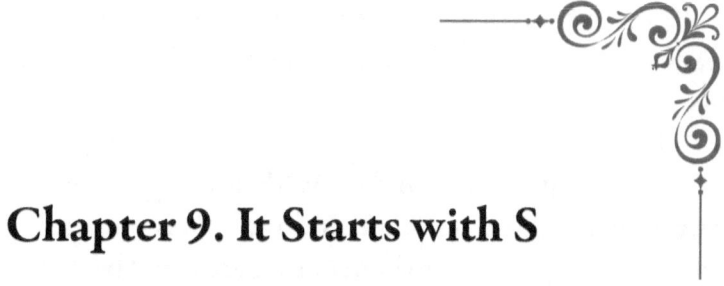

# Chapter 9. It Starts with S

His cryptic answer left me frustrated, and I could hardly wait for our next meeting. On the day we'd agreed on, Snowy and I met Kedrik in the Grove.

"Ready?" I asked him from the saddle.

"Yep." He tried to get on behind me from the wrong side.

"Kedrik, wrong side—your sword will get stuck on her flank."

"Whoops." He took his foot out of the stirrup and proceeded to walk behind Snowy, right through the kick zone, to get to the other side. Snowy snorted at his ineptitude, but was polite enough to not smack him with a hoof.

When he finally managed to swing himself behind me, he sat as stiff as a dead beaver. His posture didn't loosen as Snowy started walking, so I halted her.

"What are you, a plank of wood? Relax. Move with Snowy's movements. It's uncomfortable for her if you're so stiff."

"Uncomfortable for *her*? It's not exactly a feather bed for me either." He tried to maneuver himself into a less rigid form, but only succeeded in slouching.

"Do you ride much?" I asked.

"The Attack of the Trees was my first time. My kingdom is by the sea, remember? We're more boat-oriented people."

"It's not like SeaCrest doesn't have horses, though." Boats couldn't pull carriages, and if someone attacked the kingdom by land, the generals couldn't exactly defend their capital city by launching their battleships and hurling cannonballs at it.

"We have carriage horses and a cavalry, but my father never taught me to ride. I wasn't interested in learning, anyway, since Fyre could take me wherever I needed to go."

From his perch on top of Snowy's head, Fyre chirruped sadly, his feathers drooping. He was still too small to talk, let alone carry his familiar like he used to.

"I can teach you to ride, if you like." I was happy that I knew how to do something Kedrik didn't. With sword fighting, code making, and even swimming, he outshone me, and it was frustrating. Teaching him something would prove to both of us that I could be useful too.

"Sounds good. At least tell me how to sit properly so my—um—so I don't hurt so much when I get off."

I stifled a snicker, partly because of Kedrik's implication and partly because his breath on the back of my neck tickled.

"First lesson: move with Snowy's gait instead of resisting it. You won't get so bruised if you do that. And keep your center of balance upright, vertical to the saddle."

"I'm hardly in the saddle," he protested. "You're taking up all the room!"

"Unless you have a two-person saddle in that magic knapsack of yours, you're going to have to deal with it."

Kedrik sighed, resigned to his fate.

With Kedrik giving directions while I steered and instructed him on his saddle stance, we crossed the SeaCrest border. I was nervous about someone recognizing me, but I tried not to show it. Kedrik sensed my anxiety anyway.

"People probably won't recognize you dressed down. And if you get thrown in a dungeon, I'll come fish you out."

That was comforting. Sort of.

We came to a fork in the road.

"Which way?"

One road was cobbled and led into town, while the forest continued to shroud the other route.

"Go ahead through town," Kedrik directed. "It will be longer to go around." He didn't sound happy about it.

There were plenty of other horses on the town streets, but most were old swayback work horses that were ill-groomed and scraggly-tailed. Snowy wasn't helping us blend in by high-stepping and flaunting her pristine coat.

She was like a greyhound among scruffy mutts. Atop her, Kedrik and I looked like vagabonds in our faded sword fighting outfits. People stared. They probably thought we stole her.

But after several minutes, I realized that the glances people threw us were fearful, not suspicious. I started to think something else was drawing their attention. The village was still noisy, but everywhere I turned, there was someone quickly looking away, or in some cases, stumbling over trying to *run* away.

"What is with everybody?" I demanded, loud enough for a nearby fish vendor to hear. The man squeaked and resumed proclaiming his wares hoarsely. "What are they staring at?"

"My hood keeps falling down," Kedrik mumbled.

It took a few moments for me to realize his change of subject was actually the answer to my question. I'd become used to his appearance. But I remembered I'd been scared the first time I saw him, and he'd mentioned that people usually ran away screaming when they met him. I thought he'd been joking, but obviously not. The townspeople weren't used to his ghostly skin and hair or red eyes.

"How long do I stick to the main road?" I asked, feeling uncomfortable.

"All the way through town. We have to take a right after the last shop. Then take the path past the cliffs at the seashore and back into the woods."

I couldn't get away from the stifling confines of the noisy town fast enough. Unfortunately, we were slowed by merchant tents and pedestrians. Everyone shouted, trying to sell stuff, haggling prices, or yelling while running after customers who didn't bother to haggle and just took off with the item they wanted. It felt like I was in the middle of a beehive, except everything smelled like dead fish. Docks stretched over the sea just off the road, and sometimes the road stretched onto the docks. Snowy was nervous traveling over the jiggling wood planks, and I didn't blame her. They were damp and had colorful molds growing on them.

Finally, we escaped the bustle of town. The road rose steeply and became rockier. It returned us to the trees, first palms with dangling coconuts, and then mossy jungle trees that stood a hundred feet high and dripped with vines. Eventually, oaks, birches, maples, and poplars overtook the ecosystem.

"Are we back in Agaedith?" I asked.

"Yep. The place we're going is in your kingdom."

I was really confused now. I didn't know anyplace interesting enough in Agaedith to pay a special visit. "Can you tell me where that is yet?"

Kedrik considered a moment. "It starts with $S$," he finally said.

"A shop of some kind? A sanitarium? A saloon?"

He laughed at my guesses. "Yes, I'm taking you to get drunk."

"Well, tell me what it is! I'm dying over here."

I pestered him, but he wouldn't give in. "You'll see when we get there" was all he said.

I didn't have long to wait. Kedrik called a halt in the middle of the path. "There." He pointed. "See that rock with the squiggly line on it? That's where we have to turn off."

I steered Snowy off the road and onto a barely discernable footpath. Branches hung low overhead, so Kedrik and I dismounted to continue. Snowy lowered her head to duck beneath the branches, glaring at them resentfully. Bushes grew thickly on either side of us, blocking the view of the rest of the woods. It would have been unlikely for anyone to stumble upon the path, especially since some of the shrubs were covered with thorns. Roots crisscrossed the ground. I kept quiet, sensing that the place was secret and wanted to be kept that way.

"There's the next indicator," Kedrik said quietly, gesturing to another rock marked with a squiggly line. "The entrance should be somewhere around h—"

Suddenly, Kedrik vanished.

Dropping Snowy's reins, I knelt in front of the hole he'd fallen into. It was covered with long grass and twigs, making it almost invisible.

"Kedrik!" I whisper-shouted. I didn't want whoever made the trap to know someone had sprung it.

"That's one way to find a secret entrance!" he called up from the hole.

"What are you talking about? You mean this is where we're supposed to be?"

I pushed the grass aside to peer in, but the sun only penetrated a few feet, illuminating dust floating in the air, but nothing else.

"Yep. Come on down. Someone piled leaves and straw here, so it's a soft landing."

I looked back at Snowy and decided it was safest to leave her ground-tied. "You won't fit, girl. Stay here, all right? The trees will protect you. And don't eat any thorns."

Bobbing her head, she started nibbling on the grass at the edge of the hole.

"You hear that?" I asked the trees. "Protect her from wolves and stuff."

Patting her nose, I slipped off the edge of the hole, into the dark. Moist air smelling strongly of earth rushed by my face. Hitting the pile of soft stuff Kedrik mentioned, I slid off and crashed into someone.

"Ow," Kedrik said.

"Sorry, I can't see anything." I took a few steps away and did a nose-plant into a wall of dirt. Kedrik must have put Fyre away in his knapsack, because I couldn't find his torch-like glow.

"It's not *that* dark in here, sheesh."

"Maybe your eyesight is just better than mine, because I can honestly say I see nothing right now."

"Really? Huh. Well, the dwarves don't light the entryway for security purposes. The tunnel should be lit, though."

I'd never been invited into the dwarf tunnels before, and I'd never found one on my own. I shivered with excitement—and because there was a cold draft coming from somewhere. I started to follow the air movement to its source, but then stumbled over the pile of leaves and straw.

"This way," Kedrik called, guiding me.

I followed his voice, feeling my way along the wall until it veered left into a tunnel. At first, I still couldn't see anything. Then my eyes adjusted to a faint bluish glow emanating from mushrooms along the walls.

"Whoa." I touched one the size of a teacup. It boinged.

"If you eat them, your skin glows for an entire day," Kedrik said, stepping into the mushroom's light beside me.

"You tried it?"

"Yep. Yours might not glow as much as mine, since you have darker skin. I was like a lighthouse."

I blinked. A glowing Kedrik would be enough to scare the Intriguer right out of Clystopia.

We continued down the tunnel. Spots of glowing lime-green mold joined the mushrooms in providing light. The tunnel sloped downward and wound first one way, then another, like an earthy serpent. My boots became coated with mud, making my steps feel lumpy. Roots dangled from the ceiling and jutted out the side of the wall like the underground equivalent of nostril hair.

Eventually, the dirt gave way to rock. Layers of gray, red, and yellow stone striped the path. Red slime the color of boiling lava streaked the walls, replacing the mushrooms. In the dim orange glow, Kedrik's eyes flashed as he glanced back to make sure I was still following.

I quickened my pace until I was alongside him. "This place is so strange," I murmured. The rock amplified my voice.

"Isn't it? It's like, it should be creepy, but somehow it's just really interesting."

That was a good way to describe it. We entered a low, wide cavern with rocks like giant teeth covering it. The stalactites and stalagmites were as tall as me, and so close together I had to squeeze by them sideways. Some connected all the way from ceiling to floor, forming pillars. I felt like I was trying to find my way through a dragon's mouth. In between the stalactites hung glowing filaments like drippy stars.

"What are those?" I asked, pointing to them.

"Bug larva glowworm thingies of some sort," Kedrik said. "They aren't dangerous, but they get stuck in your hair really easily."

I was careful not to touch them.

On the other side of the cavern were a half dozen tunnels. Kedrik chose the third from the left, from which a tapping sound emanated. A few steps down the new tunnel, I breathed in a scent that didn't belong underground.

"Do you smell smoke?"

"Yes. We're getting close."

The tapping sound grew louder the farther we went, and I realized where Kedrik was taking me. "A dwarf smith," I said.

Not only did dwarves mine jewels, giving a boost to Agaedith's economies above and belowground, they were also expert craftsmen, specializing in all types of metalwork. Blacksmithing, silversmithing . . . and crafting weaponry.

"You guessed it—we're going to a dwarven sword smith."

I leaped into the air in excitement, almost hitting my head on the ceiling.

"If you want to be any good at swordsmanship, you need a real sword."

"What kind of sword should I get?" In my kingdom, only my father, the castle guards, and the army regularly carried swords. The expense was too prohibitive for commoners, and it was considered indelicate for women of any class to carry such a heavy weapon. That was part of the reason I wanted one so badly.

"They'll fit you for a sword and then forge it. No two swords are alike, just like people, so they make each one individually. All you have to do is let them measure you."

The tunnel ended in another cavern, but this one was vast, stretching all the way to the surface. Several pinpricks of daylight dotted the ceiling—to vent smoke, I assumed. Most of the light came from a hundred feet below, where the fires of the forge burned.

I counted thirteen pavilions and twice as many fires, some of which reached taller than the apple trees in my parents' orchard. More fires were encased in stone forges, and dwarves worked billows, supplying air. I wasn't sure how any of the fires were burning since a river rushed nearby, creating a sensation of clinging dampness, but they crackled away happily. A mixture of steam and smoke hung in the air, blurring the view from above.

Kedrik and I started hiking down stone steps toward the buildings, but he halted suddenly, whirling to look at me.

"Wait! You're still a girl!" he exclaimed.

I raised an eyebrow. "Nothing gets past you, does it?"

"What I meant," he said, flustered, "was that the smiths don't usually make weapons for girls."

My face clouded. I'd hoped Kedrik had found a way around that predicament. If he had simply forgotten about the custom, then I would have gotten my hopes up for nothing.

"You'll just have to go in disguise, that's all," he went on. "Don't worry, they won't ask a lot of questions. I'm giving them SeaCrest pearls, after all."

I didn't argue about who would pay—the dwarves would value gems that they couldn't mine higher than ones they could stumble over in their backyard. Plus, I found it funny that he was using money from his parents—who hated my guts—to outfit me with an illicit weapon.

My disguise was already half complete. I was still in my sword-fighting pants, which no other girl would dare wear. My face was sweaty, and I wasn't wearing makeup, so it might pass as a boy's if no one looked too closely. It was my long hair that posed the biggest problem. Even pulled back in a ponytail, it gave me away.

"Do you have any hats I can hide my hair under?" I asked.

"I think so." Dropping to his knees in the middle of the staircase, Kedrik rummaged through his knapsack. He pulled out several of the most abnormal headwear pieces I had ever seen: a pirate hat, a large fedora with a bent feather plume, a coonskin cap, a fruit hat (with fake fruit, thankfully), a jester's colorful hat with jingle bells, and a hat that resembled a chicken.

"Are you serious right now?" I demanded. "I can't wear any of these!"

"I know—just thought I'd show you my collection." When he drew out a plain brown cap, I snatched it up.

"Thank you. Although . . . it *would* be pretty hilarious if I walked into the forge with a chicken on my head."

"If you did that, I'd wear the fruit hat."

I laughed as he balanced the yummy-looking hat on his head.

"I'll spare you the embarrassment," I said, trying to fix my hair under the plain cap. But my ponytail was almost waist length, and the cap was loose and made my head look lumpy with all that hair stuffed beneath it. Even though I tucked it in as firmly as I could, it still felt like it would tumble out if I breathed too heavily.

"This isn't working," I grunted. "Could you just cut it off?"

"Cut your hair? Are you sure?" Putting away the last of his funky hats, Kedrik stood, looking apprehensive. "I've never cut hair before. Well, okay, once I snuck into Coralla's room when she was asleep and snipped off about six inches to annoy her, but that doesn't count."

"It doesn't need to be even. Grandmother can fix it later if she thinks it's hideous. I really don't care as long as it's convincing enough to get me a sword."

Fetching his pocketknife from his satchel, he tried to slash my hair off in one dramatic swoop. All he did was slice a few hairs and pull a few more out from the roots.

I winced. "Don't you have scissors?"

"Nope."

"You mean to tell me that you have an entire hat collection in that satchel, but no scissors."

"Hey, when I packed it, I wasn't thinking *maybe I'll meet a girl one day who wants me to give her a haircut so she can get a sword*. I figured I didn't need scissors if I had a knife."

I gritted my teeth as Kedrik cut my hair chunk by chunk. I half expected to be bald from all the hairs he plucked out, but when I felt the top of my head afterward, it was still hairy.

"Good enough. Thanks." With my hair cut up to my chin, it would never occur to anyone that I was a girl now. I slapped the cap onto my head. "Let's go get a sword!"

When we entered the loose ring of pavilions, no one paid us much attention. It was a welcome change from the intense stares of the SeaCrest villagers. Unlike when we rode through town, Kedrik seemed just as comfortable here as he was in the forest or river. All the smiths seemed intent on what they were doing, whether it was tending fires, heating and shaping red-hot metal, or crafting scabbards and inlaying precious stones. Not many were working together. Each person had a different skillset, so they focused on their own process.

Heat waves radiated from the flames, roasting my face. A trickle of sweat ran down my back. Steam hissed as a dwarf dipped a searing red metal rod into a bucket of water. The vapor rose, obscuring my vision.

Kedrik led me to a three-walled hut that appeared to be empty. The fire wasn't going, and no torches lit the inside.

"Smith!" he called. "I know you're in there!"

I only noticed the small man when he stood. He was completely bald, with nary an eyebrow to speak of, and almost five feet in height, which was strikingly tall compared to the other dwarves working in the forge. Much of his skin was smudged with ash, making the white of his teeth shine in comparison.

"Prince Kedrik," he growled, "I'm glad you made it on time. Is this here the young gennelman that requires our services?"

He spoke with a dialect unique to dwarves that made his words seem gruff and clipped. Dwarves had their own, private language that they didn't share with aboveground dwellers. They'd adopted Clystopian to trade with humans, but tended to blend some words together and shorten others.

It took a moment to recall that I was a boy now, and he was referring to me. He squinted at me with eyes that were bloodshot from smoke exposure. I hoped he wouldn't squint too hard and realize that I wasn't the "young gennelman" he thought I was.

"This is my friend, uh, Christopher," Kedrik introduced me.

"So original," I breathed.

"Like you could have done better," he whispered back.

"Welcome to the forge, Christopher. I'm Smith—I do most of the sword work here. You ready to be fitted for your weapon?"

"Yes, sir. Hey, was your name always Smith, or did you change it when you became one?" I couldn't help but ask.

"Ha ha, haven't heard that one before." He clapped his soot-stained hands together and rubbed them on an equally soot-blackened rag, then steered me to the center of the clearing. I felt like I was in the middle of a wheel, and the spokes were all the pavilions, fires, and forges around me. The dwarves kept working, but a few watched me out of the corner of their eye, as if they expected me to start singing or something else entertaining.

I didn't understand—wasn't I going to be measured? I craned my head around to see Kedrik, but Smith was in the way.

"Now," the blade smith said, handing me a bamboo pole. "I'm gonna test you with a couple weapons. Don't worry 'bout bein' watched, I'm just tryin' to figure out what shape, size, and material your sword should be, not makin' judgments on your skill level. The blade needs to match your form and strength, and to do that I gotta watch you in action."

"All right." Kedrik never told me what being measured for a sword entailed. I just assumed it was like being measured for a dress. This was far more nerve-racking.

I took the bamboo pole. Adjusting my grip for comfort, I slid into fighting stance. With one foot forward and one behind like a surfer, and knees slightly bent for balance, I pretended to parry, thrust, block, and swipe at a dummy made of sacks of sand.

I practiced with weapon after weapon. Sticks, metal rods, stone rods, long swords, double bladed swords, curved swords, and two-handed swords of all sizes. Sweat flowed from my body like a waterfall. I was probably going to have a visible layer of salt coating my skin when it dried.

My nervousness was soon forgotten, though. I became a concentrated machine of exhilaration and power. I ducked and spun, rolled and jumped. I faked to one side and then hacked at the dummy's arm. Spinning to get power, I sliced its neck. I danced back a few steps, pretending to defend while keeping my weapon and core balanced. I experimented with some moves that Kedrik used, and made up a few of my own. At one point, I gave up trying to be fancy and just beat the sand out of the thing.

Smith brought Kedrik over for me to practice against, but we held back on our blows since the weapons we fought with were more dangerous than the sticks we usually used.

After what seemed like only a few minutes, Smith returned to take the last weapon.

"I've got all the measurements I need. Your sword's gonna be a fine one, young lady."

Young lady? Uh-oh. Then I registered the rest of his sentence. "Wait—you're still going to make me a sword?"

"No, no," he frowned, shaking his sooty bald head. "The sword I *would've* made you would've been a beautiful, single handed, double bladed, thin long sword. And it would've been done in 'bout a month and a half. I might've even gotten my brother to make a shield to match it. But we *can't* go against policy." He winked at me.

"That sounds awesome! Thank you for, um, telling me how cool it would have been."

Beaming, I thanked him again and raced over to Kedrik, who was getting a drink from the river.

"He's going to make it!" I shouted. Catching myself, I lowered my voice, "Even though Smith knows I'm a girl, he's still going to make it!"

I was going to be the only girl in my entire kingdom with a sword! I was going to defend myself and be a swordswoman! In my excitement, I flung my arms around Kedrik in a tight hug. Suddenly, many eyes were on me, staring. Hugging the prince of SeaCrest was not normally done, I expected. Heat rising to my face, I quickly let go. All the smiths pretended to be working, and Kedrik glued his gaze to a pebble on the ground. He kicked it, his face redder than the forge fire.

Clearing my throat, I suggested that we head back.

"Yeah," he replied, turning toward the stairs. "Yeah, let's do that."

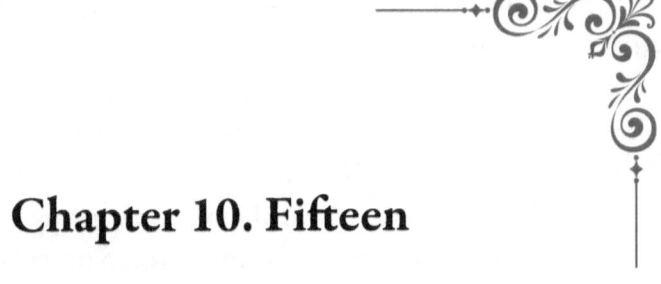

# Chapter 10. Fifteen

Soon after my sword-fitting, I visited a town in my own kingdom, this time with Grandmother Rose. I welcomed the lack of dead fish smells. No one knew I was the princess, of course. Disguised with a hand-stitched commoner dress and worn shoes, I looked like a grandchild that was helping her grandmother with errands. In fact, those who were familiar with Grandmother Rose knew me as her distant relation from the outskirts of the community. I practically was, if the castle that ruled over them counted as "the outskirts of the community."

Grandmother had laughed when she'd seen my atrocious cave haircut, and straightened the jagged edges for me so that I wouldn't make a scene when venturing into public. Or at least, less of a scene than I would have made.

Before we went to the market, we attended a church service in a tiny brick chapel. Its windows were only paper, colored to look like stained glass. The sun shone through them, giving the place a happy, rainbow glow. Prayer candles that people lit for suffering loved ones lined one wall. Paintings and wooden statues of prophets and saints decorated the area. The altar was also wooden, with images of grapevines and wheat carved into the front.

Grandmother and I squeezed into the back just before service began. It was a solemn affair, but a joyful solemn, serious in peace and assurance rather than misery or guilt. I tried not to fidget much, though being still for longer than a few minutes made me restless. Grandmother understood that I was trying my best, and didn't rebuke me when I started bouncing on the balls of my feet and staring at the candles and statues instead of keeping my eyes on the minister.

"What did you think of the liturgy?" Grandmother asked as we left, strolling next to the market.

She always asked me that when I attended services with her. I wasn't sure if she actually wanted my opinion, or if she was ensuring I'd been paying attention. Probably both.

"When the minister talked about people giving up their livelihood to follow a calling, it sounded . . . freeing. I would never be allowed to do that, though."

Grandmother only patted my shoulder, a shadow of worry flitting over her face.

The market smelled of cinnamon buns fresh from the oven. While Grandmother shopped for boring stuff like vegetables and flour, I found the bakery and bought a half dozen buns. After scarfing one, I rewrapped and stashed the rest in my satchel, intending to save them for later. On my way back to the stall Grandmother was bartering at, though, two kids dressed in rags begging at a corner caught my attention.

Even though it was rude, I couldn't help but stare. The boy was the oldest, probably around ten. He clutched his sister's hand and held out his other one to passersby. The little girl sucked her thumb. Their bare feet were caked with grime and their faces gaunt.

"Excuse me, are you homeless?" I asked the boy.

"Yeah." Dropping his hand to his side, he met my gaze unashamedly.

"Why?"

"'Cause we don't have a home," he said, speaking slowly, as though I were stupid.

Guilt crashed over me like a collapsing house. This was my kingdom, or I was heir to it, at least, and orphan children were running around towns begging for food. I gave them the rest of the cinnamon rolls and money I'd brought, and then walked away before I saw their reaction.

Situations like that were part of the reason Grandmother took me into town with her, I knew. Up in the gloomy castle, I couldn't see what real life for most people was like. However, even when I was witness to a problem, I wasn't sure how to fix it. Needlework, penmanship, and music lessons—the stuff I was taught as a princess—didn't teach me how to rule a kingdom. Whenever I considered my future as a queen, it seemed nebulous.

"Orphanage funding from the royal family was cut for this month," Grandmother said from behind me.

Turning around, I swallowed the egg-sized lump forming in my throat. "Why?"

She shrugged. "They needed the money for something else, I guess."

Seeing I was still in remorseful, confused shock, she tried to comfort me. "Next month, when the orphanage gets the regular amount of money again, it will take the children back in. Your parents are not bad rulers, Chris. For the most part, the people are content. It may seem poor compared to what you're used to, but to the commoners, times are good."

"I'd hate to see bad times."

"Me too."

The weather for the next two days stormed violently. Just when I was about to drop dead from the monotony, the rain stopped. I emerged from the cottage feeling like I was waking from hibernation and breathed in the sweet rainy air. The smell of rain was one of my favorites. Though the sky was still overcast, I was ecstatic. Being cooped up for days in a small space made me irritable.

Snowy and I trotted all the way to the Grove, bubbling with energy. Dismounting, I located Struckan and reached into the hollow knot in his trunk to reveal a scrap of parchment with Kedrik's symbol on it.

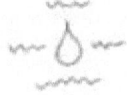

Patting the old oak tree in thanks, I decoded the message.

⟨-φ- ✳·|· ⊖✳ ∼ᵧ ]□/□✳/✳ −⊖□ ✳∼⸱✳ ⋀⋀⟩

*Terhe iz smoneoe bhneid u*

*There is someone behind you*

Pivoting, I peered into the undergrowth beyond the Grove.

"Kedrik, where are you?" I called in a sing-song voice. Treading lightly, I peered around a large rock, but found nothing but a centipede. Then I backed up against a thick shrub to survey the area.

"Grrrrraaaaaaaaaaahhhhhhhh!" Leaping out from the bush, Kedrik collided with me, and we tumbled to the leafy ground. Staggering to his feet, he laughed. "You should have seen your face!" he panted.

"Ha ha, very funny." I gave him an exasperated look and peeled a wet leaf from my arm.

"I had to show you this bush, didn't I? Come on in, it's really cool." Turning, he struggled a bit through the lush, full branches, and then disappeared. Interested, I bent to follow him. The twigs grabbed at my tunic, but I forced my way through. When I was free of the snatching plant, I stood upright. The canopy was still a few inches above my head. Sunlight filtered through the leaves, dappling the bare dirt. I investigated the space, ducking and weaving around low branches and roots. It was a small, secret world that only Kedrik and I knew about.

"This is a perfect hideaway. No one could ever find it unless they fell into it!"

Kedrik nodded in agreement. "That's sort of how I found it . . ."

"Should have guessed." My gaze swept over it again. "If travelers go by on the road, we can hide in here. There's no way anyone can see us through the leaves, especially if we keep still." We didn't want Kedrik's parents to find out the princess they hated most was hanging out with him almost every day.

"Good plan." He picked up his fighting stick, which was leaning against a protruding branch. "Let's see how well you can fight in a small space."

Pretty well, it turned out. Nimble as a squirrel, I dipped, threaded, and scurried around the new environment. Both of us tripped on roots more than once, but we always sprung up again before the other could land a "killing" blow. As we kept battling and I kept losing, fiery determination burned through me. I was *tired* of getting thwacked and bruised. I wanted to be the one causing bruises.

As a feral, unrestricted sensation overcame me, I used a branch to shield a blow aimed at my thigh and then attacked. Shuffling my feet for balance, I restrained my impulse to dive in. Instead, I used quick snaps of my stick to guide Kedrik into a tangle of roots. But he wasn't stupid—he balked, trying to escape when he saw where I was herding him. Unleashing my restraint, I spun and knocked my weapon against his shins, making him stumble into the roots and fall. To catch himself, he let his own makeshift sword clatter to the ground. I held my stick to his chest in triumph. My first win.

To my shock, when I returned home, I saw my mother floating across the lawn, ebony hair billowing in the summer breeze. She called to me. I suppressed a shudder as the sound of my flowery name assaulted me.

Father followed in the wake of her rippling blue satin gown, his smile white and even. I clashed violently with their royal image, and they noticed, because they stopped short before me.

My mother scrunched her nose at my sword fighting attire and demanded to know what I had done with my hair.

Since I hadn't expected them home so soon, I didn't have a response prepared.

"Grandmother Rose cut it for me."

They exchanged a glance I didn't like at all.

"No, wait—it wasn't her fault, I just—"

Father interrupted to say they'd missed me so much, which none of us believed for a second. The words were too practiced and held no emotion. He then asked me to join them in the parlor, where I had gifts waiting.

Standing tall, I followed them, trying not to show my apprehension. Gifts weren't a good sign. Whenever my parents gave me something, it meant they wanted something from me. Something I didn't want to give. Guilt trips and bribing were their primary parental tactics, and with my crimes at SeaCrest and the unknown gifts hanging over my head, they had double their usual power.

When we entered the parlor, a *roomful* of custom dresses, heeled shoes, hair accessories, silky undergarments (yikes), purses, jewelry, perfume, and other princess essentials confronted me.

When I didn't exclaim my gratefulness at once, my parents asked me what I thought.

What did I think? I thought I already had a shoe closet the size of the bush Kedrik and I found, filled with so many shoes that they tumbled out whenever I opened the door. My dresses were so numerous that I rarely wore the same one more than once. I never did anything with my hair except pin it out of my face, so all the hair decorations were useless.

*They needed the money for something else, I guess.* I stiffened as Grandmother's words ran through my head. Were these dresses and accessories the reason that orphans were living on the street for a month?

I scanned my parents' faces, which were bright with anticipation.

"I'm speechless," I said at last.

Mother gushed, saying she was happy that I was happy, and she knew I'd like what she and Father chose.

Father told me we needed to have a serious discussion, and I braced myself for the strings attached to all the goodies I didn't want. He squared his shoulders, as if preparing to issue a royal proclamation.

The request began innocently enough. Father reminded me that he and Mother had been abroad the past month and a half, visiting my Aunt RoseRed, her husband, the King of Tragenwood, and my cousins, SunGold and StarSilver.

I failed to make a connection between the visit and all the new clothes. Tragenwood's economy rested on lumber, not textiles. Though I'd only visited once, the memory was stark, like grass stains on a white gown. I'd been five, and my two bossy cousins had tried to force me to put on eyeliner and play tea party with them. I'd gotten so fed up with them ignoring my refusals that I locked SunGold in her own closet. StarSilver ran to her nursemaid, sobbing about how her sister was going to suffocate or starve or get eaten by a monster, and the woman tattled to my mother. I had to dust my room as punishment, which encouraged me to feel zero remorse. That one visit had prevented them from extending a second invitation.

Now, both SunGold and StarSilver were about to start their first year at the Interkingdom Collaborative University for Princesses, my father said. The boarding school had opened three years earlier and showed great promise for educating young royals and forming friendly relationships between kingdoms.

I couldn't help but smirk. "The ICUP? What kind of school name is that?"

My father ignored me. He said that princesses who attended would learn everything they needed to know to marry well.

I felt like someone had smashed a vase over my head. I knew where the conversation was headed, and everything in me rebelled. Tutors never stayed long because they said I was unladylike, incorrigible, and unfit for the title Princess Heir. The school was my parents' solution. That poorly named educational establishment would attempt to tame me so that I attracted a Prince Charming, married him, and then faded into his shadow while spouting his children like popcorn.

My parents believed the school could benefit me, my father continued, especially after hearing about the immature behavior I displayed in their absence.

I wasn't sure which of my many immature behaviors they were referring to, but I decided not to ask.

My mother said that they had tried their best to teach me, but I didn't seem to hear them. They loved me and wanted me to become a successful queen.

If that were the truth, though, they wouldn't be sending me away. For once, I wasn't indignant or boiling with frustration. My feelings were frozen, like a solitary snowflake drifting in a gray sky. The truth was that until I was docile and pretty, they wanted me out of their sight. They wanted to expunge that irritating *me* part of me, to make me a living corpse.

I said nothing.

They had made all of the arrangements, they said, and, as I could see, purchased all the necessities. I would leave for the University the next morning.

Time ran slower as I disengaged myself from my body. I saw them talk to me animatedly without hearing any of the words. My mother practically sparkled with enthusiasm, her strikingly beautiful face full of surety, like the full moon. The colorful dresses surrounding me blurred to gelatin-like blobs.

My parents looked at me expectantly.

"What?"

While I'd zoned out, they had asked me a question. Patiently, they explained it again. The University allowed each royal to bring three maids. Who did I want to accompany me?

"I don't need—" I stopped myself. Out of nowhere, the face of a tearful blonde girl floated into my head. "I'll bring Elsie with me. She works in the kitchen now."

Since I had met her, I learned that the kitchen girl was an orphan, and she had no siblings. If I brought her, she would be safe from the cook, who I knew would resume her abuse as soon as I left.

My parents objected, saying that Elsie was far too young and inexperienced. She'd only started working for the castle recently, and she knew nothing of a princess's needs.

But I was adamant. "I haven't needed a maid since I was eight. I can draw my own baths, make my own bed, and dress myself. It's not that hard. Elsie could just come as a . . . a companion."

I didn't need one of those either, but that was the first excuse I came up with. *To protect her from the cook* wouldn't have made sense to my parents.

To satisfy me, they agreed, though they chose two experienced servants, Nora and Tilly, to accompany me as well.

In a daring move, Mother came forward and squeezed my dirty tan hand in her smooth pale one. She and my father were aware that this was quite sudden for me, she said, but they were sure I would be fine. The University had wonderful credentials and was building a reputation for turning out beautiful princesses.

Slightly dazed, I headed to my room. There, I slipped beneath my bed and into the trapdoor. Flitting from passage to passage, I was no more than a flickering, silent shadow. My wanderings brought me outside the castle, but I kept moving, my feet knowing where I needed to go even if my mind didn't register what I was doing. I found myself in the stables, where Snowy, in her warm hay-smelling stall, greeted me.

Poking her head over the stall door, she nuzzled my hands.

"I don't have any treats for you this time—sorry," I apologized.

Unfazed, she snuffled my face. Leaning my head against her soft white neck, I ran my fingers through her mane, staring into nothingness.

---

Lamplight streaked across my vision, and I awoke. I sat up to find that it was still dark, and no stars pierced the night sky through my window.

That was because, I realized the next second, there was no window, and I wasn't in my bed. As I moved, the straw beneath me shifted with a soft *sssshhhh* sound. I'd skipped supper with my parents and slept curled up in a corner of Snowy's stall while she guarded me.

Dimming her lamp, Grandmother Rose let herself into the stall and sat beside me, draping a corner of her cloak over my shoulder.

"They're sending me away," I croaked.

"I know." Of course she did. She knew everything.

"They used the orphanage money to buy me a bunch of new clothes so I could become a real princess."

Grandmother stroked my hair and said nothing.

"It's true!" I exclaimed. "Buying an entire wardrobe isn't part of the normal monthly expenses." I shook my head in disbelief. "The servants say my mother was poor once, and *good*. What happened?"

"Your mother was innocent, not good. There's a difference."

I snorted.

Grandmother pulled me to my feet. "They're looking for you in the castle. I came to say goodbye."

We hugged.

"Maybe the school won't be so bad. You've always wanted to get away from Agaedith."

Yeah, until I didn't anymore. Now, I had something to lose.

"I'll tell Fyre and Kedrik what happened. Maybe you can write to each other."

Emphasis on *maybe*. We couldn't swordfight, swim, ride Snowy, or joke around long distance, though.

I turned and kissed Snowy on the nose. In the lamplight, her eyes looked like two wells of melted chocolate. "Bye, Snowy."

I knew without asking that she wasn't coming. There had been no riding clothes among the new items. My lungs felt like squeezed balloons when I thought about being so far away from her.

When I returned to my room, Tilly, my old nursemaid, was there waiting to help me dress. She'd been sent there by my parents, no doubt. I'd hardly seen her in years.

"You have an exciting day in store, Your Highness."

I kept silent.

"Do you need some help with that?" she asked, seeing that my sleepy fingers were having difficulty buttoning my traveling dress.

I shook my head and shrugged her off. Without Tilly's help, I washed my face, brushed my hair and teeth, and put my shoes on.

"My, my, Your Highness! You are getting so big, you hardly need help anymore."

Yay, I could dress myself. I was so talented.

When I reported to the entry hall, I was surprised to see Mother and Father waiting to send me off, fully dressed and primped in royal regalia.

They had one last gift for me, they said.

I reluctantly accepted the heavy, rectangular parcel. Unwrapping it, I revealed an ornate mirror with gilded roses engraved on an ivory frame. It was my mother's magic mirror—the one that had almost gotten her killed. And she was now passing it to me. Joy.

My mother said she knew I would take good care of the family heirloom and use it wisely.

"Yes, I will."

Good girl. My father patted me on the back, as if I was one of his hunting dogs.

I flinched under the touch.

The servants had done all the packing the night before, so there was nothing left to do but leave. Dumping the mirror into the bottom of the carriage, I climbed in and let the servants shut me inside. With a lurch, the journey began. The carriage bumped along the cobbles, and I stared out the window as Grandmother's cottage passed by and the scent of her herbs faded.

The carriage rolled into the woods, past Burlaku and Struckan in the Grove, the forsythia bush, and the gurgling river. Struckan might be holding a message for me, but I would never get it. Kedrik would no longer have a sparring partner.

When the wheels turned onto an unfamiliar side road, I closed the curtain. Sighing, I let the gloomy silence press around me.

"Your Highness?" Elsie, sitting across from me, spoke up. Her voice was hardly louder than a chipmunk squeak. The other two maids, Tilly and Nora, were with the luggage in the other carriage, but there was so much stuff that Elsie couldn't fit with them. That meant the poor girl had only me for company.

"Don't call me that."

"What shall I call you?"

"Just Chris."

"Okay, Chris. I should have told you before—I don't know anything about being a maid."

"You don't need to know anything, Elsie. I can take care of myself. I don't need a maid."

At first, I thought I had upset her because she let the silence stretch on so long, but when I flicked my eyes to her face, concern greeted me.

"Do you need a friend?" she whispered.

Clenching my jaw, I looked away, letting her question hang in the air unanswered.

The trip took several days, and toward the end of it, I began to hate carriages. But when I caught a glimpse of the ICUP, I decided that another month on the road would be preferable to arrival. Instead of flowers or vegetation, the road leading up to the building was marked with stone pillars like thick prison bars, foreshadowing what awaited. At the top of a hill, the square, gray brick mansion with its pointed roof stood aloof and austere, as if it believed itself too good for its occupants. Though not as tall as a castle, the school loomed ominously, waiting to swallow me. Darkness fell by the time the carriage reached the entrance, and the shadows made the mansion look even less welcoming.

Guards and footmen escorted Elsie and me into the entrance hall, which was mostly bare. The place had very little history, so there were no pictures of past headmistresses or whatever commoner schools tended to put on their walls. What drew my eyes were the flags hanging from the ceiling—one for each kingdom in Clystopia, over fifty in all. I spotted Agaedith's banner, half black, half white, with a centered red apple.

A pinched woman with a sleek iron-colored gown greeted us. She had a sour, stretched expression on her face, perhaps because of the abnormally tight bun she'd forced her gray-streaked hair into.

"You are early," she remarked, raising an already severely arched eyebrow.

Nice to meet you too, lady.

"It will be a few days before anyone else arrives, so I expect you to behave yourself while you are alone. Do you understand?"

"Yes."

"What did you say? Speak up, I cannot hear you when you mumble." Her harsh voice grated like fingernails on a chalkboard.

"Yes!"

"My name," she said sharply, "is Ms. Ann Throupé. As your headmistress, I am to be treated with respect, and that includes addressing me by name."

There was a pause. "Well?" she demanded.

"Well, what?"

If possible, Ms. Throupé's face grew even more pinched. Her slash of a mouth turned downward. "While you are here, you are a student first and a royal second. The kings and queens of Clystopia—including your parents—have authorized me and the rest of the faculty to distribute punishment as we see fit. You will do well to remember this." She widened her eyes for emphasis. Combined with her aquiline nose, the effect made her face look like a vulture's. "Follow me. I will take you to your room."

Ms. Throupé led Elsie and me up two flights of stairs and down a long hallway. Opening a plain wooden door, she ushered us briskly inside.

I gasped in horror.

"What now? This is one of our finest suites—you should be grateful for it."

I chose my words carefully. "I am very thankful for such a fine suite, Ms. Throupé, but I really do not deserve—"

"I quite agree. However, it is where you are staying. Try to keep out of the way while the porters bring in your luggage."

She didn't fall for my attempted manipulation at all. Striding out of the room, she left Elsie and me alone.

"Why don't you like the room, Chris? I think it's lovely." She sat timidly on a sofa, as if she expected someone to yell at her for defacing it. Her slim form hardly made a dent in the upholstery.

On one hand, she had a point. The room was sizable, with a carpet as thick as shaggy sheep wool, a fireplace, a canopy bed, and yep, a huge walk-in closet. If I put a coffee table and seating among the clothes, I could convince everyone it was a parlor. Rolling my eyes, I clicked the closet door shut. The architect had known what kind of quarters a princess would expect.

However, I couldn't say I was fond of the interior design.

"It's just so . . . *pink*." Everything was pink—the walls, furniture, curtains, and bedclothes. I felt like I was trapped inside a bubble of gum.

I sat on the princess-size canopy bed (which was almost twice as big as a king-size) and sank several inches into the fluffy mattress. I stayed there while the porters brought all my bags up. Elsie, Tilly, and Nora helped me organize my stuff before leaving to settle into the servants' quarters. I sat on my bed some more. After I missed dinner, Elsie brought up some food for me. It remained untouched. Eventually, the sun blinked to sleep.

Instead of sleeping, I stared up at the wispy canopy.

"Happy fifteenth birthday, Chris," I whispered to no one.

# Part 2

*"Know that I am with you; I will protect you wherever you go, and bring you back to this land. I will never leave you until I have done what I promised you." Genesis 28:15*

*"Not only that, but we even boast of our afflictions, knowing that affliction produces endurance, and endurance, proven character, and proven character, hope."*
   *Romans 5:3-4*

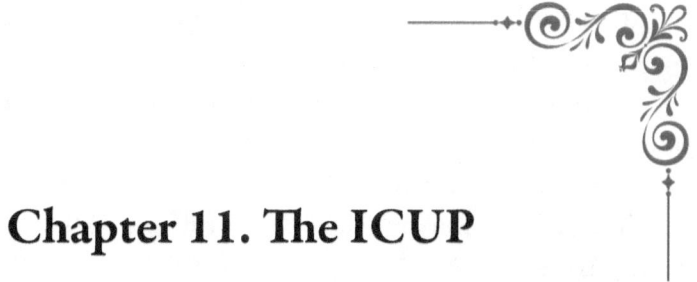

# Chapter 11. The ICUP

The school was so silent during the day that I heard a faint ringing, as if my ears were struggling to bring in sound that wasn't there. I wandered aimlessly through the halls and in the courtyard at the center of the building. It wasn't a sophisticated structure. All the bedrooms were on the third floor, all classrooms on the second floor, and the ballroom, kitchen, dining room, and parlor were on the first floor.

There were few decorations around the school. It was just as austere and unsympathetic as its headmistress. Though the food was filling, it tasted mushy and flavorless. The courtyard was all brick and gray stone except for one lone pine tree that stood bedraggled and defeated in the middle. I stared at the tree regularly, feeling kinship with it.

*Free me, free me*, the tree whispered.

"I can't. I'm just as trapped as you are," I murmured back.

A few days later, another set of carriages arrived. I watched from my bedroom window as two girls in outlandish attire were assisted from their carriages and escorted into the entrance hall. Dozens of servants scurried in their wake, unpacking luggage, tending horses, and creating a general feeling of organized chaos.

When footsteps thumped up the stairs, I went to my door and listened. Muffled sounds came from the hall, where the two girls entered their suites across from mine. I was no longer the only royal resident, but that didn't make me feel any better.

My eyes stung, and I brushed a stray tear away.

I wasn't surprised when Fairy Godmother appeared in my room a few minutes later.

"Are you okay, honey? I'm worried about you."

The words sounded foreign coming from someone other than Grandmother Rose. "Worried . . . about me?"

"Of course. Ever since you got the news that you had to attend school, you've been depressed. I know what's happened, and I just want you to be aware that I'm here for you."

"Thanks." It wasn't much comfort, though. "Hey, wait, have you been spying on me?"

Fairy Godmother pulled back her chin, affronted. The lace on her dress ruffled. "Fairy Godmothers do not spy. We merely monitor our ward's feelings. You've been at a low point for over a week. I knew something was wrong, so I did a little investigation to find out what it was—because I care about you."

That sounded a lot like spying to me, but I dropped the subject. "Do you think the Intriguer—the being behind the kidnappings—knows about this place?" I asked. "It would be really easy to capture more royals since we're all here together."

Being surrounded by brick instead of the trees' protective boughs made me feel cornered and vulnerable.

"Your cousins' disappearance is part of the reason your parents sent you away. They think you'll be safer at this remote location with guards from many kingdoms protecting you."

I didn't know who had the right instinct for safety—me or them. Honestly, I kind of hoped it was them, since I was stuck at the school.

"Have you discovered anything new about the Intriguer?"

She bit her lip. "My search hasn't turned up anything yet. If I learn something, I'll let you know. What you need to focus on now," she said, laying her arm around my shoulders, "is making the most of your time here. Try to get to know the other princesses. Some of them are probably homesick as well, and I am sure they would like to be friends with a nice girl like you."

"Doubt it," I scoffed. "They're probably afraid they'll ruin their reputation if they come too close."

Fairy Godmother gave me a sympathetic shoulder squeeze. "Chris, honey, you only think that because that's how Coralla feels about you. Hardly anyone here will know more than your name."

"My reputation precedes me, I'm sure."

"They know you were involved in an accident at Coralla's party. That's all it was, Chris—an accident. If you get to know them, I think you'll be surprised how many princesses have a lot in common with you. This is a wonderful opportunity to start fresh."

I didn't bother pointing out that I had a history of "accidents" spanning multiple social events in various kingdoms over the course of a decade. But moping around wasn't any more fun than talking to people, so I might as well give the latter some effort.

Fairy Godmother beamed, kissing me on the cheek. "I'm so proud of you, Chris. You're such a trooper."

If Kedrik had been there, we'd have laughed at her strange terms of endearment. As it was, I was too desolate to feel a sense of humor.

Later, I knocked on the door of one of the new girls' rooms. I slouched in the doorway as I waited for someone to answer it, half hoping no one did.

"Yes, yes, get in here. Honestly, Bella, I—"

As I peeked around the door, the reproving voice died, replaced with one of honeyed venom.

"Oh my, I *do* apologize. I thought you were my maid. I sent her *ages* ago to fetch my periwinkle hair ribbon from my sister. How are you, Chrisithia, my dearest cousin?"

Dearest cousin? I was SunGold's *only* cousin. Her fake warmth was obvious, but I still entered the room. I barely registered that she'd used my full name. I lacked the energy to get angry about it.

"You seem the picture of health," she went on without waiting for me to speak, "though I see your sense of style is still . . . primitive."

As always, her disdain was obvious by the arch of her carefully shaped brows. Her long golden hair was fixed in tight curls that bounced around when she turned her head, like rattlesnakes ready to spring and bite.

I shrugged. "This is comfortable."

I wore black flats and one of my new dresses. It was dappled different shades of green, like a forest in summer. I didn't see anything wrong with it. Maybe she was referring to the fact that I wore no jewelry, makeup, or nail polish.

SunGold laughed, a sound that was like a chittering flock of birds.

"You *are* funny, Chrisithia. Come now, sit here and I will do your hair. I know a style that will look adorable on you. It would never be right on me; my hair is too long."

I hesitated. I liked my hair—it was easy to take care of. But Fairy Godmother had encouraged me to make friends. Surely a hairdo wouldn't be that horrible. As long as her hairspray didn't make me go bald, I could always undo whatever style she crafted.

Seeing my uncertainty, my cousin pouted.

"I'm coming," I assured her.

As soon as I took a seat before the vanity, she attacked my head with tools and sprays. It took all my willpower not to run screaming out of her room or gag on the chemical spray that infiltrated my nose, mouth, and eyes.

SunGold was putting the finishing touches on her masterpiece when the missing maid, Bella, and StarSilver walked into the room. Or rather, Bella walked while StarSilver practically danced.

My other cousin's hair was paler than her twin's, like cream cheese icing, and straight. As she floated over (her feet never seemed to touch the ground) her hair whirled behind her like fluttering streamers. She was slighter than her twin and had a distinctive pixie look to her, though no one could doubt that she and SunGold were related.

"Here is your hair ribbon, sister! It took some time for my maid to find it because it was hidden in—oh! Cousin Chrisithia? My, I hardly recognized you!" she turned to SunGold. "That hairstyle has done wonders for her appearance."

"Do you really think so?" SunGold beamed.

"It is beautiful! Ooooooh, let's give her a makeover!" she giggled. "No one can say she doesn't need one."

They didn't bother to ask me if I *wanted* a makeover. Apparently, my opinions about my life didn't matter anymore, so why should the ones about my appearance? Before I could protest, they smeared my face with scrubs, sauces, and I think crayons, too. Pointy things ripped out extraneous hairs. I kept my eyes closed most of the time from sheer fright. When they finished and I opened my eyes, I was stunned.

I had to glance over my shoulder to make sure there wasn't someone else in the room that the mirror reflected. The face resembled artwork more than a human. It certainly wasn't my face. At least, it wasn't Chris's face.

Here, though, I wasn't Chris. Here they called me Chrisithia.

"See how pretty you look?" Squeezing my shoulders, StarSilver rested her cheek against mine and beamed into the mirror.

SunGold's hair bobbed as she tossed it over her shoulder. "That is *sooo* much better, right?"

As I drank in my appearance, I kept my face expressionless, worried I would destroy the vision like ripples destroyed the tranquility of a still pool. A rim of black called attention to my stormy eyes. Surprised, slightly parted lips glistened as red as my mother's. Framing my face was a glossy wave of brown hair, and a tiger lily barrette posed jauntily above my left ear. Fairy Godmother was right—nobody here knew me. I could be Chrisithia if I chose.

I was slightly terrified by my own reaction. Never before had I seriously considered whether I was beautiful. Sometimes I figured I was, sometimes I figured I wasn't, but most of the time I just told myself it didn't matter. Part of me wanted to reject any further diplomatic efforts, stomp back to my room, and stick my whole head in a tub of water. That's what I would have done, if I were my usual self. But my fire was out.

An idea tickled me—what if I didn't act all offended and scrape my face and head clean? Maybe it wasn't a big deal. In Agaedith, trying to be pretty was impractical since I was always scooting through passages, riding Snowy, climbing trees, or lately, sword fighting. However, I could do none of that here, so what was the point in dressing down?

After a moment of deliberation, I decided to do nothing, because it was the easiest reaction.

"You both did a wonderful job," I praised, smiling at my dearest cousins. "If you will excuse me, though, I must return to my room to prepare for supper."

"You had better not wash your face off after SunGold and I worked so hard to make it pretty." StarSilver put her hands on her hips.

"Of course not."

"Promise?" SunGold entreated.

"I promise."

I slipped back across the hall and headed straight to my closet. A pair of coppery earrings with dark green emeralds went on my ears, followed by a matching necklace. I switched my black shoes for green ones with orange flowers at the toes. They had a slight heel, but it wasn't very high, so I hardly noticed it.

As I tossed the pair of flats to the back of the closet, my eye caught something glinting. Squatting down, I retrieved an ivory frame with gilded roses and propped it against the wall. I gazed into the magic mirror. One second. Two seconds. Three seconds.

Almost inadvertently, the words squeezed themselves out of my mouth. "Looking glass on the wall, who is the fairest one of all?"

Undulating smoke appeared in the mirror, and a deep voice answered me. "Your answer will come, Chris, if you blow me a kiss."

I was too intent on getting my answer to question the request. After touching the tips of my fingers to my mouth, I lowered my hand and blew a kiss.

The mirror shimmered, but revealed nothing other than my own reflection.

"You are the fairest, my lady," it said.

A cool smile twisted my round, full lips.

"Do not tell me you are planning to wear *that*!" SunGold looked at my dress with disgust. "It does not match your style at all! Surely you have something better—that thing makes you look like a dying leaf."

As if she would know what my style was after only two days. I didn't even know what my style was anymore. I smoothed the skirt of my orange dress with bronze trim. It did sort of look like a leaf, now that she mentioned it.

"If you would like to help me, I could show you my closet. I trust you could find something suitable."

I expected her to turn up her high-bred nose and flounce away, but she didn't. Instead, she gave an aloof smile. "My thoughts exactly."

She led the way back to my room, breezing into my closet like it was hers. "Have you anything from Leather Diamonds?"

My brow creased. I hadn't examined all my new gowns in minute detail, but I knew none of them included a scrap of leather. Diamonds, yes, but no diamonds made of leather either.

"I don't believe so—"

"Ah, here! This is perfect. StarSilver has this same make. Hopefully she has not decided to wear it today as well. That would be a predicament, hmm?"

My cousin drew out a wispy purple dress with butterflies embroidered on it. On the inside of the back, a cursive "LD" was monogrammed.

"This will match the amethyst in your crown beautifully," she announced.

"Absolutely," StarSilver agreed, twirling gracefully into the room. "I have that same dress in yellow, as a matter of fact. Fortunately, I decided not to wear it today. That would have been a predicament, hmm?"

I smirked, but neither princess noticed.

"And you *must* wear these glittery shoes," StarSilver continued. "They are simply gorgeous!"

Taking my arm, StarSilver propelled me behind the dressing screen while SunGold dumped the dress in Elsie's arms and snapped her fingers at Nora, who was sitting on the sofa darning stockings.

"Help your Princess dress," she ordered them.

A flare of irritation fountained from me. Stepping away from the screen, I gently took the dress from an intimidated Elsie.

"They don't have to help me—I can dress myself," I said.

The sisters gaped at me, aghast, as if I'd just suggested we do-si-do through the hallways in our drawers.

"That will never do!" SunGold exclaimed. "You could put a wrinkle in the fabric."

"Or a rip," StarSilver added.

Their shrill voices barraged my ears. But they weren't wrong. Once, I had ripped the seam in a gown as I struggled to wriggle inside.

I suppressed a sigh. "All right, I will let them assist me. Nora, would you mind?"

As Nora hauled herself to her arthritic feet without complaint, I placed the dress back in Elsie's outstretched arms.

"Just follow Nora's instructions," I told her out of the corner of my mouth, recalling that she wouldn't know how to act like a lady's maid.

"Yes, Chris."

SunGold gaped at Elsie. "Are you going to let the girl speak to you in such an impudent manner?"

"Her name is Elsie," I said through gritted teeth, "and I asked her to address me that way."

"Whyever would you do that?"

"Because I felt like it," I said testily, more fired up than I had been since my arrival at the school. My cousins wouldn't understand, but it was too late to gulp the words back down.

StarSilver tittered, shaking her head. "Servants never make good friends," she said. "They can never relate to what it is like to be a royal. Please do not be mad at us, we only want to help you fit in."

She and SunGold looked at me sorrowfully, like hurt lambs.

"I'm not mad." I sighed, suddenly not caring anymore.

Obediently, I let myself be attired in the stylish gown. The dress was surprisingly comfortable, but the heels on the shoes made my feet ache as soon as I forced them on. I dealt with it. For the first time in my memory, I felt like a real princess—proud, beautiful, and delicate. Surprisingly, I adapted to the new me instinctively. It turned out it was easy to stand still and look pretty when I couldn't summon the effort to do anything else. I knew that not one hair on my head was out of place, my makeup wasn't smudged, and my dress fit gorgeously. I swayed in the heels naturally. It was strange—all my life I'd fought this perfection, but being a princess was in my blood. I couldn't escape it forever.

My skirt swished as I followed the twins out the door to breakfast. *Chrisithia, Chrisithia, Chrisithia*, it seemed to whisper. As I clicked the door shut behind me, I saw Elsie standing in the center of the room with her arms folded around herself, staring down at her toes, ashamed.

My shoulders slumped, and I went to wipe a hand across my weary face, but then I remembered that I'd smear my makeup, so I didn't. I started to run the hand through my hair instead, but realized I would upset the fragile waves, so I stopped. I was about to crack my knuckles for lack of anything else to do with my hand, but then I remembered that would be inappropriate and gross. Dropping my arms to my sides, I squared my shoulders and retreated farther within myself.

I gave a passable impression of being alive during breakfast—as good an act as any princess would be expected to perform. After the meal, carriages began arriving in droves. Porters rushed back and forth, jumbling luggage together and sometimes crashing into each other because they couldn't see over their huge loads.

I retreated to my room frequently to fix my makeup and readjust my hair, then returned to the growing crowd in the sitting room and pretended to be sociable. Elsie watched me come and go. She didn't say anything, but I felt her questions.

"What is wrong with you?" I finally snapped at her.

She almost jumped through the bubblegum ceiling. "Nothing. It's just . . . you're so different."

I took a deep breath, but couldn't shake the feeling that I was floating, detached from my body. "I have to be this way here."

I hardly believed the words came out of my mouth. I closed my eyes. I couldn't cry because then I would have to redo all my makeup. Being Chrisithia was the simplest solution to every problem. Chris could never rule a kingdom, but Chrisithia didn't have to. She could get a husband who knew what he was doing. That was her duty to her kingdom. She could have a son, and raise him to be like his father.

"Well, you don't have to be different around me if you don't want to," Elsie said. "I like you either way." Sitting on the edge of a chair, she swung her legs. Her feet were several inches from the floor.

She meant well, but she didn't understand. I couldn't just switch personalities on and off depending on the situation. I was trapped.

"I must go."

As I hurried out of the room, Elsie called after me softly.

"Whatever makes you happy, Your Highness."

*Happy*. I panicked at the sound of the word, not even sure how to define it, let alone be it. Wrapped in my own depressing spiral, I failed to hear two royals chatting amiably with each other around the corner. We smashed into one another with enough force to make all three of us lose our balance and dignity. I fell hard onto the stone floor. My tailbone would surely be purple the next morning, though I wasn't going to check.

Cross, I got to my feet, smoothing my dress and hair.

"Watch where you are going," I snapped, then whirled around and headed back the way I had come.

"*You* should watch where *you're* going!" a princess spat back at me.

I'd barely seen her face, only coils of black hair and eyes shaped like tilted raindrops.

"Relax, Laomi," the second girl said. I hadn't gotten even a glance at her, and I didn't recognize her voice. "She's probably just having a bad day."

Laomi sniffed. "How bad can it possibly be? Classes have not even started yet."

Stomping down the hall, I entered StarSilver's room, where she and two other princesses, Ashella and RosaLynne, were painting one another's nails and putting sequins and glitter on them. RosaLynne was an apple dumpling of a princess, all sweetness and plumpness. Meanwhile, her best friend was like a deer with big soft eyes, long legs that ended in tiny pointed feet, and cautious grace.

When we were seven, Ashella had a slumber party and invited me. Big mistake. I couldn't recall the details, but somehow, I ended up climbing halfway up the chimney in her room, searching for a flying squirrel nest. Inevitably I fell, fracturing my wrist and sending a mushroom cloud of soot into the princess's bedroom. I hadn't visited her kingdom since.

Half a year later, RosaLynne's father celebrated the opening of an extensive new garden planted in his late wife's honor. All kingdoms were invited, so I had an audience to witness me trip on my untied sash and reel into the rose bushes. I broke a few branches, but the thorns got their revenge. There'd been no reason for the King to start bawling about the dishonor to his beloved Rosamond or for my parents to shove me in a carriage and send me on the two day's journey back home by myself.

Needless to say, I hadn't conversed with the two of them for some time.

Still, RosaLynne was friendly, at least. Her bright smile showed twin dimples in her round face. "Hello! It is Chrisithia, yes?"

As if she didn't know my name. She was probably just making sure I wouldn't devour her head for not calling me Chris.

I nodded.

Her amber eyes lit up. "If you take a seat, I can do your nails . . . after . . . I take . . . a little . . . nap." With that, she conked out, sprawled across StarSilver's bed.

I blinked a few times to make sure I wasn't seeing things, but the dimple-cheeked girl didn't move. No one else seemed remotely concerned that a princess that had been perfectly fine a moment before was passed out in their midst.

"Um, does she need assistance?" I asked, jerking my head in the collapsed princess's direction.

"Poor Rosie," Ashella said, sighing. Her dark sienna complexion was shadowed further with pity. "She's developed narcolepsy." Without using her wet nails, Ashella somehow managed to reposition her friend so that her copper hair wasn't covering her airways.

"It means you fall asleep erratically," StarSilver offered in response to my blank look.

"Her mother, Queen Rosamond, was cursed to sleep for a hundred years until her true love came to kiss her awake," Ashella explained in a hushed tone. Her sheet of midnight hair cascaded over her shoulder like a dark waterfall as she leaned toward me. "It was utterly romantic, but we think the remnants of the spell were passed down to Rosie. She is afraid that she will never find a prince willing to marry her with her condition."

Ashella's dress was shorter than the usual style, allowing her petite feet to peek out. They drooped toward the ground as if they, too, were depressed for the narcoleptic princess. StarSilver, though, fussed at her reflection in the mirror, unsurprised and unmoved. She was probably glad that there wasn't as much competition for handsome princes.

RosaLynne sat up abruptly. "Huh? What did I miss?"

"You were going to paint Chrisithia's nails," Ashella prompted.

"Of course!" She patted the space beside her.

Giving her my first genuine smile since I arrived at the ICUP, I sat and offered her my hand. When she dozed again, smearing mauve paint over my cuticle, I quickly washed it off before she woke.

Coming to once again, she pushed back her silky red hair like she was surfacing from a lake to breathe. "Oh, did I go out again? I am terribly sorry—did I ruin your hand?"

"No, it looks fine, see?"

"Thank goodness. That would have been even more embarrassing." Swallowing, she took a few calming breaths, but they didn't erase the flush in her face or the frazzled look in her eyes—the same look a rabbit had when hounds were chasing it.

I wasn't the only one, then.

I swept through the hall, hoping I wouldn't be late for dinner. It wasn't my fault—I only had half an hour after RosaLynne finished my nails to don a new dress and touch up my makeup. Who could prepare themselves in that amount of time? Something told me Ms. Throupé wouldn't see it that way, though.

Rushing into the dining room, I breathed a sigh of relief when I realized no one had been served yet. But my throat constricted when I saw there was only one space left on the bench. It was next to Ashella and a girl I didn't recognize dressed in black satin. Swallowing, I slid into the empty seat between them.

Ashella and I nodded to each other, but didn't speak. Once the food was served, the girl in black did, though.

"You didn't crack your ankle when we ran into each other, did you? Your shoes look pretty dangerous." She nodded at my glittering heels.

Startled, I drew my feet beneath the curtain of my voluminous skirt. I recognized her voice as the second girl I'd rammed into, the one who told Laomi to relax. She spoke with a commoner accent. And what was with her dress? Dark colors were so not in. Among the creamy pastels and shockingly bright dinner gowns the other royals wore, she stuck out like a raven among birds of paradise.

"I am fine, thank you. And you?"

The corners of her mouth quirked upward, as if sharing an inside joke . . . with herself. Cinnamon freckles scattered across her brown nose added to the playful look. "I've been through worse, don't worry."

Her eyes flicked up to my face. "You're Chris, right? I'm Rachaella. Good to meet you."

When most royals, like my cousins and my parents, looked at me, it was as if they were seeing their own reflection in my eyes rather than me. But Rachaella's startlingly gray eyes gouged a path straight to my soul, where I imagined she was reading it like a book with every millisecond of prolonged eye contact.

"Chrisithia," I corrected, nearly choking. "I do apologize, but I am afraid I don't recall hearing your name before."

She was not a princess—that much I knew. Though there were over fifty kingdoms in Clystopia and often multiple princesses in each, I'd met them all at some event or other over the years. Rachaella must have been an obscure Lord or Lady's second cousin's in-law or something. Though the University specialized in training princesses, members of noble families could attend, even if they didn't stand a flea's chance on a hairless dog of gaining a prince's hand in marriage.

She shook her head. "No, you wouldn't have. I'm not a royal."

I was about to ask her why she was there—why she didn't run away while she still had two working legs and breath in her lungs—but an almost imperceptible movement caught the corner of my eye. SunGold shook her head slightly as if to say, "No. Don't talk to her."

Wondering what that was all about, I turned away and concentrated on my meal. The girl was weird, and I had nothing more to say to her.

She was interesting to watch, though. While the royals held their backs straight and their spoons with their pinkies out and cast demure eyes at their seafood chowder, she talked with Laomi as if she wasn't aware that her accent was wrong and ate her peas like she didn't care who was watching them fall off her fork for the third time or what they thought about it. Laomi ignored SunGold's pointed gestures to stop conversation. Instead, she and Rachaella joked and laughed like they were best friends.

I wasn't hungry. Finishing early, I excused myself and retired to my room. Classes started the next day, and I needed my beauty sleep.

# Chapter 12. The Princess Games

Stifling a yawn, I tried to concentrate as our Writing teacher, Ms. Sakura, spoke in her high squeaky voice about sonnets and feminine rhymes. Glancing around, I saw that most other girls looked even less enthused than me. RosaLynne was sleeping on her desk, SunGold and StarSilver whispered covertly to each other, and Laomi fiddled with her hair, which was arranged in an intricate, swoopy pattern stretching two feet above her head.

The rest of the morning wasn't any more exciting, because we had Music and Mannerisms classes. The teacher for Music said my voice left much to be desired. It was a nice way of saying that I sounded like a dying duck in mid-sneeze. I didn't butcher the harpsichord as badly as some of the other girls did, though. In Mannerisms class I avoided failing the first day by keeping quiet and doing my utmost to blend into the flowered wallpaper. It wasn't until afternoon break that things became interesting.

Most of the princesses relaxed outside on the hilltop, picking daisies or sitting under the shade of parasols. Rachaella and Laomi joined late, and everyone gave them a wide berth.

Rachaella didn't seem to notice. "Look!" she said to her friend, pointing to the cobblestone path.

The earlier storm had exhumed an earthworm, and it was baking on the rock in the sun, unable to return to its safe, dark home.

"Poor thing," Rachaella continued. Kneeling, she scooped the slimy, wriggly noodle into her fingers and deposited it onto a dirt patch beside the path. "There you go, little one."

"Ew," Laomi remarked.

Something shifted within me, but before I captured the new feeling, Ashella danced around the corner. A radiant smile lit her face like a firefly on a summer's night.

"There is a prince academy down the hill!" she exclaimed as soon as we were in earshot. "I can see them on the grounds from there!" She pointed to the spot she'd come from.

Instantly the princesses battered her with questions.

"Are you *sure* they are princes?"

"How many are there?"

"Are there any cute ones?"

When Ashella suggested they all check out the sight for themselves, they jumped to their feet with more energy than they'd demonstrated all morning. A stampede to see the perfect Prince Charmings thundered off.

Rolling her eyes, Laomi turned her back on them. "I could have told them there was a prince school; my brother goes there," she said.

I trailed in their wake, not invested in the situation, but not wanting to be left behind either. When I caught up, they were all jockeying for position to peer around the corner. Finding an open spot, I claimed it.

I had a perfect view of a school almost identical to the ICUP spread at the bottom of the hill. There were a few differences, most notably a training ring for weapons practice and stables for horses. A group of princes was having a riding lesson. Some of them were good horsemen, but others fell off before their mount had even begun to move. Watching them made me ache for Snowy. She was more talented than any of those training horses. I pictured her snorting in derision at the incompetence of the mounts and riders alike. Together, she and I could probably teach the class better than the instructor, who was red-faced and struggling to disentangle a royal boot from a stirrup while his mount wandered away to munch on some grass. I yearned to be high in Snowy's saddle, racing, or even just walking. Even if I couldn't ride, if I could just tangle my fingers in her mane and rest my forehead on her broad neck, whispering my confusion, I would feel better.

Unsurprisingly, the princesses were more interested in the guys than their equine companions. They took a poll to decide which prince was cutest.

"Who do you think, Chrisithia?" I was the only one who hadn't cast a vote.

I deliberated, not particularly interested in the conversation.

"The black-haired guy, on the pinto horse," I said at last. That particular prince could actually jump the horse he was riding without falling off, which was the most skill I'd seen out of any of them.

"Pinto? Isn't that some type of bean?" RosaLynne asked.

I stifled a sigh. "The brown and white horse," I explained.

"I see him! Yes, that one is attractive, I suppose," Ashella said politely.

The group finally came to a consensus on a blond prince who was continuously flipping his hair back. Suddenly, the Chosen One turned to look at us. Everyone except me shrieked and dove backward. He'd caught us, so why bother squealing like suckling pigs and pretending he didn't? Just to make things interesting, I stepped around the corner, fully revealing myself, and waved. The prince flashed his pearly whites at me and winked. Smirking, I turned and glided casually away.

Everyone was amazed by my audacity. Apparently, something monumental had occurred.

"He *winked* at you!"

"True love at first sight!"

"You two are *destined* to be together!"

"You are *so* lucky!"

I played along with them, even though I failed to see what was so impressive. I did enjoy the attention. Being admired was something I wasn't used to. It made me feel lighter, as if there were bouncy pillows on the balls of my feet.

During Dance class, the feeling of elation remained. Miss Victoria, our instructor, even complimented me on my grace. No one had ever told me I was graceful before.

After classes finished, a group of us gathered in the parlor for tea. I made sure to arrive early so I wouldn't have to sit near Laomi and Rachaella. Being too near them would diminish my popularity. But I needn't have worried. As we sipped our tea and nibbled baked goods, neither girl joined us.

Each guest took two cookies to be polite to the catering service, but ate only one to demonstrate their daintiness. I debated whether to be rude or a hog. The cookies were thin wafers with pastel icing and a sprinkling of crystallized sugar, and they melted in my mouth. I was about to decide to be a hog because I liked cookies and there were so many left over, but then I hesitated. Would the princesses stick up their noses and dislike me if I took another cookie? No one else was still eating. I would be the only one. They would know that I ate more than the rest of them—what would they think of me?

I waited too long. The servants cleared the tea and snacks, leaving us nothing to do but chat.

Gossip. Fashion. Boys. Ashella told everyone who hadn't been there what happened with the princes on the hill, and the royals showered more admiration on me. SunGold and StarSilver, who were used to being the most popular, didn't bother hiding their envy, but everyone else was captivated by my daring. Though my cousins had voted for "my prince" as cutest, they protested that he wasn't all *that* good-looking and exclaimed that I wasn't as impressive as I thought I was.

Fine—I didn't need them. They would be sorry when everyone quit hanging out with their jealous highnesses to be with me.

"Where are Laomi and Rachaella?" I asked after a while. There were around two dozen royals in our class at the ICUP, and the two of them were the only ones who hadn't stopped by.

"Rachaella was not invited," StarSilver said haughtily, tossing her silvery hair. "And Laomi is forgoing our company until we allow her little follower to join as well." She sneered, adding a mumbled, "Conceited little twit."

"Why do you dislike them?" I asked cautiously, hoping I wasn't saying something stupid.

"I am quite fond of Laomi, of course. I simply cannot comprehend why a Princess Heir of her standing would hold a commoner rat under her protection. Rachaella was not accepted into the University until the kingdom of Towers offered to pay many times the entry fee to grant her a place. Rachaella has no royal blood at all." With each word she spoke, StarSilver's eyes widened a little more, and her eyebrows shot farther and farther up her head.

SunGold expanded upon her sister's complaint. "Our parents have complained, of course, but the board members would not reconsider their decision." She was almost spitting with indignation, like a feral cat. "This is the Interkingdom Collaborative University for *Princesses*, not whoever-happens-to-be-wandering-the-streets."

I kept my face studiously blank. It wasn't hard; I didn't care who attended the school. But really, what had that girl been thinking? Attending an exclusive school for princesses was like jumping into a pit of wolves wearing a red riding hood and a sign that read, *Eat me*.

"Why would she come if she is not a royal?" I asked.

"The only reason," StarSilver informed me, "is to formalize her education so that she may be eligible to marry a prince. A prince who would otherwise have married one of *us*."

Gasps rose from the others assembled. Most of them had been unaware of Rachaella's background. I wasn't sure why they were so surprised. She didn't have the haughty royal aura or the full range of eyebrow motion, and she had a stockier, more athletic build than the average dainty princess.

"For shame!"

"Scandalous!"

"How horrid!"

"So selfish!"

"She should go marry a pig feeder in some forsaken village!"

"She should simply jump off a cliff to save the pig feeder the embarrassment!"

Historically, princes married princesses, and the bloodline stayed "pure" and "unsullied" by the lower classes. Because of the limited number of monarchs in Clystopia, that meant most royals were related, if the line was traced back far enough. In the past generation, though, increased family illnesses and odd deformities had made marriage between cousins go out of fashion. Now it was frowned upon even more than marrying one of lower class. As a result, some princes, like my father, had married outside the royal line. SunGold and StarSilver were also the result of such a marriage, though they seemed to have forgotten that.

With the fishpond of wife candidates suddenly becoming a sea, many princesses feared for their futures. Only princes, after all, would inherit a throne, unless there were no male children of the reigning monarchs. If a princess married someone of lower class than she, her reputation would sink, along with her political influence and the number of party invites she received. Her affluent way of living might even be curtailed. Unless she could find an eligible prince or wealthy lord to snag, becoming an old maid was the only option guaranteed to safeguard her lavish lifestyle. But being unmarried was the most shameful humiliation a princess above the age of seventeen could suffer.

That meant Rachaella was imprisoned in a building with princesses and ladies from fifty kingdoms who all saw her as a threat to their eternal happiness. I did not envy her.

"My thoughts exactly," SunGold said in response to the horrified outbursts. "I am glad we are in agreement. There will be no objections to the plan my sister and I have devised to make Rachaella quit the University, I presume?"

"Of course not!"

"Oooh, you have a plan?"

"Do tell us!"

I blinked, slowly. All the fake-polite voices battering my eardrums were giving me a headache.

The twins shared a glance. "We plan to make her residence here as miserable as possible! Eventually, she will see the futility of her actions and leave, returning to the hole she crawled out of." StarSilver clapped her hands with giddiness, as if she was explaining details for a party she was organizing.

"How will you make her miserable?" Ashella asked. "I would like to help."

"Oh, well, you know—I mean, we could start by not speaking with her, of course," StarSilver mumbled.

SunGold tried to help her out. "And by not inviting her to events such as this. After those, um . . . perhaps we could write notes to push under her door, telling her to go away. And insult her if she approaches us."

"Insulting her should not be difficult," RosaLynne said in her dreamlike, lilting voice. "She has worn the same abysmal black dress for the past two days. It makes her look frumpy."

"Wait," Ashella protested. "I thought we were not to speak to her at all."

"Obviously, you may speak to her if you are insulting her," SunGold explained.

Ashella put her hands to her temples. "This is sooo confusing."

A bark of laughter squeezed out of me before I could stop it.

Twenty-one pairs of raised eyebrows swiveled in my direction.

"Pray tell what is so humorous, cousin," SunGold said, miffed at my interruption.

My lips twitched. "It's just . . . none of you have any idea how to play this game, do you?"

"What are you talking about?"

"Yes, what 'game'? This is serious!" my cousin protested.

"Exclusion? Hate mail? Alternating between ignoring and poking fun at her? Come on, that's not how you prank someone."

"I assume you have some suggestions, then?"

I folded my arms in front of my chest. "Pour her ink into her writing desk. Lick pieces of hard candy and stick them to her back and hair. Put something wet, like syrup or sauce, on her seat before she sits down at dinner. Take her stuff and hide it in random places when she isn't watching. Get caught receiving a note in class that makes fun of the professor with her signature as the sender. Push spiders or crickets under her door, not notes. A dead snake would be even better."

I paused when I realized that everyone was riveted to my words.

I shrugged. "That should be enough to get you started."

"Wait, what was the first thing again? You said everything so fast!" Ashella exclaimed.

I patiently went through the snippet of my extensive repertoire of pranks again. I had experience with all of them, either because I'd pulled them on Ben or he'd done them to me. That was the game. The game, I knew, was very effective at making both of us miserable. It would work on Rachaella too, I was sure. Once she started returning the pranks, though, things would get intense. Some of the princesses would freak. As for me, getting jelly dumped over my head or pine needles and stones hidden in my dancing shoes couldn't make me any more miserable than I already was. At that point, it would be a test to see whose will was stronger—the royal girls', or the wannabe-queen's.

A few days later, I stood with a squadron of princesses outside a classroom as they prattled on about nothing. Soft footsteps came toward us, but I was facing away, so I couldn't see who it was. I glanced at Ashella, who winked one dark brown eye and then the other in quick succession. That was the signal. The talking continued undisturbed, while I strained to tune them out and concentrate on the feet treading closer.

We'd pulled so many successful pranks already that I'd lost count. I kept expecting retaliation, but none had come yet. In fact, Rachaella hadn't given any indication that she resented what we were doing. Either she was stupid and thought all the spills, missing items, and chilly stares were unintentional, or she hoped that if she ignored us, we would stop.

I waited for the right moment, then stuck out my heel, as if I was going to leave the circle of princesses and go to class. The timing was perfect. Her foot met mine, and I pivoted just in time to see quills, papers, and a book lurch through the air.

Rachaella, however, didn't tumble into a tangle of limbs and petticoats like I'd expected. Instead, as she headed toward the floor face-first, she stuck her arm out over her head in the shape of a half moon and *rolled*. I blinked, and she was on her feet again.

"Whoops," she said. Her curly hair hadn't even pulled out of its ponytail.

I froze, transfixed. One moment, she'd been about to nose-dive into the floor, the next, she was brushing nonexistent dust from her skirt.

This time, I recognized the feeling I got when I observed her: curiosity. I forgot about the rules of engagement and started to ask her a question. But before I got a single syllable out, two arms looped through mine. Ashella and RosaLynne steered me away from our victim, smiling conspiratorially. They must not have seen the stunt Rachaella had pulled. Their talk dimmed to a buzz in my ears as I looked back over my shoulder.

Rachaella hadn't bent to pick up her spilled items. Instead, she watched me watch her and smirked as if we shared an inside joke.

After entering the classroom with the rest of the frilly flock of royals, I sat. Rachaella's desk was several rows behind mine, so I didn't see when she finally arrived. And I didn't turn around, even though I was dying to. The girl was an athlete. Where was she from? What did she do when she wasn't parading as a royal in a school for princesses? I only half-believed the idea that she was there to become polished enough to marry a prince. What was the true reason for her attendance? And why did I care?

Things were simpler when I didn't care. During class, I dutifully listened to Ms. Sakura as she talked about poetry. I read aloud from the book of poems when it was my turn, and I worked on my assignment when she distributed it—all without caring.

The whole time, curiosity about Rachaella nagged at me like a corset strung too tight. I hated thinking about her, because when I did, I started to question myself. When I wondered what she could do, I couldn't help but ask myself what I was doing. When I thought about what she really wanted to become, if not a prince's wife, reflections about what was I becoming forced their way into my head. When I pondered who she was, I blanked at the question of who I was.

My mind was entirely addled by the time class ended, though, of course, I was too refined to show it. Porcelain dolls didn't show their imperfections until they dropped on the floor and shattered.

Being thrust against the brick wall right outside of class didn't help my nerves either. I exhaled sharply as Laomi shoved her face close to mine, her dark eyes glittering menacingly. She was shorter than me, but with her heels and the mountain of straight black hair piled on her head, she seemed bigger.

"You. Listen. I know what you are doing to Rachaella, and I will not stand for it. She is here, and she will stay here as long as she likes. Get over it."

I stared at her through dead eyes, recalling a time when her ferocity would have resulted in me lashing out in return. "Are you finished?" I asked in a voice that wasn't mine.

Taken aback at my lack of irritation, Laomi regarded me with her head tilted to the side. Her hair wobbled precariously. "Are you drugged?"

I wasn't sure how to respond to that, so I didn't.

"Never mind," she said. "This is the only warning I'll give. Leave. Her. Alone."

Backing away, she stalked down the hall.

I made my way to the next class, unfazed. Her threat didn't mean anything—what could she do to me? Whack me with her braid? She hadn't threatened any of the other royals—not even my cousins—so she somehow knew that I was the one coming up with the ideas for the pranks, even if I didn't personally execute all of them.

So far, at SunGold and StarSilver's insistence, we'd restricted the pranks solely to Rachaella. But we could be more effective if we made her only friend suffer as well. Laomi might not be so supportive of her commoner lackey if the haughty royal woke up one morning with fifty pieces of chewed gum in her hair.

That evening, I raided the kitchen with a few especially devoted followers. Along with a bottle of milk, eggs, and a wheel of blue cheese, I took a few fruit pastries. The pastries were to snack on. Everything else was prank supplies.

"You made it!" StarSilver whisper-giggled as we bundled ourselves into SunGold's room with our absconded food items.

"What took so long? I was afraid you had been caught," SunGold said.

I looked down my nose at her. "Of course not."

In fact, the job had been easier than I expected. All the kitchen assistants had been busy washing dishes, so the three of us just meandered in, grabbed what we needed, and left quietly.

When I knelt to put my load on the coffee table, SunGold squeaked.

"Not there! Take it out on the balcony. It will stain and smell if it spills."

"It has to be here," I objected. "Setting up outside would draw attention."

As I finished setting my prank supplies down, SunGold pursed her lips, but didn't object again.

"Mmmff," Ashella murmured as she set down the cheese wheel beside the milk and eggs. She rolled her shoulders. "That cheese must weigh as much as I do. I hope my arms do not become larger after carrying that thing up three floors."

My eyes skimmed the cheese package. The label read *10 lbs*.

RosaLynne set the pastries on the opposite side of the table, and then she and Ashella left to fetch the remaining supplies from their rooms.

"What are those for?" SunGold snorted, pointing at the baked goods.

"Eating. I figured if I was going to sneak into a kitchen, I might as well steal something good." I took a cherry pastry and bit into it.

My cousins regarded me with wrinkled noses as jelly squirted out the sides and crumbs dropped to the table.

"I have to watch my waist," StarSilver muttered.

I shrugged, feigning indifference, but once the other two princesses returned, I set the half-eaten snack to the side and didn't touch it again.

Ashella and RosaLynne dumped old jewelry boxes and purses next to the food. The containers were filled with grass, thorns, burrs, and wet leaves. A few, the ones that I'd filled, contained spiders, ants, and wasps. For the past several days, I'd encouraged the girls to use part of their free afternoons to gather stuff we could use to design pranks. Some were reluctant to touch things they considered gross, but most participated. Ashella and RosaLynne had "courageously" volunteered to store all the stuff until it was needed.

"Who is coming across with me?" I asked.

"I have terrible balance, you know that. My feet are so small," Ashella said, excusing herself. "And Rosie cannot accompany you, either. She might become too stressed and fall asleep halfway across."

RosaLynne nodded solemnly at her best friend's assessment.

Fair enough. "Cousins? Do either of you dare to join me?" They didn't have balance problems or narcolepsy.

SunGold smoothed her hair. "No, thank you. If it is all the same to you, I will stay here."

"As will I," her twin said, not meeting my eyes. "We will help toss things over to you when you reach her balcony, though."

For a moment, I froze, looking from one girl to the other. When I came up with the idea, I'd never thought I'd be doing it alone. But it was too late to back out, so I ventured onto the balcony and stood on the railing by myself in my stiletto heels, arms spread wide for balance. I could take the shoes off, but I wouldn't. I didn't need to.

I scurried across the four-inch strip of brick between SunGold's balcony and the next, which happened to be Rachaella's. We'd discovered that the bolts on the balcony doors were surprisingly easy to slide from the outside. Once I reached Rachaella's balcony, gaining access to her room would be easy.

"Do *not* fall!"

"Oh, but she is so high up!"

*Careful, careful*, whispered the tree from the courtyard.

I ignored them. If I fell, I might break a bone or two, but I wouldn't die. There was no reason for them to be so dramatic.

With my clique unhelpfully cheering me on, I bridged the gap. Stepping from brick to railing, I dropped to the balcony, turned smartly, and curtsied. The others applauded.

As I slid back the bolt in the glass door, Ashella, RosaLynne, and my cousins tossed over the bag full of prank materials. I heard the eggs crack as the cheese landed on top of it. Kicking in the flimsy door with my heels, I got to work. I hid huge chunks of smelly blue cheese, made puddles of milk, sprinkled grass everywhere to attract bugs, scattered bugs everywhere to accent the grass, and poured the cracked eggs over the bed. When Rachaella returned, she would have to clean the mess herself since she had no maids.

The room was mostly barren of knickknacks, but as I drizzled jelly from an untouched fruit pastry onto her dresser knobs to make them sticky, I spotted a portrait positioned on top next to a vase of wilted wildflowers. It wasn't a miniature of herself, which some princesses displayed in their rooms, but that of a bearded man with smiling eyes crinkled against the sun. Intrigued, I examined it, wondering who Rachaella cared about enough to display a portrait of. A relative, perhaps—though at first glance, he didn't look much like Rachaella. He had windblown brown hair instead of tight black curls, blue eyes instead of gray, and his skin tone was much paler than her light brown hue. But as I looked closer, I recognized the heart-shaped face, cinnamon freckles, and mischievous smirk. Her father, perhaps, or a beloved uncle.

The e asygoing, f riendly g aze i n t he f rame d isconcerted m e, a nd I moved to the other side of the room to avoid the feeling of being watched.

I was about to nestle a duo of spiders among Rachaella's pillows when I caught sight of the wall behind her bedframe. It was decorated with colorful strips of paper. As I peered closer, I saw quotes had been copied with a neat hand onto each strip. After t he q uote, t here w as a b ook, a chapter, and a verse written: 1 Corinthians 10:13, Isaiah 35:4-6, 1 Kings 19:12.

Momentarily distracted, I read my way up the wall, drinking in words that provided comfort to someone who felt lonely, offered love to someone who felt abandoned, and called to action someone who was confident that their life had purpose, even though they didn't know what that purpose was. Warm memories of attending candlelit church services with Grandmother Rose stirred in the back of my mind. Near the ceiling, one paper arched over the others.

"I give you a new commandment: love one another. As I have loved you, so you also should love one another." John 13:34

I exhaled, long and slow. Then I backed away, off the bed, to the door. Phase Two of the plan was to mess with her belongings—strewing clothes over the floor, making a mess of face creams and toiletries in the bathroom, and hiding her jewelry.

I didn't do Phase Two. Shame washed over me. I started to understand that what I was doing wasn't a game. I took the spiders with me when I left, releasing them over the edge of the railing into the courtyard below. Then I returned to SunGold's balcony and pretended, as princesses often do, that nothing was wrong.

# Chapter 13. Rekindled

A note fluttered onto my desk during class from SunGold. I opened it and read.

*You are no longer any fun at all! Where were you for the jelly prank?*

It was the third prank I'd missed since the room invasion. After my epiphany, I had no desire to torment the poor girl anymore.

I scribbled a reply.

*You were no fun on the balcony when you made me cross by myself. I need a break.*

After reading my answer, she pursed her lips and turned away.

I returned my attention to the letter I'd recently received from my parents. Their communication wasn't interesting. They talked about their latest vacation, the unseasonably warm weather, and their new chandelier. But the pages fixated me, because in the bottom corner was Kedrik's symbol.

Somehow, for some reason, he'd hidden a message to me within my parents' letter. I scoured the tedious words repeatedly until I noticed something off about the writing.

My parents were precise to a fault, yet there were two ink blots hovering over the words "entirely" and "company." Puzzled, I tried to conjure various meanings for the chosen words.

After ten unfruitful minutes, the obvious answer hit me: those weren't the chosen words. The blots were *under* the words "in" and "visibly," not over the other words. Invisible! Kedrik had written his message on the back of the parchment with invisible ink.

I couldn't concentrate during the rest of the morning classes. In Speech, I was reprimanded for staring into space, and then yelled at again for saying "Whaaat?" instead of "Pardon me, could you please repeat that?" In Art, I accidentally gave Ashella's portrait red eyes.

"Chrisithia!" she protested. "I am *not* that hideous!"

Personally, I didn't think red eyes were hideous, but I didn't say so. Apologizing, I started over. When we were dismissed for midday break, I headed to the library and found a book on espionage with a section on invisible ink. Kedrik had mentioned it before, but all I remembered was something to do with lemons. Flipping through the volume, I read about so many types of invisible ink and ways to reveal it that I'd have graduated by the time I tried half of the strategies.

Removing the carefully folded message from my handbag, I scrutinized every letter again.

*Dear Chrisithia,*

*We hope this letter finds you well. Your father and I recently returned from a holiday in SeaCrest—only you were banished, of course, not us—and I must say, I am pleased to be home. The dolphins we saw at sunset were quite lovely, but SeaCrest is far too sunny, which of course wreaks havoc on my skin, and though sand is exfoliating, it is difficult to remove once it invades every crevice.*

*It seems as if the climate has followed us back to Agaedith, unfortunately. Though it is supposed to be autumn, the stifling Heat has been nearly unbearable. At least the orchard seems to be enjoying the weather. The royal agriculturalist has forecasted a record harvest this year.*

*We have a few new sapphire sculptures and a new chandelier hanging in the drawing room . . .*

The letter regaled the extravagance of the new crystal ornament before moving on to other mundanities. The letter concluded with:

*Make us proud.*
*Queen Snow White and King Orrluxe*

There w ere n o q uestions a bout h ow I w as c oping w ith t he jarring transition to school life, or even a *Happy belated birthday!* Overlooking the irritating tone of the correspondence, I scrutinized it once again for discrepancies that would show me how to make the invisible visible. I read the stupid thing three more times before I noticed that "Heat" was capitalized.

Rushing to my room, I lit a candle and held the paper over the flames, careful not to set the whole thing on fire. Soon, brown letters appeared, spreading over the back of the parchment like water spilling. Hungrily I read, even though I knew it was pathetic to hold on to scraps of paper and ink so desperately.

Hey Chris!
The day you left, I stopped by Grandmother's cottage to see why you hadn't shown up to sword fight, and she told me the news. Attending a University for princesses sounds awful. Grandmother said your parents instructed the school to intercept any communication from her (apparently they think she's a bad influence?), so we forged a letter from your parents so we could keep in touch. FYI, fake royal seals are scarily easy to come by.

Of course they had forged the letter. My parents never wrote me when they left me at home; why would they write when they sent me away?

At least Coralla isn't there to bother you. Our parents want her to have a "personalized education," so they didn't send her. She had a jealous fit when her friends left, and I somehow got blamed for it. I can't help but wish she'd gone and you'd stayed.

I haven't heard of the Intriguer kidnapping anyone else, and the trees haven't experienced it trying to break into their consciousness again. No sign of the wolves either. I mean, they're around—the trees can sense them—but they haven't bothered Fyre or me. I don't think they've given up, but the trees are looking out for us, so they haven't had an opportunity to attack. Have you spoken with Fairy Godmother again? If you have, let me know if she mentioned any new information about the Intriguer.

I hate to tell you this, but Snowy is sick. She won't eat anything, and she won't let anyone ride her. Grandmother's doing the best she can to treat her, though. She's pretty handy with all those plants. Try not to worry too much. Your horse is awesome, and with Grandmother helping her, I'm sure she'll be all right.

Fyre is almost full-size now, and he's working on endurance flying so he can visit you. What's the school like? Are there any princesses there you haven't punched in the face? What classes do princesses even have to take to be considered "finished"? Don't forget to keep up with your sword fighting!

Also, I heard it's your birthday. Well, it won't be your birthday when you read this, but let it be known that I wished you a long-distance "Happy Birthday" on your birthday. I hope it actually was happy, and not boring. If you had given me a heads-up, I would have even mailed a gift. But now it's going to be a little late—meaning, I don't have anything yet.

The Grove isn't as fun without you. When is your first break?

I felt like I was breathing fresh air after being water boarded to the point of drowning. Reminiscing about the time Kedrik, Fyre, Snowy, and I had spent together, I sighed. I hadn't forgotten about the Intriguer or wolf pack either. But at the ICUP, they didn't seem as real. Reading about what was happening back home brought what mattered to Chris into the forefront of my mind. I clenched my jaw to keep it from trembling.

I read Grandmother's note next.

Dear Chris,

I miss you! Your parents have forbidden communication between us hence all the secrecy. Kedrik was helpful in that regard—he's a smart, creative young man, and I can see why you two get along.

For some reason, the King and Queen think I am a bad influence. I don't think they liked it when you came home directly from the forest in grass-stained boys' clothes and short hair. They want you to be kept indoors and pampered, like some caged songbird. I couldn't stand not hearing from you until next summer, so unfortunately, I've had to go behind your parents' backs. But only because this is an extreme circumstance. In all else, of course, I am their humble subject.

Like Kedrik mentioned, I'm doing the best I can for Snowy, and I am hopeful she will recover soon. The Intriguer hasn't shown itself, and I am worried that means it is on the move. Don't let your guard down. Make safe choices.

Your birthday gift is arriving soon in a separate package.

I'm so proud of you, Chris, and I love you so much. I look forward to hearing how you are doing. Stay strong. Love you.

My eyes were watering by the time I finished, and my apathy dissolved. Flint struck stone within me, and sparks of liveliness lit upon the cold ashes of my being. A roaring fire of emotions burned, and the ice around my frozen heart melted and evaporated.

Breathing deeply, I rose from a kneeling position to my full height, clutching the letter. I looked into the magic mirror hanging on the wall. There was a beautiful girl in there. She was stylish, popular, and coldhearted, but not who I wanted to be. I screamed, almost making my blood bubble.

Elsie rushed into the room, stumbling over the hem of her dress.

"What is wrong, my lady?"

I stared straight through her, feeling manic. "EVERYTHING!" I shouted.

Eyes wide, Elsie slowly backed into the hall.

I tore the mirror from the wall and threw it facedown into the back of my closet. Snatching up my heeled shoes, I banged them on the floor until they broke. All the containers of hairspray and gel were dumped. The perfume I detested but wore anyway because everyone else thought it was delectable got splashed off the edge of my balcony. For good measure, I threw the crystal bottles off, too. They thumped onto the grass below.

I smeared my glass balcony door with makeup and lipstick to get rid of it. The rain would wash it away within a few days. Finally, I scrubbed my face and combed my hair out. I didn't need a mirror to reassure myself that I was Chris again, free from the shackles I'd put on myself to meet the impossible beauty standards that society held princesses to.

I detested myself like a wart. How had I let myself slip away for so long? This place wasn't good for me. The people here weren't good for me. I needed to go home.

"Elsie?" I called. "Are you still out there?" I opened my door to see her sitting with her back to the wall right outside. "Sorry if I scared you. I'm, uh, me again."

She swayed to her feet. "Really?"

"Really."

"Good." She fiddled with her skirt, unsure what to say next. Guilt sliced through me. The reason I'd brought Elsie to the ICUP was to protect her from the cook and help her have a real life. But all I'd done since arriving was ignore her and make her act like a lady's maid. I knew nothing about her.

"How old are you?" I asked. Hey, I had to start somewhere. "Eight, nine?"

"I'm twelve."

Twelve? My eyebrows shot up. She was so small. Surely she wasn't only three years younger than me. But she met my gaze steadily, and there was no reason for her to lie. Plus, her eyes, solemn and blue, looked as if they'd lived through thirty years of the world's sorrow, not just twelve. Those eyes shouldn't have belonged to a child. The rest of her features were soft and young. She might be quiet, but she was someone who saw things—who *knew* things, and absorbed information, processed it, and stored it away for when it might be useful for survival.

She was also a wholly good person, and I was glad I brought her with me. Since I no longer had my crown stuck up my highness, maybe we could get to know each other.

"Will you forgive me for having an identity crisis?" I asked.

"Sure. You never did anything wrong to me, anyway."

I bit my lip, swiping a hand through my hair. Maybe I hadn't mistreated *her*, but I had others.

Arriving late for Dance class, I burst through the double doors of the ballroom and locked eyes with a dozen startled princesses as they beheld me for the first time. I was Chris: plain dress, flat shoes, hair down, no makeup. It was no wonder everyone faltered in their dance steps, abandoning their manners to gape at me like baby birds asking for food. Hardly anyone had seen me as me since I'd arrived at the ICUP. They'd better brace themselves. They would be receiving a double dose of Chris energy and boldness from now on.

Striding into the room, I took my place in the line of dancers, unabashed.

"Princess Chrisithia—"

"I hate that name," I interjected, "and I don't know why I ever let anyone call me by it. Just call me Chris."

My teacher, Miss Victoria, scowled. "Class is halfway to completion. Where have you been?"

"In my room."

"Doing what, pray tell?"

"There's no point in praying—I won't tell you either way. It's none of your business."

Dead silence. Clearly, Miss Victoria had no idea what to make of me. She was used to submissive, delicate princesses, but I no longer fit that description. I had no reason to care about her class anymore. Dancing was a good workout, but not my preferred method of exercise. The only power she held over me was the threat of getting sent to the office for a tongue-lashing by Ms. Throupé.

The girls beside me in line edged away, as if my sudden lack of style and etiquette was contagious.

Unexpectedly, my teacher smiled. Her grin was wide and toothy, like a predator's when it pulled back its lips to avoid getting its mouth all dirty while it devoured a bloody carcass.

"It is very much my business when you are late for my class. Come."

Strolling to a cupboard, she opened it with a flourish and gestured inside to the rows of corsets.

"Nice underwear collection," I said.

Her face grew, if possible, smugger. "These corsets are specially designed. Take one. We are learning to dance in them today."

I was already wearing a corset, loosely. Though I couldn't tell the difference between it and the ones on display, there must have been one, otherwise the teacher wouldn't be looking at me like a wolf ready to take a nice juicy bite of deer. I debated whether to listen to her, but her smile was like a challenge, and I couldn't back down. Feigning indifference, I snagged one off the hook and stalked behind the dressing screen.

The first thing I didn't like about the new garment was that I couldn't put it on myself—a servant had to assist me. After half stripping, the servant arranged the hard piece over my upper body. As it closed around me, I suddenly felt claustrophobic, like I'd been shut in a coffin. I sucked in my breath as the servant yanked on the laces. "Easy there, killer, you aren't juicing an orange."

"Make sure it is tight enough, Melinda!" Miss Victoria called.

The servant pulled several more times while I tried in vain to fill my lungs to give myself some space. I felt like a mouse being constricted by a snake. As the corset crushed my waist and ribs, I resisted the urge to cry out. When I at last emerged from behind the screen, the condescending stare of Miss Victoria met me.

"I'm ready to dance now," I said, though I had no idea how to do so without the ability to breathe.

"Well then, we shall resume."

And the torture began. The music was upbeat, and the choreography demanded fast, twisting movements. There were rapid spins, high kicks, and skipping leaps every few seconds. My head spun as the room popped in and out of focus.

I wasn't the only one struggling with the unusually strenuous routine. Unable to keep up with the tempo, Ashella tripped over her small feet. Meanwhile RosaLynne flushed, gasping for breath even more than me. Miss Victoria had over-tightened her laces as well, forcing her body's naturally round shape to conform to a more traditional hourglass.

After a few minutes, I stopped.

"What seems to be the trouble, Princess Chrisithia?" my teacher asked with honey dripping from her mouth like a grizzly bear's drool.

"This is stupid. I'm done."

"Your classmates are dealing with it."

"If they want to make themselves faint, that's their issue." I'd learned my lesson about playing games. "Now, how do I get this thing off?"

Miss Victoria's chin thrust upward. "You may remove it once class is dismissed."

Forget that. Whirling around, I swept from the room. The war was on.

Returning to my room, I found Elsie tidying up after my earlier rampage. While she scrubbed at a makeup stain on the rug, she hummed to herself. Nora and Tilly were nowhere to be seen. They were probably off in the servants' quarters. I wondered idly why Elsie didn't spend more time there, rather than in my room.

"You don't have to do that," I said. "I'll clean everything later—or now, since I'm done going to classes for the day."

"I know I don't have to, that's why I'm doing it." She straightened. "Is something wrong?"

"Yes. I need your help getting this corset off."

I would throw it over my balcony into the growing trash pile.

To my frustration, Elsie couldn't undo the tight, complex knot Melinda had tied. There were no scissors or knives anywhere, and nail clippers didn't work. I spared Elsie when she offered to use her teeth, and she refused when I suggested she try burning it off.

The supper bell rang, and I still wore the horrid device. I didn't talk to anyone while eating. The twins gloated from the other end of the table, but I wasn't bothered. The relief at being myself again was too great.

Luckily, I didn't catch sight of Miss Victoria during the meal, or I would have been convicted of murdering her by shooting poisoned daggers into her from my eyeballs.

I would have liked to say something to Rachaella, but she wasn't sitting near me. Glumly, I wondered what state her room was in, and if she'd been bitten by any ants or stung by any wasps I'd left there. I resolved to make it up to her. She deserved that and more. The other royals would stop pestering her if I insisted, and if her room still had stains or pest problems, I'd help clean it.

After that, I didn't plan to stay for long. Everything I cared about was back in Agaedith. I would show the school board that not all princesses could be tamed, and that I was far more trouble than I was worth. It wouldn't take long to get myself expelled.

It was time. I placed my feet softly, treading silently. I couldn't be punished before I left my room, but it was better that no one knew I was awake, and a creak in the floor could disturb a light sleeper.

Turning my knob slowly, I opened the door just enough to peer into the sleeping corridor. Everything was black—no lights under any doors. Once lessons had started, the princesses became too exhausted after the "vigorous" classes to stay awake late. The school had guards, but none were stationed in the middle of the hallway. At least, I'd never heard any patrol closer than the stairwell.

Stealthily, I entered the hall, sucking in my breath to squeeze between the door and frame. The gesture was pointless, since my gut was squeezed as far as it could go already by the corset.

Creeping down the edge of the hall, I brushed my fingers along the wall. Rachaella's door was two to the left of mine and straight across. At least, I was pretty sure that was hers. I would laugh out loud if I went through all this secrecy only to burst into the wrong girl's room.

My hand hit a bump. I had reached the first door. Stepping carefully, I lifted my legs over the space of floor in front of the door. The spots people walked over most often were more likely to creak.

When I came to the second door, I crawled ever so slowly to the other side of the hallway, careful to always balance myself on three points. Standing, I loomed over Rachaella's doorknob. I tried turning it carefully, and discovered it was unlocked.

It would have been polite to knock, but I didn't want to risk the noise. So instead, I peeked past the door, holding the knob so the hinges wouldn't squeak. It was Rachaella's, all right. The faint moonlight of the window outlined her as she hung a damp black dress across the curtain rod. She sang softly to herself, something about roses in a window.

I almost jumped out of my corset when something moved outside, but it was only the lone pine tree swaying in the wind despondently. I heard it whispering and beckoning to me. *Free me. Free me.* I shook my head, ignoring the summons. There was nothing I could do for her, after all.

No horrid smells or sights greeted me as I slid inside the doorway, so I assumed Laomi had instructed her servants to clean the room. Cautiously, I closed the door behind me and made my way over as Rachaella finished her song.

No matter how I approached her, it was going to be awkward, so I just cleared my throat, said "Um, hi," and waited for whatever happened next.

"So you came to talk and not to jump me, then? That's a relief." She turned her steady gray eyes on me. This time I met her gaze without flinching.

"You knew I was here?"

She pointed at my reflection shining in the glass door. The clarity of it made me feel silly. Good thing I wasn't actually trying to sneak up on her.

Folding her arms, she cocked her head, waiting for me to tell her what I was doing sneaking into her room after lights-out.

"I'm sorry," I said, getting straight to the point. "It was me who trashed your room, and I came up with most of the other pranks that we pulled on you." No explanation, because there was none. No excuses, because there weren't any good ones.

"Apology accepted."

She stuck out her hand, and I regarded it for about three seconds before considering that maybe she wanted me to shake it, so I did, and she seemed satisfied. I'd never shaken anyone's hand before. Princesses got their hand kissed or were bowed to. Shaking a hand was much friendlier, though. I should try it more often.

"I can tell if people are lying, you know," she went on. "You aren't."

"I'm a terrible liar, so I've no choice but to be honest."

She seemed to find this funny. Laughing, she beckoned me to a comfy chair in front of the coffee table and sat across from me on the sofa.

"Laomi told me some stuff about you, like how you're usually the odd one out, like me."

I shrugged. "Laomi's right—but the last couple weeks I just didn't, I mean, I don't know, I was depressed, I guess, so I tried something else." The words tripped over themselves on their way out, but I kept talking. "And it turned out to be a bad idea, so now I'm back to being the odd one out."

She leaned back on the sofa and swung her foot, relaxed. As she did so, I realized how stiffly I was sitting and tried to loosen my muscles. It was hard not to feel self-conscious while sitting in the room of the person I'd victimized, especially since she was pretending like none of it ever happened and we were acquaintances.

"There's a lot of poison in the world, you know?" she said thoughtfully. "Some of it you have to take even though you don't want to, and some of it you want to take even though you don't have to. But we can't expect to be exposed to poison all the time and not get sick."

My taut posture unwound as I exhaled. She understood. She *understood*. "And the royal atmosphere is more toxic than most," I said, stringing along the metaphor. "But you know that, now. Why are you still here?"

"I had to get away from my life for a little while." Swallowing, she examined her fingernails, suddenly nervous. "Some stuff happened, and I have to make some decisions, but I'm not ready yet. I wanted to experience something different first, so when my best friend Laomi said she could get me a spot here with her, I said sure."

"I see." Except I didn't. She couldn't have been vaguer. It wasn't like I was her friend, though, so I couldn't expect her to pour out her soul. "Too bad it turned out the way it did."

"I like some parts, like learning to dance and sing and make art and write poetry. Most of the things I've learned before have to do with survival. Art makes me think about the beauty of life, not just how to keep living it. The princesses don't actually bother me much."

I snorted. "How can they not? They—we—have been trying our shriveled little hearts out to make you miserable."

"I'm a commoner, Chris. I've been through worse. Getting tripped in the hallway is nothing." She flicked her hand like she was shooing away gnats.

It was almost funny, how easily she dismissed the weeks-long effort and obsession of the petty princesses. But what suffering had she gone through to pay for that invincibility? I recalled the orphans on the street I'd given some baked goods to, and the children watching the parade who wore flour or potato sacks instead of clothing. There had also been adults with bare feet standing in scorching sand, skin turned to leather by working in the sun, and mouths sagging from trying to be strong throughout a lifetime of hardship. Maybe it made sense why being here, painting, writing, and dancing, would be an oasis for a commoner.

"Well, I'll still make sure they quit bothering you," I said.

I stood to leave, but just as my hand reached for the knob, a thunderous knocking pounded through the door. I reeled backward, automatically looking right and left for somewhere to hide. Rachaella's saucer-size eyes met mine. No one would knock that loudly unless they weren't afraid of getting in trouble. That meant a faculty member or guard must have heard us talking.

Rachaella gestured for me to hide under the bed, and I obliged as fast as I could. A bit too quickly, in fact, because as I dove toward the floor, my head hit the bed frame with a dull thud. I stifled a low groan and rolled under the bed skirt.

When the door opened, I heard a soft sigh of relief over the pounding on my forehead. "Oh, good, it's just you. Why were you knocking? A guard might hear you."

I peered out from under the bed to see a princess in a metallic gold nightgown with volumes of hair spilling from a messy bun the size of a watermelon.

Laomi folded her arms as Rachaella shut the door behind her. "Just me? I am not 'just' anything. If there were any guards around, they would have heard *you* ages ago. I overheard you speaking with someone, and I wanted to join the party. If it's anyone who's not welcome, I will help you get rid of them."

I didn't know why Rachaella was so relieved. She was friends with Laomi, but I wasn't. I didn't know her from scrambled eggs, and I certainly didn't trust her half the length of her hair.

"I don't need help getting rid of anyone. Thanks, though."

"Well, who were you talking to? I know you talk to yourself sometimes, but there were definitely two voices."

"Chris." She beckoned to me. "You can come out now. Laomi's safe."

Since she'd revealed me, I'd no choice but to come out, even if I was mistrustful. Feeling a sense of déjà vu, I tried my best to look respectable when crawling out from beneath Rachaella's bed. I made a mental note to choose a new favorite hiding place as I pulled a cobweb out of my hair.

Laomi wasn't impressed. She curled her lip as if Rachaella had just revealed a skunk.

"Why is *she* here? Do you want help tossing her out? I'd be happy to ensure she never bothers you again." She put her hands on her hips, glaring at me as I stood. Without her heels on, she was more than an inch shorter than me, not counting the snake nest bundled on her head, but that didn't make her any less menacing.

"Laomi! We can't go around beating people up," Rachaella scolded.

"We can if they refuse to do what we want."

"We've already talked about this—the answer is *no*."

I had no idea what they were talking about. If they could beat people up, why didn't they defend against the bullies who picked on Rachaella? My hairline throbbed where I'd hit it off the bed frame, but I refrained from rubbing it.

"So what is she doing here?" Laomi demanded.

"None of your business," I said, matching her glare.

"I wasn't talking to YOU!"

"Keep it down, someone will hear!" I hissed.

"Make me!"

I gritted my teeth, holding back a string of abuses. Laomi and I continued to glower at each other. She looked like an angry cat. I could almost see her hackles rising.

"Relax," Rachaella intervened, stepping between us.

Realizing I had my fists clenched, I forced them open, breathing deeply—as deeply as I could, anyway, with the dang corset on.

"She wants to be our friend, Laomi."

Whoa, hold up—Rachaella was nice, but Laomi? I never said anything about being *her* friend.

Laomi's voice was dangerously low. "Chris does not have friends. She is a loner, and she cares for no one."

"That's not true," I blurted. "I do have friends, they're just not vain, proud, stupid idiots like you."

"Vain? Yes. Proud? Rightfully. But an idiot?" She sniffed, somehow managing to keep her hair balanced while sticking her nose in the air. "You could not accomplish half of what I have if you lived twice as long."

I rolled my eyes. "Like what, keeping your neck from snapping under the weight of your ego?"

Both of us moved forward, lightning and fire crackling between our eyes, but Rachaella came between us again.

"Both of you, stop," she interrupted, placing a hand on each of our shoulders. "You're going to wake up the whole floor."

Breaking eye contact with Laomi, I seethed inside. I hated her. I hated her voice, I hated the condescending looks she shot my direction, I hated the way she flounced and preened even while standing there in her nightgown. I hated her for making me lose my cool. I'd come to apologize properly, and instead I'd caused a scene. I was ashamed, and I hated Laomi for that too. She reminded me of Coralla.

I was on the verge of giving Laomi a roundhouse kick to the face. I wasn't sure exactly what a roundhouse kick was or how it was done, but it sounded painful, which was the goal. I didn't care about getting into trouble. In fact, I needed to get into loads of trouble if I wanted to get kicked out of school, but it wasn't fair to drag Rachaella into it.

Giving one last disdainful sniff, Laomi pranced out of the room, slamming the door to her suite.

Forgetting Rachaella beneath my pent-up anger, I stalked back to my own room without saying goodbye, and then screamed into my pillow. This place was killing me.

# Chapter 14. Blood and Ketchup Go Flying

I took the time to finish penning a covert reply to Grandmother Rose and Kedrik, so I arrived late to Writing class. Ms. Sakura never took attendance, so I didn't get in trouble. She simply greeted me and took my homework. I seated myself to listen to the rest of her lecture.

"Each of you will now write your own haiku," she finished, rattling the beads on her eyeglasses. "Keep in mind what we have discussed. Attempt to find the extraordinary in the ordinary and capture the essence of your fascination in the few words allowed in the form. Turn in your finished poems to me at the end of class. Tomorrow we will move on to acrostic poems."

Lips twitching, I worked diligently on my assignment.

> This is my haiku
> It is really, really dumb
> See? I told you so

> Another haiku
> This one is worse than the last
> What did I tell you?

> My one last haiku
> This is extremely boring.
> Finally! I'm done.

Signing my name with a flourish, I turned it in and left early.

The next class, Music, was hardly a challenge.

"I have a horrid cough!" I protested hoarsely to Mrs. Warbler.

Each princess was supposed to sing a solo that day. I didn't feel like singing. All the songs in the songbook were about star-crossed lovers, or long-lost lovers, or waiting to find true love. They were the same song with different words, and none of them were good.

"Sing to the best of your ability, and I will not take points away from you, Chrisithia," she encouraged. Mrs. Warbler was elderly and probably half deaf anyway, so even if I sounded like hens being attacked by a fox, she'd still likely give me a passing grade.

My voice sharpened to a razor blade. "My name is Chris." Then, remembering I was in the thrall of sickness, I coughed weakly.

"Will you sing, or shall I have to send you to the headmistress?"

*"Nooooo!"* Everyone except the teacher flinched.

"I am sorry, what did you say?"

Wow, she really was deaf.

"I said no. I will not disgrace myself by singing while I am sick."

Mrs. Warbler's wrinkled old face scrunched together regretfully. She hated disciplining her students. But she wasn't stupid—she knew I was lying. "Then I am afraid I have no choice. If you insist on being difficult, I must send you to Ms. Throupé's office. You may explain to her what you told me."

"Very well." I scooped my music stand and songbook up and hightailed it out of there before she changed her mind or got suspicious of my willingness to visit the office. When I darted past her desk, Rachaella looked away, stifling laughter.

As soon as the door shut behind me, I ripped my songbook to shreds and scattered the pieces in a halo around the classroom entrance. Then I made warped, abstract art from the music stand and hung it on the doorknob.

Mrs. Warbler assumed my honor would take me to the office. Her mistake. After surveying my work, I returned to my room to form a battle plan for the afternoon classes.

As I strolled into Fashion class later that afternoon, Madame Annabelle clutched her heart in shock. Her hair, looped on top of her head, bobbed precariously. She almost tripped over the hem of her red velvet dress.

"Madame!" I exclaimed in fake surprise. "Whatever is the matter?"

"Daaaaaahling, your attire is simply ghastly!" she responded, blinking rapidly in a futile attempt to clear the image of me from her mind.

Inside, I was in hysterics. Some of the other students were smiling broadly and trying to hold back peals of laughter. I was becoming a staple source of entertainment. Everyone looked amused except Laomi, who was glaring at me as if she'd like to wring my neck like a chicken's. Fashion was her favorite class. She was teacher's pet.

I couldn't reveal my true emotions, though, because that would ruin the effect I was going for. Instead, I opened my mouth into an *O*, pretending to be highly offended. "I beg your pardon! In what way is my wardrobe unsuitable?"

Recovering her composure, my teacher waved her hand dismissively. "Your sense of fashion has altogether disappeared, daaahling!"

"You really think so?" I asked. Scrutinizing my apparel, I nearly cracked up. I wore an unadorned burnt orange dress that was slightly too small, showing off my ankles and wrists. On my head sat a white sailor hat that must have somehow escaped Kedrik's satchel and found its way into my suitcase, and underneath it my hair was freshly washed but damp, like limp noodles. I had fuzzy slippers on my feet instead of shoes. My earrings were giant electric blue triangles. Three twisty metal rings wound their way around the fingers of my right hand, and wooden beads encircled my left forearm halfway up to my elbow. No jewelry could be found on my neck besides the glowing fire charm that Fairy Godmother gave me, and that was invisible. A spacious canvas drawstring bag dangled over my shoulder. I was fashion's antihero.

The rest of the class period, Madame droned on about trend setting. Often she would glance at me, the words dying on her lips. After a few seconds of staring, she'd shake her head and continue the lesson.

After class finished, Rachaella and Laomi walked beside me as they made their way to dinner.

"Will you change out of that before you eat?" Laomi asked, turning up her nose.

"Why bother?"

"Because it is heinous! I am embarrassed to be seen in your vicinity!" she blurted.

"Then go away."

"You go away!"

"You can't make me."

"Want to bet?"

"Laomi!" Rachaella warned. She moved between us. "Are you trying to get yourself kicked out of school or something?" she asked me.

"Yep." My bracelets clunked cheerily as I strode down the hall.

"Why?" Laomi demanded.

I didn't owe her an explanation. But I didn't mind anyone knowing, and I was trying to tolerate Laomi for Rachaella's sake.

"There i s n othing f or m e h ere." I  j erked m y h ead i n Rachaella's direction. "Last night, you mentioned that classes were a nice break from your real life. Well, this 'break' is all a princess's life is, and I can't stand it anymore. I want to actually learn something useful, and have a goal that doesn't revolve around marrying a prince. If I graduate from here, that will never be possible."

"What kind of useful stuff do you want to learn?" Rachaella asked.

"Sword fighting." The words jumped out of my mouth before I could stop them. I hadn't planned to reveal so much about myself. It was too late to gulp the words back down, though. "I was learning sword fighting, herbal healing, and encryption back home."

"Sword fighting," Laomi repeated. She didn't look like the crown jewels were stuck up her royal patootie anymore. Instead, her mouth was an intense line, and she seemed to appraise me anew with her gaze.

"Let's all say it a few more times," I grumbled, forgetting that I was trying to be polite. "I don't think the princes down the hill know yet."

"We won't tell the whole world," Rachaella promised.

"What are we not telling the whole world?" It was Ashella. Somehow, she had snuck up behind us without our realizing it.

I forced a peal of high-pitched laughter. "Ashella! I suppose I *could* tell you as well, but only if you *promise* not to tell *anyone*."

Ashella could barely suppress an excited squeal. "I promise!"

Yeah, right. I knew that as soon as I told her, it would scald her brains out until she passed it on to someone. Or everyone. Gossip was one of the few ways princesses could amuse themselves.

I beckoned her close to talk in her ear. "Miss Victoria wears a wig because she's actually bald," I whispered. I'd no idea if it was true, but that was the beauty of gossip—it didn't matter. And if the rumor spread, it would serve the woman right for trapping me in this abominable corset.

Her mouth gaped open as she stepped back. "No!"

I nodded conspiratorially.

"I was not aware of that!"

"Remember what I said." I put my finger to my lips.

"Of course." Giving me a dazzling smile, she danced happily ahead of us to the dining hall.

"What did you tell her?" Rachaella asked.

"I'm sure you'll hear about it soon enough." I smirked.

"It's pretty creative, the way you're trying to get expelled," Rachaella admitted. "Better than pulling a knife and waving it at the teacher, like some people do."

"I don't want to *hurt* anyone." The implication that kids in commoner schools used weapons against teachers and other students was alarming. "Besides, if I had a knife, you wouldn't find me still wearing this torture device." I pointed to my corset.

"Did you try soaking in the bath? Fabric expands in water," Rachaella said.

I nodded. "It does a little, but not enough to wiggle out of it. There are hard pieces in it too, not just fabric." A flush crept up my neck. Discussing how to escape my underwear was embarrassing.

"You sound pretty desperate to me," Laomi cut in.

"I am desperate. I can hardly breathe in this thing."

"Not that—I mean you getting yourself expelled. If you succeed, your prospects in the long run will not be promising."

I scowled, folding my arms. "Prospects" was a euphemism for "handsome princes willing to marry you." Obviously, they wouldn't be promising if I got kicked out—that was the point.

We entered the noisy dining hall. I sat at the end of a table, several chairs away from those who were already seated. They ignored me and I ignored them, which was fast becoming a habit. To my surprise, Rachaella and Laomi sat across from me.

I tensed, scrunching my toes up inside my slippers. My focus remained on my plate as the servant filled it.

A few girls cast regretful glances at Laomi across the berth between the three of us and the rest of the class. No doubt they wondered why such a sophisticated, fashionable princess—one of *them*—would choose to sit with Rachaella and me.

"You don't have to sit near me," I muttered.

Laomi tossed her head. The movement reminded me of the way cats flicked their ears when they were bored with something. "See? She does not want our company. We should leave. We can sit farther down the table. The royals will not bother you with me here, I promise."

Rachaella ignored her friend. "Of course we don't *have* to sit near you. But maybe we want to."

"Speak for yourself," Laomi grumbled.

Rachaella elbowed her.

I didn't know what to say to that, so I took a bite of steamed green beans.

Ignoring her food, Rachaella propped her chin in her hands and peered at me with her penetrating gray eyes.

Gravely, she asked, "What is your favorite animal?"

I swallowed a lump of vegetables. "Um, horses. Though I really like dragons too."

"Dragons!" Rachaella's eyebrows rocketed skyward. "Why?"

"They're giant, fire-breathing powerhouses that can fly. What's not to like? I kind of hope I see one someday."

"But they burn people's homes and crops, steal livestock, and kidnap and eat princesses," she reminded me.

"If you ask me, we could do with fewer princesses."

Rachaella giggled. Laomi choked on her potatoes, spat them out into her napkin, and then smothered her smile behind it.

Since I'd utterly failed at it so far, I decided to renew my effort to be polite. "What are your favorite animals?"

"Cats," Laomi said at once.

"Of course it's cats," I said, more to myself than her.

She glared at me, sure I'd insulted her. "What did you say?"

"Nothing. So, why do you like cats?"

"Well, specifically, I like mountain lions. House cats are all right, but mountain lions have a more significant presence, you know? I like the way they move."

Nodding, I stuffed my face with more food before I said anything else that she might interpret as offensive.

"I like wolves," Rachaella said.

My fork clattered on the porcelain as I dropped it.

"I think they're misunderstood," she continued. "They're wild, and can be dangerous, but they can be playful, too, with their pack family. Their social hierarchy is complicated, and they have an entire language. They're really intelligent and—what's wrong?" she asked me.

I probably looked like I'd just swallowed a mouthful of salt. "Wolves almost killed me!"

"Really?"

"Tell the story!" Laomi commanded, leaning forward and looking interested for the first time.

I told them about almost drowning in the river with who-knew-what kind of water monsters ready to eat the corpses of Kedrik, Snowy, and me, and how we found shelter in a cave that happened to be a wolf den. There were, of course, some holes in the story.

"What were you doing in the river?"

"And wasn't there another spot where you could climb out? Why did you need a cave?"

I was more hesitant to talk about the trees attacking us, my cousins disappearing in a vortex, and the Intriguer. But there was no reason to keep a monstrous evil power roaming Agaedith and SeaCrest a secret, and if they thought I was crazy or lying, I couldn't help that.

"You made that whole thing up," Laomi said after I'd finished. She scowled, seeming disappointed that my almost dying five times over couldn't be true.

But Rachaella shook her head. "No, she's telling the truth."

"Are you sure?"

"I'm sure."

"Hm." The princess studied me with narrowed eyes, but didn't comment further.

"I think it's brave of you to want to go back," Rachaella said softly. I hardly heard her over the shrill twittering of the rest of the hall's royals. "Some people in your situation would be glad for a chance to run away."

Laomi jerked her head to face her friend. Her hair wobbled precariously. "That is not what you did."

"That's exactly what I did—what I'm *still* doing."

Before I comprehended which narrow dirt path they'd steered the conversation onto, servants whisked our plates away—the signal that it was time to go to the next class.

For the rest of the afternoon, I concentrated on my goal. I blew charcoal dust all over the Art teacher and skipped needlework altogether, because how could I annoy anyone without resorting to stabbing people with embroidery needles? I tried not to think about Rachaella or Laomi. Sure, they'd been nice (or at least, Rachaella had been). People sometimes were nice to me, but then they'd forget I existed, or quit being agreeable, or find someone that interested them more. Kedrik was the exception because we'd both been alone. For everyone else, a conversation at lunch meant nothing more than a conversation at lunch.

So, aside from ensuring Rachaella wasn't bullied anymore, I didn't need to think about them, or their favorite animals, or the way they'd asked me questions and actually listened to the answers, or whether they'd believed my death-defying story. Because if there was one thing I was sure of, it was that they wouldn't be thinking about me.

"Look at me, I'm Rachaella. I like to role-play as a crow!" At the far end of the table, the princesses mocked Rachaella's black dress.

"What is this delectable morsel of food, fillit-mig-non? How exquisite! I've only ever eaten boiled mutton and raw potatoes."

"Except for the occasional crow." The princesses tittered among themselves.

Their victim studiously ignored their hateful comments, chewing her supper methodically. She and Laomi had, inexplicably, continued to sit near me at mealtimes. Probably for lack of anywhere or anyone else better.

I, however, was fed up. I was tired of the self-centered princesses, tired of the inadequacy of the school administration, and *extremely* tired of eating soggy green beans every meal.

Forming a lump of the mushy stuff into a ball, I slapped it onto the end of my salad fork. Taking careful aim, I let it fly.

The gloppy mess plopped onto StarSilver's poofy satin sleeve and began to dribble down her arm. Not quite a bull's-eye, as I had been aiming for her leering face, but it was enough to let the whole group know that the fork was strong with this one.

"EWWW! I hate you, Chris! This will never come out! Do you have any idea how long I had to wait for this dress to be made?" Spluttering and crying, she tried to wipe off the stain but only succeeded in smearing it around. SunGold and her other companions tried to console her while shooting me venomous looks.

"This dress is part of the newest line in Leather Diamonds!" Her face flushed as she hyperventilated. "And it was personalized for me by special request! Now I can never wear it again!"

Hands folded over my fork, I blinked at her without comprehension. She tried to tarnish Rachaella's spirit over and over without remorse, but when I dirtied her dress, it was unforgivable. She was flipping out as if I had just murdered her sister.

". . . you could never understand," she went on, growing even more heated. "You're too selfish and arrogant and—"

In a flurry of furious motion, she sent a handful of mashed potatoes in my direction, heedless of her pearly white gloves. Of course, mashed potatoes probably wouldn't leave a stain. I ducked just in time, though it didn't matter, as the food soared well over me and hit an older princess from another table square on the noggin.

The mashed potato recipient put her gloved hand to her curls and withdrew some of the mush. Whipping her head around and splattering the princesses around her with white flecks, she glared at our table.

"Which one of you threw that?" she demanded. When no one spoke, her eyes narrowed. "Fine—if none of you will reveal the culprit, then you shall *all* pay!"

And so began the ICUP's inaugural food fight. At first it was mostly one-sided, with older girls from one table hurling casseroles, meatloaf, and salad at our table (most of the princesses at my table were too scared to retaliate). But then someone accidentally hit an innocent bystander from a third table, so more joined in.

Soon the whole dining hall was in an uproar. The table teams dissolved, and it was every princess for herself. When available artillery ran out at one table, royals dashed madly to another like bystanders running after candy thrown from a parade float. Sometimes they grabbed ammunition right off a fork suspended in mid-bite. It was hard to tell if everyone was angry or enjoying the respite from stiff backs, high heads, and dainty airs.

I laughed out loud as I launched a pork projectile, reveling in the anarchic chaos I'd caused. Looking around, I saw Laomi wearing a furious look, sloshing milk at anyone who came too close. I estimated about three bottles of conditioner would be needed to get all the sticky apple tart out of her hair. Her navy-and-silver dress stained with vinaigrette was a hopeless case. To my other side was Rachaella. She glanced at me, amusement shining through her quirked smile. Ketchup was smeared on her cheek and arm in a way that looked like blood.

A glob of smeary something smacked my cheek and slid down my neck. I scooped the gravy away before it slithered down my corset. Turning, I faced my attacker: Laomi. She was livid. Her hair was more sauce than style, and she was clawing at her ear, where some mashed potatoes were trying to take up residence.

"You . . . how could you?! This place is a war zone. All these dresses that took *weeks* to create are destroyed. Look at us. We're not princesses—we're less civilized than common grackles."

"So? Everyone here can afford to feed all their dresses to a horse and buy new ones." Why was she so enamored with clothing? "And being civilized all the time is no fun," I finished.

"The money isn't the point! Clothing is wearable art. Thanks to you, an entire gallery has just been demolished." She traced her fingers over the ruin of her silky sleeve.

Gonging from the bell tower rang out over the chaos. As quickly as the fight started, it stopped. Remembering who they were and what they were doing, everyone dropped their weaponry and marched out of the dining room, keeping their heads low and letting the teachers usher them outside.

Once we assembled on the lawn, Ms. Throupé, sporting the latest fashions in cranberry jelly and salad dressing, marched up and down our ranks, ranting about the "desecration of respectable society." She shrieked like a buzzard fighting for carrion.

"Such indecent behavior proves to me that you all have abysmal self-control and total lack of class!"

My attention drifted. It was hard to take her seriously when, unlike a buzzard, she had no talons. She could yell all she wanted, but that was it.

Most of the other royals weren't focused on the lecture either. The princes down the hill were out and about, and no one wanted to be seen in their messy state. Girls tugged on the potatoes and gravy smashed in their hair, casting distraught glances toward the potential beaux.

I was distracted for a different reason—they were having a sword fighting lesson.

Interested, I watched as the princes practiced, my eyes following their technique easily. Most were clumsy, though a few showed at least *some* promise. Kedrik and I could probably take five of them on at once without getting a bruise, though. Their instructor barely seemed to care, shouting encouragement rather than instruction.

When he did offer guidance, it wasn't well received. After correcting the stance of a blond prince who was wearing a vermillion jacket more suited to a ballroom than a training ring, the stubborn prince resumed slouching as soon as the instructor's back was turned. Others argued that their skills were perfect already and the way he was training them was all wrong. Some just didn't care about learning and chatted or spun their wooden practice swords like batons. Princes, I saw, were just as vain as princesses, but somehow even lazier.

Didn't those stupid boys realize how lucky they were to be learning something useful? I'd willingly take a tongue-lashing by Throupé every day if I got a tip or two on my own sword fighting technique in exchange.

If I hadn't been completely swamped with instigating mayhem and trying to get kicked out of school, I'd try plotting a way to get sword fighting lessons. But Snowy was sick and needed me, the Intriguer was still in Agaedith, and the wolf pack was patiently awaiting my return so they could kill me. Kedrik and I could practice sword fighting when I got home.

Even so, I wished I could learn a new move to pull on Kedrik. It was hard to beat him when he knew every skill I did.

I was almost disappointed when Throupé finished her lecture and we returned indoors. Casting a regretful glance over the hill, I followed Rachaella and Laomi up to our rooms.

"Who were you staring at the whole time?" Laomi asked as we trooped up the stairs. "Your eyes were obviously glued to *someone*." She smirked, but then her expression suddenly soured. "It was not my brother, was it? That would be so gross."

I scowled at her. "For your information, I was watching the sword fighting. That way I can learn how to chop off the heads of people who annoy me."

"Of course you were." The sarcasm practically dripped from her lips.

"What's so funny?" I snapped at Rachaella, who was convulsing in silent giggles.

"You two." She grinned. "You know why you bicker so much, don't you?"

"Because she's so annoying!" Laomi and I blurted in the same instant.

"No." She shook her head. "You're so *alike* that you can't stand each other. Both of you are extremely tough, firm in your beliefs, passionate about your interests, independent, and maybe a bit short-tempered." She counted off the traits on her fingers.

I didn't believe a word of it, but neither Laomi nor I had an adequate response, so we lapsed into silence.

"See you later," I said as I slipped into my room.

Elsie was waiting for me, trying to stoke an indignant fire. Haziness wafted around at eye level. When I closed the door behind me, she stood. Ash smeared her hands, cheek, and knees where she'd been kneeling.

"I tried to start a fire, because it's been getting cold in the evenings, but it won't burn," she said, almost in tears.

"Let me help." I dropped onto my hands and knees and added kindling and dried grass to the spaces. After cracking open the balcony door to get a draft, I relit the whole thing. The flames livened under my care, crackling and emanating a halo of comforting heat and light.

"It takes a bit of practice, but you'll get the hang of it," I said.

She nodded, biting her lip. "I picked up a package in the mail room for you this afternoon—it's from the King and Queen. I put it on your bed."

She was still standing attentively, watching me play with the fire. Her shoulders and back were so tense I felt like I should say "at ease" like a general commanding a foot soldier. It was my own fault if she couldn't relax around me, though. I hadn't exactly proven that I was reliable since we'd come here. If I continued to be casual, though, hopefully she'd pick up on my vibe and unwind.

"Cool, thanks." As I moved toward the sleek box situated on the mattress, I realized something was amiss. The string tying it together was scraggly, and part of the lid was bent upward.

I trailed my fingers over the broken lid, looking questioningly at Elsie. "Do you—"

"I promise I didn't touch it!" she blurted. "It was like that when I went to pick it up." The poor girl was trembling. I didn't blame her. The cook had probably beaten her for smaller mishaps than this.

"I believe you," I reassured her. "I was just going to ask if you knew who might want to go through my mail, or why."

My letters might have been read, too. Good thing my notes from Grandmother and Kedrik were in invisible ink.

Elsie exhaled, relieved that I hadn't accused her. "I'll go back to the mail room later and see if I can learn anything," she offered.

"Thanks." I beckoned her over to help me undo the strings on the box.

Grandmother and Kedrik had promised to send something my way, so although the royal seal was on the package, it was probably from them.

Undoing the hastily redone wrappings, I discovered an old purse with missing gemstones, filled with candy. Next to that was an herb pouch with separate compartments stuffed to the brim with various plants from Grandmother's garden. Breathing in the scent of earthy spices made me yearn for home.

"Ah-CHOO!" Elsie rubbed her watery eyes. Her face was tinged a rosy color. "Sorry—allergies."

"It's probably the marigold," I said, tapping the dried remains of a yellow flower. "I'll just keep the herbs wrapped until we need them." An herbal tea on a chilly autumn evening would be enormously satisfying.

I dumped the purse to sort through the candy Kedrik had sent and was surprised to feel something hard remaining in the purse's lining. It was flat, and longer than an ear of corn.

With a great tug, I ripped the purse's seam apart.

"What are you doing?" Elsie exclaimed in horror.

"Hang on . . ." I rummaged around, sticking my hand into the new pocket. "I'll show you—got it!" I triumphantly pulled out a knife. Pulling it from its sheath, I revealed a blade shaped like an arrowhead, though much longer, about the length of my hand from wrist to fingertip. It was a beautiful emerald green that flickered in the firelight. The tang flowing from the blade was shaped like a dog bone—a simple round cylinder with a nub at the end. It was wrapped in leather strips for better handling. The weapon fit perfectly in my hand.

"A knife! Wait—knives aren't allowed here!" Elsie looked anxiously at the deadly weapon, as if it might start shouting its presence to the faculty.

"Shh! Keep it down. How can you look at this gorgeous weapon and the first thing you come up with is 'knives aren't allowed here'?"

"Well, they're not. What if someone finds out you have it?"

"As long as I don't go bragging to the whole school or attack someone, they won't."

I touched the edge of the blade, still marveling at its unique shape and color.

"AH!" Blood gushed down my arm from my finger, dripping onto the bed.

"Chris! What did you do?" Rushing forward to help, Elsie whipped off her apron and wrapped it around my finger, slowing the flow. I hadn't expected the knife to be so sharp. No knife I'd ever seen could cut like that one just did. The slice itself had barely felt like anything, but I watched the blade cut deep into my skin. I looked at the apron, which was already turning dark. Was my finger even still on? It must have been, because it was throbbing.

I said nothing, only blinked. Something inside me lurched. There was so much blood everywhere . . . my blood . . .

One second I was feeling woozy and lowering myself onto the bed. The next second—

# Chapter 15. I Fail at Failing

Kedrik and I were sword fighting. He kept beating me, over and over.

"It's not fair!" I wailed. "I'm wearing a dress! You should wear one, too, that would make it even."

Kedrik laughed. "No way! That's just an excuse. A real warrior never makes excuses."

I took a deep breath. It felt good. I hadn't breathed properly for some time because of my corset. Looking down, I realized that my constricting dress had been magically replaced by a billowy tunic and pants. I was so light and free!

Launching myself at Kedrik with renewed vigor, I resumed the battle. Just as I disarmed him, an uncomfortable stinging sensation burned my cheek.

"Ow!"

"Good round," Kedrik said as he retrieved his weapon.

The stinging came again, this time on my other cheek.

A sound like a dragon roared in my ears.

I opened my eyes, and the roaring faded. It was a dream. In the back of my mind, I had known that, even though I hadn't completely accepted it. Sword fighting in the Grove with Kedrik was too fun to be true. But that didn't explain what Elsie was doing standing over my bed in the middle of the night while I visited dreamland. Disoriented, I tried to figure out what was going on.

"You passed out, Chris."

Oh, right.

I gulped air, feeling woozy. Strangely, the corset didn't restrict my lungs at all. Elsie must have sliced the strings with my knife. She'd also bandaged my finger well enough to stop the bleeding.

"Do you want some water? Or maybe a piece of candy to wake you up?"

"Okay." My voice sounded like a sick child's, but my strength started to seep back.

"You really scared me." Elsie's curls bobbed as she knelt and grasped my good hand. Her blue eyes seared me with their distress.

"It's sharp" was all I managed to say. I was concentrating on trying to sit up. Nothing was blurry or spinning, but my muscles were weak. Finally, I managed to prop myself up on a pillow.

I was a mess. Between bits of food from the fight, blood, and sweat, my dress was ruined and I was all sticky. My hair clung to my face like leeches.

"Oh, the knife was sharp, was it? Who would have guessed?"

Was that timid, quiet Elsie being sarcastic? She must have been pretty upset. If bleeding all over myself and the floor and passing out in a heap was what brought her out of her shell, though, it was worth it.

"Were you slapping me to wake me up?"

Turning pink, Elsie didn't answer, choosing instead to hand me the note she said had fallen out of the purse lining where the knife had been hidden. In it, Kedrik revealed that the knife was actually a Mountain Dragon's tail blade that he'd found in the river. Its tip was the sharpest known material in the world and harder than diamond.

I was constantly impressed with the vast amount of knowledge that guy had. The knife was in its sheath on my nightstand, the blade hidden from sight. I smiled at it. It was a perfect weapon for defending myself, though part of me wished Kedrik had kept it for his own protection. The wolves and Intriguer were in Agaedith, after all.

"Is Prince Kedrik your friend?" Elsie asked. "I've never heard of him. What kind of friend gives a weapon as a present?"

"He keeps a low public profile," I said. "But he knows me well enough to realize that I would like this kind of present."

"Either that or he's secretly trying to murder you."

"He's not. Stop worrying."

When I got to my feet, I wasn't shaky. In fact, the short nap left me energized. "I'm feeling fine now—thanks for your help. I'm going to go take a bath."

Elsie nodded, saying nothing. Her presence had shrunk and faded again, as if I had regained my strength by sapping hers.

I touched my fire necklace, trying to think of something to say that would break down her walls. The necklace was warm, like the spot on my forehead after Grandmother kissed it goodnight. After ten awkward seconds of silence between us, I gave up and escaped to the bathroom.

I removed my soiled clothes, gratefully pulling off the wretched corset. Once I got all the dried blood and food off myself, I put on a sea-green nightgown with ruffles that looked like a mermaid's fins. It felt wonderful to move freely again without restraint or chafing, though I winced as the cloth brushed against spots on my skin that had been rubbed raw.

Wandering through my closet, I dug around for some slippers. Out of the corner of my eye, I saw a flash of movement. I turned to see the corner of the magic mirror poking out from beneath some hair accessories, reflecting my own motion. I grasped it firmly, heaving it up and setting it against the wall. Cascades of ribbons, broken jewelry, and half a lace doily flowed off it. I hadn't touched it since I ditched Chrisithia. On impulse, I asked it The Question.

"Looking glass on the wall, who is the fairest of them all?"

When I blew a kiss toward the mirror's surface, the glass swirled, twisting my image, then grew dark, as if stained with ink. When it cleared, it only revealed me from behind, kneeling in front of the mirror.

"You are, my princess," the mirror replied in a deep voice.

I snorted. "You're just a flirt, aren't you?" There was no true answer to such a subjective question. It probably always declared the asker the fairest to avoid another fiasco like SnowWhite's.

"I beg your pardon!" it exclaimed. It didn't deny it, though.

A banging on the closet door startled me. The mirror wobbled.

"Good gracious!" it called out. "Please, do *not* let me fall!"

"Chris, are you all right?" Elsie's muffled voice asked from outside. "Who are you talking to?"

"I'm fine! Just talking to the mirror!" It wasn't until the words left my mouth that I realized how weird that must have sounded. Poor Elsie—she probably thought I was certifiably insane, what with me starting food fights, slicing myself open, and having discussions with my reflection. "I'll be done in a minute!" I added before turning back to the magic mirror.

"So, can I ask you some other questions? Because I think the 'who's the fairest' is getting old."

"I quite agree. Ask me any question you like." The mirror swirled and went dark again in preparation.

"Ohhhh, you were talking about the magic mirror." Elsie said, appearing over my shoulder. "What are you going to ask it?"

"I don't know. What's for dinner, maybe?"

Elsie pursed her lips.

"Okay, okay. How about this: Who is the best swordsman in all of Clystopia?"

"Please phrase the question as a rhyme," the mirror requested.

"Why?!"

"It is more entertaining that way."

Elsie and I stared at it.

"What? It is!" it protested.

"Whatever. Looking glass on the wall, name the best swordsman of them all."

"You'll get the answer, I swear, if you give me three plucked hairs."

I frowned at the new request, but tore three hairs from my head and let them drift over the mirror. Fizzing, they dissolved. But the mirror remained cloudy and silent.

"Um, hello? Anyone home?" I rapped on the glass.

"Yow! Can you wait one minute? These things take time!"

Elsie and I waited. I stretched out, hands behind my head, while Elsie tugged a lock of her curly hair nervously.

"King Nicholas," the mirror finally answered. The glass cleared to reveal a tall, bearded royal with a teal-blue cape holding a sword aloft.

I nodded, staring at the image. So he was the best, huh? I wondered how long it took him, how many hours he'd practiced, and how many battles he'd seen.

Time for another question. "Looking glass—"

"Can I ask a question?" Elsie blurted.

"Sure," I said.

"Of course, my lady," the mirror replied.

Elsie flushed. "Thank you." She cleared her throat. "Looking glass, I don't mean to be a bother, but please tell me the name of my father."

Her voice faded as she spoke, and the last word of her request was hardly a whisper.

"Your answer will come in a little while, if you will give me a smile."

Elsie acquiesced, tipping her head and smiling tentatively at the mirror.

My eyes narrowed as I regarded the glass held in the gilt frame. "You're kind of creepy, you know that?" First a kiss, then hair, and now a smile. The requests made the mirror's aura seem a bit . . . off.

There was an audible sigh. Clearly, it was weary of me and my attitude. "It's not a personal fetish. Payment is required to answer a question, and the price varies."

Its explanation didn't ease the wariness blooming in me.

Meanwhile, Elsie waited, teeth clenched, while the mirror processed her request.

"Elsie, breathe. You're turning purple."

She took a shaky gulp of air. I felt sorry for her. I had known she was an orphan, but not that she'd never known her father. Had she not known her mother either? Did they die? Or did they leave their baby on the step of the orphanage, cold and uncaring? I couldn't believe it. Elsie would have been an adorable baby. Not even a troll living under a bridge could have parted with her willingly.

"Your father's name is Hans."

"Hans," Elsie said to herself. When I looked at her face, it was obvious that she was no longer in the roomy closet of the school, working for a princess—she was somewhere far, far away, a beloved child of Hans and her mother. In an alternate reality, would she have had siblings? A home with a little vegetable garden in the back? Would she have gone to school instead of slaving away every day as a cook's helper?

"Hey, wait a second," I said. "Did you say his name *is* Hans? Is he alive?"

"He is very much alive."

"Oh!" Elsie's face became as white as a wedding gown, then tomato red, then white again. It looked like she was going to pass out.

"Easy," I said, standing to give her support. I led her to the couch (yes, there was a couch in the closet, placed there just in case anyone exhausted themselves trying to choose an outfit). After wiping her sweaty curls from her face, I brought her a drink of water.

She sat up, sipping obediently, though she was clearly agitated. "I never knew he was still alive. Please, ask the mirror where he is!"

I did as she asked, offering more hair as payment, but the answer it gave was a kingdom on the opposite side of the realm.

"I will find him! I must! Say you'll let me look—I'll die if you forbid me!"

"Of course you can look for him," I said, trying to keep the uneasiness out of my voice. If her father was alive, why was he traipsing around the other side of Clystopia instead of raising his daughter? The idea of a father was agonizingly enticing, but if I knew anything about adults, it was that they were never as reliable as they should be, with the notable exception of Grandmother Rose. "We've got to get out of here first, though, remember?"

"Yes, I guess you're right." The glowing coals of hope in her eyes faded, but didn't go out entirely. Somehow, she didn't look like such a forlorn orphan anymore—more like a fairy maiden.

I decided it was a good time to stop playing with the mirror. The change that had come over Elsie—and the reason behind it—troubled me. "I'm going to head over to Rachaella's. Do you want to come?"

"Rachaella's?"

"Yeah, to her room—Laomi might be there, too. We're just going to talk for a while. I'm sure they would like to meet you."

She swallowed. "I don't know . . . maybe." She averted her eyes, but her lips curved into a shy smile. For the first time, it occurred to me that maybe she hung out in my room so often because she wanted to spend time with me.

"Okay then, you're coming."

I stuffed the mirror back under the junk. "Thanks for your help," I told it.

"Anytime," came the dry reply as I set a stocking on it.

———— ∽ ————

For the rest of the week, I disrupted class, annoyed my teachers, and ignored summons to Throupé's office for lectures. I felt the imminent reckoning fast approaching. Soon, I knew, my comeuppance would be at hand. I'd be kicked out of the ICUP, and everyone would live happily ever after.

Elsie energetically supported me in all my endeavors, sometimes staying in my room longer than the moon remained in the sky to dream up schemes. It was she who brainstormed a more daring and dangerous idea than anything else I'd attempted. So dangerous, in fact, that when we told Rachaella and Laomi about it, they nearly refused to help. But when I said I was going to do it anyway, with or without them, Rachaella gave in. She would feel horrible, she said, if I hurt myself and she could have prevented it. Laomi did everything Rachaella did, so she reluctantly agreed to go along.

"Ready?" I asked after the four of us gathered in Rachaella's room. She had the only balcony that overlooked the courtyard. Mine and Laomi's faced outside the school.

"No. But I don't suppose it matters," Laomi complained.

"You're right, it doesn't. Let's go."

Thick darkness squeezed the air. Over my head, I wore a mask made from a pink pillowcase with two holes cut into it for eyes, and soft slippers on my feet for stealth. My dragon blade was tucked into my belt.

Laomi and I crept onto Rachaella's balcony. She stayed in the shadows near the wall, handing me the tip of her hair, which was braided into a thick rope. I took it and stole into the moonlight, creeping to the railing. Swinging over, I let Laomi lower me toward the ground. She grunted as she struggled to keep me from splattering all over the stone.

"You could stand to lose a few pounds," she hissed through gritted teeth.

"You could stand to gain a few muscles," I said in reply.

I touched the ground before she could drop me. Drawing my knife, I stepped toward the lonely pine tree at the center of the courtyard. It beckoned me with its branches.

It hadn't ceased its entreaties to be set free, reaching out to me every time I passed a window or ventured into the courtyard. When I told Elsie about being marked as a tree friend and hearing the tree's voice, she had taken me more seriously than I'd anticipated.

"You should help it," she'd suggested. "It's all alone, after all. There's no one else it can turn to."

So there I was, standing in the courtyard next to a scraggly tree, ready to commit vandalism.

"I'm here," I said to it.

*Come. Free me*, the tree whispered. Her voice was like a bowl of sprinkles being stirred—a soft, trickling sigh. Her name was Anastia.

"I can't get you back to the forest," I told her. Talking to a tree during the day would have made me feel uncomfortable, or even unhinged. But in the cold rock courtyard among mystic moonlight and shadows, the unusual felt normal.

*I know. What I ask, you can do.*

I knew what she was asking, and I'd come prepared. I looked down at my knife. It looked deadly, glittering in the silver light. That was good—it was about to become deadly.

I squeezed the hilt tighter, but hesitated. I didn't want to cut her down. It would feel like murder.

I steeled myself against the feeling. She was a tree, not a person. Besides, she was obviously not happy there, without even a blade of grass for company.

On my hands and knees, I crawled under her branches to the trunk. The needles were sparse and dry, breaking off easily. The scent of pine hung in the chill air. Anastia groaned. I put my blade at the base of the trunk, level with the ground, on my side. I did not want her to fall on top of me when she died.

Despite the cold clouding my breath as it left me, I was sweaty. I pulled the hood off my head. There was no point in wearing it anymore. No one would see me against Anastia's trunk. I put the blade back against the bark . . . and hesitated again.

*Cut.*

"I can't. I can't do this to you."

*You would leave me to my torture?*

I took a long, shaky breath. "No. I'll make the cut."

*Thank you. And get a move on. If you don't do it soon, the suspense itself will kill me.*

"Then maybe I should wait . . ."

*No! Cut, please.* Anastia was filled with a hope she hadn't had in years. I couldn't fail her.

I sliced into her trunk as swiftly as I could. Beneath the blade, it felt no harder than a tender steak.

Anastia screamed in agony, a high-pitched screech that echoed inside my head like a witch being burned at the stake. Gasping, I cried out, doubling the rate of cutting. Back and forth. Back and forth. Sap smeared over my hands and gummed my knife. It was Anastia's life blood. I was thankful that tree blood wasn't red, or I would have surely passed out. As it was, the sharp scent of sap made me dizzy.

Finally, she stopped screaming. With a groan, her limbs went rigid, beckoning no more, and she toppled over. Branches scraped my face as I scrambled away from the trunk and back to the balcony Laomi's hair still dangled from.

"You got sap in my hair!" Laomi exclaimed once we were safely back in Rachaella's room. "Now I'll have to stay up all night while Marie cleans it, and if she misses a spot, everyone will think *I* cut the tree down!"

Rachaella, though, took one look at my face and enveloped me in a hug.

"It was awful," I mumbled, the fading echoes of Anastia's scream still lingering. "You couldn't hear her, but it was awful."

"It's okay, Chris. It's over."

I took a shaky breath. It was over—over, over, over—except in my head, where Anastia's scream wouldn't die. My hands were still sticky with pine blood, and the smell made me nauseous.

Taking a seat on the bed, I stared at the wall above the headboard where all the Bible verses were posted and tried to gain control over my emotions. Without saying anything, Elsie sat next to me, shoulder to shoulder, offering me her own form of silent comfort.

*Hope deferred makes the heart sick, but a wish fulfilled is a tree of life. Proverbs 13:12*, I read.

I blinked. "Where did you get these?" I asked Rachaella, gesturing at the multicolored strips of paper stuck to the wall.

She shrugged. "They're all verses that jumped out at me while I was reading the Bible," she said.

"How much of it have you read? It looks like you have the entire book posted up there."

She jumped onto the bed on my other side and wrapped her arms around her knees. "I've read it once through. Now I'm going back to read my favorite parts again. But I like to choose some verses to put on the wall. Seeing them helps me, when life feels impossible."

"They're nice." The words of faith reminded me again of Grandmother Rose. I could almost feel one of her comforting hugs.

"Both of you are such silly idealists," Laomi scoffed, folding her arms.

"Maybe so," Rachaella admitted. But she caught my eye and grinned, as if we'd just found out we belonged to the same secret club.

I folded my sticky hands in my lap. They'd stopped trembling. I felt a little better.

For breakfast, Madame Bellafonte decided to teach our Etiquette class table manners by hosting the meal in her classroom. The lesson was less intuitive than I expected. It wasn't as simple as saying *please* and *thank you* when I wanted the salt or keeping my elbows off the table. Madame grilled us on which of the half dozen forks to use for which dish, how to fold napkins across our laps the proper way, and what to do with our pinkie fingers while holding different utensils. I dutifully memorized and did the opposite of whatever she instructed.

"I wonder what God's favorite food is?" Rachaella wondered aloud.

"Does God even eat?" Laomi asked, delicately sipping her tea.

"I suppose he could if he wanted to," I said.

"Hmmm . . ." Rachaella took a bite of hash browns. "I'll have to ask him about it when I die."

"You should give Laomi and me the answer in a dream, so we can bribe him with it to get into Heaven—it's the only way we'll make it in."

Rachaella narrowly escaped snorting juice out of her nose as she stifled laughter.

As I scooped eggs toward my mouth, the door burst open with a *bang* like a cannon. Several of the princesses flinched, jostling the table. My spoon leaped out of my hands and landed on my lap, scattering its contents. Since I hadn't folded my napkin properly over my lap, my dress got scrambled-egg-ified.

The intruder was Miss Victoria, wearing a bandana on her head. She glowered at me, clicking her fingernails together like a predator preparing for the kill.

Marching over, she grabbed my arm and pulled me upright.

"She is to come with me," she explained to Madame Bellafonte. "Immediately."

Without further ado, she dragged me out the door and slammed it behind her, muttering all the while.

". . . think you're so clever, hmm? Well, this time you went too far! I *shall* see you punished . . ."

I twisted my arm back to make her let go. "I can walk by myself, thanks," I grumbled. Ever since she'd trapped me in the corset, Miss Victoria had been the teacher I most despised.

"Impertinent, as always. I will soon remedy that. You shall be gone before you can say 'pomegranate.'"

"Pomegranate," I mumbled. "Oh darn, I'm still here."

Miss Victoria practically ran through the hallways, the red bandana over her head flapping behind her like a flag. From Madame Annabelle's class, I knew that bandanas were a fashion nightmare, so I had no idea why she was wearing one. It contrasted sharply with her jangly earrings, dark makeup, and gray satin dress with black trim.

I had to jog to keep pace with her long legs. It was a good thing I wasn't still wearing the corset—I wouldn't have been able to breathe.

Miss Victoria came to an abrupt halt. I barely managed to skid to a stop before slamming into her. Square bold letters across the heavy door before us read:

## MS. ANN THROUPÉ, HEADMISTRESS
## INTERKINGDOM COLLABORATIVE UNIVERSITY FOR PRINCESSES

It was time. I said a silent, desperate prayer that I would be deemed unfit for civilized society and expelled.

Miss Victoria knocked politely on the door. There was a pause, and then it slowly opened. The final confrontation was at hand.

We entered.

The office walls were unadorned and gray. The naked stone floors were gray. The desk was overbearing and gray. Ms. Throupé was austere and gray. Even the thin light filtering through the tiny window was a hopeless, bleak gray.

Inside, I leaped for joy. It was the perfect setting for a dramatic expulsion.

With a wave of her hand, Ms. Throupé indicated for me and my adversary (savior?) to be seated. Once Miss Victoria and I placed ourselves in stiff (and naturally, gray) chairs with jutting corners, Throupé adjusted her spectacles and addressed my teacher.

"Well?" she demanded. Her voice grated, making the hair on the back of my neck stand on end. "What is *so* important that you must disturb me at such an unnaturally early hour? How can a young pupil, a girl, cause so much trouble that you, a trained educator, are unable to subdue her?"

Miss Victoria, to my satisfaction, swallowed nervously before setting her jaw firmly to her task. "Extreme cases call for extreme measures. Though I regret interrupting you, immediate action is necessary to suppress this student's disruptive behavior!"

Ms. Throupé raised an eyebrow. "And you cannot address the issue yourself because . . .?"

"The most severe remonstrations have no effect! The other teachers allow her to reign over their classroom, fearing the consequences if they attempt discipline. You have heard the reports. I alone have stood my ground. The result? The little beast has broken into my quarters and stolen my . . . my . . ."

She gestured around her head with both arms, her face bright pink. It was the only colorful thing in the room.

That was when I realized why she wore the bandana.

A snorting squeal of a laugh escaped me. I couldn't help it. My fabricated gossip was actually true—Victoria *did* have a wig! And someone stole it! I would pay big to find out who it was before I left. A thank-you was in order.

Her baldness was only hilarious because she had been so nasty for so long. I'd managed to stumble upon her one weakness, the chink in her armor, by complete accident. It was sad, really, that someone as young as her had to suffer from hair loss, but she would find no sympathy from me.

Someone cleared her throat. Mirth still tugging at my mouth, I met the grim looks of Ms. Throupé and a hairless Miss Victoria.

"You seem to believe that your deed was humorous," Throupé said.

"Indeed," I agreed heartily.

"Silence!" she squawked. I jerked back in surprise.

"I believe that the accusations you describe have merit. More of a concern, though, is the other crime she has committed."

"What other crime?" I asked, feigning innocence.

"The destruction of the courtyard tree."

"I don't know anything about that. I thought the school finally decided to get rid of the eyesore."

"Do you recognize this?" From a desk drawer, Throupé drew a pink pillowcase with two eyeholes cut into it.

I swallowed, feigning nervousness. "That's not mine."

"Really? I have a master key to all the suites. Can you guess which room had a pillow missing its pillowcase?"

I breathed shallowly, looking away and pretending that I hadn't left my hood there purposefully for her to find and trace back to me. This was too easy.

"You have been warned, Princess, that if ever another teacher complains to me again—"

"But Headmistress!" Miss Victoria interrupted. "Have we not dealt with her impudence long enough? She should be expelled at once!"

I couldn't have agreed more.

"Silence!" Throupé glared down her beak-like nose. Miss Victoria reeled backward as if slapped. "As I was saying, the princess in question will remain at the University over the summer if she fails her classes and her behavior is not remedied."

Summer school? My shoulders stiffened. That was the opposite of what I wanted. Throupé had just signed her name on my blacklist. Crushing the armrests in my grip, I seethed.

"Is that understood?"

I tilted my chin up. "Challenge accepted," I said.

# Chapter 16. One Down, Two to Go

I stomped through the empty corridor, my footfalls echoing on the cold stone. Somehow, it was too crowded. I passed the courtyard window, where a team of guards were cutting up Anastia for firewood. She had escaped, but I was still imprisoned. Her idea of freedom wasn't for me, though. She had had no hope for the coming centuries. I had two legs, a quick mind, and I was far from helpless. I turned away from the scene and kept walking.

Flinging a window ajar, I sucked in a lungful of crisp autumn air. Then I climbed nimbly through to the open world outside. Doors were overrated.

Lying in the damp grass, I stared up for a long time at the sodden clouds above. The sky had never been so dreary at Grandmother's cottage or the Grove.

The bells in the tower rang to signal a change of classes. I didn't move. The corridors writhed with the teeming mass of princesses and perfume. They talked and giggled and swished their skirts. None of them noticed the solitary girl beneath the open window. I was relieved when classes began and all went quiet again.

"There you are!"

My dozing eyes cracked open, and I rolled onto my stomach. Rachaella and Laomi were clambering through the window, making more noise than a flock of geese.

"Ow! That's my foot."

"I'm stuck, my dress snagged on the edge."

"Your hair is attacking me!"

"Whoops, there goes my other shoe."

I cleared my throat. "Ever heard of stealth?"

"I doubt . . . people who practice . . . espionage . . . wear full-length gowns . . . on the job!" Rachaella puffed, finally pushing through and plummeting to the ground. She maneuvered to kneel beside me while Laomi unsnagged her dress. "When you didn't come back, we worried that you got expelled and left already." Rachaella put a hand on my arm.

"No. Instead of expelling me, Throupé threatened to make me stay over the summer."

"What? Can they even do that?"

I jerked a shoulder noncommittally. "I don't know. I'm not concerned, though." Throupé's threat was an empty one, I was sure. All the teachers knew they would suffer hell if they stayed the summer with me. Still, being thwarted that morning was rankling.

Rachaella nodded sympathetically. "I'm kind of glad you weren't kicked out, though. I'd miss you."

"I might have, too," Laomi drawled, "but seeing you moping around feeling sorry for yourself is making me sick."

"That's not what I'm doing." I crushed a clump of grass in my hands, glaring at her.

Laomi sniffed, unconvinced. "As long as we're all skipping class, would you like to watch some sword fighting? The princes are practicing down the hill now."

Sitting up, I blinked at her. For the first time, I felt like she saw me. And I saw a little bit of her, beneath the haughty, prickly princess mask she wore. Maybe we *were* more alike than I had realized.

"Let's go."

When I returned to my room after spying on the princes' sword fighting lesson, I found Elsie sitting on the edge of my bed, swinging her legs and looking like a little angel. On my bedpost was a familiar curly brown wig.

"I should have known." I laughed, sitting next to her. "How did you do it?"

"It wasn't hard. Rumors travel fast, and the servants hear all of them. One of Miss Victoria's maids said it was true—she hates her mistress. She let me take the wig when I asked her."

"You're sure no one else knows it was you?" The last thing I wanted was for her to get into trouble while I wasn't around.

"I'm sure. Even if they found out, they would think you told me to do it."

True. I nodded at her reasoning.

"So, did it work? Did you get expelled? I heard about Miss Victoria dragging you to Ms. Throupé's office."

"Not yet, but I'll get there." I cracked my knuckles, staring at the inanimate pink fairies dancing on the rug.

"I picked up another letter for you in the mail room this morning. It doesn't look opened, but I can't tell for sure. Maybe it'll make you feel better to hear from home," Elsie said.

"Thanks."

"No problem." Bouncing off my bed, she skipped out of the room. Off to cause more mischief, no doubt.

I found the letter waiting on my desk. The seal sported my family's royal crest: a red apple with a half white, half black background. Elsie was right. The letter didn't look tampered with at all. Relieved, I ripped it open and held it to the heat of the fireplace.

Brown letters revealed themselves.

Dearest Chris,
I'm so sorry. Snowy died last night. One of the stable hands must have forgotten to lock the door, and wolves got in. Kedrik and I think it was the pack with the Speaking Wolf alpha. It was over quickly, so she didn't suffer much. She runs in the meadows of Heaven now.

I hurt for you, Chris. I hated writing this letter. I am so, so sorry, and I love you and miss you so much. More than anything, I wish I could be there for you.

Love,

A tiny sound escaped me as I sank to the floor. No. *No.* Pain stifled me. Waves of it drenched me from the inside out. My heart was carrion. Coherent thoughts left me, leaving feelings to tear me apart.

After an interminable about of time, the door opened. "Chris," Rachaella said, "Laomi and I are going—what's wrong?"

I was sprawled on the floor, limbs scattered. The fire had gone out at some point, and the autumn chill was creeping in. I hadn't noticed until she came in that I couldn't feel my fingers or toes.

"She's dead," I croaked. "My horse, Snowy. She's dead." Dead. Dead. Dead.

Rachaella sat beside me and took my hand. "I'm so sorry," she whispered. "She was special, wasn't she?"

I mouthed the word *yes*, but no sound came out.

I clenched my fists in anger as I pictured Ben leaving the stable for the night, strutting and whistling and carelessly leaving the door wide open. My chest throbbed as the image came into my mind, unbidden, of Snowy's pure white coat running with blood. I imagined the alpha wolf, eyes gleaming, leaping through the stable door. Snowy screaming, rolling her eyes in panic.

I refocused on reality when a teakettle whistled. There was a pillow under my head. I watched Rachaella and Elsie mutely. One of them brought me some tea. I sat up, took a sip, and burnt my tongue. Then I drank some more and burnt myself some more.

I cried, though I knew Fairy Godmother wouldn't come with Elsie and Rachaella present. Their sympathy was preferable anyway.

I had so many questions, mostly starting with *why*. Though I asked none aloud, Rachaella still sensed them spinning like tornadoes through my head.

"There isn't always an answer," she said gently, sitting shoulder to shoulder with me. "Or if there is, we don't always know it right away."

I sighed.

"I know," Rachaella said.

Elsie came to sit on my other side and leaned her head against my shoulder.

Trying to make sense of what happened was useless, but the desperate thoughts wouldn't leave me alone.

A drop of wetness landed on my finger. Astonished, I watched tears stream down Rachaella's cheeks. The gray of her eyes was nothing like the dreary, foreboding atmosphere of the headmistress's office. Her eyes were filled with love and sorrow and light at the same time. *I know*, she'd said. I wondered who she cried for. I squeezed her hand, feeling solidarity in knowing that I wasn't the only one who'd lost someone.

I sent up a prayer that something good could be twisted out of the bad.

That night, I sat on my balcony for hours, staring into the heavens. The clouds had given way, and a pelt of silver swathed the sky. Sipping herbal tea, I wondered if Grandmother or Kedrik were looking at the sky too. I doubted it. But I wasn't alone—Rachaella, Laomi, and Elsie were with me, and I would be okay.

The letter hadn't ended with Grandmother's goodbye. I hadn't noticed Kedrik's short message at first, but after I recovered from the afternoon's shock, I reread the letter and saw his postscript.

P.S. Hey Chris, it's Kedrik. The wolves left a mark on the stall door:

The trees told me that the pack has left the woods, heading northwest. Be careful.

Kedrik didn't attempt to explain the marks that the wolves left. He knew they would be clear to me: one down, two to go.

Taking a deep breath of the smoky-scented fall air, I brought my eyes down to earth. There were no sounds of crickets, no flashing fireflies. A cold wind blew through the red, gold, and crimson trees, stirring the fallen leaves.

Shivering, I went inside.

"I'm going to go watch the sword fighting this afternoon," I announced a few days later during lunch. Skipping class was easier than coming up with ideas to disrupt it, and it communicated the same message. "I don't care to learn about 'the history and use of the fan.' Do you two want to come?"

"No thanks," Laomi answered.

"It was kind of a one-time thing for me, too," Rachaella said. "Besides, it's freezing outside today! I want to curl up beside the fire with a cup of cocoa, not hike around the woods."

I shrugged. "Suit yourselves."

A cacophony of girlish giggling broke out at the other end of the table. SunGold, StarSilver, and their string of followers were whispering and casting meaningful glances toward Rachaella. Though Laomi and I did our best to shelter her, the bullying hadn't completely subsided.

I scooped up a spoonful of squash threateningly.

"Don't, Chris." Rachaella gave me a penetrating look.

Angrily, I stuffed the orange mass into my mouth.

"How can you stand it?" I asked after I had choked it down.

"It helps if you wash it down with a glass of milk."

"No, how can you stand *them*?" If they talked about me like that, right in front of my face, I'd start a fight.

"I don't care what they think about me, or what they say. I almost feel sorry for them."

I sighed. Leave it to Rachaella to view her bullies as the victims.

Standing, I stretched. "I'm off to take my hike. See you guys later."

Dumping the remains of my meal, I headed to my room to change into something less conspicuous than the neon orange dress I was currently wearing.

"Finally! You're here!" Elsie exclaimed as I opened the door.

"What? What's wrong? Did the bathroom flood?" For whatever reason, that was the first emergency that occurred to me.

She giggled. "No, nothing like *that*. But I did some spying, and I think I found something important." She paused dramatically. "They're going through everyone's mail."

"Who is?"

"I don't know, but someone in the school is monitoring you and the other royals, gathering intelligence about all the kingdoms in Clystopia. Official wax crests are even replicated. I bet they could murder you and have their spies draft a whole year's worth of letters to your parents, and they would never guess what happened!"

"It wouldn't take much to fool my parents," I mumbled. "But slow down and tell me exactly what you saw."

"Okay." She took a deep breath. "Across the hall from the mail room is the mail sorting room. All the mail is dropped off, picked up, and organized there.

"I haven't been there, but go on."

"When I went in looking for anything suspicious that might explain why some of your mail seems tampered with, I noticed the room size didn't match up with where the room next door began. There should have been extra space. So I went back during lunch break when it was empty—"

"Hold up," I interrupted. "You mean there were people around the sorting room when you were snooping around?"

"Well, yes, they work there."

"And they didn't say anything to you? Like, 'hey, you're not supposed to be here'?"

"No. I just acted like I was supposed to be there, and they didn't even notice me."

I digested this. Every time I walked into a room, everyone noticed me. It was standard for princesses. Servants rushed to show they were at my service, royals nodded or sniffed disdainfully, and commoners cheered or bowed. One of the reasons I liked the passages in Castle Agaedith so much was that I could escape all that unwanted attention. What would it be like to walk into a room and be just another person? Being invisible might be Elsie's talent, but I wasn't sure if I should be jealous or pity her. Either way, it was useful.

"So what happened when you went back during lunch?"

"I found a hidden section of the room. There were a few opened packages—two of them were for your cousins—and a stack of mail. The wax seal replicas were in there. There were also some half-copied letters lying around. They matched the handwriting of the originals, but some of the words were altered."

"Were you able to get a good look at any of the letters?" Falsifying royal mail was a capital offense in many kingdoms regardless of what was sent, but knowing what was written in the fake letters might help us determine the sender's motive.

"I—I can't read," she stuttered.

"Oh, right." Since Elsie was a commoner raised in an orphanage, she wouldn't have had many education opportunities. I made a mental note to ask her later if she'd like to learn.

At the moment, though, it was important to focus on the issue at hand. "Are you positive no one saw you?" I asked. I found it hard to believe that if illicit spy activity was going on, the involved persons would leave so much evidence that a twelve-year-old could find it.

She nodded. "I'm positive."

"But you don't know who is involved."

She shook her head.

So it could be anyone—teachers, guards, servants, royals . . . or all of them.

"I wonder what the motive is," I murmured.

I started pacing back and forth in front of the fireplace. I heard somewhere that's what people did when they were trying to think hard about something, so I decided to give it a try.

The most obvious reason was that one kingdom was spying on others to gain an advantage in commerce—or start a war. Best not to jump to the second conclusion right away, though.

The secret room was built into the school itself, so the culprit would likely be whichever kingdom was involved in constructing the ICUP. The problem with that idea was that the school had been a collaborative effort. That was why it was called the Interkingdom Collaborative University for Princesses. How did one kingdom sneak in an extra room? If that was even what happened.

Elsie plopped down into the cushy sofa near the fire, her striped maid's dress and apron fanning out around her and her curls bouncing.

The mystery of the intercepted mail piqued my interest. At the same time, I was aware of the danger that our knowledge put us in. I was bold, but I wouldn't just walk into class and say, "Hey, Mrs. Warbler! Would you by any chance be involved in a conspiracy to intercept all the royal mail and gather private information about Clystopian kingdoms?" My throat would be slit while I slept.

I stared into the flickering fireplace.

"Good job spying," I finally said, patting Elsie's arm. "Why don't we just lie low and think about what our strategy should be from here?"

Elsie's eyebrows shot up. "Lie low and think? Who are you and what have you done with Chris?" she teased.

I laughed. "I know it's not traditional policy, but we're in danger now. If the spies knew that we're aware of what they're doing, they would try to get rid of the evidence—or us. We have to be careful." I hated the ICUP. Now everyone else had reason to hate it too. If we notified the right people about what was happening, the place would be shut down. I would never have to come back, Rachaella wouldn't have to worry about being bullied by princesses again, Elsie could search for her father, and we would all be safe. Until I got into some other trouble, anyway.

For now, though, we were vulnerable, and had to proceed cautiously. I looked around my pink room with all its accessories and comforts and felt like I was being gagged.

"I've got to get some air, or I'll start screaming and tearing people's limbs off," I said.

"Don't let me hold you up." Elsie edged away, holding up her hands in mock surrender. It had taken a while, but she was becoming much more comfortable around me. I was glad.

After switching my bright orange dress for a more discreet tan, I gave her a feral smile before darting past, out the door.

I inhaled my first lungful of real air for the day. The woods rustled softly, preparing for the drowsy winter months. I proceeded down the hill toward the prince's training ring, trying not to step on crunchy dead leaves that would give my presence away.

Sneaking around in the woods was much more difficult than indoors. Even with the camouflage dress Laomi had loaned me, I felt exposed. The trees didn't have many leaves left to hide among. I kept an eye on the forest surrounding me and carefully placed my feet. Down the hill, the princes trickled into the training ring. Closer . . . closer . . . I stopped.

The back of my neck prickled, putting me on alert. It was suddenly quiet. Unnaturally quiet, until the trees creaked a warning.

I knew that as soon as I turned around, I would see something very bad, but I couldn't avoid it by ignoring it. Clenching my jaw, I unsheathed my knife and whipped around, sinking into a defensive stance.

A low snarl sounded from the alpha wolf as the pack stepped from the shadows. Their matted coats looked like dirty carpets and stunk worse. I'd forgotten how massive the Speaking Wolf was. He could crush my head in his yellow-toothed jaws or squelch it under his thick-clawed paws—easily. It occurred to me that he was probably planning to do exactly that. I almost choked on my heart.

"Hey, girlie," the alpha rumbled.

I recalled the slashes in the barn door—one down, two to go.

Fyre wasn't here this time—or Kedrik, or Snowy. I was alone.

The wolves moved in, taking their time. They knew they had me, so they were going to have a bit of fun playing with their food before they ate it. I saw the tartar on their teeth and the manic gleam in their eyes. I backed away, an adrenaline surge making my brain go a million miles a minute.

It was three to one. There might be others circling around to make sure I didn't get away, but I couldn't sense them. I had a knife, and they had two-inch claws and teeth. They could run for hours, and I could run maybe a hundred and fifty yards before I started to slow. Did I have any hope? Not really.

I backed against something hard and stopped. I was trapped . . . or was I? I felt the ridged bark behind me and smiled. I wasn't outnumbered, the wolves were—by thousands. No matter how far they ran, there would be trees ahead for miles.

"Forest," I whispered. I knew I didn't imagine the trees stirring at my voice. "You made me a promise. Help me now."

I moved on to the next part of my supremely off-the-cuff plan. Spinning around, I sprinted away, screaming bloody murder. Which it *would* be in a minute, if I couldn't escape.

Barking, the wolves lunged after me, scrabbling in the leafy debris. Tremors shook the ground, and the trees around me came to life. A maze of roots and vines crafted a pathway for me. It closed behind me as I ran, blocking the hunting beasts. I heard pained yelps as the wolves tried to follow, running into trees or getting their pelts stuck in thick undergrowth. Chancing a glance back, I saw nothing but vegetation crisscrossing over itself. My feet pounded a rhythm with my heart, and I ran with the speed only possible to those who might wind up dead if they went any slower. I leaped over bushes and rocks with the knife still in my hand.

Taking a risk, I launched myself up the nearest tree, expecting fangs to close around my ankle any moment. Scrambling up the trunk like a terrified chipmunk, I stood in the boughs panting, knife at the ready.

A triumphant barking erupted behind me. I whipped around, slashing. The blade sank into flesh, and the barking turned into yips of pain.

As the branches and leaves settled, I climbed higher, conscious of the monsters prowling beneath. They were mad now. Both their dinner and their revenge had gotten away.

The woods quieted again, except for the snarling and scraping at the base of the trunk and my lungs wheezing. I was out of shape.

Another wolf leaped up, trying its luck, but fell short. I thanked God that wolves weren't granted the ability to climb trees. Steadying my breath, I considered my next step. The wolves had me treed. I wasn't dinner for now, but I couldn't stay in the boughs forever. Waiting for the beasts to go away wasn't an option. As soon as I descended, believing they were gone, one could pop out of a bush and clamp its jaws around my neck.

I had plenty of time to think of something worth trying—no pressure. Maybe the trees would bend closer and let me walk across them to the edge of my balcony. Or I could try to swing from tree to tree using vines, never touching the forest floor. It would be horrible if one snapped, though. Hmmm . . . maybe I could fashion some wooden spears with my knife, if the trees didn't mind.

"You're not going anywhere," the alpha growled. He placed both forepaws on the tree's trunk.

Even though I knew he couldn't reach me, I instinctively inched my way higher.

"We will wait as long as we need to." Our eyes met, and he bared his teeth in a grin. "And while we're waiting, I can tell you all about how your horse died."

# Chapter 17. A Posse of Princes

I went rigid.

"All the beasts smelled us before I even unlatched the door." The alpha's whiskers quivered as he spoke. "They started screaming. I was concerned at first that the noise would draw the humans, and they'd shoot us full of arrows before we could seek our revenge, but we had plenty of time. Your kingdom should invest in new latches for your barn doors if you want to keep *me* out. Humans complain about wolves stealing their livestock so often, but they're the ones who make it so incredibly easy for us to grab a snack whenever we want."

"I'm not listening to you," I interrupted.

"Yes, you are—you can't help it."

Pointedly, I turned my back and climbed higher. But the alpha wolf's gravelly voice carried.

"The horses panicked. It was quite the party. I spotted Snowy right away. She remembered us and was trying to kick down the stall door. Stupid animal—that would have made our goal even easier."

"Shut up," I hissed. He was baiting me. I *knew* he was baiting me, but I couldn't help my rage from building.

The alpha licked his lips. "Her eyes are—*were*—really pretty. Especially the whites. There was a lot of white surrounding her eyes. She was terrified. They were like droplets of milk, but tastier."

I clapped my hands over my ears and almost fell out of the tree as a result.

The alpha waited with half open jaws, but I steadied myself. He scored his claws over the ground in frustration, growling again.

"By far the most tender part of her was her neck, though," he continued, regaining his composure.

I started humming to drown out his words. My body was shaking with so much fury that the leaves of the branch I stood on vibrated. I wanted to kill that wolf. Sticking my blade down his throat, or into his jaw and up through his face—that would shut him up. My knife hand was sweaty, even though the breeze promised winter.

"It quivered even after she was dead, and all that blood made it extra juicy . . ."

My humming turned into a scream of rage.

"There was a lake of blood all over the stall. But don't worry, my pack mopped up most of it with their tongues. She had delicious blood. Unfortunately, the humans came before we could finish the meal, but her body gave us the energy we needed to come find you. I'm not sure what the humans did to clean up the half-eaten carcass, but I envy them." He licked his lips again, as if remembering Snowy's taste.

At that point, I snapped. Yelling incoherently—names, obscenities, another language maybe—I jumped like a squirrel to the branch below me. A wolf jumped up, and I kicked at it, but I missed because I was still too high up.

A shout suddenly rang out that wasn't mine. Distracted, I peered through the canopy and spotted a dozen boys—princes—rushing heroically toward me. As they drew closer, the sight of their silver swords raised in the air and threateningly gleaming brought me back to myself.

I groaned. How embarrassing. I didn't need a princely rescue party—I was handling the situation perfectly well. I had never in my life been a damsel in distress. I was the one who distressed the damsels!

The wolves below glared at me through yellow slits. The alpha crouched, and then launched himself at me before I could blink. I wasn't ready for the speed or power of the jump. He soared like a furry cannonball straight for me and would have tackled me off the branch if the tree hadn't moved a bough in the way, clotheslining him.

Yelping in surprise, the wolf fell on one of his brethren, squishing him. The smaller wolf squirmed, trying to escape.

"Fear not, young maiden! We've come to rescue you!"

The oh-so-brave-and-valiant young princes drew closer. I cringed.

"Until next time, then," the alpha barked. "We'll be waiting."

The alpha signaled to his pack, and the outnumbered wolves melted into the shadows.

"Oh, cut it with the theatrics!" I snapped as the princes arrived. "I'm fine. I would have been fine even if you didn't race over here waving your swords around like a bunch of chickens with their heads cut off." They clustered around my tree, shading their eyes to look up.

"I beg your pardon?" Obviously, the crowd beneath me was wondering why the weird girl in camouflage was throwing insults at her rescuers. Charm and flattery were probably what they expected, and their huge egos couldn't comprehend any female who didn't worship them.

I was still furious at the wolves, but even more than that, I was furious with myself. I would have gotten myself killed because of my stupid temper if the trees hadn't been looking out for me and the princes hadn't scared off the pack. And since my pride was wounded and the alpha's words made me heartsick, I needed someone to take out my anger on. The princes were readily available.

"Look," I said, starting over. "It was a nice gesture for all of you to come over here, but I don't need your help. Run along now and do princely things."

I was too emotionally unstable to watch the sword fighting lesson as I'd originally intended. I wanted to get to my pink room as soon as possible and tell Elsie, Laomi, and Rachaella that the wolves had come to the ICUP for me. They killed my horse because Snowy and I had accidentally trampled their pups. The alpha wanted me to feel his pain before I died. Therefore, anyone I cared about was in danger.

"How did you get out here?" one of the princes asked, ignoring my plea to leave. "It is miles to the nearest village!"

"It doesn't matter." I was glad they didn't recognize me as a princess.

Impatient for them to go, I sheathed my knife and began to maneuver my way down the tree. There were more knots and branches than most trees had. It was almost as if it had put extra bumps there on purpose to help me down.

"Do you have need of assistance?"

"How many times do I h—" My sentence was cut short as the tree suddenly shifted the branches and footholds out from under me. It was a cruel prank. I plummeted into a pair of waiting arms. Thanks a lot, dumb tree. Just what I needed to prove to them that I could take care of myself so they'd go away.

The tree gave a rustling chuckle as I squirmed against the prince who caught me. *Go with them*, it said. It wanted me to go with the princes who had decided to "save" me without an invitation? Well, I would j—

I blinked dizzily at the prince who was still holding me. The sun shone behind his head, giving his coppery skin a glow and making a golden halo for his dark hair. A pair of concerned emerald eyes met mine. Wow. Those eyes were obviously designed to hypnotize every girl who caught sight them. But since I recognized their ability, I managed to shield myself against the spell. For the most part.

"Put me down. Now, please."

He righted me, and I held out my arms to steady myself.

"You are injured!" someone exclaimed.

I looked to where they all were staring. My hand was covered in sticky, drying blood.

"It's not mine."

Had I stabbed one of the wolves? I couldn't remember, but I must have. I rubbed my eyes with my clean hand, hoping that I wouldn't pass out. I managed that, at least, which was a relief. The very last thing I wanted was to awkwardly faint into someone's waiting arms.

I started to wipe my hand on my dress, but then stopped. Laomi would kill me if I brought her outfit back bloodstained.

"Here." Green-Eyes dropped a handkerchief into my open palm.

"Er, thanks." He did something helpful, finally.

I recognized a few of the princes, Green-Eyes included. His name was Prince Arcturus, but I'd never caused a catastrophe in his kingdom, so we didn't know each other well. Perhaps that was why he was still smiling at me.

"Good work, men!" The instructor, a bald man with a shiny face, caught up to his exuberant class. "You found a victim, identified the problem, assisted with courage, and conquered! You all pass your first test.

Now, let us return to the training field and resume practice. Keep your real swords handy—you will need them if the wolves return."

He clapped his hands, and the horde moved off—all except Arcturus.

"You *are* coming back with us, right?" he asked. "We don't know how far the wolves have gone."

"I was just about to suggest that!" boomed the instructor.

"But I—"

"Not another word! It is dangerous in the woods for ladies like yourself! Come!" The overbearing man hooked my arm in his and steered me back with the group before I could ask exactly what kind of lady he considered me to be like. He guided me to a wooden bench just outside the training ring. "Have a seat here!"

He practically shoved me onto the bench. Ugh—I had ventured out to see sword fighting, and now I had a front-row seat. But all I wanted to do after the wolf encounter was go back to my relatively safe room and talk with my friends.

The princes might have scared off the wolves with their numbers, but when it came to actual sword fighting, they were terrible. I watched for a painful two minutes before rolling my eyes and heading to the weapons shed. I was here, and I couldn't leave until I was sure it was safe, so I might as well practice instead of sitting around. Peering into the shadowed hut, I waited for my eyes to adjust. It was dank and musty. The tiny amount of sunlight that streamed through cracks in the wooden wall illuminated millions of dust particles.

Ignoring the stench of damp rust and fungus, I carefully sifted through the weapons. Most were just wooden practice swords and shields, but chipped spear tips, bowstrings, and random splinters of wood were littered among them on the floor, gathering mold. The sword racks themselves were practically empty. I hefted each weapon and tested it for size and moldiness by giving a few swings. One was so decomposed that it broke as I gripped the handle. Finally finding a newer weapon that fit, I made my way back through the obstacle course to the door and surveyed the training field.

Two sparring partners were throwing their wooden swords into the air, trying to make them spin and then stick into the ground. Another two had dropped their swords and were wrestling in the grass, grunting like wild boars. The remaining princes were gathered around the wrestlers shouting, "Fight! Fight! Fight! Fight!" As I watched, one boy pinned the other down. Though he struggled like a turtle that had fallen onto its back, he couldn't regain his feet, and the fight ended.

"Darn it!" Stomping his foot, one of the onlookers slipped a few coins into another's outstretched hand. The receiver grinned and pocketed the money.

I rolled my eyes. Where was the instructor during all this? Nowhere to be found, of course.

Marching over, I called out, "Who will fight with me?" I held my practice sword up so they understood I wasn't looking to start another wrestling match.

A dozen eyes swiveled to stare with blank expressions. Everyone got quiet. If there had been any crickets around that time of year, they would have been chirping.

"But . . . you are a girl!" one of them exclaimed incredulously.

"Aren't you a smart one?"

Still, no one stepped up.

"A *real* warrior never backs down from a challenge. I've just issued a challenge. Now, who will fight me?"

I heard a deep sigh, then the victorious wrestler, a prince with dirty blond hair (dirty both in color and because he had just been rolling on the ground) stepped forward and swiped up a fallen weapon. Tossing his head back to dramatically swish the hair out of his eyes, he gave a radiant smile. "If that is what you wish, then."

My stomach clenched. I recognized the guy. The way he smiled and carried himself so confidently reminded me of a day, not so long ago, when I waved to a prince, who waved back and smiled, tossing his dirty blond hair. I narrowed my eyes. I was *so* going to beat this guy.

I slid into my sword fighting stance. "I'm ready when you are."

"Take it easy, Valiant," Arcturus advised as the blond boy stepped up.

I gritted my teeth at Arcturus's chauvinism. At that moment, though, I couldn't afford to spare him even a venomous glance. Concentration was key—the stakes were life or death. Well, maybe not in this particular situation, but I had to practice like the real thing, right?

Valiant (what kind of name was that anyway?) gave a clumsy, half-hearted swing in my general direction. Fine. If he wanted to be dumb and listen to Arcturus, he could. But he would regret it.

I parried his blow easily and went on the offensive, swiping sideways with enough force to break his arm. He blocked it just in time, but his eyes grew large as the vibrations of the jarring blow traveled through him. Before he fully recovered, I feinted an overhead strike, then went into a side cut. He dodged, but his balance was off kilter. He jabbed, I stepped aside. I cut, he practically tripped. I jockeyed my feet nimbly, staying balanced, and monitored my breathing, exhaling when I swung to land heavier blows. He stood tall and jabbed wildly, sucking wind and occasionally tossing his hair back. That darn hair of his—he just couldn't leave it alone.

There was only one way for the fight to go, and it was time to end it. I attacked with short, quick blows that he could block, but allowed me to move closer. When we were only a foot away, I swung for his neck, and he barely managed to parry. Using my momentum to turn out of the blow, I scooted behind him and kicked him in the back of the knees so that he fell, dropping his sword. I poked him in the back of the neck with my weapon, and then allowed him to return to his feet.

Sticking my sword point down in the ground (that was the custom at the end of a practice fight, so that both participants understood that the fight was over and quit hacking at each other), I extended my hand. He shook it, embarrassed and dismayed though he was.

"Man, you just got *owned*!" teased a tall prince with curly dark hair and freckles.

"Do *you* want a go?" I challenged him. I wasn't even winded. "Bring it." Freckles shut up really quick.

"Anyone else? No? Okay. I'll be back next practice. Until then!" I waved.

"Wait, what about the wolves? They might still be out there." It was Arcturus again. That guy annoyed me.

"I'll be fine. I'm sure they've moved on by now." I couldn't tell him that the trees were beckoning me back, telling me it was safe—he'd think I was crazy. "And if they *do* come back, I'll climb another tree and scream for help." Saying that last part almost killed me. I would never do such a thing.

"No, you won't," he said, seeing through my lie. "You'll probably pull out some more battle skills and send the wolves running. After what you did to Valiant, it wouldn't even surprise me." The other princes had meandered away, but Arcturus was still running his gob. "You look familiar. What's your name?"

I was taken aback at how easily he read me, and masked my face carefully before answering his question. "My name is Christina."

"Chris*tina*—got it." He nodded skeptically, but didn't say anything else.

Gulping, I whirled around and ran into the woods. Once the training ring was far behind, I leaned against a birch.

Why couldn't I have thought of a better name? I was such a terrible liar. Arcturus was going to blow my cover to smithereens. It wouldn't take more than a prince's brain for him to figure out that I wasn't a lost villager, but Chrisithia, princess of Agaedith and daughter of SnowWhite.

Something tickled my ear, and I whipped around, half expecting a whisker attached to a muzzle full of sharp, yellow teeth. Instead, a tree vine trailed over my shoulder, though there was no breeze. As I watched, bewildered, the tree morphed, forming a ramp into the canopy.

Issues with Arcturus forgotten, I glided up the thick branch. Another bough morphed, forming a pathway to the next tree. Prickly twigs moved out of my way, and bumps flattened so I wouldn't trip. Full of wonder, I walked from tree to tree, never setting foot on the ground. I rose higher and higher, until only the sky was above, and sixty feet of air and leaves separated me from the ground. My prison school squatted below, looking dull and unimportant. I gave it a patronizing smile.

There was nothing like the thrill of being so high up that I'd die if I fell.

I told Laomi, Rachaella, and Elsie about my encounter with the wolves. Laomi and Rachaella had heard about my earlier problems with wolves, but the story was new to Elsie, so I explained about the Intriguer, and how I accidentally killed the pack's pups when hiding in their den, which fueled their quest for revenge.

"The alpha said he'd be waiting for me. He killed Snowy just so he could torture me by describing . . . well, he just did it to torture me." I didn't have to torture myself by rehashing the details. "That means he might go after you too."

"Before we talk more about wolves that want to eat us, I want to hear more about the Intriguer," Elsie said. "You said that's what kidnapped your cousins, right?"

I nodded. "That's what Grandmother Rose said. Kedrik and I just got too close, so it drove us away. I don't know anything else about it, though."

"You know that they weren't the only royals kidnapped recently, right?" she asked.

"Um, what?" That was news to me.

"The servants mentioned it at the start of your classes. Two other princesses were supposed to attend, but they both disappeared on stormy nights."

I caught what she was implying. Maybe the storms hadn't been natural, but vortexes like the one that took my cousins.

"Maybe the Intriguer is responsible for spying on the school, too," Elsie suggested excitedly.

The idea was worth consideration, but we didn't have enough information to confirm her theory. Before I figured out a way to say that nicely, Rachaella spoke up. "Wait a second—who said anything about the school being spied on?"

Elsie described what she found earlier in the mail sorting room.

"It would make sense for the Intriguer to be behind it," she finished. "Getting information from letters between royal families would be the perfect way to plan kidnappings."

Her logic was sound. If the Intriguer was powerful enough to scoop up royals with storms and control trees, surely it could also sneak into a secret room in a school for princesses.

Laomi nodded thoughtfully. I was surprised at how calm she remained during our revelations. They were full of alarming, nearly unbelievable information, after all. But she accepted my and Elsie's stories without question and delved straight to the point. "It's a good theory," she said.

"Can we prove it, though? If the Intriguer is as powerful as you say, we can't beat it alone. To get help, we'd need proof."

"That's the problem," I said. "It's a huge unknown, which makes it dangerous. But . . ." A thought popped into my head, so obvious that I felt like smacking myself. "I know how to get proof. Well," I corrected myself, "we can prove it to *ourselves*, anyway. I don't know how many other people will believe it."

I jumped off my bed and threw open my closet door. Striding to the back, I pushed dresses and boxes aside. Where was it? Frowning, I dug deeper through shoes, stockings, and hair ribbons.

"Ow!"

I froze.

"If you do not mind, would you be so kind as to get your *foot* off my *face*?"

I looked down. There it was! I picked up the magic mirror, trying to wipe off the footprint on the glass.

"Ouch! Stop it!" The mirror huffed. "You abandon me yet again, and then I have to suffer the indignity of being stepped on!"

"Sorry. Listen, I need to ask you a question—it's important."

"After *that* treatment? I think not!"

Ignoring it, I stuffed it under my arm and lugged it back to the others on my bed. I set it in the center of the thick pink comforter, and we all clustered around.

"And how will a *mirror* help prove anything?" scoffed Laomi.

"This," I said, "is no ordinary mirror."

"I should say not!" it piped up indignantly.

Laomi and Rachaella's eyes widened. Elsie bit her lip, stifling a giggle.

"This is my mother's magic mirror," I explained. "It used to belong to an evil queen, but after she was killed, SnowWhite inherited it."

"So that's the mirror that can tell you who the fairest in the land is? Is it still your mother?" Laomi had a hungry curiosity in her face as she sat up. I looked at her stylish gold-with-black-trim dress, her shining ebony hair, and her perfectly applied cat-eye makeup, and I wasn't surprised that she got distracted. I couldn't blame her though—that's the first question I'd asked the mirror too.

"Um, that question doesn't work anymore," the mirror mumbled. "Broken from overuse."

Disappointed, Laomi slumped.

"But we can ask you different questions?" Rachaella spoke up, talking directly to the mirror.

"Certainly."

"Okay then . . . what exactly is the meatloaf in this place made out of?"

The mirror darkened, contemplating, and then swirled as if in disgust. "Are you sure you want to know?"

She hesitated. "On second thought, no."

"Hey, wait a second!" I fumed. "She didn't have to give you something or make her question rhyme! Why were you going to tell her the answer?"

"Stop whining," the mirror said. "She was more polite than you. Besides, it was fun to watch you struggle."

I glared at it. "You'd better watch it, or I might be getting seven years of bad luck really soon."

The laughing splashes of color dissolved off the glass instantly.

"Could we ask the important question now?" Elsie asked, obviously dying to know the answer.

"Sure—sorry, Elsie." I cleared my throat. "Looking glass, will you please, tell me who spies on students at ICUP?"

The mirror swirled with black and gray. "You shall not ask in vain, if you give me a shout of pain."

Elsie gasped in surprise, but I'd kind of been expecting a shady request. The information was valuable, after all.

"Here, pinch me." I held my arm out to Laomi because I knew she would do it.

She did, but not with pleasure. A grimace slashed across her face as I shrieked.

Then we all held our breath, leaning toward the swirling surface in anticipation. The mirror darkened, but revealed no picture. It stayed that way for almost five minutes. I was just beginning to think I'd broken it when it spoke.

"It is difficult to tell," it answered at last.

"What kind of answer is that?" I asked, rubbing the sore spot on my arm.

"Was it this uncooperative for the evil queen?" Laomi whispered in my ear.

"I doubt it."

"I heard that!" the mirror snapped.

"Please, magic mirror," Rachaella implored, "we're ready to listen to your explanation. All the kingdoms in Clystopia could be in danger, and it is up to us to reveal the truth. We need your help."

If Clystopia's fate was resting in the hands of four girls and a stubborn mirror, we might as well torch the place and move out. But I kept that thought to myself and nodded solemnly to support Rachaella's plea.

"Oh, very well. What I meant," the mirror amended, "is that many spies with various interests are taking advantage of the school's information density. The most imminent threat, however, is from . . . an anomaly."

The breath left me. "What does that mean?"

For once, the mirror answered my question without theatrics. "The being is a singular creature. Such power has no equal in all the realm. It has many names and many forms, for its art is in deception and manipulation. Truth becomes fiction and fantasy a reality whenever it is around. It uses its powers of illusion to twist minds. Though it has been subdued before, happily ever after never lasts. It always returns. It has been called many things, but you know it as the Intriguer."

# Part 3

*"But Moses said to God, 'Who am I that I should go to Pharaoh and lead the Israelites out of Egypt?'" Exodus 3:11*

---

*"Be brave and steadfast: have no fear or dread of them, for it is the Lord, your God, who marches with you: he will never fail you or forsake you." Deuteronomy 31:6*

# Chapter 18. Unwanted Answers

We were so dead.

All noise hushed after the mirror finished speaking. Instinctively, I clutched the glowing fire orb around my neck. Its warmth gave me a little comfort. Though I had assumed the answer even before asking, it was still a shock to hear it. The mirror's statement made it more real.

Even though we knew it was partly responsible for the school's security breach and a menace to everyone who resided here, the Intriguer still had no identity, no face to recognize. How could we know what it was when we saw it? How could Clystopia defend against an intangible enemy? How could we beat something as flighty as smoke?

"Was the Intriguer also the one who kidnapped Chris's cousins and the two princesses who were supposed to come to the ICUP?" Rachaella asked.

"I will answer what you inquire, but three drops of blood do I require."

Before I could think about it too much, I drew my knife and pricked the tip of my finger. Squeezing my eyes shut, I stretched my arm in the general direction of the mirror, hoping blood was coming out but not wanting to check. After a few moments, a soft handkerchief covered my hand.

"I could have done that, Chris," Rachaella murmured, wrapping up my finger.

"No worries," I gasped. When I deemed it safe, I peeped open my eyes.

The mirror's answer was simple. "Yes, it was the Intriguer."

"What did it do with them?" I asked.

After I gave it another blood donation that made me positively light-headed, the mirror said, "It has taken them to its fortress of illusion, to play with their minds."

I shivered, horrified. My mouth ran dry, and I couldn't think of an adequate response. The Intriguer may not have killed its victims—yet—but mental torture might be even worse.

"If I may ask, whose form does it have at this school? Or who is its host?" Elsie's voice was shriller than usual.

"Good question," I murmured. If we knew the forms the Intriguer had taken on, we would be a step closer to defeating it.

The payment to answer it, though, was not simply more blood.

"Your query shall not linger," the mirror said, "if you but give me a finger."

I drew a sharp intake of breath and almost choked. Rachaella grabbed my wrist, as if she thought I might hack off a phalange then and there.

"I wasn't going to do it," I muttered.

"Just making sure."

We tried to pry for other information, like more details on what the Intriguer was, how it could be defeated, and who was strong enough to defeat it. But the mirror asked for an eyeball, spleen, and pituitary gland (whatever that was).

I was about ready to show the mirror a very particular finger indeed when Laomi threw up her hands.

"We're getting nowhere!" she exclaimed. "Unless we're going to make a human sacrifice, there's not much more we can ask."

"At least we know that the Intriguer exists and it's behind the kidnappings and spying," Elsie pointed out.

Bringing my knees to my chest, I rested my forehead on them. The responsibility of even the little knowledge we'd gained was overwhelming. I took one, two, three deep breaths, trying to ignore the pretzel knots that my intestines were forming.

"Okay," I said, trying not to choke on my words. "Here's the plan. Step one: don't die. Step two: look for a way to send a message back to our families without it being intercepted. Step three: continue to not die and wait for a reply. Step four: keep the mirror safe."

I raised my head to see their reactions. Rachaella nodded, Laomi set her mouth in a determined line, and Elsie, bless her, was looking at me like I was her salvation. That was terrifying.

"We can do this," Rachaella encouraged.

"Maybe the Intriguer wanted us to find out. Maybe it's already too late." Leave it to Laomi to be a downer.

"Let's not dwell on it too much," I said, worried that Elsie was going to faint. Either it would find out what we had been talking about and kill us, or it was our responsibility to save all of Clystopia's royalty. Either way, dancing lessons and table manners were now the least of my concerns.

"It might not be as bad as we think," said Rachaella, "The Intriguer isn't all-knowing, otherwise it wouldn't need to spy. And if its power was limitless, it wouldn't have to rely on illusions to manipulate people. This will work out. We just have to keep quiet and focused, and look for an opportunity to deliver our message."

She wasn't wrong. Even so, we were still prisoners at the ICUP, and because the Intriguer was monitoring our communication with the rest of the realm, we had no way of knowing when we'd get the opportunity to tell someone the truth. Maybe not until we went home for Christmas break. I wasn't thrilled at our odds of staying alive and un-abducted until then.

There was a real chance that we would be captured, or killed, in the meantime. That fear nagged me—the fear of dying. If I was alone, I could not have endured it. But sharing the secret with people I trusted was a great comfort. For each other, we could be strong.

Nonetheless, I sent up a prayer for our safety.

From then on, it was even harder to endure the school's inanity, knowing what I did. One night, after drinking what felt like a gallon of tea to help me relax, a relentless tapping noise interrupted my uneasy slumber.

*Tap tap. Tap tap.*

I rolled over.

*Tap tap. Tap tap.*

Burrowing deeper under the covers, I shoved my head under the pillow.

*Tap tap. Tap tap.*

I ignored it. If it was the Intriguer, hopefully it would kidnap me soon. Keeping me awake was unnecessarily annoying.

*Tap tap. Tap tap.*

"What the *heck* is that?"

Fed up, I threw the covers off and stood abruptly. Black spots danced around my eyes as I went from horizontal to vertical too quickly.

There was a fluttering noise on my balcony. Peering through the glass doors, I spotted a familiar bird with flaming feathers. Fyre had grown from a fledgling into a magnificent creature with a six-foot wingspan in only a few short months. The effect of his shifting red and gold plumage against the moonlit, powdery snow on the balcony was dazzling.

Forgetting my fatigue, I lunged for the door. The cozy, fireplace-warmed air in my room was stolen away by the biting wind when I finally managed to open the frozen door.

*Finally! You sleep like a rock!* Fyre said in my head as he shot inside. *Do you have any idea how long I've been trying to get your attention?*

His voice was back. I was torn between being happy to talk with him again and dreading all his sarcastic comments.

"Do you have any idea how irritating it is to have someone incessantly tapping on your window while you're trying to sleep?" I retorted.

*Oh, the pain and suffering you've endured.*

He had no idea. I threw a nearby couch pillow at him, which promptly caught fire.

*Smooth.*

I struggled to smother the burning fabric. Lucky for me, Fyre's flames didn't burn people unless he wanted them to, otherwise I would have become a cinder.

I wasn't truly mad, I just felt like pretending I was because he woke me up. Privately, I was thrilled to see a familiar face and excited about the new possibilities his arrival offered. With Fyre able to fly the distance from home to the ICUP, I could get the news about the Intriguer to Grandmother. It was unlikely that anyone would intercept the phoenix and read my message.

I stroked Fyre's head with a single finger. His feathers felt like warm, silken air. Closing his eyes, he made a cooing noise deep in his throat. He looked up at me with his deep black eyes.

*I missed you.*

"I missed you too, Fyre."

He flitted into the fireplace, where he settled into the glowing coals. Knowing his wish, I stoked the fire until the flames were roaring. His feathers blended with them until I could only see his beak and liquid eyes, reflecting the tendrils of flame around him.

I glanced outside. The ground was dark, but the sky was beginning to lighten. It was the time of absolute silence before dawn when the birds hadn't awoken yet, and the nocturnal animals were just drifting to sleep. The time when magic was most potent, and the air had a spell weaver's cast to it.

"How is everything back at home?" I asked Fyre softly, not wanting to disturb the peace with my horrific news just yet, even though it was eating my insides in its need to get out.

*All right. Grandmother Rose still isn't allowed to communicate with you, but as you know, your parents' enforcement of that is a failure. Her health is great, considering her age. Kedrik is fine, but lonely, though he won't admit it. He misses you a lot. That kid has a big heart, but not a lot of good people to fill it with. You're very important to him; I hope you know that.*

His flickering gaze turned to a searching glare, as if he were waiting for me to dismiss Kedrik as someone trifling that I had forgotten about.

"He's my best friend!" I said quickly. "I can't wait to see him again."

He relaxed, closing his eyes and becoming invisible amid the feathery fire. *Some people change when they go away for too long.*

I swallowed, not allowing myself to be haunted by the change that had come over me when I'd first arrived. Fyre was right—people did change. But I hoped most of my changes since then were for the better.

*Your parents are fine too. They have been home ever since you left, hosting parties and redecorating that million-room castle. They're getting ready for . . .*

"For what?" I asked. Go figure, they would only stay home and have fun when I wasn't there. I burned with bitterness. "What are they getting ready for?"

*I should let them tell you when you come home. Like I said, everyone is healthy. The news isn't urgent. Have you been using the herbs Grandmother gave you?*

Even though he changed the subject without even trying to be subtle about it, I answered his question. "Yes. Tell Grandmother they've been really helpful. I'm almost out of chamomile, though."

*I'll bring fresh stock up with me next time I come.*

"Great!" Letters never came fast or often enough. Plus, there was that minor issue of them being intercepted and read.

*Speaking of bringing stuff, Kedrik asked me to give you this. It's a new invention of his.*

Separating himself from the flames, he bent and picked up what looked like a thin rectangular slate. The rope that had tied it to his leg was a charred wisp of ashes. I hadn't noticed it before, probably because Fyre himself was so magnificent to look at. The stone was cool when he handed it to me, even though it had been resting on embers. Suddenly, Fyre spat a fireball in the dead center of the slab. I jumped back in surprise. When it dissipated, glowing letters in Kedrik's handwriting were revealed. Wow! Fyre-induced invisible ink!

Hey Chris,

Like my new invention? It's a lot more secure than the old invisible ink method for sending messages. Since Fyre is so much bigger and stronger now, he'll be able to carry news back and forth much faster than some dude on a horse.

Coralla's acting really weird—well, weirder than normal, anyway. She stays locked in her room whenever there isn't some stupid tea party or dress fitting to go to. When I walked down the hallway her room was in, she flipped out and screeched at me to quit "snooping around." For the record, I never "snoop". I spy—there's a difference. Also, it's a strange experience for me to be accused of spying when I was wasn't. I was actually on my way to the storage room for an innocent paper clip. Well, it was innocent, but now it's part of the detonator for one of my smoke bombs. But I digress. Coralla's hiding something she doesn't want me to know about. So when you come back, you have to help me find out what it is.

Other than that, things have been quiet here. The wolves are gone. No sign of the Intriguer either, though I heard a few royals in other kingdoms have mysteriously vanished. I doubt it's just a coincidence.

Remember that sword you got fitted for a few eons back? It's almost done! It needs a few modifications for stealth (I doubt the ICUP allows four-foot-long lethal weapons if they don't even allow scissors), but it'll be ready for you for Christmas.

How are things at the school? I'm sorry your plan to get yourself kicked out hit a blockade. You'll get there, I know it. Is Laomi still annoying you? That girl is one of Coralla's best friends—I've never liked her.

I'm glad you got the knife I sent. I was worried it would be confiscated, but it sounds like the candy worked to disguise the rest of the bag's contents. Have you used it yet?

To reply, wipe the rock hybrid with a cloth damp with salt water, then write your message in oil. Cover the whole thing with egg white, and let it dry.

"Egg white?"

*You wouldn't believe how many different sealants he tried before he found one that worked. Tree sap, milk, spit, slug slime, avocado juice, and chicken grease, just to name a few.*

"His dedication is impressive." I hadn't realized until too late that I'd said it out loud.

*I'll have to convey your compliments to him.*

I snorted to cover up my embarrassment. "And make his head swell up? Not smart, Fyre."

*True.*

Though I hated to spoil our reunion by bringing it up, I couldn't delay conveying the recent Intriguer developments any longer.

"Listen, Fyre. I need to tell you some things that are extremely important. It might affect the lives of all the royals in Clystopia."

Fyre cocked his head, listening intently.

I told him how the magic mirror confirmed that the Intriguer was not only running loose and kidnapping royals, but also infiltrating the school to spy on the kingdoms of Clystopia.

*I need to go back*, Fyre said as soon as I'd finished.

I called for Elsie to filch raw eggs, oil, and salt from the kitchen while I hunted around for a brush to write with. Elsie brought the ingredients at once, but didn't stick around. I figured she was tired. Though I felt bad for waking her, she could move around without being noticed a lot easier than I could. Princesses weren't allowed out of their rooms after hours, but servants were expected to run errands for their mistresses whenever needed, so she wouldn't draw attention. After wiping the slate clean, I scrawled as many details onto it as I could, slathered it with gooey egg white, and then tied it to Fyre's leg with a hair ribbon.

*Not as much of a break as I'd wanted, but this can't wait.*

"Who are you going to give the message to?" I asked as he readied his flight feathers. My parents probably wouldn't listen—or Kedrik's parents, for that matter.

*Grandmother Rose, of course. I'm not stupid. No offense to your parents or anything...*

"Give them all the offense you want." I didn't care. Grandmother Rose would know what to do—that's what mattered. "Please hurry, so we know how to help."

*We?*

"Me, Elsie, Rachaella, and Laomi."

*You dragged your school friends into this?!*

"I didn't drag them anywhere! This affects them, too. They deserve to know what they're up against, and I trust them."

*Don't tell anyone else.*

"I won't. But speaking of keeping secrets, you still haven't told me what my parents are preparing for. They aren't likely to tell me anything—you know that. Is it important?"

*Don't worry, it isn't about the Intriguer. Your parents, as far as I can tell, know nothing of it. I still don't think I'm the right one to tell you this, but the suspense is killing me, so I'm going to anyway. Your parents are preparing for a new baby. Your mother is pregnant.*

With that, he took off through the door in a whirl of flaming sparks.

My mind screeched like a rusty door as it struggled to interpret Fyre's news. As the phoenix receded into the cloudy sky, I stared after him, holding the balcony door open. White flurries coated my hair and eyebrows, and my slippered feet grew numb. Finally, something registered in my brain: I was cold. After bolting the door, I went to stand by the fire.

Me, a big sister. Was that good or bad? The changes a baby would bring were a mystery. Would my—well, *our*—parents go gaga over it and spoil it to death? Or would they leave on vacations as usual, ignoring the baby and leaving us alone? Becoming a babysitter was a scary thought.

I might not even be around when the baby came—the Intriguer might have kidnapped or finished me off by then. It certainly came close before, and it hadn't even been trying. One of these days I might run out of luck. I closed my eyes, touching my fire pendant.

My door creaked open. Jumping to attention, I whipped around to face the intruder. I drew my dragon knife from where I always kept it, safely hidden in its cleverly disguised sheath on my waist, ready to face whatever trespasser threatened me. A wide-eyed, white-faced Elsie carrying a breakfast tray was not what I'd expected.

"Oh. G-good, you're still up," she stammered.

"Elsie, um, hi." I sheathed my weapon. "Sorry about that, I was expecting . . . never mind."

"Don't worry about it. All of us are edgy. I just wasn't prepared for you to come at me with a knife when I brought you food, that's all." She smiled, a little color returning to her cheeks. "Since we're both up, I figured we might as well have a snack."

I cleared my throat. "Yeah, good idea."

We sat down to eat. The formal breakfast in the dining hall wasn't for several hours, but I doubted I would sleep anymore after the night's excitement, so the food was welcome. Sharing a quiet, companionable meal with a friend calmed me. Besides, she had taken a risk in nicking the food, so I could certainly take the time to eat it.

Throughout our meal of bagels, cream cheese, and wild berry jelly, I kept opening my mouth to tell Elsie the news about my mother's pregnancy, but eventually I decided that I'd rather stuff my mouth than spit out words for the time being. I'd let myself digest the news before sharing.

My thoughts distracted me so much that my class disruptions that day were mostly accidental.

"Chris, would you quit tapping your quill like that? I'm trying to concentrate!" Laomi glared at me. She wasn't the only one I was irritating. We had an essay test in Ms. Sakura's Writing class, and I was making the only noise in the otherwise quiet classroom by tapping ink blots onto my desk instead of writing words. I hardly noticed the difference myself, because the air was stretched with the tension of students who hadn't studied. It was a very loud quiet.

"Sorry," I said anyway. A minute later, I forgot and started up again.

I had issues in Fashion class as well.

"Chris, *dahling*! A lavender silk gown does *not* match black knee-high boots and orange glitter eyeliner!"

"Oh." I looked down at the random assortment of items I had picked from the make-believe wardrobe of the test scenario. "Perhaps I'm starting a new trend," I suggested breezily.

Madame Annabelle was not impressed.

Later, in Speech class, I mumbled as I read aloud from a stuffy romance epic. "O, how your skin doth gleam, with a radiance that rivals that of the sun."

"When speaking," Miss Twitter interrupted, "it is considered rude to mumble. Enunciate what you are saying. Be proud of your vocabulary, for it is part of what distinguishes you from the vulgar peasantry."

"But your silken hair is dark, the swirling vortex of night that I long for!" I continued, increasing my volume.

Finally, my turn to read ended. Sighing, I massaged my temples.

"What's wrong, Chris?" Rachaella asked after class. "You seem . . . distracted."

"I am distracted. And stressed." The truth, just without an explanation.

"Is it about whatever new development you've been keeping to yourself all day?"

My steps faltered in surprise.

"You're easy to read. So? Are you going to tell us?" she asked.

The four of us met in Rachaella's room to talk, because I didn't want to discuss any more important death-defying plans in my obnoxious, fluffy pink quarters.

"I really want to meet Fyre," Rachaella said when I'd finished telling the story. "Seeing a phoenix would be amazing—I doubt there are more than a handful in Clystopia. Kedrik's really lucky."

"Yeah . . . he can be pretty annoying sometimes, though."

"Who, Kedrik or Fyre?" Elsie asked.

"I meant Fyre. Kedrik's perfect."

"Ooh, he's perfect?" Rachaella wiggled her eyebrows at me.

I hadn't meant to say that; it just spilled out. Flustered, I searched around for a comeback.

I was saved unexpectedly by Laomi, who said, "Does Fyre ever lose his feathers? Or would he mind if you took a couple? Phoenix feathers would be the neatest accessories."

"I don't know. I don't think he'd be very happy if you plucked one out of his tail, though. Anyway, you guys are missing the point! Fyre's taking the message back to Grandmother Rose. She'll know what to do. If he can make it there and back without getting intercepted, we'll have a way to communicate with the outside world, and we'll be one step closer to saving everyone. Am I the only one who is about to have an anxiety attack about this? What if it doesn't work?"

Elsie raised her hand. "I'm about to have an anxiety attack."

"If it doesn't work, then we'll find another way," Rachaella said, setting her jaw.

She and Laomi exchanged a look.

"What if there isn't another way?" I demanded. "How can you be so sure things will work out?"

"I'm not sure things will work out, but I'm going to do what I can, and then quit worrying about the parts I can't control. We're not heroes. It's not up to us to save the world. We're just regular people trying to make a little bit of difference. So don't worry so much, okay?"

We stared at each other, her gray eyes boring into my stormy ones.

Finally, I swallowed and looked away. Rachaella was the only person I'd met who could outstare me. "It's hard," I said.

"I know."

It was hard because bad things happened, and they could happen again, and what if one of my infamous screw-ups was what caused the catastrophe?

"I'll try."

"Good."

I pictured myself back home with the burden of handling the Intriguer on someone else's more qualified shoulders, preparing for the arrival of my new brother or sister, and hanging out with Kedrik and my other friends in a relaxed, non-life-threatening environment. It would be bliss. I wanted that life more than anything.

But there was nothing I could do about it but wait—and wait, and *wait*—and try to believe that everything would work out.

I lay in the grass, looking up at the blue sky dotted with clouds. The day was amazingly mild for so late in the year, and everyone took the chance to get outside during afternoon break. Most of the princesses sat on blankets in clear view of the princes' horseback riding lesson, but Rachaella, Laomi, Elsie, and I were sprawled on the sun-kissed earth, our heads close to one another's, and our hair tangling together.

The last several days had been peaceful. No one had tried to kill or kidnap us. Fyre hadn't returned, but it was still too early to expect him. Because no vortex had slurped us up for sending the message yet, I started to calm down—somewhat.

"Look at that cloud!" Rachaella exclaimed. "It looks like a dragon breathing fire."

I pointed to the one next to it. "That looks like two mushrooms salsa dancing."

Rachaella and Elsie laughed, and even Laomi gave a small chuckle under her breath.

"That one's shaped like a heart!" Elsie said.

"There's a bunny," Laomi added.

It was Rachaella's turn again. "Hmm . . . that looks like a lion drinking at a pool of water."

"I thought it looked like a guy with an Afro falling into a huge bowl of pasta," I said.

There were a few more snickers before Elsie went. "Those three by the tree line look like flowers," she said.

"There's a bunny," Laomi added.

"That's what you said last time!" I protested.

"I can't help it! They all look like bunnies to me! Big, white, fluffy bunnies."

"That one isn't a bunny," Rachaella said. "It looks like Noah's Ark, with all the animals lining up to get on."

It was funny, how such a silly game was made enjoyable because of the people playing it. No matter what the activity, I enjoyed it more when I did it with them.

"There's one that looks like a soft pretzel being eaten by a jellyfish."

"There's a long string of pearls." The sunlight made Elsie's hair glow like a halo. She was more relaxed too—about the Intriguer and about hanging out with royals all the time.

"There's—"

"Let me guess," I interrupted Laomi, "a bunny."

"No, actually, that one looks like my Uncle Lou."

I blinked up at the cloud in question. "He has an awfully big nose."

"Exactly."

We played the game until we grew tired of it, and then Laomi said, "I love the sky. If I could fly, I'd be up there all the time. Sky blue is my favorite color." She shifted in the grass, her face tilted up in wonder. In that position, she didn't look as chiseled or haughty as usual.

"It would be neat," Rachaella agreed. "It's like a whole new world up there—a reverse ocean you can breathe in." The way she said it made it sound like she'd visited that world before.

"My favorite color is the sky too!" Elsie exclaimed.

For some reason, I couldn't picture Laomi loving light blue so much. Maybe because she never wore the color.

When I asked her about it, she said, "It doesn't suit my complexion." That seemed like a strange reason to me.

"My favorite color is orange," I offered. It was the color of fire and sunsets.

"I like lilac," said Rachaella. "Lilacs are my favorite flowers too. What about you guys?"

"Bleeding hearts," said Elsie.

"Tiger lily," said Laomi.

I thought for a minute before answering. "Dandelions," I said finally.

"What? Why?" Laomi sat up, looking at me incredulously. The proud expression was back. "Dandelions are weeds, not flowers."

Rolling to face her, I rested my head on my elbow. "Because they *are* weeds. No one realizes how beautiful they are. Everyone hates them and tries to get rid of them, but they refuse to die."

Sitting up, Rachaella pushed her dark hair away from her face and lifted her arms to the sky, stretching. "I like dandelions, too," she said. "In a sea of grass, they stand out spectacularly. They aren't afraid." She knew I hadn't been talking about just flowers. It was nice, having someone understand me so well. "Plus," she added, "when they turn white and fluffy, they grant wishes."

"Are you saying that when I'm old and fat I'll be a Fairy Godmother?"

"Maybe."

I stuck my tongue out at her.

Something in the background caught my eye. Ashella and RosaLynne were situated near the castle, away from the other princesses for once. They plucked pieces of grass idly and watched Rachaella. When they saw me watching them watch her, they averted their gazes and resumed whatever conversation they'd been having.

I kept the corner of my eye on them for the next few minutes. RosaLynne fell asleep, slumping into her friend's lap. Ashella caught her, setting her head onto a pillow (brought outside expressly for that purpose, no doubt), and brushed the hair out of her friend's face. Taking one limp hand in two of hers, Ashella patted it protectively.

Rachaella's eyes followed mine. She tilted her head thoughtfully. "I don't think they will be happy with princes," she murmured.

A harsh laugh drew my eyes to SunGold, who was staring at the two girls with scorn.

I didn't understand what was going on. Ashella and RosaLynne were followers of SunGold and StarSilver—or they had been. Something must have happened to ostracize them.

I soon forgot about their drama because it wasn't on my list of things I considered important. But that night, I got within three steps and one bad decision away from stabbing them.

I was in bed, staring at the canopy as silvery shadows slipped around me, meditating on escape. When I heard voices, I rose and pressed my ear against the hall door. All princesses were supposed to be sleeping. We would be punished if we were caught out of bed. I'd never heard anyone aside from Rachaella, Elsie, Laomi, or an occasional servant moving around so late. But neither of the fuzzy voices in the corridor belonged to any of them.

I cracked open my door, straining to make out words, but the silence in the rest of the hallway roared in my ears. It would be impossible for me to go to sleep without knowing who was breaking the rules, so I slipped into the blackened hallway. The darkness was so thick I could have drowned in it if I breathed too deeply.

A door clicked shut—Rachaella's. Concerned about bullies trying some new abuse, I drew my dragon blade.

Slinking over, I pressed my ear to the crack between the door and frame. At last, I recognized the voices: Ashella and RosaLynne. What were they doing breaking the rules and sneaking into other people's bedrooms? My sleep-fogged brain and the suffocating darkness made me jump to the worst conclusions. Was it really them? Or was it the Intriguer disguised to *look* like them? It was even plausible that the Intriguer was forcing them to harm Rachaella to keep from being kidnapped themselves. I couldn't imagine a situation where the Intriguer wasn't involved. There was no other reason for the two princesses to be risking their reputations by skulking around in the dead of night to visit the most unpopular person in the school.

I wouldn't let them hurt her. Or if it was too late, I'd at least avenge my friend. I'd gone as far as grasping the knob and turning it when I heard what the two girls were actually saying.

". . . that we know they were lies. You never planned to marry into royalty, did you?" Ashella asked.

"No." Rachaella's voice, for the first time.

"We believe you. We refused to perform a dishonorable task that SunGold and StarSilver asked of us, and since then they have been spreading rumors about us, too."

RosaLynne spoke up. "We wished to apologize before, but you were always near Laomi and Chris. Neither of them thinks highly of us."

"They just want to make sure I'm not being bothered anymore," Rachaella said. "They're both good people."

A pause.

"Well, we are sorry for causing you trouble. Our treatment of you was disgraceful."

"Apology accepted."

"We should go," one of the princesses whispered.

The doorknob turned beneath my hand. I jerked back.

"If you want," Rachaella called after them, "you can sit with us tomorrow at lunch. I'll tell Chris and Laomi you're all right."

"No . . . well, perhaps."

"We will consider it."

I didn't hear any more of the exchange because I was tearing back to my own room, heedless of squeaky boards. I almost missed the door and ran into the wall.

There was nothing wrong—nothing except the hurricane of adrenaline racing circles through me and my twitching hand that still held my knife. No danger. I'd almost seriously injured two princesses who weren't even up to no good.

I paced, still gripping my weapon. I didn't want to let it go, even though it helped nothing. Stressed and confused, I stared into the fireplace embers and tried to take deep, slow breaths.

# Chapter 19. Princess Prodigy

"Christina!" Arcturus waved to me from the training ring, where the fresh snow had been shoveled to clear the area for weapons training, or rather, mess-around-with-a-sword-or-just-hang-out-time. I'd joined the princes for practice several times, and very little swordplay ever happened.

Climbing down from my perch in a poplar tree, I joined him and the other princes who were competing to see how far they could throw their swords like spears across the field. I had an idea that some exercise would help me with my rising anxiety levels. I expected Fyre to return any moment, and my patience was wearing thin. I hoped the phoenix realized that this was no time to take a whimsical detour to the beach.

"See how far you can throw it!" Vance, a prince with a cleft chin and flaming red, pointed eyebrows that matched his hair, handed me a spare sword.

"Two niblets says she makes it to the top three," Ronnoc whispered out of the corner of his mouth to Valiant. Ronnoc, a ropey boy with dark curly hair and freckles, would bet on anything, like how many snowflakes he could catch on his tongue in thirty seconds. The final number had been seven.

"All right." Valiant and Ronnoc spit in their hands then shook. Ew. Some guys were disgusting, even the ones who were supposed to be all refined and princely.

Taking the makeshift spear, I balanced it in my hand, took a running start, and hurled it. It landed toward the front, but around fifth place.

Ronnoc shook his head forlornly and sighed. "You let me down, Christina, you let me down." He parted with his money with a dejected expression that I knew was just for show. Like any royal, he could make bets far larger and more often than he did without financial worries.

I shrugged. I'd never thrown a spear before. It seemed pointless unless there was a target. The princes declared Laomi's twin brother Lanovan the winner. He was a lean guy with shaggy black hair that was forever hanging in his eyes. I supposed he didn't need to see to throw a spear far.

A chorus of chuckles broke out behind me. Turning to see what was so funny, I spotted a tired-looking prince with mussed hair and wrinkled clothes stumbling over to the field. His chubby cherub cheeks stretched into a yawn.

"Hey, Bean!" Arcturus called. "Finally decided to join us, huh?"

"I didn't sleep at all last night!" Bean complained. "*Someone* put this under my seventh mattress." He held up an uncooked green pea.

Arcturus's smile gave him away. "How long did it take you to find it?"

"Only about ten minutes, but I didn't start looking until this morning. Last time, you used my thirty-second mattress, so I knew it would be near the beginning this time."

"Well, what took you so long to get out here, then? Practice is half over!"

"I had to leave a present somewhere in your room, of course."

Arcturus's face took on a startled expression. Bean sauntered past him, looking smug.

*Fweeeeeeet!*

The piercing whistle made everyone grimace.

"All right, everyone! Practice started twenty minutes ago! What are you all doing standing around staring at the clouds?" It was the instructor, who had decided to show up for once. Though no longer completely bald, his hair was buzzed so close to his head that I couldn't determine the color. Even though the temperature was below freezing, he wore a single tight, long-sleeved tunic to show off his muscles.

The princes responded immediately, falling silent under his commanding glare. We trudged off to get the swords we had thrown.

"Everyone pair up and duel!" the instructor announced once we had gathered around him with our weapons.

Just like that? Hello, everyone, and welcome to swordsmanship class! Grab a partner and start chopping away at each other! My lips formed an unimpressed line.

"Ah—little miss?"

Since I was the only girl on the field, I couldn't pretend I didn't know he was talking to me. It was tempting, though. "What?"

"I see you have come to visit our class again—welcome back. You may have a seat on the bench over at the edge of the ring if you wish to watch."

I clenched my jaw, remembering that the instructor hadn't been around to see me beat up Valiant during the first training session I'd crashed, and go on to win nearly all the contests the princes devised in later ones.

"I came to train," I said shortly, marching off before my fiery temper resulted in a confrontation.

His footsteps pursued me, thumping loudly on the frozen ground.

"For your own safety, I am afraid that I cannot allow you to—"

"I don't need your permission." Despite his size, the instructor didn't seem especially bright, and he didn't intimidate me. I didn't care about his policies or rules.

When he tried to grab my arm, I thwacked his fingers with my practice sword and kept walking.

"Listen here, young lady!" he barked. "I do not know where you have come from or what inappropriate behaviors women practice there, but here, ladies such as yourself DO NOT USE WEAPONRY!"

I caught up to the princes, who fidgeted as they watched the exchange, uncertain. A few cringed slightly when the instructor yelled.

I smirked. "Watch me."

I didn't bother turning around, though I was sure the expression on his face was priceless. I left him, still flustered, behind me. I knew his type. Bluster was the only method he knew to get people to do what he wanted. With guys, it would work because he could back it up with physical force if necessary. But people like him never knew how to deal with girls. I was ninety percent sure he wouldn't attempt to forcibly drag me off the field. I waited, but his rough hand didn't touch me again. Good thing, too, or I would have broken his fingers.

Prince Rohith, a short boy with deep brown skin, curly hair, and a scar splitting one eyebrow, was the only one without a partner at the moment, so I faced off with him. A few yards away, Vance flipped a coin to Ronnoc, who pocketed it.

Seeing me view the exchange, Ronnoc winked. "I knew Coach would see things your way."

Coach blew the whistle, and we began. My skills were no longer a surprise, but I still managed to beat Rohith fairly easily. His feet were quick and his blows hard, but he lacked creative skill. Then I battled Bean, whose form was sloppy. I hardly needed to attack him—he tripped over his own feet and sprawled in front of me. Arcturus's defense was solid, but he lacked the fire of competition. After a few minutes, he gave up and declared me the winner.

"Why do you do this," he asked when we finished, gesturing to the ongoing sparring matches, "when no one expects you to?"

I squared my feet, still panting. "Because when I fight, I know that I'm alive."

I headed toward my next bout without waiting for a response.

After two more wins, I nearly gave up hope that anyone would challenge me, but then I dueled Lanovan. He had everything—agility, power, and creativity. He didn't go easy on me either. I started out with a powerful swipe upward, which he blocked easily and swung out of before coming at me from the side. I managed to get my sword down in time, but my arms strained at the strength of the blow. Out of all the princes I'd dueled, that kind of power had only been matched by Kedrik.

He faked a thrust and took a swing at my legs, but I jumped, connecting my weapon with his on the way down. With the extra power of gravity behind me, I wrenched the sword out of his hand. But before I could do anything else, Lanovan lunged forward and grabbed the hilt of my sword, placing himself between me and my weapon and twisting it out of my grasp. I dropped to the ground as he swung the wooden blade in a wide arc. Now *that* was a move I wanted to try on Kedrik.

Snatching up his fallen sword, I rolled to my feet in a ready stance.

*Chris, where are you?*

"Hold up." I stuck Lanovan's sword into the ground to show that I wasn't up to any trickery, and then did a quick spin.

"Fyre?" I whispered, though I didn't see any flaming feathers against the snow. Huh, I was positive I'd heard his thought-speech.

*I've been waiting on your balcony for fifteen minutes. Someone will see me if you don't let me in. I'm not exactly inconspicuous.*

It *was* Fyre!

"Sorry, I've got to go. We'll finish later?"

"Sure—you're a skilled fighter," Lanovan said.

"You are, too."

I ran up the hill toward the forest.

"See you, Christina!" Arcturus waved, then turned back around and finished off Bean with a swoop of his sword.

Ronnoc glanced over his shoulder at me. "Are you coming back next practice?"

"Bet on it."

He grinned. "I will!"

As soon as I was out of sight, I took to the trees and raced back to the princess academy. I never thought I'd be so excited to run *toward* the place.

The icy air made me look forward to my fire-warmed room. My breath puffed in billowing clouds. Becoming comfortable with traversing the rounded branches so high up had taken a while. There wasn't much snow stuck to the barren trees, but occasionally I came across a dangerous-looking ice patch. Eventually, my legs adjusted to the rolling and shaping of the branches, and I practically sprang through the treetops.

When I arrived at my destination, Fyre peered at me with beady eyes.

The maple beneath me stiffened to her regular position, and I climbed easily to my railing, careful not to snap any brittle branches.

*Thank you!* I thought-called to the trees, then jumped onto my balcony and into three and a half feet of accumulated snow. Typical—after making it through an entire forest without stepping in an inch, I manage to soak my entire bottom half in the last three steps of the journey.

*I see the trees have given you power, too.*

"Yep!"

Wading to the door, I turned the knob—locked, of course.

*Way to go, genius. Now we're both trapped outside.* Fyre fluttered over to perch on my dry shoulder.

Ignoring his remark, I peered inside, but saw no one. Elsie was probably snitching food or spying on suspicious-looking persons.

"Hold on."

Drawing my knife, I slid it through the crack in the door and used it to push the bolt back. Then I opened the door with a flourish, bowing.

"After you."

*Princesses are supposed to curtsy*, he sniffed, hopping inside.

I smirked and followed him, removing the grating before the fireplace and bowing again to annoy him.

Ruffling his feathers, he jumped into the warm coals.

"So? What's the news?"

Fyre gave a long yawn before answering. *Oh, I forgot. Your herb package is still outside. Sorry if the plants are a bit soggy.*

Leaping up, I retrieved the damp bundle from the balcony.

"Thanks for bringing it. What was Grandmother's message?" I asked as I set out the herbs to dry.

*It's all written down.* He held out his leg with the slate attached to it.

I flipped my knife out and sliced the already burning string. Fyre blew a fireball at the thin rock, and when it dispersed, I read the short note.

Hang in there. We will come for you.
We have allies. Be ready at all times, and tell no one.

The letters burned away, leaving me frustrated. Who was this "we" coming for me? What allies? When would they be here? How should I prepare for their arrival? Did they expect me to leave my friends behind while I made my escape? I could never do that!

"She didn't tell me *anything*!" I exclaimed.

*I know. She knew you wouldn't be satisfied, but the less information you have, the less the Intriguer can gather if it takes you.* Fyre preened his feathers calmly, as if he had just commented on what lovely weather we were having instead of prophesying my doom.

My blood chilled. "Do you think that's likely?"

He ducked his head. *I don't know. I'm not sure how it chooses its victims. But you've been here, in its power, for several months now, and if you keep investigating it, there's a good chance it will notice.*

At least he didn't sugarcoat it. Fyre's blunt honesty was disquieting, but he didn't keep secrets to protect me, which I appreciated.

"What about everyone else at the school? Will they be rescued?" I never liked SunGold or StarSilver, but they didn't deserve to be held captive—or worse.

*Not everyone can be saved, Chris. Not everyone will want to be saved—they won't necessarily believe what's going on. I'm sorry. There's not much we can do until we get the truth out. And to do that, we need you with us—and that mirror.*

I understood. A disreputable princess declaring that everyone was in danger wasn't evidence. The ICUP was a high-security fortress with guards from all the Clystopian kingdoms. It was hard to believe that a secret room was snuck in during construction to intercept communication and exploit royal secrets. It was even harder to believe that the Intriguer responsible for it was abducting royals by whisking them away in magical tornadoes. But if the mirror corroborated my story, my parents would be convinced of the truth. They could then use their influence to spread the word and save everyone.

But still . . . "I can't leave my friends."

Fyre was silent.

"Did you hear me? I'm not leaving without them!" I clenched my fists. My knuckles cracked.

*I understand. Pick only the people who know about the Intriguer and you trust with your life. Everyone else will have to stay for now. To make the mission successful, we need to move quickly, and having fifty princesses who don't want to get their hems dirty will slow us down.*

Scowling, I looked away, hating the idea of abandoning anyone to the mercy of the Intriguer. But Fyre was right—mobilizing a band of princesses and trekking through the woods in winter was worse than impossible. The

Intriguer would laugh itself into hysterics, and then pluck us up like ripe blueberries from a bush.

"Okay. It'll be me and three others." I described Elsie, Laomi, and Rachaella.

*All right, we will try to bring them as well. But—*

"No trying. No 'buts.' If they don't get rescued, I'm not coming."

*You must promise not to tell them anything about this conversation or the rescue party,* Fyre continued, ignoring my protest. *The Intriguer might find out, and then we'd be in even more trouble. Just make sure they are prepared to leave at a moment's notice.*

"How am I supposed to prepare them when I'm not allowed to tell them anything?"

The tower bell clanged, and the sound of numerous high heels tapping toward dinner filled the hall.

*You'd better change before leaving—you're soaked,* Fyre said instead of answering. *Someone might realize you're up to something.*

After throwing on a new dress, I stoked the fire some more.

"Will you be safe here?"

In response, Fyre tucked his head into his wing, instantly becoming seamless with the real flames of the fire.

I left him to his nap, feeling even more dissatisfied than before he'd arrived.

"Hi, Ashella, RosaLynne . . . you both look nice this evening," Rachaella said as she sat next to me at the dinner table.

It was the most awkward conversation starter I'd ever heard. I was almost embarrassed on Rachaella's behalf.

The princesses smiled nervously and looked at their food. Ashella mumbled something that vaguely resembled "thank you." The newest royal rejects sat two seats down from us, in that uncomfortable area where we could listen to each other's conversations, but we didn't have to talk to one another because we weren't technically sitting together.

Taking a vial from her purse, RosaLynne dripped three drops of bright blue liquid inside her stuffed pepper. As she did so, she cast a furtive glance around and saw me watching.

"This is a potion that will stop me from falling asleep when it is undesirable." She chewed on her lip, as if afraid I was going to challenge that statement.

"Nice. Does it work well?"

She shook her head. "I only received it two days ago. It can take up to a week to become effective. Currently, it has only prevented me from falling asleep during the night."

I munched on my pepper solemnly. "Well, I hope it works out for you."

"Me too."

Ashella shifted to give her friend an encouraging smile, which RosaLynne returned with something that was more like a grimace.

When Rachaella, Laomi, Elsie, and I escaped, the two of them would be left behind with the Intriguer. The thought made my food taste like mud. I struggled to swallow.

Laomi plopped down on my other side, startling me. Her face was lit up with excitement. I immediately became scared.

"Did you tell her?" she asked Rachaella, glancing back and forth rapidly between us.

Rachaella shook her head. "I knew you would want to."

Laomi beamed. I nearly shivered with fright. "Chris, I have the best news. Guess what was put on the announcement bulletin while you were gone!"

I perked up. I loved guessing games. "The head chef got caught mixing bird plop in with the biscuits and gravy this morning."

"Eeew! No! There's going to be—"

"A snowball fight? Losing team gets strung up by their toes?"

"No, a—"

"Ball? Where we wear extra-poufy dresses with extra-high heels? And dance until our feet fall off?"

"How did you know?" she asked, deflated.

"Wait, really?" I had been kidding. Princesses were traditionally inaugurated as debutantes on their sixteenth birthdays when they hosted a "coming out" ball. There were many princesses at the ICUP, myself included, who were too young. I never dreamed the school would hold one.

Laomi must have missed my tone of panic, because she continued to prattle on excitedly. "It's going to be the week before Christmas, and the princes from the school down the hill are going to be our guests! I'm designing our dresses, of course, so I'll need you and Rachaella in my room after classes to get your sizes."

"Oh . . ." was all that trailed out of my mouth.

Sighing in ecstasy, Laomi exclaimed, "This is going to be so much fun!"

Oh yeah, fun, fun. I needed to be excused to go puke for joy. Slogging through a day of princess boarding school without screaming, I could handle, barely. Saving Clystopia from the Intriguer infiltrating the boarding school, not so much. Dressing up in outrageous attire and participating in a formal dance, *not at all.*

I massaged my forehead as it began to pound.

From the other side of the dinner table, my cousins left their clique and sashayed to Laomi.

"Good evening, Laomi," SunGold said, giving a fake leer of a smile.

Flipping her ribbons of hair over her shoulder, StarSilver copied her sister.

Laomi regarded them coolly. "To what do I owe the pleasure of your attention?"

They missed the sarcasm dripping from her words.

"We heard that there is a ball planned for the school next month," StarSilver said, "and we were wondering if you would do us the honor of designing our gowns."

Cocking her head, Laomi considered. "I suppose I will have time to design two more personalized gowns once I finish the ones for my friends," she said, gesturing to me and Rachaella.

My cousins preened. "How wonderful!"

"We are truly grateful—"

Laomi interrupted them. "Pardon me, did I say I would give you the dresses?"

"Well, of course, we will pay a considerable amount for your work—we would never expect you to *give* them to us," StarSilver said. "How does five hundred marks sound?"

As they waited, wringing their hands, Laomi sipped her water and eyed them. "That sounds like a perfect amount to start off the bidding."

"Excuse me?"

"You are excused. I shall have cards for the silent auction of two personalized Leather Diamonds ball gowns displayed on the bulletin board soon. Feel free to stop by and place a bid."

With that, she turned her back on them.

Rachaella shook with laughter as soon as they were gone, but I didn't know what was so funny.

"What just happened?" I asked. "Why did they want you to design their dresses?"

Laomi barked out her own laugh, but when she saw how confused I was she looked at me incredulously. "Oh, wait, you were serious."

Before I could ask what I was missing, she reached over and turned my sleeve back to reveal the tag stitched there. The tag had the letters *LD* in intertwining cursive embroidered on it.

"What does that say?" she asked me.

"*LD.*" I wasn't a toddler, geez.

Then she showed me her own sleeve, which had an identical tag. Rachaella pulled her sleeve back too—*LD* again.

"What does *LD* stand for? Lame dress?" I joked. I didn't appreciate being treated like an idiot, so I felt like making a snide comment. I was fully aware the tag held the logo for Leather Diamonds, a dress brand so popular even I'd heard of it. Their dresses were actually some of my favorites, since they were designed for comfort as well as elegance.

Laomi's brows furrowed into her familiar scowl. She looked ready to slap me.

The reason suddenly dawned on me. "Wait—did you . . . make these?"

"I designed all three of them. In fact, nearly every royal in this room is wearing clothing that I created. I am considered a prodigy dress designer. My pieces are the height of fashion throughout Clystopia."

"True story," Rachaella said.

I was still wrapping my head around the idea that there was such a thing as a prodigy in dress designing, so I said nothing.

"My fabrics and the style of every dress are designed to be both comfortable and classy. There is no equal to them anywhere for style or durability. Why do you think they never bothered Rachaella when I was near her? Why do you think they refused to pull pranks on me? They were afraid I would quit selling to them. As the queen of their fashion identity, I have power over them."

"I had no idea. Sorry for insulting your work. I actually really like this dress."

"Hmph. I suppose I will forgive you this once, since you were ignorant."

I bit my lip to keep back a sharp retort. It was still hard for me to understand sometimes how the gentle, caring Rachaella was friends with the prickly princess. I couldn't even imagine how they'd crossed paths.

Leaning back in my chair, I folded my arms. "How did you two meet?" I asked, changing the subject.

"Laomi and Lanovan were kidnapped once, when they were little," Rachaella explained. "My parents saved them. I was really young, obviously, so I don't remember much. But after they returned them safely to the castle, our families stayed in touch. You could say the three of us grew up together."

Her explanation left out a lot of details. It occurred to me that even though I trusted the two of them with my life, in some ways, I barely knew them.

Uncertainty about the future continued to plague me. At night, peaceful shadows crept over my legs where I sat on my bed, inviting me to sleep. I drew my knees up sharply, away from their serpent tongues and toward the thin moonlight filtering through the window.

I didn't *want* to sleep. I couldn't. There was too much to think about—the Intriguer tightening a noose around the school, the rescue party on its way, the ball, how long it would take Miss Victoria to realize that someone had broken into her locked cabinet and slit all the corsets.

I stroked my knife fondly. It was undoubtedly the second-best present anyone had ever given me; Snowy had been the first.

Hugging my knees, I gazed, transfixed, at the ever-expanding shadows when suddenly, the moon went out.

There was no light anywhere. I was drowning, suffocating under the shadows that twined around my throat, trying to choke me. Sliding off the bed, I stumbled toward where I knew the balcony door was.

A faint glimmer caught the corner of my eye. Fyre awoke from his slumber beneath the ashes and extended his wings, illuminating the room with a golden red glow. The darkness retreated, hiding in the corners, but my entire body remained taut and ready for action.

I peered through the glass door, but saw nothing outside—a void of darkness still pervaded.

*Something is very wrong.*

Though Fyre spoke only in my mind, his voice seemed to echo forever in the gloom. Gritting my teeth, I reached for the doorknob and pulled with all my might against the frozen door. I had no idea what possessed me, but I wanted to do *something* besides stand there. I needed to know what was happening.

Out in the darkness, there was a flicker of light. It was a lantern, held aloft by a girl I recognized from class—a princess. She was illuminated like a ghost against the night surrounding her. What was she doing? Her nightgown and hair whipped in the wind as leaves, sticks, and stones spun circles around her.

The vortex began to lift her.

I pulled in vain against the door, making the glass rattle. I didn't know what I could do, only that I had to try.

*Don't, Chris! That's a bad idea,* Fyre warned.

But it didn't matter. The door was stuck, either from cold or because the Intriguer didn't want interference.

The girl's lamp snuffed out. When the peaceful moonlight returned, she was gone.

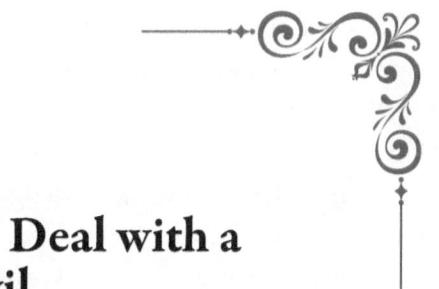

# Chapter 20. A Deal with a Devil

"Chris!"

I was up, out of bed, and had my knife drawn in a split second, my reflexes sharp. But everything looked fuzzy, and my head pounded. All night I'd had horrible dreams about tornadoes and doors that wouldn't open.

I squinted against the weak winter sunlight venturing bravely across the threshold. It was late morning, but since it was Sunday, there were no classes.

Elsie stood before me, wringing her apron.

"Elsie? Whaza problem?" I asked blearily.

My friend was shaky, and despite the chill, sweat dampened her hair. Taking a breath, she swallowed. "It's getting worse. A student is missing, and . . . Rachaella's sick."

It took me a few seconds to register what Elsie said, but when I did, my heart started thumping out of rhythm. Because of the previous night's events, I already knew a girl was gone. Rachaella's predicament was a new concern, though. From Elsie's distress, I could tell she was talking about more than a cold. I ran a hand through my unkempt hair. I couldn't afford a panic attack. I had to assess the situation.

"Where is she?"

"In her room, in bed."

"Anyone with her?"

"Laomi."

"Who else knows?"

"No one, yet."

I took a breath to calm myself, but all it did was make my eyelid twitch. It could be a coincidence that Rachaella got sick the same day a girl disappeared. The Intriguer had never caused disease before—not that I knew of, anyway.

I had herbs and knowledge on how to use them, thanks to Grandmother. This problem, at least, I could do something about.

"I'm going over to see her symptoms," I said.

Rushing down the hall, I knocked, but then strode inside without waiting for an answer. Elsie trailed me. Laomi sat next to the bed, helping Rachaella drink some water. The usually immaculate princess was still in her nightgown, her long hair trailing on the floor in a messy, unbrushed braid. No makeup disguised her puffy, stressed eyes.

I sidled over to observe Rachaella. She was flushed with heat, even as she shivered. Her breathing rasped; each time she inflated her lungs, it sounded arduous. Her throaty cough ruptured the air. Some water dribbled down her chin, and she pushed the cup her friend offered away.

"It's just a cold—I'm not dying. Don't look at me like that." Rachaella folded her arms and tried to look exasperated, but she couldn't quite pull it off.

"You sound like a grizzly bear with a smoking problem," I told her. "It doesn't look like you've slept. You have a wet cough, your color is off, and . . ." I paused to place the back of my hand against her forehead, "You have a fever. What else is wrong?"

"Should she talk with a cough like that?" Laomi asked. "She is having difficulty just breathing. And what are you, anyway, some kind of healer?" She folded her arms, too, pulling off the irritated look much better than Rachaella had.

"I'm not a healer, but my grandmother is. She taught me some remedies." I turned back to my patient. "Rachaella, I need you to tell me what hurts, because you're the only one who can feel it."

She nodded weakly, blinking with the slowness of a drowsy tortoise. Opening her mouth to speak, she instead let forth a cacophony of raspy coughs.

"Sorry," she rasped when her body had stopped shuddering.

"Shhhh . . ." Laomi soothed, holding the cool cup of water to Rachaella's lips again. She stroked her sick friend's hair. I had never seen Laomi distraught to the point of becoming gentle and not caring about her appearance. She did care for Rachaella, even if she seemed annoyed with her, me, and the rest of the world most of the time.

After sipping more water, Rachaella spoke. "It hurts everywhere when I move. My head is throbbing. My throat is sore. I can't breathe through my nose. I'm so . . . cold . . ." Feebly, she nestled deeper into her layers of comforters, and then closed her eyes, breathing through her scratchy windpipe as if to catch her breath.

"And sometimes she coughs up . . . stuff." Elsie added, grimacing in spite of herself.

I nodded, drawing Elsie and Laomi toward the fireplace so we could have a private discussion. "It's the flu, I think, or something similar. She'll be fine if I treat her." Hopefully. "Let's keep this quiet. I don't want the doctors here getting hold of her when I don't know what they're like."

Common treatments in the medical world included leeches, cod liver oil, mercury supplements, dousing the patient in alternating boiling and ice water, adorning them with charms, and heroin. At best, unhelpful, and at worst, lethal. Not all doctors were incompetent, of course, but without knowing one way or the other, it was better to keep Rachaella away from them. Grandmother Rose knew what she was doing. Her treatments would heal Rachaella, as long as I remembered how to administer them properly.

A tortured groan came from the bed, and Laomi flew to her friend's side again. I sped out the door to fetch my herbal supplies.

"Fyre!" I called, bursting into my room.

*Huh? Wha . . . ?* He blinked groggily. *I don't feel so well, bad night's sl—*

"It's important—wake up! Rachaella's sick. I think I know how to treat her symptoms, but I want Grandmother's advice, too."

Fyre pushed out of the fireplace, trailing ashes and hopping around like he was drunk. Extending his wings, he flapped experimentally a few times, preparing for flight. He knew how dangerous sickness could be if not treated properly. Even if he was worn out, he had to get going to update Grandmother about the Intriguer's moves and ask her advice about

Rachaella. I explained the details to him, and within minutes he was off, leaving me to gather and sort herbs.

Herbal treatments weren't as simple as some people thought. I couldn't just give a patient some leaves to chew on like a cow. Some herbs could be eaten, of course, or steeped in tea. Others were more useful as poultices, tinctures, or salves. Some plants had leaves that healed, and roots that were poisonous. There were also herbs that couldn't be mixed with certain others, or their effects would be nullified.

I grew up surrounded by these plants since I often stayed with Grandmother Rose and helped with her gardening. With her as a mentor, I helped heal scrapes, burns, bites, chills, allergies, infections, and various illnesses. She taught me how to use each herb, the proper dosage, and what to do if treatment had little effect on the patient or they had a bad reaction to it. I had every reason to be confident in my herbal knowledge. But treating a patient by myself, without Grandmother's guidance, set me on edge.

I returned to Rachaella's room with a steaming pot of tea. It included steeped thyme, chamomile, and peppermint leaves.

Since Grandmother wasn't there to do it, I murmured her prayer of healing over the concoction. "May my action and Your power work together to nourish and heal."

After adding a touch of honey, I helped my friend sit up, and then gave the fresh-smelling drink to her, sip by sip. Elsie and Laomi sat by and watched with mournful expressions.

"Chris?" Rachaella croaked after drinking, "Is this serious?"

"The fact that you're strong enough to ask that is a good sign. A flu feels terrible, but you were right, you aren't going to die." Probably.

It was a few minutes before she answered. Chamomile had many attributes, including that of a sedative. I knew it was still too early for it to work, but I couldn't help but hope that she had fallen asleep. Rest was key to fighting sickness.

"Well, if I do die, that's okay. Don't feel bad—I've never been afraid of dying. This *pain* though . . ." She thrashed about in bed, trying and failing to get into a comfortable position. Finally, out of breath, she ended her convulsions in a twisted position.

"Try to rest," Laomi urged. "Chris said you would be fine." She squeezed her friend's hand before laying it gently back on the pillow.

"Read to me," Rachaella requested. "Something happy, to distract me. No sickness or death, please."

My throat clogged with emotion. Yes, she would be fine, eventually. But in the meantime, I hated seeing her so miserable. I reached for the nearest book on the end table blindly. The Bible—of course it was. Flipping through it, I found a reading from Psalms that sounded good. I hadn't perused the Bible much before, but I'd always liked the Psalms when they read them in church. They were melodic and often contained comforting messages. The rhythmic stanzas might help her fall asleep, too.

"'O Lord, how many are my foes! Many are rising against me; many are saying of me, there is no help for him in God.'"

Laomi crossed her arms. "You call this happy?"

"Just shut up and listen. It gets better."

Rachaella scowled at me.

"Ah, I mean, *dearest Laomi, please* just shut up and listen," I corrected myself.

Both of them stuck their tongues out at me. I smiled.

It took me a moment to find my place again. "'But thou, O Lord, art a shield about me, my glory, and the lifter of my head. I cry aloud to the Lord, and he answers me from his holy hill. I lie down and sleep, I wake again, for the Lord sustains me. I am not afraid . . .'"

Rachaella fell asleep before I finished the chapter. By the time I closed the book, my eyelid had stopped twitching.

Rachaella was sleeping relatively peacefully when Elsie arrived with an armload of muffins and fruit. Splayed across the comfy purple sofa chairs, Laomi and I looked up tiredly.

"Oh, hey," I said. "I was wondering where you went." At the sight of the muffins, I perked up. "Food!"

Relieving her of the burden, I dumped it on the stained-glass coffee table, and Laomi and I dug in. The scent of the chocolate in the muffins overpowered the odor of sweat and sickness.

"What's the matter?" Laomi asked, staring at Elsie. The golden-haired girl sat at the edge of a chair, not eating.

"The princess is still missing." She kept her eyes glued to the ground and played with the fabric of her skirt nervously. "Her friend went to her room to say good morning, but she wasn't there. Her door and windows were open, and her room was ransacked. The whole castle was searched, but she wasn't found anywhere."

Laomi wrinkled her brow. "Did they check the grounds too?"

Elsie nodded. "There was no sign of her. The storm last night wiped out any traces."

"She's gone," I said. "The Intriguer took her—they aren't going to find her anywhere."

An apple slice hit me in the face. Gritting her teeth, Laomi grabbed a new piece of fruit, glaring at me.

"What?" I asked. "Was that too blunt?"

"A bit!"

"Sorry."

"Just quit saying stupid, unhelpful things."

Laomi draped her arms around Elsie, trying to comfort her.

I tried again. "How about I go ask the trees if they saw anything?"

Elsie gave me a hopeful look.

Sighing, I got to my feet and stretched. "I'll be right back," I promised.

"Be careful!" Elsie exclaimed.

Princesses milling in the hallway gave me strange looks as I marched back across the hall, barefoot and still in my nightgown. Ignoring their loudly whispered comments, I headed to my room and closed the door.

This time, the balcony doors opened easily. Stepping outside, I surveyed the battlefield spread below me.

Branches, dead leaves, and other debris—a lantern that had been blown off someone's balcony, some roof shingles, and a curly brown wig—were scattered over the torn earth. Boughs hung to mother trees by a few slivers of wood, and bushes were so ripped and crushed they were no more than piles of kindling. With all the dirt strewn everywhere, the slushy snow was more brown than white. The forest moaned in pain.

"Maple, what happened?" I asked the tree nearest me. "Was it the storm last night? The Intriguer caused it, didn't it?"

*No storm did you hear. The one you call Intriguer came, collected its dues . . .*

"Its dues?"

*A girl ventured outside in the dead of night. She—eeeeEEEEEIIIIII!!!!*

The reverberations of the tree's screech almost knocked me off my feet. I clung to the balcony railing, knuckles white. Frantically, I blocked my mind before it could be burnt up by the tree's thought-screams. The snowy silence was a relief. I crinkled my toes, which were getting cold in the ankle-deep snow I stood in.

That's when I heard a sound that wasn't in my head. *Scritch scritch. Scratch. Scraaaaape.* And a growl.

"Hello, girlie."

I reached for my knife before remembering I'd set it on Rachaella's nightstand and forgotten it. I tried to gauge the distance between me and the ground. Could the alpha reach me? No. Otherwise, he would have broken in and devoured me already. Still, I took an involuntary step back.

The alpha barked a laugh. "Afraid I'll jump up there and nibble your toes?" he taunted.

Along with the alpha, three other wolves circled below. Two more attacked the maple tree I'd been speaking with, ripping bark from the trunk and sending their blunt claws deep into her wood.

"Stop it!" I shouted at them, leaning over the railing.

"Make us," the alpha barked. His yellow eyes glittered.

"Guards!" I called over my shoulder.

"Ha! We'll be long gone before those beetles arrive. We can return at our leisure to continue debarking this fine tree here."

"What do you want?" I snarled.

The alpha blinked. "To kill you, obviously. I thought I'd made that clear by now."

"Well, I'm not going to jump off the balcony and let you tear me apart. Sorry to disappoint."

He chuckled, a sound like bubbling blood. "Not yet, anyway."

"What's that supposed to mean?"

With a swish of his tail, he signaled his two pack members to quit torturing the tree. "What Woody was trying to tell you is that princess girl was fulfilling her end of a deal."

"How would you know anything about it?" I narrowed my eyes, suspicious.

He bared his teeth. Against the putrid snow slush, they looked pearly. "The whole forest heard her scream before she was taken, begging to be forgiven her debt."

I started to shiver. "Is this true?" I asked the maple. I wouldn't believe a word the alpha said if it wasn't backed by someone else.

The tree shuddered a sigh. *Yes.*

"Told you—the girl made a deal with a devil. Now she's in its thrall."

I reeled backward, shaking, almost falling on my butt in the snow. My eyes darted, unfocused.

The alpha watched me steadily. "Your Intriguer knows what it's doing."

Turning his back on me, he began to pad away.

"What do you mean, 'my' Intriguer?" I demanded.

But he and his pack vanished into the broken forest without answering.

The watery winter sun melted over the horizon, but Rachaella's sickness remained unchanged. Her fever raged, and she alternated between curling into a shivering ball and throwing the covers away in a violent flash of heat. With no way to help, the rest of us paced, stared out the window, and repeated the same conversations over and over.

"Who would be dumb enough to make a deal with the Intriguer?" Elsie asked for the umpteenth time.

"That girl, apparently," Laomi snipped.

"Maybe she didn't realize what she was doing," I suggested. "Maybe she was tricked into the pact." It couldn't be that hard to trick a princess. Most of them weren't the brightest flames on the candelabra.

"We have another thing to worry about too." Elsie brought her pacing to Rachaella's bed, replacing the damp cloth on the sick girl's forehead with a new one. Rachaella stirred, rolling over and murmuring feverishly.

"You mean something other than getting sick or kidnapped?" The only powerful allies I had, the trees, had gotten themselves torn up by the Intriguer. There was no safety, even with them.

"Rachaella isn't going to get better before tomorrow, and if she doesn't go to her classes, the faculty will take her to the infirmary and set the doctors on her."

Laomi and I knew the implications of that. Rachaella could not, under any circumstance, fall prey to the alchemists and butchers that were charged with healing. Since this was a school for the richest people in Clystopia, I would have thought we'd have access to adequate health care, but we'd found out that wasn't the case. The ICUP was staffed with fashionable doctors that followed healthcare trends, rather than performing effective treatments.

"There's only one thing to do, isn't there?" Laomi raised her chin defiantly. "Are you thinking what I'm thinking?"

She was right. There was only one option that could possibly work. "We'll have to poison them, so they're too busy caring for themselves to experiment on Rachaella. And let's take out Ms. Throupé too, while we're at it."

"What?" Shocked, Elsie clapped her hand over her mouth and backed away from me. "That's crazy!"

She took me too seriously sometimes.

"I am going to strangle you with my hair." Laomi put her hands on her hips. "Be serious!"

"Oooh, now I'm terrified." I pretended to hide behind my arms, smirking.

"You should be—my hair is feared throughout the land as a deadly weapon."

"Anyway, I know what Laomi meant," Elsie spoke up, getting us back on track. "We need to hide her."

Laomi nodded. "She'll become the next missing girl. Everyone will probably assume the same thing happened to her as that princess. No one will suspect us. I know a perfect hiding place, too. And once the guards finish searching her room, she can go right back in her bed and hide under everyone's noses until she heals."

Under the cover of night, we one-third carried, one-third dropped, and one-third rolled Rachaella onto her quilt, which was spread out over the floor. She wasn't that heavy, just difficult to hold with three people. None of us had ever hauled a limp body around before, so we weren't very good at it.

Once positioned on the blanket, we dragged her out the door, down the hall, and into Laomi's room, keenly aware of the noise the blanket made against the wood and our loud breathing. Every second we remained exposed, I expected a guard to jump out at us.

Finally, we made it safely into Laomi's room. We took a few seconds to catch our breath, and then continued dragging our friend to Laomi's spacious closet, which came complete with an extra vanity, two lounge chairs, and a coffee table, plus plenty of space left over.

Shoving loaded clothes hangers aside, Laomi felt along the back wall. Something clicked, then something else popped, and then a piece of the wall swung open, revealing a hidden compartment.

"Nice." I was impressed. No one would think to look there. I wondered if everyone had one of those hidey holes in their closets, or if Laomi was just special.

Elsie crawled inside to check it out. I popped my head in after her. Though the ceiling was low, there was plenty of room lengthwise to lay Rachaella. It was neither drafty nor stuffy, but smelled of wood and mothballs. We wasted no time maneuvering Rachaella inside.

The rest of the night, the three of us kept watch over her in shifts. Rachaella woke a few times while I was tending her, but she wasn't up to any intelligent conversation. I barely slipped her a few sips of tea or water before weakness made her lie down again.

"It feels like I'm dying," she mumbled once.

"Well, you aren't. You'll be better soon." But her words sent a stab of fear through me.

Hearing the clip-clip of brisk footsteps, I awoke, rolling over. Laomi's servants almost jumped out of their petticoats when they saw a sleep-deprived creature with bloodshot eyes and a mane of frizzy hair arise from their lady's couch. After several days of constant attention, Rachaella still wasn't getting better, and my own body was feeling the punishment of very little sleep.

When I drunkenly tottered into my own room, Fyre was waiting for me. I hadn't expected him back so soon. With a strangled whimper, I flung myself at him and buried my head in his warm feathers. They caressed my dry cheeks. Enclosed in his protective wing, I was sheltered from all the suffering and fear I'd been experiencing. I would have doused him with tears of relief if it wouldn't have hurt him. Too soon, he hopped out of my embrace to offer a vial clenched in his claws.

*Make your sick friend drink ALL of this.*

"What is it?" I asked, hoarse.

*A magic potion.* He winked.

Though grateful, I scowled as I accepted the vial. I hated the secrecy. There were some treatments Grandmother Rose wouldn't share with me because they were too dangerous to make, or something dumb like that. But I felt that if a potion was for healing, I should know about it, regardless of the risk. I needed all the knowledge I could get in case I was in a life-or-death situation. If this vial wasn't enough to cure Rachaella, it would be helpful to know what was in it so I could make another batch.

But all I said was, "Thanks."

I rushed back into Laomi's room, only to skid to a halt when I saw the servants tidying up.

"Laomi?" I called. I wanted to get the potion to Rachaella as soon as possible.

"Sorry milady, Princess Laomi just went to breakfast a moment ago," said one of the maids, curtseying politely.

"Oh, well, I just wanted to get the dress she was going to let me borrow. It's in the closet," I said, thinking fast.

"We're terribly sorry, but Princess Laomi specifically told us on her way out not to go in the closet. I think she has one of her new designs in there.

If it got messed up, she would be mighty unhappy." The other maid showed me to the door and swiftly closed it in my face.

Argh! If they hadn't been innocently doing their jobs, I would have marched back in there and shoved them out of my way. But Laomi obviously didn't want them to know about Rachaella—servant gossip spread faster than butter in the sun.

My friend was so close, safely locked away in her little cubbyhole with Elsie tending her, but I couldn't get to her without making a scene. I would have to run downstairs and grab Laomi, and by the time we made it back upstairs, shooed away the maids, woke Rachaella, and gave her the potion, breakfast would be over. My stomach growled in lamentation, but there was no alternative.

Dashing down the steps, I careened into the breakfast room and practically dragged Laomi to her feet.

"What is wrong with you, Chris?" With the lack of sleep, she was even more irritable than usual. "And why are you still in your nightgown? You look like a street urchin."

A few girls giggled, but I didn't shoot them the glare that I normally would have. "I really want to borrow that one dress of yours with the golden sequins, but your maids won't let me in the room. You promised."

Laomi picked up on my meaning immediately. "Come on, then. We can't have you walking around in public looking like *that*." She swept her curtain of hair aside and grabbed a few pieces of toast.

On the way back up, I swallowed two of them practically whole before deciding some should be saved for Elsie and Rachaella, if she woke up.

Laomi didn't ask questions. She knew by my agitation that something important had happened. After dismissing her maids, she led me to the back of the closet, where our friends sheltered in the cubbyhole behind a dozen gowns.

"She's awake!" Elsie exclaimed when we pushed the dresses away and popped open the door. My heart lifted with hope. I kneeled beside the hole in the wall, and Laomi crouched behind me.

"Rachaella?" Laomi whispered.

"Hi," a throaty voice rasped.

"How are you feeling?" I grasped her clammy hand with both of mine.

"Okay." As if she'd ever admit it if she wasn't. She was probably about to pass out, throw up, die, or all three at once.

I pulled the vial from the folds of my nightgown and held it up. "Grandmother Rose sent a potion especially for your sickness. It might taste rotten, but you've got to drink it *all*, okay? It's going to help you get better."

Rachaella nodded and let us help her sit up. I uncorked the top of the elixir.

"May my action and Your power work together to nourish and heal," I said, putting all my welling feelings into the words.

I held the vial to Rachaella's cracked lips. Without any windows, the closet was dark. The only light came from a small lantern Elsie had beside her and faint rays from the outer room. Even so, the potion seemed to almost glow like condensed sunlight.

"Ready? Bottoms up." I emptied the contents into Rachaella's open mouth like I was feeding a baby bird. She swallowed, then licked her lips for any traces of the liquid. The rest of us stared at her, waiting for a reaction, even though I knew herbs could take over an hour to start working. But the elixir had been so mysterious and different from any other herbal remedy I'd seen that I felt something would happen soon, though I didn't know what. Would she start laughing hysterically? Faint? Begin speaking in tongues? Go feral?

"It tastes like chicken," she finally announced.

We all let out a collective sigh of relief.

"Chicken?" Laomi queried. "How can weeds taste like chicken?"

"I don't know, but I feel a lot better already. Whatever your grandmother put in that, Chris, it works!"

She looked from one face to the next, completely lucid. She seemed more refreshed than the rest of us. Stretching both arms above her head, she yawned. "Excellent. Is there anything to eat around here? I'm starving."

Laomi handed over the toast, too shocked to make a smart-aleck comment.

"Is there anything else you need?" Elsie asked.

"Nope. I think I'll just sit here and relax. Thanks, though."

I had to force myself not to gape like a dead fish. Her voice was filled with her normal cheerfulness, her breathing was even, and the dark shadows under eyes had greatly receded. What had Grandmother done? That remedy was unlike any other I had ever heard of. Nothing I knew granted such immediate results.

Rachaella scarfed down the toast like a chipmunk stuffing its face with nuts.

It was nearly time for classes to begin, so Laomi and I had to go. Though we were hesitant to leave her, Rachaella insisted that we arrive at class on time. "They might suspect you're up to something if you're not," she pointed out. "Besides, it's not like I'll be alone. Elsie's here with me."

As we retreated from the cubbyhole, she hummed contentedly. When I went to leave the closet, though, Laomi grabbed my arm.

"No. You are done embarrassing me by walking around like . . . that. You asked me to find you a dress, and I am going to."

"That was just an excuse!"

"It was a pitiful cry for help. Only a complete boor would think that people wore *sequins* in this day and age. Honestly, Chris, you are killing me."

# Chapter 21. Modeling Dresses and Other Death-Defying Feats

The familiar whisperings of the forest tickled my thoughts. I darted from shadow to shadow beneath the branches, swaying with them as they moved in the wind, heading to the last sword fighting lesson of the semester. Leaving the school was always a risk because of the wolves, but I'd managed so far—one more class couldn't hurt. I knocked on a tree with my fist for good luck.

Rachaella gained strength every day, though she still hadn't resumed classes. She was as perceptive as ever, though. She'd noticed I'd missed a few sword fighting lessons, and, thinking it was because of her sickness, had persuaded me to go to the last one of the semester, if only to get out of the castle for a while. She sensed my fidgetiness from being inside too long. Since it seemed she was past the dangerous time when she could suffer a relapse, I didn't worry too much about leaving her.

A dense fog covered the arena when I arrived, sheltering the princes from view. The chilliness and humidity made for an odd mixture. Shivering, I left the tree line and made my way into the arena only to discover that no one was there yet. I tossed my hair back. No matter—I'd get my pick of the weaponry. Last time I had been stuck with a sword that had a broken hilt.

I chose a sturdy practice sword from the shed, swiping it through the air a few times to make sure it was balanced, and then returned to the ring.

The fog started to clear, leaving drops of frigid dew on the droopy winter grass. Training would be muddy that day—if anyone showed up. Where were they? I hadn't arrived that early! But there were no shouts of rambunctious princes coming from the direction of the school or whistles from the instructor trying to rein them in. It didn't make sense; lessons were never cancelled. Even when the weather was abysmal, they still trooped outside to gain "experience."

I peered through the fog toward the foreboding school building, but the moisture was still too thick to see it well. As I struggled to penetrate the gloom, a pair of yellow eyes appeared, hovering in the mist, and met mine. I froze, the hair on the back of my neck rising.

As I watched, it seemed like the fog condensed, forming a monstrous shaggy beast with jaws that could snap my leg in half. The alpha's eyes never left mine as it emerged from the mist, not wanting its prey to escape.

"Time to die, girlie."

Cursing myself for letting my guard down, I drew my knife and prepared to run back to the trees. But before I took a single step, the wolf threw back its head and let loose a spine-tingling howl that paralyzed me. As I internally screamed at my body to move, four howls on all sides of me answered the first. The wolves trotted toward me, forming a diamond that cut me off from the frantically beckoning trees. Knowing that I was slippery and liable to get away if they slacked off in the hunt for even a second, the wolves approached quickly.

I let out a shout, brandishing my weapons, but I might as well have been flourishing feather dusters for all the good they did to slow down my soon-to-be killers. They were close; I saw the saliva dripping from their fangs.

A shout answering mine surprised the wolves as much as me. All of us paused and stared as Arcturus careened toward our group with a rock in one hand and a dead branch in the other. I think we were all wondering whether he had a death wish.

Taking advantage of the distraction, I snapped into action and lunged for the nearest wolf. Conking it on the schnoz with the practice sword, I darted past as it yelped and flinched. Pumping my legs, I sprinted straight for Arcturus.

"RUN!"

Heeding my command, he whirled and fled alongside me. Snarls and barks pursued us, gaining every millisecond. We gasped, trying to make ourselves go faster, but the trees were uphill. Four legs were stronger than two—there was no way we would make it to the woods before they overtook us.

Twisting around, Arcturus hurled the rock toward our chasers. To my great satisfaction, a yip along with a crunching noise resulted. But it wasn't going to be enough. I didn't look back, but I was sure I wasn't imagining the hot breath on the back of my legs. What would they do when they captured me? Bite my neck and kill me quickly, or take me down and begin to devour me alive, heedless of my screams of torture? If it was the latter, I would surely kill at least one and maim a few others before I died.

I braced myself for my final battle when I became aware of another person running alongside Arcturus and me. Even though I'd hoped she would respond to my hastily squeezed-out tears, I almost stumbled when I saw Fairy Godmother. Her bizarre appearance nearly overwhelmed the urge to keep running.

"Careful, honey," she said, as if we were simply on an afternoon jog through the park.

Though I managed to keep my legs moving, I couldn't help but stare at her at the same time. She looked so out of place—a plump, white-haired lady in a full-length hot pink gown, puffing and beaming as she ran, even though there were murderous beasts a few feet behind. The image just didn't compute.

"When I say 'go,' turn and run back to the shed," she instructed. "GO!"

Whoa! What was wrong with "on the count of three"?

Coming to an abrupt halt, I grabbed Arcturus's arm and pivoted to face the ravenous wolves.

"Argh!" Arcturus yelled as I jerked him around.

*Zap! Zap! Zap!*

Bolts of light shot out of Fairy Godmother's wand, disorienting the wolves. They stumbled and shook their heads, momentarily blinded. I jumped out of the way as one beast hurtled past me, heedless of where it was headed.

All we needed was a moment to race past them.

Breathing heavily, Arcturus and I pounded back the way we came with Fairy Godmother right behind us. My chest screamed as it cramped from lack of oxygen, but I pushed past the pain. Obscured by the fog, I only spotted the weapons shed when we were practically on top of it.

Arcturus reached the door first. Wrenching it open, he scooped me inside before diving in himself. Both of us tumbled to the dusty floor while Fairy Godmother secured the door. My knee slammed onto a fallen arrowhead, and I winced when I stood. For a moment, everything was quiet aside from our gasps entering the frozen air in clouds.

"Will they be able to get in?"

*BAM!*

I leaped into the air as the whole structure vibrated.

*BAM! BAM!*

Feral snarls and the scraping of claws against the flimsy wooden door came in intervals after the slams. My question didn't need to be answered. The unstable shack that couldn't keep out a draft wouldn't withstand the muscular battering-ram bodies of the wolves for long.

What to do . . . What to do . . . Hey! Weapons! What a convenient coincidence.

*BAM! CRACK!*

There wasn't much time left. I hefted a long, thick rod with a spearhead strapped to the end. Seeing me struggle to maneuver it, Arcturus rushed over to alleviate some of the weight.

*BAM!*

The whole building groaned in pain. The crack in the door widened, and a muzzle poked inside, baring teeth in a snarl before disappearing. The next wolf would likely slam itself right on top of the gap, shattering the door completely.

"When the next one comes, we'll shove this through the door!" I yelled to Arcturus.

"Got it!"

Dust and a few rotting planks rained from the ceiling as forceful clawing racked the walls. Then the noise subsided as the previous wolf stepped aside to allow its partner the final crushing blow.

"NOW!"

At a run, we thrust the spear through the break in the door just as a matted body of fur hurled toward it. I closed my eyes, clenching the weapon with all my might. A weighty force hit the spear, and I barely managed to keep from staggering backward or toppling over. The body made a squelching sound as it slid the length of the weapon.

It wasn't the alpha. Disappointment skewered me—if the alpha died, I knew the others would give up the hunt. But now, I worried that the pack would keep after me until the last member went down.

Yelps of pain erupted from the impaled wolf as it twitched in midair. The others whined, concerned and uncertain how to finish the task since one of their own was blocking them.

Was it wrong that I held no pity for the dying animal? It had tried to kill me, but only because the leader of its pack ordered it to. If anyone, the alpha should feel guilty for leading the non-intelligent animals under his protection on this vengeance hunt. Still, it was in pain now, paralyzed, waiting for its end.

The remaining pack members circled their companion, sniffing him. One whined. Sluggishly, more fog crept in, encroaching on the remaining animals as if to swallow them. I watched through the cracks in the shed, shaking with tension.

The snarls and yips of the wounded wolf became gurgles, and then the body went limp. I slid my gaze to the alpha wolf, who watched his companion die with an unreadable expression. He stood as if turned to wood, not a hair on his pelt shifting.

When he finally moved, he did so all at once, whirling about and signaling to the others to retreat. They loped away, tails twitching. The last thing I saw before they disappeared was the alpha's eyes as he glanced back at me. They had hunger and hate written clearly in them. I had slighted him one too many times. I shivered.

For several moments, I watched after them. Sun pierced the mist, slowly melting it into the atmosphere. Warm streams of light highlighted the dust motes in the shed, making them shine. The suddenly cheery atmosphere was only belied by the dead wolf body drooping over the threshold.

Letting my shoulders slump, I leaned against the wall. "Good teamwork, Kedrik," I said before I could stop myself.

Confusion clouded Arcturus's face.

"Er—I mean, Arcturus."

I looked away, a pang of homesickness sweeping over me.

"Those wolves," he said, "aren't normal. They were the same ones that attacked you that first day, weren't they? Do *not* lie to me, Chris," he warned, seeing my mouth open to object. He didn't call me *Christina* now that the others weren't around. "I want to know what is going on. It gets a little personal when I almost get eaten."

"Fine. My friend and I were in their den last summer and I accidentally killed their pups by trampling on them. They already killed my horse, and since then, they've been after me." I slid down the wall until I sat on the floor with my knees drawn up to my chest.

"That is definitely not normal for wolves." He sat next to me, leaving a little space between our bodies.

"The alpha is a Speaking Wolf."

He tensed. "A Speaking Wolf? Why is there no hunting party out there trying to bring it down?"

"I killed its pack's children, Arcturus. It shouldn't be punished for that."

"It is an animal."

"It is intelligent."

"Well, you did just kill another one," he pointed out, nodding toward the dead wolf suspended right outside.

"As long as they keep hunting me, I'm going to defend myself. But if they want to leave me alone, I'll let them go."

He shook his head, obviously not understanding.

"What were you doing out here, anyway?" I challenged, changing the subject. "And where is everyone else?"

"You're changing the subject."

"I know I am!"

We stared each other down for a minute. The flicker in his eyes revealed that he had a temper too. Then he blinked, giving me a wearily amused smile.

"Okay, you win," he said, tucking a stray piece of hair behind my ear delicately.

I struggled and failed at keeping my gaze hard.

"Practice was cancelled for today," he said, "because of an assembly, but you wouldn't have known because you don't go to our school. I didn't care to hear about 'The History of Parchment,' so I snuck out for a walk. Then I thought I'd come down and tell you practice was cancelled, if you were here. That's when I saw you being surrounded."

In the opposite corner of the shed, something stirred. "Oh, don't mind me, dears! I'll just recover from that painful exertion quietly over here while you talk amongst yourselves."

Arcturus started. "Who's there?" he asked, as if he hadn't noticed her until now. I wasn't sure how he could miss Fairy Godmother in that hot pink gown, though.

"The guardian of the toolshed," she said dryly. "Who do you think? It's me, sweetie! Your Fairy Godmother, here to save your lives—for the second time, in Chris's case."

"I'm sorry!" I exclaimed, rushing over. "Are you okay?" She was flushed, and her hair had been smooshed to one side.

"I will be in a moment, honey, thank you. Some types of magic just wear me out."

"How did you know we were in trouble?" the prince asked.

"I let the wind blow tears out of my eyes," I said, "and she came to rescue us." It was only luck that she'd made it in time, though. "I'm glad you came," I said, returning my attention to Fairy Godmother. "Arcturus and I would be dead if you hadn't."

"Yes, thank you for saving us," the prince echoed.

"Happy to help—though you do seem to have a knack for trouble, honey. Be a dear and try to stay safe from now on, hmm?"

"I'll try." But no promises.

"Now then," Fairy Godmother said, rising and brushing her skirt off. "Chris, why don't you hop up a tree and run along back to the school. I need to give the prince his wish. The way is perfectly safe now. Don't worry, they won't come back."

I didn't know how she could be so sure the alpha wasn't lurking right outside the door, but the nearby trees confirmed that the pack had moved off.

"You attend the school? So you *are* a royal. I knew it." Arcturus flashed his teeth in triumph. "Princess Chris of Agaedith, right?"

"Thanks for blowing my cover." I scowled at Fairy Godmother.

"You did that yourself when you summoned me," she pointed out. "Only a royal could do that."

I folded my arms in a huff and turned back to Arcturus. "You won't tell anyone, will you? I have a reputation to maintain."

"I'm no snitch."

"Thank you. And thank you for running to help me, instead of running away."

"Glad to. I'll see you at the ball in a few weeks. Save me a spot on your dance card, okay?"

Sweeping up my callused, dirty hand, he planted a gentle kiss on the back.

Dumbstruck, I mumbled something unintelligible to even my own ears and scrambled outside through the splintered door, almost tripping on the body of the dead wolf. That shed was way too stuffy and cramped.

"That was quick," Elsie said as I entered my room through the balcony.

"Yeah. Practice was cancelled for an assembly." I didn't go into details. She already had plenty to worry about, and anyway I was fine.

"Did you fall?" She raised her eyebrows at my stained dress.

"The fog made it slippery."

From his perch on my bedpost, Fyre scrutinized me, unbelieving.

*We need to talk later*, he said.

I nodded to show that I'd heard.

"Anyway, Laomi's maids finished crafting the dresses for the ball this morning. Laomi wants everyone to meet in Rachaella's room to try them on." She stared at the floor while she spoke, like she was a real maid instead of my friend.

"Okay. Is something wrong?"

"No." Her toes shuffled closer together.

My brow furrowed. "I'll be right over," I said. "You can go ahead if you want." Casting a concerned glance at her, I disappeared into my closet to change out of my muddy training clothes.

I remembered Laomi mentioning that she wanted to design our dresses for the ball, but the stress from the Intriguer, wolves, and Rachaella's sickness had brushed it from my thoughts. We'd never even given Laomi our sizes—I only half-believed that they were already done.

Once ready, I meandered into Rachaella's suite with Elsie, who had waited for me despite my suggestion. The gowns were hidden in garment bags hanging on the curtain rod. My stomach flip-flopped. Laomi had kept the designs an absolute secret. What if my dress was horrid, but I was obligated to wear it because she was my friend? Hopefully, she didn't mess up on the sizing. I pictured being in the middle of a dance and either feeling like a sausage or twirling right out of the dress—either way, not good.

"Finally!" Laomi exclaimed, even though I hadn't been gone longer than half an hour. She was pacing back and forth in anticipation. Upon spotting me, she grabbed my hand and steered me to a chair.

I sat down with a loud *thump* and grimaced, forgetting that the chairs in Rachaella's room weren't cushioned like the ones in my and Laomi's rooms. A bruised butt was not something I needed.

She narrowed her eyes at me disapprovingly. "I thought you'd *never* get your butt in here!"

My injured one, thanks to her.

"Thanks for waiting," I said politely. This was important to Laomi, and if I soured the mood with sarcasm, she would never forgive me. Laomi wasn't someone I wanted holding a grudge against me.

She acknowledged me with a dismissive wave. "Let's get started. Rachaella, you're first."

Taking one of the garment bags from the curtain rod, she laid it gently on the bed where Rachaella, still tired from her illness, was splayed out. Fingers fumbling, Rachaella managed—with quite a bit of help from an overenthusiastic Laomi—to undo the various buttons and peel the bag away.

Her face lit up. "Laomi . . . I love it!"

They were blocking the view, so I couldn't see a thing. Elsie, seated on the couch, strained her neck to catch a glimpse, then gave up and ran to the bed.

"Oh!" Her eyes grew wide, drinking up the sight.

Curiosity getting the better of me, I followed, peering over her shoulder.

I was impressed—Laomi had created a masterpiece. The layered skirts were shaped like overturned flowers of the palest purple hue. Stitched into the outer layer were tiny amethysts in swirling, intricate patterns. Darker purple ribbons wove in and out of the gems, making the design pop into focus. The sleeves consisted of many fluttery strips of fabric, carefully matching the petal theme. A light dusting of white and purple glitter made the dress shine. The elegant yet modest style matched Rachaella's personality perfectly. On anyone else, the cut would be too plain, but the mixture of beauty and simplicity suited her.

"It's a lilac, isn't it?" Rachaella breathed. "My favorite flower." Leaning over, she gave her friend a tight hug. "Thanks so much."

Laomi responded with a tight-lipped smile. "I haven't even shown you the coolest part yet! Look."

Lifting the skirt, she revealed a pair of lilac-colored breeches and short under-tunic that were stitched into the dress. "If something happens and you need to escape, the outer skirt can be removed to run faster. And here—" She fumbled for a second on the outside of the dress. "Is a secret pocket with slippers inside. No one can run fast in heels."

"You really thought of everything, didn't you? I can't wait to put it on!"

Handling the dress carefully, Rachaella disappeared behind the dressing screen.

Two minutes later, she returned, looking like the spirit of springtime. When she smiled, her expression radiated even more joy than usual. No trace of sickness was evident.

We admired her for a while, and then she said, "Okay, my turn is over. Are we going to see Chris's next?"

"Sure." Laomi swept up a bag and opened it with a flourish.

I didn't have time to prepare for the moment of truth, and I involuntarily flinched as the contents of the bag revealed themselves. Then my eyes riveted to the dress, and a slow smile spread over my face. Did I say dress? It was a covering of fire. Swirls of red, orange, and gold were mixed with licks of blue and green. When I touched the fabric, the colors shimmered and moved as if alive. Encircling the waist and trailing long enough to touch the floor were several strings of flame-colored beads, ribbons, and sashes shaped like tongues of fire. The neckline and sleeves ended in a flame pattern.

"Whoa," was all I could say.

"Go try it on!" Laomi urged.

Alight with an anticipation I'd never associated with clothing, I did so. The whole situation felt surreal. One hour I fought for my life against a wolf pack, the next I modeled formal gowns with my friends. My life was absurd.

The gown was sturdy and fit well. Too often, gowns restricted the wearer's motion, which made no sense for a dance. How people acted graceful in dresses that wrapped their legs tightly, or ones that weighed half a ton because of all the gems, embroidery, and ruffles, was beyond me. But in this dress, I knew that if I suddenly had to move, I could *move*.

The dress swathed me in confident, fierce power. And I looked dang good, if I did say so myself.

After everyone oohed and aahed over me, Laomi took her turn as the model. Her dress was smooth and formed close to her body, showing off her curves. It had only one strap, her other shoulder left bare. As she moved, the iridescent colors switched, like viewing an opal from different angles. Transfixed by the shifting patterns, I once again wondered how she managed to capture personality so well in her creations.

"I wish I was a princess," Elsie breathed. Her voice was hardly above a whisper, but we all heard what she said. She looked ready to cry.

As Rachaella, Laomi, and I turned to look at her, she clapped a hand over her mouth, mortified. "Did I just say that out loud? That's not what I meant! It came out wrong! I just wanted to say that . . . well, those gowns are so pretty, Laomi, and—" She stopped, her face not pale for once, but as red and blotchy as ketchup.

For the first time, I caught a glimpse of feelings that Elsie had barricaded deeply within herself. I'd spent the last several months with her near-constant presence, but I was at once acutely aware of how little I knew of her. She was always helping me or listening to what I had to say—she never spoke about herself. And I had never asked her. The only time she had revealed her innermost desires was when she asked the magic mirror about her father.

It was only natural that she felt left out. As a young orphan among three rich (even Rachaella, compared to Elsie, was rich) ICUP students, she could only quietly listen when we talked about classes, teachers, and events of the day that she wasn't a part of. And while the three of us attended a fancy ball, she would be with the maids, doing whatever it was maids did when they weren't waiting on their princesses. What *did* maids do every day? I'd never thought to ask how her day went when I was done with mine. Did she have other friends? She had never spoken of any, but that wasn't surprising. What kind of horrible friend was I?

Laomi gave the poor girl a sympathetic look. "Of course you want to be a princess, Elsie! Anyone in your position would. Now, I can't help you with that, but I can help you go to the ball."

The redness ebbed away as confusion replaced Elsie's embarrassment. "But . . . maids don't attend."

Laomi scoffed. "Says who? You're no more a regular maid than I am a regular wild pig!"

"She's a very irregular wild pig," I agreed.

"Shut it, Chris, or I'll impale you with my tusks." Tossing her mane of hair, she pointed to the shadowed side of the room. "See that bag over there, Elsie? Go on and open it. It's for you."

Hesitantly, Elsie made her way to the dark corner where a fourth bag I hadn't noticed sat waiting. Without opening it, she delicately picked it up and slipped behind the screen to dress.

When she came back out, it was like looking at a different person. I had never noticed before how her maid uniform sapped her natural beauty. She shone brilliantly in her sparkling white and sky-blue dress. The tulle skirt poofed out like a cumulus cloud. She was like a little bird, flitting through the sky.

Flying across the room, she threw herself at Laomi. "It's the most beautiful thing I've ever seen in my life!"

As her whole being sparkled with delight, my heart melted. Though I had never cared much about pretty clothes or jewelry, it was easy to imagine that Elsie, an orphan girl forced into servitude at a young age, might. After all, I already had everything I could ever want, so I took my possessions for granted. Elsie had nothing.

"Wait—" Elsie wore the horrified look of someone who had been told they could fly over a waterfall, but instead had crushed themselves against the spiky rocks at the bottom. "I can't go to a ball! Everyone will know I'm just a maid, and then I'll get thrown in the dungeon!"

"We won't let that happen," Rachaella soothed. "Besides, I don't think the school even has a dungeon."

Elsie nodded insistently. "You didn't know? Some princesses send their servants there when they are angry with them. I've heard there are rats and sharp glass and it's cold and wet and smells like mold and—"

"Calm down," I said, patting her arm. "No one is throwing you into a dungeon for going to a party."

"The place will be packed," Laomi added. "Not everyone will know everyone else. The older princesses will think you're a younger princess, and vice versa. Teachers will just assume they don't have you in class. No one will ever know! I wouldn't have made the dress if I thought you would be in danger. Come on, you have a chance to be Princess Elsie, mysterious Cinderella of the ball. Who could pass that up?"

"Okay." Though she was still nervous, Elsie's eyes reflected undisguised longing. She clenched her fists in excitement. "I'll do it."

*That took longer than I expected.* Fyre's voice invaded my head as soon as I returned to my room.

I jumped, dropping my gown and half drawing my knife before I realized it was him. As if anyone else would be speaking directly into my mind.

I relaxed, unclenching my jaw. "We're princesses—we love fussing over dresses and acting like models."

Fyre made a noise halfway between a guffaw and a snort.

"You sound like a dying chicken," I commented.

*Could a dying chicken barbeque you if you annoy him too much?*

I rolled my eyes. "Actually, the gown she made me is pretty cool—look." I held it up for him to see.

*Hey! It looks like me!* He clacked his beak in appreciation.

The corners of my mouth lifted as I laid the dress over a chair.

*Have fun at the ball, Chris, but be careful.*

"I always am."

He blew a puff of smoke in disbelief. *You, always careful? That's a joke. Seriously, I probably won't be here to back you up if something happens, so be extra vigilant.*

Right, like the time he'd "backed me up" when I tried to stop the Intriguer's storm from kidnapping that princess—or earlier today, when Arcturus and I were locked in a shed with wolves clawing at the door trying to eat us. But instead of mentioning those times, I just asked, "Where are you going?"

*THEY will be heading out soon, and I need to show them the way.*

My heart started to pound like a blacksmith's heavy hammer against my chest. The rescue party was coming. I wished Fyre could tell me who was in it, but it was probably too risky, and it didn't matter as long as they busted us out.

"All right, good luck. We'll be ready," I said, trying to contain my anticipation. We would finally be free soon! And I would never have to go to class again! And Throupé and Victoria could kiss each other's butts! Ha ha!

Taking a breath, I told myself to calm down.

*Oh, one other thing.*

"Yeah?"

*Do not leave the grounds again. You could get yourself killed. Then all the time and energy spent trying to rescue you would be wasted. I don't have time to hear about what happened this afternoon right now, but don't let it happen again.*

I swallowed as his hard black gaze bore into me. "Got it." It didn't matter anyway, since sword fighting lessons were over. There was no other reason for me to go wandering around.

Satisfied, Fyre whirled his wings and flew off in a shower of crackling sparks and flames.

# Chapter 22. Lying and Dying in Holes

The howling wouldn't stop. For the first few minutes, I thought I was dreaming. In that half-delusional state between sleeping and waking, the sound hypnotized me. It engulfed my mind. Shivers tingled down my spine, and goose bumps sprouted on my arms and legs despite my layers of blankets.

When I realized the sound was real, that the wolf pack was actually outside my balcony howling, I burrowed deeper into the bed, scared. They had to go away eventually, or the guards would drive them off. That was the guards' job, right? They protected the school from beasties of the wilderness. But after an hour of the incessant, otherworldly sounds, the wolves didn't go away, and the guards didn't come.

I got mad then. I liked sleep. Did they think that because they couldn't kill me, they could sit outside my door all night and annoy me instead? I wouldn't stand for it. Throwing off the covers, I grabbed my knife and stomped outside. Flakes of snow drifted from the inky sky, but I was too irked to notice the cold. To my surprise, only the alpha was there. The pack was probably farther in the woods, waiting for the signal to come and eat me.

"Finally," the alpha growled.

"Go away," I growled back.

"No. You need to . . . I have—" Frustrated, he cut himself off, snapping his jaws together with a click.

Tail twitching, he paced back and forth beneath my balcony. He shook his head as if trying to loosen pesky thoughts. I watched him silently for thirty seconds. Then my bare feet started to get cold, and I got sick of wasting time outside when I could be in bed, so I headed for the door.

"Wait," the alpha barked. "I have a proposition for you."

"Don't care," I said, but I stopped.

"My beta is dying. If you help her, I swear I will stop trying to kill you. We've hurt each other enough. I don't want to lose her."

It was a trap.

"You think I'm an idiot, or a bleeding heart. Or both. Forget it." I opened the door. Warmth from the fire crept out.

"I know the old lady taught you healing. My beta has a wound, and it's making her sick. This isn't a trap." I heard him scoring his claws over the frozen ground.

"You're lying."

"He's not lying." To my surprise, Rachaella walked out onto my balcony. It was so dark inside that I hadn't seen her. She too was in bare feet and a nightgown. Puffy purple shadows beneath her eyes stuck out like bruises on her brown face.

"Sorry for listening in. I came over to ask for more chamomile—I couldn't sleep. Then I heard you out here. He's not lying, though. I can tell when people are lying, remember?"

"You can ask your rustling, bark-faced friends, too," the alpha growled.

I would have to ask Rachaella later how she was in my room at all, when I knew I remembered to lock the door before I went to bed. For now, I looked from her to the trees, who whispered the alpha's truth. There was a she-wolf sheltered in the woods who was very sick. That didn't mean that after I healed her, the alpha wouldn't change his mind and bite my head off, but if there was a chance his pack would leave me alone after I saved her, I wanted to try. If I didn't, and the alpha's second-in-command died, he would be after my blood that much more.

"Fine. I'll help."

After gathering a bundle of herbs, some clean rags, and a pitcher of water, I threw on a cloak and boots and climbed down the tree next to my balcony, followed by Rachaella. She insisted on coming along.

"Why?" I asked. "You don't know healing, you're still weak from being sick, and the wolves might change their minds about not eating me."

"You might need an assistant who has hands instead of paws. Plus, I can be there for moral support. I don't want to let you do something stupid all by yourself."

"So you agree that this is stupid?"

"Duh. But it's also an adventure."

I shrugged. "I can't stop you, I guess."

"Exactly."

As my feet touched the ground and I released the tree, I felt exposed. The alpha towered before me, his yellow eyes searing my skin.

"This way," he said. Flicking his tail, he trotted into the woods.

Shouldering my pack of supplies, I followed him. Fyre's words echoed suddenly in my mind. *Do not leave the grounds again. You could get yourself killed.*

*Sorry, Fyre*, I thought. I'd do my best not to die.

By the time we reached the rest of the pack, I was regretting that I hadn't brought gloves. Rubbing my fingers together, I breathed on them, trying to regain circulation.

"Here," the alpha said.

Their new den was not a sheltered cave like the old one, and it didn't have soft sand to dig into beds. A makeshift hollow scraped into the side of a hill was the best way to describe it. There was some thick brush on one side, which most of the wolves clustered under. They piled on top of one another in a snuggled heap. The ground was stiff. The pack had managed to push most of the snow into a pile to block the wind, but the frozen ground still didn't look comfortable.

There was a single tree arching over the hollow that provided the only shelter from rain and snow. It wasn't impressive. In summer, the area likely flooded often because of the low elevation and nearby stream. The soil around the tree's roots was eroded away, and nestled beneath them was a lone, reddish pelt.

When Rachaella and I entered the den, the pack leaped up, yapping, growling, and licking their chops. Before they could tear us apart, the alpha stepped between us and snapped. Curling back his lips, he showed his teeth. His hackles stood up like porcupine quills. The wolves settled down at once and let us pass. The alpha then guided us to the tree roots where the beta wolf lay motionless.

She was the only one who hadn't jumped to attention at our arrival. All she did when I knelt before her, in fact, was flick her ears. Her eyes remained shut. The alpha threaded his way through the roots and nosed her cheek, an act of affection that surprised me. He curled up behind her, so his body gave her more shelter, and licked her ears.

"Fix her," he entreated.

I examined the furry body. The she-wolf was larger than the others, but not Speaking Wolf size. She was sinuous where the alpha was blunt. Her red coat was sleek and soft against my cold hand, except for the six-inch gash that oozed pus and infection. The wound was undoubtedly the source of her sickness.

I bit my lip. The alpha should have asked for help a week ago. There was nothing to do, though, but get to work. After speaking the prayer of healing over my remedies, I tried to get the sick wolf to lap up a powerful bunch of sleeping herbs so she would feel less pain while I tended her wound. She was too delirious to eat much. As I cleaned out the infected scrape, though, she barely twitched.

A light dusting of snow fell as Rachaella and I tried to save the wolf. The reflection of the moon off the whiteness provided all the light we needed. Shadows stretched and grew over the course of the night. The alpha sat still, watching us with his yellow eyes the whole time to make sure we didn't bring additional harm to his beloved pack member.

I tried to feed the she-wolf herbs again—this time mixed with some that would fight off infection from the inside. She didn't eat any, but she opened her eyes. She stared at me, and as I stared back, my breath caught in my throat. Her eyes were dark chocolate brown, reminding me of Snowy's.

"Rachaella," I said. It was the first time either of us had spoken above a whisper since we'd arrived.

"Yes?"

"Could you go back to the school and get more water?"

"Sure. I'll be back as soon as I can."

She disentangled herself from the tree's roots and jogged out of the den.

It hadn't been a lie. I hadn't said that I needed more water, just asked if she could bring some.

Fifteen minutes later, the she-wolf died. I'd known since I saw the wound that she was a goner. It was rotten deep on the inside, and nothing short of magic or Grandmother Rose herself could have saved her. I wasn't my grandmother. I'd hoped that maybe, if the alpha could see that I at least tried, he would let me go. I didn't get so lucky.

When the sick wolf's chest rose and sank for the last time, he stiffened. Taking his eyes off my work, he nuzzled her, trying to get her to move, to breathe again. A faint whine drifted through the air, like a far-away echo of a whistle, saying goodbye. I tried to back away slowly without making any noise. If I climbed the tree above us, I would be okay. The roots shifted slightly to give me easy access.

That's when the alpha struck. With a snarling bark, he launched himself at me. The force of the blow carried us both out from beneath the tree's shelter, into the middle of the hollow. I landed on my back with a thud. There wasn't enough snow to soften the landing, especially with a wolf on top of me. He'd knocked the wind out of me, and I struggled to breathe, struggled to say something, but his giant paw just pressed harder on my stomach.

"I will tear your throat out just like I did your precious horse's. Except yours is tender and quivering, like a rabbit's. It will be easy."

I felt his hot breath on my neck, smelled the musk of the woods on his fur. He was going to kill me. An unnatural feeling of calm flooded through me, and I met his glare with my own hard gaze.

That gave him pause. Instead of tearing me to pieces, he sniffed. "You have no fear-scent. Why?"

"I am not afraid of death. The next life is bound to be better than this one."

He snarled. "Are you afraid of pain, my brave prey? Because I can easily make your journey to Heaven a lot slower than you'd like. Or maybe I'll just bite you and wait for the full moon, when lots of interesting things will happen. You'll wish you *were* dead, then."

I didn't flinch. I didn't look away from him. There was so much rage in him, but there was also pain. And the pain was feeding the rage, and I was sorry that I'd helped to cause a lot of it.

"It was an accident," I breathed. "Killing your pups."

"What." His claws dug into my cloak.

"We were being chased by the Intriguer. It possessed the trees, and we jumped into the river to escape. We climbed into your cave to seek shelter. I never knew the pups were there."

He sniffed again. "You're not lying."

"No. So if you want to blame someone, the Intriguer is the one that is actually responsible." A thought struck me. "Unless you *are* the Intriguer, in which case you might as well kidnap me now, because there's no way I'm escaping out from under your oversized paws."

The wolf gave a watery gravel laugh. "You think I'm the Intriguer? You think I possessed a forest and kidnapped royals? Okay, fine—you got me. I'm the Intriguer. Just tell me this, girlie. If I'm so powerful, how come I couldn't even kill *you* until now?"

I was stumped. "Good point." I didn't like the sound of that "until now" part, though.

Like I'd said, I wasn't afraid of death. However, I'd rather not die right away if I could help it. Not much I could do about it, though, as his claws were still sunk into the front of my cloak. So I just lay there awkwardly as snow melted into my clothes, hoping he'd decide to kill me quickly rather than slowly.

"When the Intriguer gets involved, humans don't see straight." The alpha broke eye contact, instead looking far off, to another place or time. "They start blaming each other for things that go wrong. They don't want to admit they have a much more powerful enemy, so they refuse to see the truth. Maybe I fell into that trap. Maybe I just wanted an enemy I had a chance of defeating, so I chose you."

Then, amazingly, the weight of his paw lifted from me.

"Go home, girlie."

I stood, wobbling slightly, and shuffled a few steps.

"I said GO!" he barked.

I almost fell over.

"I don't want to smell your fluffy princess scent around here anymore!"
I broke into a run.

I'd thought I was dead, but I was alive. I ran two hundred yards through the woods before climbing a tree and running some more through the branches. I only stopped when I saw Rachaella leading an army of guards into the forest.

"What the . . ." I mumbled to myself.

There were dozens of them—Rachaella must have practically left the castle unprotected. Swinging down, I landed in front of her. Surprise and fear appeared on her face. Instead of screaming, though, she kicked me in the chin. My head snapped back, and I fell backward for the second time that night.

"Oof."

"Chris! I'm so sorry! I didn't realize it was you—I just reacted! Are you okay?"

She skidded to her knees beside me, brushing the hair out of my face.

"It's a good thing I didn't bite my tongue off," I said. "How can you even get your foot up that high?"

"I'm very flexible," she admitted. She helped me to my feet and dusted snow off my clothes.

"So . . . are you on your way to fight a war?" I asked, eyeing the burly armored men behind her.

"We were coming to save you," she said. "I knew the she-wolf was dying, and that's why you sent me away. Once she died, I thought the alpha would kill you. So I came back and got help. I'm sorry it took so long, I gathered everyone as fast as I could. But . . . it looks like you don't need us."

I shook my head.

"You escaped your kidnapper?" one of the guards asked, astonished. "What did he look like?"

I blinked. "Who?"

"The man who kidnapped you," Rachaella said, raising her eyebrows for emphasis.

She hadn't told the guards the whole story. I could protect the alpha and his pack, if I chose.

"Oh yeah, that guy," I said, trying frantically to come up with a description. "Um, he was wearing a mask, so I didn't see his face. His clothes were . . . black. All black." That narrowed it down to all evil villains in the history of villainy.

The lead guard commended me for my escape and promised to hunt my would-be captor down as well as redouble the vigilance in and around the school. I barely listened to his claptrap as we returned inside. I was tired and cold and wet, and there was wolf blood on me.

The guards walked Rachaella and me all the way to my room, as if they weren't sure I'd remember where it was, then marched back to their posts.

My door was locked. Well, of course—I always locked it before I went to bed, and I'd left from the balcony, so it would still be locked.

"Great," I mumbled. I would have to go outside, walk around the building, and climb up the tree and onto my balcony to get in my room—and explain why to every guard I met along the way.

"Here, I can help," Rachaella said.

Before I could ask how, she pulled a few bobby pins, a bent metal clothes hanger, and a penknife out of her coat pocket, and set to work picking the lock. In less than a minute, the door was open.

"Well, that answers one of the questions I was going to ask you." I ran a tired hand down my face. "Do you want to come in?"

She hesitated. "I do really want to know what happened, but if you're too tired, it can wait for tomorrow."

Her eyes were wide, sparked with curiosity. My body was heavy with fatigue, but I had a feeling my near-death experience would prevent me from getting much sleep.

"I can talk now; it's fine," I said.

I locked the door firmly behind us. Then I stoked the fire, shuffling the embers until they lit the new kindling and logs. I took the quilt off my bed, and Rachaella and I curled up on the couch with it to watch the flames. I told her what happened after she left.

"Even though we couldn't save the beta, I was glad you came to help," I told her once I'd finished. "And it was really good of you to come back for me with all those guards after I sent you away. I don't deserve a friend like you." The last part ended in a whisper.

"You sent me back to the school when you knew the wolf was going to die, so that the alpha wouldn't kill me. Don't tell me you don't deserve a friend. That's one of the bravest things anyone has ever done for me."

I smiled. "Oh yeah, you were so thankful, you kicked me in the face."

She covered her face with both hands. "It was an accident! I told you I was sorry."

"How do you accidentally get your foot higher than your head and connect it with someone's chin?"

Uncomfortable, she sank deeper beneath the blanket, pulling it around her neck.

"How do you automatically roll when someone trips you?" I asked softly. "How can you tell when people are lying? Where did you learn to pick locks? And even just *reading*—most commoners, even some knights, can't read."

She swallowed. "I'm a Draigarian." The words were so quiet I barely caught them.

"A Draigarian?" I tried the word out in my mouth.

"Shhhh! Don't ever repeat that word to anyone, even Elsie."

"Okay, but what does it mean?"

She sighed, sitting up again. The light of the flames flickered across her face, reflecting in her eyes. "It's a group my parents founded. They helped people when no one else was around or had the ability to. They and their friends taught me stuff like self-defense, how to get into a locked room, and how to tell if people are lying. It was training for when I was old enough to join them."

She nodded her head a few times, as if telling herself it was okay to keep going. I waited.

"But then my dad died." She started rocking back and forth, eyes closed. "It was the most painful moment in my life—finding out. I knew their job was hazardous, but my parents and their friends had always been bigger than the danger. I never worried about them until Dad was suddenly gone. And then I didn't know anymore whether I wanted to be like them, risking myself and my family to help people. So I came here, just to get away and experience something different."

She gave a low, forlorn chuckle. A tear streamed down her cheek. "All of that followed me, of course. The Intriguer is here, and people need to be saved. I guess I can't run away from what I'm meant to do. But I'm scared—the Intriguer has powerful magic, worse than what my parents ever fought, and I don't even have my glinkga yet."

I had no idea what a glinkga was—an award? A title? A weapon?—but I wasn't going to question her anymore when she was in such distress.

"You don't have to fight it alone," I promised her. "I'm here. Elsie and Laomi are, too. *We* are going to save everyone." As I said it, I believed it for the first time.

"I hope so. We can give it our best shot, at least." She fiddled with the end of her braid. "Even though I'm scared, I'm not confused anymore. I know this is what I'm supposed to do. And I *want* to do this. I want to help people, like Dad did. What better way to prepare for the next life than helping people in this one?"

I didn't say anything else. She didn't need advice. She just needed to know that I was there for her. Reaching over, I wrapped my arms around her in a hug. I wasn't used to hugging people, except for Grandmother Rose. The one embarrassing hug I'd given Kedrik was the only time I remembered initiating one with someone my own age. But something in her face, her strength, her sorrow, urged me to reach out.

Rachaella hugged me back, the tension in her body easing. Our breathing settled into a rhythm—when she breathed out, I breathed in. It was nice, hugging.

"The alpha knows stuff about the Intriguer," I said suddenly, letting go. "And he has reasons to hate it. Maybe we can get his help, too." A Speaking Wolf would be a powerful ally.

"You think so? Even after what happened tonight?"

I recalled what the alpha said, about how maybe he had confused me with the real enemy. He also said he never wanted to smell me again, but that was a minor detail.

"It's worth a try," I said.

"Okay then. Tomorrow?"

"Tomorrow. Or rather, later today—I think it already is tomorrow."

We continued to talk and stare into the fire, and before long, I woke up with her feet in my face and mine in hers. We'd both passed out on the couch.

I rolled away with a grunt and got to my feet. Outside the window was a blur of white—a blizzard. I guessed visiting the alpha would have to wait.

By the time I got dressed, Elsie arrived with food.

"Morning, Elsie. Thanks." I took a bite of oatmeal and almost gagged. It was a disgrace to the word *oatmeal*. I missed Grandmother Rose's cooking. After three bites, my appetite vanished, but Elsie cleaned her bowl. Rachaella stirred right as she finished.

"Oh! I didn't see Rachaella there. I'll go get more food," she offered.

"She can have the rest of mine. I'm not hungry."

I shoved my bowl into the awakening Rachaella's hands. "Classes start in fifteen minutes—better hurry."

Her eyes widened in alarm.

"When did she come over?" Elsie asked as Rachaella shoved food down her gullet.

"Last night—it's a long story. We'll tell you on break when we can get Laomi over here too. We've got some work to do if we want to save everyone."

Unfortunately, further efforts to save everyone did not take place that day. Or the day after that. Or even the day after that. It was three days, in fact, before the blizzard slackened enough to allow anyone to venture outside. By that time, so much snow was on the ground that even opening the door was a hassle.

Rachaella, Elsie, and Laomi had all wanted to come with me when I sought out the alpha, but they would have had to tunnel through the snow like rabbits. Alone, I could travel the treetops. There was snow up there, too, and it was slippery, but I was confident that I could manage. The trees always made it easy for me.

The others reluctantly agreed to remain while I searched for the wolf pack. After stepping off my balcony onto the maple, I strode along the treetop path in the direction the alpha had led me three days before. I figured the best place to start looking for the wolves would be their makeshift den.

Five minutes later, I had no idea where I was. Everything looked the same covered in snow. There were no landmarks. Sighing, I placed my gloved hand on the branch beneath me.

"Can you show me where the alpha wolf is?" I whispered.

*He is no friend. He will hurt you.*

"I need to ask him some questions about the Intriguer."

*You cannot trust what he says.*

"Well, I still need to talk to him. Can you please just show me the way?" I was fed up with everyone either being overprotective or trying to kill me.

The branches rearranged themselves, creaking, while snow slushed off into piles below. The twig tips pointed the way.

"Thank you."

I skated my way from tree to tree, following the forest's directions. The trees led me back to the den, which was completely enveloped in snow, and deserted. But the trees stopped directing me, so I knew this was the place they meant.

I gritted my teeth. "I know the wolves were here before, but where did they go next?"

*Home.*

I froze. "Home? You mean Agaedith?"

*Back where they came from.*

I slumped against a tree's trunk, my legs dangling over a branch in the air. I was too late. Just when I was beginning to hope for some real knowledge and strength to help us with the Intriguer, the opportunity was snatched away by a dumb blizzard.

*Except for the alpha.*

Before I could react, the mound of snow piled at the base of the tree I sat on shifted. A black snout poked out, followed by a front paw. Then the snow fell to the side, revealing the massive body of the alpha, his dark pelt frosted with white.

Instead of insulting me or jumping up to bite my leg off or even just telling me to leave, he settled back down among the roots of the tree without even acknowledging my presence. Curling up, he tucked his nose into his tail, making him look like an oversized puppy.

It took me a minute to work up the courage to say anything. "Um, alpha?"

No response.

"Hey, I know you told me to get lost, but I need to talk to you."

I crept down the tree to get closer—but not too much closer.

"Are you listening?"

"Whadayawant?"

I jumped five feet back up the tree. My lungs almost came out my throat. "I, um, what are you doing?" It occurred to me how odd it was that he was curled up there in the snow while the rest of his pack was headed home.

"I'm dying in a hole—what does it look like I'm doing? You should be ecstatic."

"Why?"

"I don't know, maybe because I've been trying to kill you for several moons."

I shook my head. "No, why are you dying?"

"Lone wolves don't last long. A wolf's strength comes from its pack, and they're gone. I sent them away. I have nothing and no one left. It's winter, and the prey is gone. I used all my strength to fight you, and now that I'm not fighting you anymore, I've nothing to live for and no energy to go back."

*Wretched*—that's the word that came to mind as I looked at him. His coat was damp and stuck up in scraggly bunches, and his limbs were stiff from disuse. The piercing yellow gaze that usually cut through me was gone. He wouldn't even glance in my general direction. I tried to suppress the pity welling inside me.

He was a beast, I reasoned with myself. He killed Snowy. Even at that moment, he was probably manipulating me.

"Fine then—die. Just remember it wasn't me who killed you. It was your stupid vengeance."

I skied away through the treetops, but not before I noticed a second mound of snow beside the alpha and thought of the reddish fur and sightless brown eyes beneath it.

As soon as I returned to the ICUP, I marched into the kitchens, intending to filch a ham or beef leg or mutton haunch or something. The cooks chased me out. Elsie had trailed me, waiting for me to tell her what happened in the woods, and she saw the whole ordeal.

"What are you trying to do?" she asked.

"I need raw meat . . . for the alpha."

Without asking questions, she placed her hands on my shoulders confidently. "Go back to the room and wait. I will get some."

I did as she said. Rachaella and Laomi passed me in the hall and demanded to know what happened in the forest.

"You promised you would let us know as soon as you got back!" Laomi complained.

"I don't remember saying that. But nothing's happened yet." I told them about the pack leaving, and the alpha staying behind. "I have to make sure he doesn't die before I can get his help with the Intriguer. He said lone wolves don't last long, especially in winter."

"Will he accept food that you give him? He's not a pet, and it sounds like he wants to die," Rachaella pointed out.

"I don't know!" I snapped. That was what I was worried about, too. I couldn't help him if he didn't want help. I couldn't save him if he wanted to die.

Elsie slipped inside the room, staggering under the weight of two plucked turkeys.

"Perfect!" I rushed to relieve her.

"Ew," Laomi said.

The turkeys were at least fifteen pounds each. All I had to do at that point was drag them a mile and a half through the canopy and give them to the alpha. I tied the birds together and draped the rope over my back so one turkey hung in front, and the other behind. It was awkward, but I didn't know a comfortable way to carry thirty pounds of featherless fowl.

"Are you sure you don't need help?"

I didn't know why Rachaella bothered asking. She couldn't travel through the trees without a turkey, let alone with one.

"I'll be fine." Taking a few deep breaths, I strode out the door and off my balcony again.

Talk about a workout. I was breathing heavily before I traveled through five trees. If the turkeys hadn't been raw, I would have taken a break and snacked on them. As it was, I pushed onward, grumbling under my breath about the stupid, heartsick wolf.

"He'd better still be there, and he'd better eat these, otherwise I'm going to kill him myself. I'm not dragging bear bait all over the forest just for him to not have an appetite."

After another fifteen minutes, I had to quit talking to myself because I was too busy heaving lungfuls of frigid air. Taking a break, I braced myself against the bark of a tree to relieve some of the extra weight. The rope dug into my skin. Removing it, I set the birds on a branch and rolled my shoulders, trying to loosen the burning muscles. I had to be careful not to throw my back out. That would be an embarrassing injury story to have to tell Grandmother Rose.

After a brief respite, I shouldered my burden again and kept trudging. It was another hour before I made it to the wolves' old den. I skidded from the tree's branches to the ground. Then I tripped, fell on my face, and sent the turkeys flying. They couldn't remain airborne without feathers for long, though. They landed with a thump next to the alpha in the snow. He was still curled in the same place I'd left him.

He raised his head at the noise, and I quickly got to my feet. Even though he'd let me go one time before, I wasn't positive that he wouldn't change his mind and eat me instead of the turkeys. But his gaze swept over me without coming to rest and settled on the meat. Now that I was there, I didn't know what to say. How could I make him eat?

"No dying allowed," I said lamely.

To my astonishment, the alpha chomped a turkey leg. He ate mechanically, as if it was a muscle reflex instead of something he actually wanted to do. I watched him for a few minutes as he devoured the first bird.

"Must be nice to be at the top of the food chain," I muttered.

His ears flicked, picking up my words. "You don't know anything—humans are higher up than wolves . . . usually." He paused and actually grinned at me, turkey skin dangling from his jaw. "But there are still some things above both of us."

"Yeah, that's actually what I wanted to talk to you about," I said, scooting closer. His bulk intimidated me, as well as his claws and the fangs that were tearing the turkey to shreds, but I felt compelled to stay there, on the ground, rather than hide in the trees and call down to him. He was volatile, wild, and intelligent, and I was soft, probably chewy, and naive, but I wanted to be on equal footing with him. I wanted to prove my boldness, my earnestness—and my desperation.

Without warning, he whipped his head around, closing his jaws around my hand. There was a sharp pain and a scraping feeling, but before I could cry out, the alpha turned away and went back to eating again, ignoring me.

"Ow! What was that for? I just fed you!" I cradled my hurt hand close to my core, afraid to look at it and catch the sight of my own blood.

"Exactly. Mercy is a weakness that must be torn from you. In the wild, the weak die." He snapped a bone between his teeth.

"Is that it? You scared me a second there. I thought you were going to kill me after all."

"Ha! No, I can't kill you, girlie. You're too fun to mess with."

"Maybe it isn't mercy that makes me want to keep you alive," I retorted.

"You want my help in battling the Intriguer."

I squared my jaw. "You have just as much reason to hate it as I do, maybe more."

"You might as well enlist the help of a hedgehog to fight a dragon," the alpha growled. "My strength is nothing against its magic."

"I still want your help."

"Only because you are nothing more than an ant. A hedgehog's partnership would benefit you more than fighting the dragon alone."

"You know more about the Intriguer than I do. You're a wolf; your senses are sharper than a human's." My feet were getting wet from standing in the snow for so long, but I wasn't going to give up.

Fairy Godmother and Grandmother Rose thought the Intriguer was something new, but the magic mirror said it had been subdued before, though never defeated. The alpha wolf was the first living thing I'd met who seemed familiar with it.

"I don't know much more than your tree friends do, and you don't have to risk your skin talking to them." Finished with his meal, the wolf began to lick his paws for the last shreds of flavor.

"Help me," I insisted.

"Why should I?"

"Because you've nothing better to do."

He gave a bark of surprised laughter. "Best argument you've given yet. Fine. I'll tell you what I know about your Intriguer."

I suppressed the urge to remind him that it wasn't "my" Intriguer. He was really trying my temper.

"You might have heard that its specialty is the power of illusion. But illusion doesn't just mean sight. It can recreate other senses as well. It can make you taste, hear, feel, and smell things that aren't there. And it can confuse more than one person at a time, manipulating whole communities. What is real? The only way we know reality is through our senses. If those lie, then everything is in question. Its ultimate goals are not always clear until they're within its grasp, though."

"How do you know when it's manipulating people? How can you tell when it's messing with their senses and when something is real?"

"I am a wolf. When the Intriguer is confusing humans, it does not always make itself invisible to those whose senses are sharper than human ones. It could confuse me, too, if it tried. But I've lived on this earth longer than most humans, and I am still not old for a Speaking Wolf. Sometimes there is a blur, a scent of magic, a taste of unreality—I don't know how else to describe it. Then I know that the Intriguer is there."

"But what *is* it?"

The alpha flicked his ears dismissively. "It can be whatever it wants. Maybe that means it isn't anything."

I scowled. "Well, you're utterly unhelpful."

"I try."

Shadows were stretching. The sun hadn't broken the clouds all day, but the cooling temperatures informed me that it would set soon. There was no stillness like the stillness of a winter night. Standing, I started back toward the tree, still holding my bitten hand close. "I might think of more questions tomorrow. Will you be here?"

"Maybe."

I rolled my eyes. He was infuriating.

"Take care of that hand. You wouldn't want it to get . . . infected." Swishing his tail, he stalked away, leaving the pile of cracked bones behind him.

His words froze the blood in me. What had he told me, just last night as he was preparing to torture and kill me? *Or maybe I'll just bite you and wait for the full moon, when lots of interesting things will happen. You'll wish you were dead, then.*

Maybe he hadn't killed me because he'd decided to do something worse.

# Part 4

*"But the day of the Lord will come like a thief, and then the heavens will pass away with a mighty roar and the elements will be dissolved by fire, and the earth and everything done on it will be found out." 2 Peter 3:10*

———— ✦ ————

*"Like a lengthening shadow I near my end, all but swept away like the locust." Psalm 109:23*

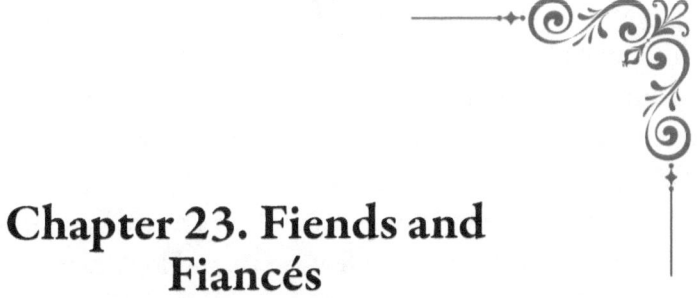

# Chapter 23. Fiends and Fiancés

I sat in the middle of the ball. Once more, for emphasis: I sat in the middle of *the ball*.

It wasn't half as bad as I'd imagined. Kind of boring, really. Fiddling with the dirt in the potted plant beside me, I sipped my punch idly.

Everything in the great hall was frosted with white glitter, and the fake cotton snow and stringy icicle thingies that people put on Christmas trees were hanging everywhere. The chandelier had been dusted and polished until it tossed glittering sparkles into the far recesses of the room, and, to my dismay, several pine trees had been felled and decorated to fit the theme. I couldn't stand too close to them, because the scent of their sap-blood was overwhelming.

Amid the snowy winter decor, my fiery ball gown stuck out like a sore, broken, swollen, bleeding, blistered thumb. It pleased me.

Speaking of sore, broken, swollen, bleeding, blistered thumbs, my hand was perfectly fine. The alpha had barely broken the skin with his bite. I was still concerned about what exactly would happen on the full moon, but that wasn't for a few weeks. I had enough to figure out already without worrying about that, too. Still, the question sat in the recesses of my mind—another thing to slowly gnaw away at my sanity.

I'd visited the wolf almost every day since he bit me, bringing food that Elsie stole from the kitchen. Rachaella showed me how to build snares to catch game, too. I'd set a few up in the forest, but at this time of winter, they weren't effective at catching more than the occasional bird. Whenever I visited the alpha, I asked new questions about the Intriguer, but I hadn't gleaned much useful information yet.

I yawned, glancing around for my friends. Rachaella and Lanovan were in animated conversation, which I found odd at first, because Lanovan usually kept to himself, but then I remembered he was Laomi's twin. He and Rachaella probably knew each other well. Elsie sat next to them, listening.

At the same time, Ronnoc and Bean greeted Laomi, bowing, and asked her to dance. After saying a few words and looking from one to the other, she took Ronnoc's arm and started to sashay to the middle of the dance floor. Turning his head, Ronnoc stuck his tongue out at Bean, and then stuck out the hand Laomi wasn't holding behind him. Sighing, Bean parted with two gold coins.

Laomi and Ronnoc were skilled dancers. They added their own personal flair to the moves, stepping gracefully. Laomi's hair swooped dramatically behind her.

Valiant and Vance also caught my attention, dancing vivaciously with SunGold and StarSilver. Those two royal pains in the neck took the cake for most outlandish gowns and makeup, and second for hair. Laomi got first in that category, of course.

SunGold's dress looked as if it was made of real gold plating, layered one piece on top of another. When she moved though, the gold seemed to liquefy, proving it wasn't as stiff as it first appeared. It was as if a metallic river wound around her body. StarSilver's gown was so tight and covered with white gems I didn't know how she could dance. At times, it seemed dangerously insubstantial, like moonlight. Both girls had been infuriated when they had lost the dress commissions Laomi was auctioning off, but obviously they'd found an alternative dressmaker.

Downing the rest of my punch, I leaned back, staring at the arched ceiling splattered with white star-speckles. Admittedly, it was my fault I wasn't having any fun. I wasn't comfortable with the setting. It felt like someone had thrown me into the middle of a deep lake when I hadn't taken enough swimming lessons to learn how to blow bubbles. I'd rather stab stuff with a sword any day. Being a wallflower was safe, at least. I wasn't likely to embarrass myself or ruin anything.

My vision suddenly went dark as a pair of hands covered my eyes. They were gentle, so I didn't freak out and draw my knife.

"Guess who?" a voice said.

I pretended to puzzle over the answer. "Jim Bob? Is that you?"

"Close enough." Arcturus let his hands drop, laughing. "You looked bored over here, so I thought I would come say hi."

"How did you know it was me?" I had been holding onto the hope that no one from sword fighting would recognize me all dressed up. So far it had worked. I wasn't concerned about getting in trouble with the school—the more trouble I was in, the better—but I'd finally earned a modicum of respect from the princes as a commoner swordswoman. If I revealed myself as a princess, that could change.

"Easy—I just looked for the prettiest girl here."

I almost snorted punch out of my nose. "How many princesses have you tried that line on?"

"Only you—otherwise it would backfire so quickly."

I rolled my eyes, not fooled. I knew what he wanted to talk about. He had questions, surely, about the wolves and why they had attacked us. "Arcturus," I began, and then hesitated. ". . . About the other day, I can—"

"Don't worry about it," he interrupted, "if it makes you uncomfortable."

Confused, I looked up at him. He looked quite nice in his neat black suit and green tie patterned with golden feathers.

"I thought that's what you came to ask about."

"Nah, I just wanted to know if you would like to dance."

Suddenly nervous, I swallowed. "Sure," I said, taking his arm.

Walking onto the floor, we waited for the line to end. Then, with a flourish, we stepped together into the dance. I found that my feet placed themselves naturally in the pattern across the floor. Thanks to Miss Victoria's hellacious dancing lessons, I didn't have to think about the steps at all. Dancing was . . . *fun*. When I didn't have someone glaring at me for my mistakes, shouting corrections, or playing fast-paced songs while I was laced too tightly in a corset, there was little to aggravate me. Plus, Arcturus was an enjoyable dance partner. We both made mistakes and laughed at them. His friendly demeanor made me relax, and he dipped me backward without dropping me.

For a little while, I forgot about the Intriguer. Yes, truly forgot, and my mind was a happy blank. His warm-but-not-sweaty hand was in mine, his other one clasped lightly around my waist. Our surroundings blurred into a swirling mass of white sparkles. Sounds of conversation were muffled. Only Arcturus and the floor beneath us seemed stark.

Several songs later, we were breathless and ready for a break. Elsie came to check on me, and I introduced her to Arcturus.

"Oh!" she said, turning pink when he kissed her hand.

They danced a few songs together while I tried to hunt down Rachaella and Laomi, but my other friends were nowhere to be found.

Unconcerned, I returned to the edge of the dance floor, where I met Ronnoc and Bean. They didn't seem to recognize me, which was a relief. I danced with each of them, but Arcturus cut in before long.

"Okay, you guys," he said. "Don't steal my dance partner."

They laughed and moved on. That was all right with me—I liked dancing with Arcturus best, too.

As he twirled me around, a thought struck me—did Kedrik know how to dance? Somehow, I doubted it. I couldn't picture him indoors among the finery and dressed in a suit. Sure, his parents hosted parties, but from what he told me, he had never been allowed to attend. The thought was unsettling, and I pushed it aside, trying to focus on enjoying myself.

When the tower bell rang twelve times, indicating midnight, I tensed as if waking from a spell. The Intriguer existed and was in the school itself, most likely watching us all that very minute—stalking us, waiting for its chance—and I was too busy dancing to stay alert. I stilled, breaking the rhythm.

Before I could say anything, a flurry of movement caught my eye. Ashella pranced away from her dance partner, who, angst-ridden, doggedly followed her.

"But wait!" he cried. "I don't even know your name!"

Fleeing without reply, Ashella kicked out, trying to leave her undersized slipper behind in a careless, elegant fashion. Instead, the shoe flew up and whacked the prince upside the head. Reeling backward, he clutched his jaw.

I ogled, trying not to draw attention by cracking up.

"Er . . . right." Arcturus's lips twitched.

Most of the other onlookers smiled or even chuckled out loud, but I spotted one exception. RosaLynne gazed after Ashella's retreating figure, her shoulders slumped in resignation and her eyes filled with heartbreak. I swallowed, suddenly recalling Rachaella's words that fall afternoon when we saw them together: *I don't think they will be happy with princes.* Their meaning was clear now. But even if Ashella and RosaLynne were in love, their responsibility to marry princes and carry on their bloodlines came first—it wouldn't matter what they wanted. My jaw clenched at the unfairness.

"Do you want to get a drink?" Arcturus asked, cutting into my thoughts.

"Yeah, I'm kind of thirsty." The mini punch cups just didn't hold enough liquid for hydration.

Arcturus offered his arm, but I shied away, preferring to walk independently. The idea of touching even his elbow when it wasn't required for a dance made my heart thump uncomfortably. We began to stroll over to the refreshments, but then I spotted something that made me come to a screeching stop: a warm, delicious, melty, oh-so-un-nutritious chocolate fountain!

*Halleluiah! Halleluiah!* I sang in my head. How had I not noticed it before?

Immediately, I made a beeline for it.

"Chris, what—oh." Arcturus headed after me.

Gathering a plateful of fruit, I sighed in ecstasy. *Dear God, thank you for chocolate!* I prayed as I took my first bite of a chocolate-covered strawberry.

"Do you really think it's a good idea for *you*, of all people, to be eating so much sugar? You literally bust through walls without it." My dance partner's lips tugged upward in amusement.

"Don't be ridiculous," I said through a full mouth. "Of course it's not!"

He eyed my plate of fruit. "Let me grab some before you sit down. I want to try it too."

Taking an experimental marshmallow, he let the thick, addicting liquid run over it.

"Mmmm, this stuff *is* good!" he said after popping it into his mouth.

"Told you!"

We stuffed ourselves with lusciousness, procuring quite a few strange looks in the process, but hey—we were having fun. Seating ourselves at a table for two barely large enough for our plates, we devoured the rest of our snack.

"You know," Arcturus commented after swallowing, "most of the time I can tell which royals are related, but I would never guess your mother is SnowWhite if I didn't already know. Not that that's a bad thing," he added quickly.

I shrugged. "My parents travel a lot, and even when they're home, I don't see them often. My grandmother raised me, so a lot of my personality probably comes from her." Eager to change the topic, I asked, "Are you like your family? I don't remember them."

I'd seen Arcturus at social functions only rarely, and his parents never. The fact that he had never tasted a chocolate fountain before was telling. They were all the rage at Clystopian royal parties. His parents must have been very private people.

"They don't get out much. Because of a curse, my father's right arm is a swan wing. My mother was a goose girl before she married him. Both of them are more comfortable around things with feathers than the royal scene. They've been abroad most of my life."

We exchanged a wry look of solidarity—absentee parents were something we had in common.

He hesitated, as if debating whether to say something more. Then, "Could you come closer for a moment?"

Standing, I took two steps to his side, my shoes clicking on the marble floor.

"May I take your hand?"

I narrowed my eyes warily, but offered my hand. It wasn't likely he would bite my fingers off.

He placed my fingertips over the back of his blazer, next to his shoulder blades, and traced them down his back. There was a bump, like a roped scar, and next to it, his back alternated between ridges and softness, almost like . . .

"Do you have *wings*?" I asked, astounded.

He grinned, but put a finger to his lips. "Not many people know that I'm part swan too."

"Why not?" Then, quieter, "If I had wings, I'd be flying all over the place to show them off. You can fly, right?"

"Sure. I don't do it when I'm around people, though. When there's something that makes you different, everything is more complicated. You know that."

"If people don't like who you are, wings and all, then they don't deserve your time," I said.

"It's not as simple for me as it is for you."

Simple for me? Ha! He should have seen me at the beginning of the semester. "It's not simple at all. I just know I'll never be happy unless I'm me."

"If you say so, *Christina*." His green eyes glittered.

He had me there. "Fair point."

"Knowing royals, can you honestly say that I would be accepted if I revealed my secret? And what about the common folk? Would they recognize someone like me as their future leader if they knew the truth?"

I opened my mouth to offer him encouragement, but then closed it again, remembering Kedrik. What people didn't understand, they feared. And what they feared, they rejected, even condemned, without consideration.

The prince sighed, twirling the fondue fork in his hands. "As the heir to the throne, I have too much to lose. I can't risk it."

Either because of the injustice, or eating too much chocolate-covered fruit, my stomach grew queasy. "Do you want to go outside for a few minutes?" I asked.

"Sure."

On our way to the courtyard, we skirted SunGold and StarSilver, who were in a heated argument. Without warning, it exploded into a shouting match.

"I hate you!" SunGold screeched at her sister.

"Well, I hate you more!" StarSilver yelled back at her.

The noise in the room died as everyone turned to watch the twins having hissy fits. It wasn't clear what they were fighting over. My guess was some prince. Arcturus and I edged away, but we didn't get far before SunGold started screaming insults.

"You are a yellow, snot-bellied, crumple-faced swine who should go eat your own dung!"

"Oh, yeah? Well, *you* are a warty, pickled frog who deserves to have goopy pustules sprout all over your face!"

SunGold turned maroon trying to think of a retort. "Your *mom* is a warty pickled frog who deserves to have goopy pustules sprout all over her face!" she finally shouted at her twin.

StarSilver opened her mouth, but then paused, probably thinking that was not the best comeback her twin had ever thought of.

I turned away, trying not to snigger. A few teachers rushed over and broke up the argument before one could call the other a lazy-eyed, stubby-toed dogface or something equally outrageous.

Leaving them behind, Arcturus and I went to the center of the ICUP's brick-and-stone courtyard. A circle of bushes had replaced Anastia the pine tree. Fortunately, I didn't feel poorly enough to make a partially digested offering to the shrubbery gods. After gulping some fresh air, my rioting innards soothed.

The place was full of wintery silence. No other ball goers had ventured out. Unlike inside, where it only looked like winter, outside it felt like winter, too. It even smelled frosty. The wind blew unevenly over the top of the school, making eddies of snow swim down to where we stood.

"I'm certainly glad neither of *them* is my fiancée." Arcturus glanced back inside at the twin pouters.

It was an odd thing to say, but I only chuckled and replied, "Me too."

He must have misinterpreted what I meant, because a faint smile touched his lips. He regarded me with half-lidded eyes.

Whoops. Had I just inadvertently flirted with him?

"As soon as I saw you, Chris, I knew you were an interesting person."

"Well, yeah—how many princesses are there who take sword-fighting lessons?"

He shook his head. "I was actually talking about the parade—Coralla's birthday parade."

Ugh. Why did he have to bring that up? Embarrassment and indignation didn't fade with time.

I cringed. "You were there?"

Arcturus's brows knitted, his smile vanishing. "I was in the float right in front of you."

I bit my lip, trying to remember. There had been lots of floats, but why couldn't I recall the one directly in front of me?

"It was blue, and it had clouds and lots of birds on it," he prompted.

"Right, I remember now," I said, even though I didn't. I just couldn't stand that sorrowful expression anymore, as if someone had just killed his dog, his dog's mate, and their litter of a dozen puppies.

"I saw you behind me, up in a plaster tree. You looked bored and rebellious. Everyone else was so fake. I felt bad when those bees started attacking you."

"I wasn't bored anymore when they came," I grumbled. "Wait a second, if you were right in front of me, then yours must have been the float mine ran into! I'm really sorry about that." It was a very belated apology, but I meant it.

"You weren't to blame. I wanted to tell you that at the party that night, but I couldn't find you or your parents."

That was because we hadn't been around. My parents had fled the scene in humiliation. I'd been busy punching Coralla, meeting Kedrik, and yelling at Queen Aquanetta. Good times, good times.

"The way we actually met was better, anyway," he continued. "We got to know each other more than we would have with a staged introduction."

He took my cold hand in his. "It is truly a relief to know that my fiancée is someone I can get along with."

My face gave a little spasm. I yanked my hand back. "What did you call me?"

"My fiancée—that is what you call someone you are engaged to." He gave an awkward chuckle.

"We're not engaged." I started to back away.

"What do you mean? Months ago, your parents met with mine and negotiated a trade deal that was highly beneficial to both countries. The whole contract hinges upon us marrying when we turn sixteen . . . They never asked you?" It was his turn to look stunned.

So that was why my parents had insisted I attend Coralla's birthday parade and garden party. We were supposed to have been introduced that day. And the reason I was attending the ICUP at all was so that my improper tendencies could be tamed, and I would make a suitable wife. *His* suitable wife. It felt like the ground was spinning.

"No! But they asked you? And you *agreed*?" I was shaking with cold, but also shock and anger.

"Of course I agreed! It's what is best for my country. As Prince Heir, it's my responsibility to serve my subjects in whatever way necessary, including through marriage."

"You sound like you're reciting lines," I sneered.

"That's what a mantra *is*." His jaw was set, stubborn.

It was like looking in a mirror.

My desire to scream at him dissipated. The situation wasn't his fault. He hadn't come up with the contract without my input or kept it a secret from me. Resentment cut me up from the inside, but it wasn't directed at him.

I closed my eyes, counting to five to steady myself. "I didn't mean to dismiss your goals," I said when I opened them again. "Wanting to be what is expected of you is just strange to me."

He relented, too. "I am sorry this is how you had to find out." He rubbed his temples. "Just so you know, I would never force you to marry me. If the time comes and you still can't stomach the idea," he swallowed, "we can call it off."

"You would be okay with that?"

"You're not a bird, Chris. I'm not going to put you in a cage."

I shivered. We had been outside long enough for my ears to start burning and my fingertips to become stiff. Goose bumps sprouted on my arms as the frigid air attacked my body.

"I'm going back inside," I said.

I didn't invite him to follow me, and he didn't.

As I reached for the door, a mass of red and white roses came flying out of the ballroom, running into me. Reeling backward, I managed to keep my balance, but my flowery adversary wasn't so lucky. She spun away to the opposite side of the courtyard and then slumped to the ground, mumbling incoherently. Recognizing the rose-patterned dress as one of the two Laomi had made by commission, I rushed over to see if the princess was all right.

"Are you okay?" Arcturus asked me.

"I'm fine, but I don't know if RosaLynne is." Poor girl, what had happened?

Bending down, I brushed a piece of hair off her face to see if she had fallen asleep or been hurt.

"No!" Her eyes snapped open, and she grabbed my wrist like an eagle grasping a fish. "Don't take me! I didn't know! It's not fair! Don't . . . Don't . . ." She slumped back, asleep.

"What's wrong with her?" Arcturus demanded.

Frowning, I disentangled my hand and stepped out of grabbing range. "She has narcolepsy," I said shakily, "so she often falls asleep suddenly at inconvenient times. I thought she had a potion that managed it, though." This time, my shiver wasn't from the cold. Who had been chasing her? Though I stared through the glass doors to the silver glow and friendly chatter within, no pursuer revealed themselves.

Let's see . . . an invisible chaser who wanted to kidnap—or control—a princess? There weren't a lot of suspects. Suddenly, I really wanted to get back inside.

Without warning, an angry gust of icy wind slammed the doors shut and nearly ripped my hair out of my head. Frost crept over the glass, making it opaque. The only light in the courtyard had been from the sparkling ballroom. Without it, darkness pervaded, thick and menacing.

I lunged for RosaLynne's arms and started to drag her back toward the entrance.

"Arcturus! Try to get the doors open!" My voice was nearly lost in the howling wind, but he understood.

No matter how hard he pulled against the door or hammered his hands on the glass, it wouldn't budge, and no one noticed the three royals trapped outside.

The wind screamed through my bones, and my skin burned with cold. The storm was coming. Trying to haul the unconscious princess to the door was like trying to climb up an ocean wave. My steps took me nowhere.

I looked skyward. Swirling black clouds formed a massive spinning vortex with the courtyard dead in the center. Glowing red eyes and gaping jaws within it leered at us and drew closer . . .closer . . . I was paralyzed with icy terror. Despair surged over me like a blizzard, peppering me with bits of hopelessness.

Some piece of swirling debris whipped against my face. A flower of pain blossomed. It was enough to snap me out of the trance. Breaking away from the mesmerizing eyes of the storm, I released RosaLynne and tackled Arcturus. Once both of us were freed from the sadistic spell, we crawled to the pathetic shelter of the courtyard shrubs at top speed. Breaking glass and terrified screams made me chance a look back. All the windows and doors to the ballroom were shattered, and the vortex had frightened the candles and fireplace flames to smoke. Shadowy shapes moving frantically were all that I could see of the dancers.

The worst sight of all, however, was at the edge of the courtyard, where Arcturus and I escaped from seconds before. RosaLynne, helpless in her slumber, was swallowed up in the vortex's gaping jaws. There was no way we could have saved her or fought against a being of cold and dark wind, but the sight drew a strangled scream from me. Her flowery dress whipped around like a flag of blood right before she disappeared into the void.

Hunger sated, the monstrosity melted into mist. The howling wind ceased.

My ears rang in the unnatural silence. Clouds covered the moon, so no light came from the sky. Everything was as dark as an oily mixture of ink and charcoal.

After a few minutes of no sounds but our breathing, Arcturus and I rose shakily to our feet.

"What was that?" the prince questioned, hoarse.

I snorted. "It was the chicken we all had for lunch, come back to wreak revenge on those who ate it. What do you *think* it was?"

"Nothing good, that's for sure."

I stared at him in disbelief. "You mean you really don't know?" I would have thought Fairy Godmother would have told him at least a little bit.

"I know that it seems to be a hazard to hang around you."

"It is, isn't it?" I said, realizing that it was true. None of the other princesses had experienced so many near-death encounters. At least, they'd never mentioned it. Was I just always in the wrong place at the wrong time? Yeah, right—that was as likely as my parents giving me a bow and quiver full of arrows for Christmas. Coincidences didn't happen often. More likely, I was one of the Intriguer's next targets.

I rubbed my fire-orb necklace, wishing Fairy Godmother could give me some answers. But crying couldn't bring the type of solution I searched for.

Cautiously, we ventured back through the stone courtyard that was conspicuously bereft of sleeping princesses. I tried not to imagine what the Intriguer might do to RosaLynne. As we stepped over the shattered glass door, it was like going through a sound warp. Chaos reigned. In the darkness, people ran about, knocking over and trampling one another. Bits of broken glass littered the polished marble floor, interspersed with droplets of a thick, viscous liquid that definitely wasn't punch. We hesitated to move farther inside, unwilling to add to the panic or get rammed over.

"SILENCE!" Ms. Throupé shouted her favorite word from her perch on a tabletop. "Listen to me!"

No one paid attention, but the headmistress's voice was loud enough to be heard over the royals' screaming, which was impressive. "All princesses will proceed to their suites immediately, and princes shall go to the front of the building! Their carriages will be there to return them to their own school! Go in an ORDERLY fashion!"

Grabbing my shoulders, Arcturus spun me around to face him. His voice wasn't as loud as Throupé's, but I clearly saw him mouth the words *be careful*.

Well, duh. Giving his arm a reassuring squeeze, I left. He would learn soon enough that worrying about me was a waste of energy.

Though I searched the throng for Laomi, Rachaella, and Elsie, I couldn't recognize anyone. It was too dark, and the halls were too dense with sweat, fear, and poofy dresses. When I finally made it to my room, though, Elsie was waiting for me, already changed out of her gown. She had lit a few lamps to dispel the darkness with a golden glow.

"Elsie!"

"Chris!"

I threw my arms around her, my relief enormous. I had been terrified that she, as little as she was, had been trampled.

"You didn't get cut by any glass, did you?" I held her at arm's length, inspecting her for injuries.

"No, I'm fine. I was with Laomi's brother, and he helped me. Laomi was with us too, but I lost track of her."

That wasn't a good sign. "What about Rachaella?"

"She went to bed early—she said she wasn't feeling well. So she wasn't around when it happened."

I guessed partying wore her out easier than the rest of us, since she was still weak. "Let's check on her just in case she needs anything."

On our way to Rachaella's room, we stopped to knock on Laomi's door, but the maids answered and said she hadn't come back yet. I bit my lip.

I almost pounded Rachaella's door down when she didn't answer immediately. Finally, she opened at the umpteenth knock.

"Yes?" she said, blinking away sleep. "Hi Chris, Elsie. Is the dance over?" Her linen nightgown and disheveled hair made it clear that we had woken her up. "It was fun, but I was just too exhausted to stay until the end."

"Sorry to wake you. We just wanted to make sure you were okay," Elsie said.

"Everyone's going to bed now," I added. "A storm just blew through all the windows in the ballroom. Glass is all over the place."

The sleepiness left Rachaella at once. "Really? I've never seen a storm like that before. And I didn't hear a thing. Are you sure it wasn't some prank or . . ." She trailed off as I gave her a meaningful look. A flash of realization lit her face.

Confused at our exchange, Elsie glanced back and forth between us. "What? Tell me! No keeping secrets."

"It wasn't just a storm," I murmured under my breath.

Elsie gasped. "The Intriguer?"

I nodded. "RosaLynne is gone this time."

Silver starlight tears glistened in Rachaella's eyes. "Where is Laomi?" she asked suddenly.

"She hasn't come back yet."

Without another word, Rachaella joined us in the hall, and we sprinted for the stairwell.

*BAM!*

I slammed into someone coming up the stairs. Both of us hit the floor, then Rachaella and Elsie tripped over us.

"Aaaah!"

"Ugh!"

"Ouch!"

"Watch out!"

"Whoa!"

"Sorry!"

After getting sufficiently kicked, rolled on, elbowed, and bruised, I jumped up, brushing myself off.

"Laomi?" I asked the figure I ran into hopefully.

"Young ladies!" The figure rose.

Nope, not Laomi.

"I am astounded at you! You were ordered to return to your suites at once and remain there!" Miss Victoria glared at us. "Turn around and return this instant!"

"But Miss Victoria," Rachaella protested, "our friend hasn't come up yet!"

"That has nothing to do with you!" Victoria snarled at us. "If she is unable to follow instructions, that is her own problem!"

I considered decking her and running past, but then a familiar voice called out from behind us.

"What are you all doing? Get in here, I need you!"

Whirling around, I grinned with relief at Laomi's head sticking out of my doorway. "Geez, have a little patience, will you? We're coming!"

Hoisting the two girls beside me to their feet, I ushered them inside my room and locked the door. That done, I rounded on Laomi. "Where were you? We almost had simultaneous heart attacks!"

"Chris . . ." Her voice was strangled, painful. "I need your help." She revealed her arm, which she'd been holding close to her stomach.

Elsie gave a sharp intake of breath as the lamplight hit it.

Blood oozed from several scrapes stretching from her elbow to her wrist. The light illuminated flecks of glass lodged in her skin, where swelling had wedged them firmly. More than anything else, it looked like a cougar had clawed her.

I clenched my jaw. "Elsie, please light a few more lamps and bring them closer. Rachaella, would you grab some tweezers from the bottom shelf of the cabinet in the bathroom? And get a few wet and dry towels, if you could."

Both girls hurried off, tight-lipped.

Kneeling, I examined the injury. The cuts were long, but they weren't too deep, so blood loss wasn't a concern. It didn't look like anything vital had been severed, which happened sometimes with cuts like hers. All the bits of glass concerned me, though. There could be particles that were too tiny to see in there that could cause infection.

"How's the pain?" I asked.

"Bad."

"I mean on a scale of one to ten."

"I don't know!" she snapped.

"Do the best you can to guess."

"I don't want to!" She paused. "Seven."

"Okay, sit tight. I'll be right back."

"Like I'm going anywhere."

I didn't respond. If her mood was even less pleasant than usual because of her injury, I couldn't blame her.

Gathering herbs, clean bandages, and a cleansing solution infused with aloe vera and calendula, I prayed over them, and then returned.

I handed a piece of willow bark to Laomi. "Chew on this—it will help with the pain."

She took it without comment, though she grimaced when the bitter flavor seeped onto her tongue.

I used the tweezers Rachaella brought to fish out all the glass pieces I found. The task was even more challenging than it should have been because of Laomi flinching whenever I touched her and the other two exclaiming "Don't hurt her!" every other second.

"I'm not trying to hurt her!" I finally shouted, losing my temper. "If I don't get all the glass out, it'll get infected and she'll most likely lose the arm!" That last part was an exaggeration, but it made Laomi sit still, so I didn't correct myself.

Next, I used the infusion to rinse and clean the cuts before gently patting away the blood and moisture with the towels. Lastly, I soaked a bandage and some burdock leaves in the infusion and wrapped them together around her arm tight enough to stop any extra bleeding, but not so tight that it would cut off all circulation. That would be bad—then her arm really *would* fall off.

Laomi exhaled. "Thank you, that feels a little better. I knew you'd do a better job than the doctors. Plus, I would have had to wait forever in line. There are a lot of injuries. They'll probably run out of supplies." Her voice cracked at the end.

"How did it happen?" Rachaella asked.

"There wasn't any warning," Laomi grunted. "One second everyone was having fun—Lanovan was talking to Elsie and I was eating little pink hors d'oeuvres—then the next second the windows caved in and all the lights went out. Everyone started screaming and running in every direction. The three of us headed for the stairwell, but my hair came loose and some idiot stepped on it and made me fall. As you can tell, there was glass all over the floor." She scowled at her bandaged arm, and then slumped in her chair, exhausted. "At least *you* made it back safely, Elsie."

"Yeah, it was a complete nightmare," I added. "I was in the courtyard." I couldn't help but be a *little* dramatic. I deserved it.

"*What?*" Laomi looked at me incredulously.

"So that's how you knew it wasn't a regular storm." Rachaella folded her arms. "What happened out there?"

When I told them the story, they all had something to say.

"You have really bad luck, don't you?"

"Poor Rosie."

"Was the guy you were trapped with cute?"

The last question came from Laomi, of course.

"What kind of stupid question is that?" I demanded.

"True. He was a prince, so he had to be cute."

Argh! That wasn't what I'd meant! When I opened my mouth to say so, though, Rachaella spoke first.

"Come on, Laomi, concentrate on the problem here, which is *not* how cute Chris's boyfriend is."

"Arcturus is *not* my boyfriend."

"Are you sure?" Rachaella smirked. "You were spending quite a lot of time with him . . ."

"Of course I'm sure!" He was not my boyfriend—and he was definitely not my fiancé.

"Whatever," Laomi said. "Anyway, since there's nothing we can do against the Intriguer, I'm going to bed. Might as well get some sleep while I wait to be abducted."

"I think that's a good idea," Rachaella said. "Going to bed, I mean, not waiting to get abducted."

As if I could sleep if I went to bed now. Nothing we could do would hold a candle to what the Intriguer could achieve. I had known that before, but I'd pushed the hopeless thought down. Seeing the Intriguer's storm take RosaLynne made the terrible truth surface. Even after we escaped, finding someone who would help who was a match for the Intriguer would be nearly impossible.

Still, running would be better than waiting to be kidnapped. I had to believe that the rescue party would arrive soon, and we would make it to freedom.

The three of them headed for the door, tired and dispirited. But as Laomi and Elsie disappeared around the corner, Rachaella hung back.

"You're hiding something again, Chris. Why are you always hiding something? You know we only want to help. Don't you trust us?"

I looked away, facing the glass door. "It's not you I don't trust, it's the school itself. Plus, I promised I wouldn't tell. It's for your own safety." Her intense stare prickled the back of my head.

"Fyre is leading a rescue party here, isn't he? You're going to escape into the woods," she whispered.

I whipped my head around. How did she guess? Too late, I realized that I gave myself away. "Not by myself," I said. "I would never leave without you and the others."

"You mean just Laomi and Elsie, not the whole school."

"Well, yeah—the element of secrecy would be blown to smithereens if I took the whole school."

She chewed on her lip, then blurted, "I don't think we should go."

My eyes widened in surprise. "Because we'd be leaving people behind? Rachaella, we can get help for them, but we have to get out of here first."

She was being unreasonable. Just because we couldn't rescue everyone at the same time didn't mean we should stay and suffer with them, waiting to be kidnapped.

"It's not that. It's just . . . there may be another way out—an easier way, that will save everyone. Everything will work out if we hold on a while longer, trust me. Can you do that?"

I peered at her, studying her like I would study a locked box. Her breathing was raspy, and sweat glistened on her nose and forehead, but her wide stance and determined gaze were confident. Curly black hair spilled over her white nightgown and partially shadowed her face. Her gray eyes shone like deep pools with secrets at the bottom. Many, many secrets.

"Now who's hiding something?" I asked, regarding her coolly.

"Like you, I hide things for safety." Her lips quirked upward. "It's a heavy responsibility sometimes."

"Does this have to do with being a Draig—"

She was at my side with a hand over my mouth before I finished the word.

"Don't say it. I should never have told you, but I trust you. Just don't say it."

I shoved her hand away. "Fine, it if means that much to you." Sheesh. It was just a word, *Draigarian*. I didn't even know what it meant.

I ran a hand through my hair. "What am I supposed to tell Fyre when he comes? That he and the rescue party should turn around and go home just because my friend said everything will be okay without them? That's ridiculous."

"Sometimes what seems ridiculous actually makes a lot of sense when you see the whole picture. I can't tell you the whole picture, but I know it will work. Please believe me."

I hesitated, closing my eyes. I wasn't sure what the right choice was—which strategy would ensure our escape. But there was one thing I did know. "I can't leave without you," I finally said, letting out my breath. "If you're staying, I will, too."

She gave me the smallest, most hopeful smile, and then quietly left, like a thief in the night.

That girl—she meant so much to me, but I didn't get her.

# Chapter 24. As Flighty as Smoke

My sleep was restless. The layers of blankets twined around me as I convulsed tirelessly. Sparkling lights and superficial laughter morphed into broken glass that looked like black water and the terrified screams of stupid, innocent royals. A black wolf with yellow eyes glared at me, growling.

*What will you do next?* it asked. *Kill, or be killed? There is no mercy here. Mercy is weakness.*

At that, he leaped at me, snarling. I spun around to run away through the woods, but the trees were black and still. Smoke drifted through the otherwise unmoving forest, causing my throat to sting. As I raced away, the fallen leaves and undergrowth beneath my feet were replaced by hot coals. Embers floated before my eyes. The wolf didn't care. Its footsteps thudded closer as I struggled to maintain my footing. Feet burning, I tripped, sending hungry sparks into the air and searing pain into my hands. The sparks formed a sharp mouth with a forked tongue of flames.

Then the fire spoke: *Princess. Tree friend. Tamer of wolves. What is your next move? Better act quickly . . .*

The wolf caught me, grasping my neck in its teeth and shaking me like a sack of feathers. The fire's roar echoed in my head, and I awoke.

My nightmare was real. Or was I still dreaming? Wisps of smoke hanging in the dead air blurred my senses. The stinging in my throat intensified.

Rolling out of bed, I hit the floor and stayed there. Untangling myself from my quilt shackles, I crawled to the door, coughing. The smoke stung my eyes, so I closed them, and as a result, it took me ten times longer than normal to reach my door because I kept bumping into things.

323

At last, I made it to the door and felt the bottom with the back of my hand. It was warm, but was that because of fire outside, or the heat from the fire in my fireplace? I had no idea what a normal door temperature was, so there was no way to tell if it was safe beyond. If it wasn't, I could escape from the tree by my balcony. But what about Rachaella and the royals who didn't have an easy escape route? Her balcony was on the inside of the school. The only place she could escape was the courtyard. Stone wouldn't burn, but if the school surrounding it was on fire, it was a death trap.

I gritted my teeth, berating myself. The fire wasn't necessarily that serious. Some clumsy cook could have burnt a piece of toast. Of course, I wasn't sure why someone would be making toast in the middle of the night, and it would have to be practically on fire to cause so much smoke . . .

Deciding to take my chances, I stood and threw open the door. A haze of choking smoke greeted me. The black cloud was floating up from the stairwell. There was no way that was toast smoke. Though I couldn't see the fire, it spoke to me in its crackling, sizzling voice.

*Burn, princess. Dissolve in my flames.*

Magical speaking flames—maybe I was still dreaming. Or perhaps the Intriguer was responsible. Could the thick smoke be nothing more than an illusion? I wasn't counting on it.

At any rate, I didn't catch any more words the fire spat after that, because sonorous screeches erupted from SunGold's room across the hall.

"We're all gonna diiieee! We're all gonna diiieee! We're all gonna diiieee!"

It was a good thing she wasn't panicking. Staying calm in an emergency was key to getting to safety.

Princesses rushed out of their rooms toward the stairs, only to realize that the fire was rising up them. Not knowing where else to go, they clung to one another, jumping up and down and having coughing and screaming fits. I couldn't make out Laomi or Rachaella. Elsie was downstairs, beyond my ability to help. The maids' quarters were on the ground floor, so at least it would be easier for her to escape. She could simply hop out the nearest window.

The smoke scratched my eyes and throat, Elsie's absence needled at my mind and heart, and the screaming was killing my ears. I couldn't do much about the first two, but I would certainly try with the last one.

"SHUT UP! No one's going to die! Everyone get in my room *now*; there's an escape route."

Breaking into a fit of coughing, I withdrew back into my room, not waiting to see if anyone would follow. I tripped over the couch and flipped over it, sprawling out on the other side. Picking myself up, I continued until I hit the balcony doors. Flinging them open, I gulped lungfuls of relatively fresh air. It felt like millions of tiny people were branding the inside of my lungs with hot iron rods.

As the smoke hurried out to the atmosphere beyond, I saw the shapes of the first princesses coming into my room.

"Over here," I croaked.

They struggled over, coughing and wheezing. A few stumbled over the couch like I had. No one spoke when they made it outside. It was probably too painful. Royals weren't accustomed to pain.

To my intense relief, I spotted Laomi at once, in a blood-red satin nightgown, holding coils of her braided hair.

"Laomi, you first," I said hoarsely, indicating the maple tree just off the balcony. "Help them from below, and see if Elsie made it out."

Nodding curtly, she swung into the thick boughs, deft despite her recent injury. I relaxed a bit as she clambered down. One safe.

"I'll go get the others," Rachaella said from the doorway.

My mouth worked furiously, but no sound would come out before Rachaella vanished back into the smoke. I wanted to run after her and drag her back, but I knew it was pointless. The best thing for me to do was get everyone down, and then go help her. Rachaella and her stupid helping-people obsession. What sort of idiot ventured farther inside a burning building?

The other princesses formed a massive pack, hungry for air. They jostled each other and pushed toward the edge of the balcony, where the air was freshest. That could get dangerous. Not all of them could fit on my small balcony, and those inside were shoving hard to get out. Someone might get pushed right off the edge.

"Sit down!" Of course, no one listened.

Grabbing the nearest princess, I helped her get from the railing to the nearest tree branch. It took an excruciatingly long time. As I helped one after another, it became painfully apparent that few royal ladies were used to doing any sort of climbing activity. They were meticulous with their thin nightgowns, not wanting to smudge them or catch the edge on a twig, and they kept messing with their unkempt hair instead of concentrating on their descent. These annoying occurrences became especially tiresome when the whole faculty and student body from the prince's academy came up the hill to help. Then the silly girls kept glancing toward the ground instead of watching where they put their hands and feet.

One princess saw how high up she was and froze, jamming the entire railing-to-tree transfer. Finally, Laomi clambered up and literally detached the girl's hands from the tree for her. Another girl grabbed only thin air and almost fell. As it was, her foot was wedged into the tree, so she only sprained her ankle instead of breaking her neck.

My whole body began to ache from lack of fresh air, and my fingers became thick, unwieldy logs. Every time I thought *okay, almost done, almost everyone is out*, someone else would stumble over, led by Rachaella. She was as flighty as the smoke, only staying long enough to take a few quick breaths before plunging back into the school. Slowly, she made her way through the corridor, emptying the rooms of their inhabitants and bringing them to safety.

My movements became mechanical, like a door hinge in desperate need of oil. Whenever I spoke, my voice cracked. Sometimes I couldn't hear myself at all. It was drowned out by the sledgehammer in my brain. It was like a gong declaring time was almost up. A hissing, crackling sound intensified, and I knew the flames were closing in. Stupid wooden floors—why couldn't the builders have made the entire school out of brick?

Dimly I thought again of Elsie. Laomi had never told me if she was safe. Then again, Laomi had her hands full with the unruly princesses. I could only pray Elsie had made her way out.

There was one person, however, that I should have been keeping an eye on. I hadn't seen her for several minutes, and growing panic made me practically push the last person off the balcony. I whirled around to face the smoke still streaming out of the building, bringing a fresh wave of pain to my eyes and lungs.

"Rachaella!" I called, except with my worn-out lungs, it sounded more like, "Ra-ay-a!"

There was no answer except the roaring of the fire coming closer. I dove back into the thick gray cloud on my hands and knees. Now I was the stupid idiot. But there were no professional firefighters around, and once I left, no one would come to look for her. When it came down to it, what I had told her a few hours ago was true—I couldn't leave her behind.

I crawled as fast as I could, feeling like a cockroach that was about to be stomped on. The heat was far more intense now, as the flames had moved up the stairwell and started devouring the hallway. The fire was obscured by smoke, but the heat made my face feel like it was going to melt off.

*Hide and seek, princess,* the fire roared. *Who will find her first?*

Through the layers of swirling gray, I detected something solid and edged toward it feebly. It was a body. I reflexively tried to scream when soft flesh met my hands, but it came out as a series of cacophonous coughs.

My bloodshot, watery eyes could hardly make out who it was. No wait, who *they* were. StarSilver had collapsed face-first, and her hands were pointed like an arrow toward Rachaella, who had seemingly tried to drag her along before sinking down in front of her.

I only had the strength to save one.

Grabbing Rachaella around the waist, I hauled her back toward my room. Every inch of my body screamed in agony, but I forced myself to keep going. Not for myself, but for Rachaella. She needed to live. She *deserved* to live! All she wanted to do was dedicate her life to helping people. Over and over, every day since I'd met her, she'd proven that. She had so much left to give to the world, and there was so much the world could do to be better for her. Blank spots appeared in my vision and grew larger as my limbs relaxed. I fought the darkness and pressed on, trying to ignore my body's screams for fresh air. Every time I greedily snatched a breath, it burned my lungs, my heart, and my blood even more.

An eternity of suffering brought me to my room and around the couch. I followed the drifting smoke to my balcony, but couldn't lift Rachaella over the railing. Using my own weight as leverage, I at last managed to drape her over it. After that staggering feat, my body overcame my will, and I found nothing but empty space where the tree should have been. I tried to hold onto Rachaella as she fell beside me, I really did. But when the sturdy branch of the maple closed around my waist, slowing my fall, Rachaella was so far, far away.

There were lots of voices all around me—sobbing, shrieking, commanding, yelling, searching. The roar of the fire never ceased, but it was at a safe distance now. I lay on the ground, unable to move except for breathing in and out, in and out. My lungs were ragged, shriveled lumps of useless gray flesh. I wanted to give up trying to use them, but my body forced me to keep going.

Though my eyes burned, they were too dry for tears.

Feet crunched the dead grass close by. Through slitted eyes, I thought I spotted a very long braid and a boy with fuzzy slippers, but I wasn't sure. Strange arms lifted me, carrying me away from the wreckage and noise and unclean air. Someone held my hand as if they never wanted to let go. As we drew farther away, all the sounds grew muffled, except the wind in the barren trees and soft, desperate crying on my left. It was too painful to find out who it was. I concentrated on gulping the ever-freshening air. It was the cold that hurt my lungs now.

Whoever carried me brought me into a building slightly warmer than the outdoors. There were lots of echoing halls to walk down and lots of doors to open and lots of stairs to climb. Multiple pairs of feet thumped along after me, and the hand squeezing mine never let go. Throughout the journey, I kept my eyes closed.

The most comfortable bed in the world rose to relieve my carrier of their burden. I lay there, going in and out of consciousness, until a cup of water that tasted like it was from the very fountain of life touched my lips. I inhaled it like a kid given free reign over an ice cream shop.

Still, I didn't try to open my eyes or speak. Flopping back onto my pillow after the drink, I concentrated on concentrating on nothing. Though there were no clear thoughts to get rid of, my mind had no intention of resting. The smoke in the school had permeated my brain, and it felt like flames were still dancing beneath my eyelids. *Burn, princess. BURN!* they screamed in mocking tones. Swirling vortexes swept my friends away, but no matter how fast I ran, I couldn't reach them. The Intriguer took them to the far corners of the earth, leaving me to search desperately. I had to choose one to save—there wasn't time for the others. The anguish brought me to my knees. On the cold stone, StarSilver and RosaLynne splayed side by side with no breath in them. When I drew close, they sat up, capturing me with their undead gazes.

*You killed us, Chris.*

"No!"

*You didn't save us; you let us die.*

"I tried! I couldn't . . ."

Torturous scene after torturous scene flew by, where I was alone and hunted by both evil and good. Shunned forever, I hid alone in a cold place where it always rained.

I couldn't scream out loud, so instead I thrashed about in the bed, squeezing the hand that never left mine until it was probably more mashed pulp than appendage. And I couldn't stop coughing.

After an eon of feverish visions, respite came. A song started as a single angelic note, then grew to a harmonious symphony of peace. The dying embers in me came to life, not hissing and crackling like the evil fire, but warm and flickering—the flames I knew and loved. A dream, yes, but a good dream. When Fyre at last soared into the room and perched on my bed, whispering, *Go to sleep now, Chris,* I listened effortlessly.

I ceased kicking, banished my cough, and stayed completely still, wanting to hear every note of Fyre's life-giving music. He stopped before I slipped beneath the waters of sleep completely. I had just enough time to hear a short exchange in the real world, next to my bed.

"Will she live?" Though the voice was hoarse with anxiety, and probably smoke, it had a familiar ring to it.

"I'm sure she will," another voice I knew responded. "Chris is a survivor."

I opened my eyes, letting light flood in. It made me tear up. As my eyes adjusted, I saw Elsie, curled in a wobbly wooden chair, fast asleep. Meanwhile Arcturus, head resting on the edge of the bed, still had his hand in mine. Slowly, so I didn't wake him, I removed my hand.

"Awww . . . why did you go and do that? You two look so cute together!"

Startled, I looked up to see Fairy Godmother pop into view at the foot of the bed. "You're too independent," she went on, tutting. "Though I suppose that can be a good thing."

I wasn't in the mood for the boy-teasing. Actually, I was never in the mood for it, but especially not right then.

"Rachaella's dead, isn't she?" I said, not daring to hope otherwise.

Fairy Godmother gave me a measured look, as if she was assessing my current physical and emotional state. My desperate eyes, probably bloodshot enough to look redder than Kedrik's, waited with bated blinks for the answer. Could it be possible she was still alive? Had I gotten her out soon enough? Had she survived the fall? Despite myself, I let hope rush in exactly when I didn't want it. Rachaella would probably be battered much worse than I was, but I would care for her. I would stay here forever if it meant she would be okay. The rescue party could take Elsie and some other princesses back. I knew Laomi wouldn't go unless I knocked her out and had them drag her. Or maybe they would wait for us in the woods, and when Rachaella was well enough, we could bring her. Maybe we wouldn't even need the rescue party, if Rachaella had another plan. She had *promised* me everything would be all right, and I trusted her.

At first, it didn't register when Fairy Godmother said, ". . . Yes. Yes, she is, honey."

"She is what?"

"She is dead."

As the world came crashing down around me, I kept myself held in a state of disbelief. I wiped my eyes, making sure nothing was there. There wasn't. It wouldn't do to cry over someone who wasn't even dead. Fairy Godmother was mistaken. I stared over her sparkly, black-sleeved shoulder, silence eating me alive.

"Sweetie, you need to understand, it was her time. People like Rachaella . . . don't last long in this world. It's too harsh, and they're too idealistic, too selfless."

I shook my head, making my ears ring. "But . . ." There was something wrong with what she said, but my mind was too fogged to complete my thoughts, and my voice was transient, like sifting sand.

"I'm so sorry. Grieve now, honey, while you have the time."

Fairy Godmother faded.

Tormenting thoughts violated my mind. Had Rachaella known she would die when she volunteered to gather the stragglers? What had she been thinking while dragging the unconscious StarSilver—her enemy!—through the hall? I clamped my teeth shut and clenched my fists, but nothing eased the pain. When I closed my eyes, it was even worse. The image of her limp body was burned into the back of my eyelids.

I shifted in bed, and Elsie and Arcturus awoke. One look at me sitting up, eyes open and alert, and Elsie burst into tears. Arcturus turned away, so I couldn't see his face. I was touched by their concern.

"I'm okay, guys," I said, my voice sounding like a bullfrog being strangled by an excited young child. I gathered Elsie to me, stroking her hair as she sobbed against my shoulder. Holding her seemed natural, after what we'd been through. Somehow, Elsie had become like a little sister to me, and weak as I was, I would protect her.

"Where are we?" I asked Arcturus, who still wasn't looking at me. I heard him sniffle.

"In a spare room at the prince academy, near the hospital wing," he said. "The fire was put out. You're safe." He said the last part more to himself than me. As if in pain, he finally turned his head. His eyes were glistening. Oh, geez, I hoped he wasn't expecting me to stroke his hair too.

Nothing was really "safe," I knew. There was no way I—or any royal within a hundred miles—was safe. People were injured, possibly kidnapped, and even dead. I had no doubt that the Intriguer started the fire. There was no other explanation for the evil flames that crackled their voices in my head. It reveled in chaos, drawing entertainment from sorrow and fear.

Elsie was taking gulping breaths like a drowning person, trying to calm down. If she cried much more, she *would* be a drowning person. "Last night . . ." she began.

I tensed, not wanting a replay, but I didn't interrupt her. She had to let it out. It was like telling a nightmare to someone you trusted—it didn't seem so bad after you told the story.

"Mary, Laomi's maid, ran into our sleeping quarters, yelling that there was a fire. I didn't see anything, but it smelled smoky, and I was scared. I followed everyone outside through the kitchen, and when we came around front, there were so many people running around, shouting. I saw the smoke coming out of the top floor, and the girls climbing down the tree, and I knew th-that was your balcony. Y-y-you were up there." Though she trembled, she didn't stop talking. "There were so many people around, and I wanted to help, but I didn't know how. There weren't enough buckets or water, and the ground was frozen, so I couldn't use dirt. All I could do was stand there and watch . . . Laomi was helping people down, but they were going so *slowly*, and you and R-Rachaella weren't out yet. There was no one left on the balcony, and I thought you were gone, but then you both came back and fell through the air. I ran over, and oh, oh, she was . . . it was horrible. I knew. I knew. And you were . . ."

I hugged her tighter, as if I could squeeze all the bad memories out of her. They were just as vivid for her as for me. Nothing would make them fade.

"I'm here," I murmured into her hair.

*BANG!*

Still holding Elsie, I jerked my head up as the door opened forcefully, slamming into the wall. Laomi stood in the doorway, shoulders drooping and ragged hair dragging on the ground. She looked like she had paced the school all night. Without hesitation, she joined the small party on my bed.

Asking "Are you all right?" would have been stupid, so instead I said, "Your bandage fell off. You should let me put a new one on." The wound beneath was clotted and oozing.

"I took it off. The pain keeps me sane."

Reaching over, I squeezed her good hand. Instead of pulling away like I expected her to, she clenched my hand tightly in return.

"Come with me."

Standing, I followed her, with Elsie in tow. The three of us made a fragile chain. Arcturus watched us go, but didn't follow.

Laomi guided Elsie and me through the halls that must have become familiar to her during the night. The drafty corridors and silence of our slippered steps reminded me of a tomb, as if all of us were dead and buried together under a mound of stone. Hardly anyone in the school was awake. After the previous night's ordeal, rest was much needed.

Only one room, when we passed it, had anyone awake in it. Through an open door, I spotted Ashella, seated in a chair with her head in her hands. She was sobbing. Next to her was RosaLynne's crystal vial with the blue sleeping potion. I bit my lip as we swept past.

We entered an unadorned white room with no chairs. There was only one dirty window, but the bare walls reflected plenty of light from the fresh morning sun.

She was there, lying on the only bed. She didn't look like she was sleeping; she looked dead. Rachaella normally slept with her limbs thrown about haphazardly, not neatly on her back with her hands folded. It was wrong, and I almost wanted to dump her on the floor to put her in a more natural position. If she were there, she would have laughed at my thoughts.

Her nightgown was no longer an angelic white, but smudged with soot and smoke. Framing her face was her curling dark hair, but her gray eyes were closed, never to fix me with their knowing look again.

I turned around and stared through the doorway, as if expecting another Rachaella to be there, looking at us with a raised eyebrow and playful smile. My emotions swelled. After this, I would never see her again. She was gone. Gone. Gone. I would have to memorize her face, even though I hated memorizing it the way it was, or it would fade from my memory forever. She wouldn't read from her little red Bible with the gilded pages or help me enact crazy plans to chop down a tree or give medical treatment to a wolf in the dead of night anymore.

My heart pumped poison through me, and with every thump anguish threatened to rip me apart. I wanted to throw up. I sank to the floor, releasing Laomi's and Elsie's hands and clasping my knees instead.

Without Rachaella's body before me, Fairy Godmother's announcement of her death had been abstract, questionable. But now there was no dodging reality, and I couldn't stand under the full truth of it. Grief leaked out of me as tears.

Elsie sat beside me, crying quietly.

Laomi looked vacant, as if there was no one home upstairs. "She should never have come here," she murmured. "She should never have put up with all those stupid royals. And she should *never* have gone back into the burning school."

She collapsed next to me in a heap. "It didn't have to be this way!" she shouted, pounding a fist into the stone.

The mix of my own emotions made me want to scream too. Death was unknowable from this side. There were no answers—only questions that would never receive a response until it was my own turn to die. No words were good enough to soothe Laomi's misery, or mine. There was an empty cavern in my heart where Rachaella used to be, and it hurt and itched and threatened to break the thread on my already tenuous hold on reason.

I looked at Rachaella one last time, taking in her calm, trusting face that would never know suffering again. Surely, she was she at peace. Surely, she was somewhere happier, where she didn't have to struggle so much. It wasn't fair for her to be dead. But death, from her perspective, had never been a bad thing, only a natural thing.

The three of us remained on the floor, huddled close, sharing sorrow and warmth. Laomi's fists were clenched, her eyes scorching with fury even as they dripped salty water. Elsie cried quietly while clinging to the sleeve of my dress, as if I was the anchor that kept her from blowing away.

As a survivor, I would continue to survive, and continue to be there for the sake of those around me. If all I could do was offer my presence, I would. But was that really all that I was capable of? Hanging on? Waiting for rescue? As a princess, it was surely all that was expected of me.

If Rachaella had allowed someone more qualified to help the princesses escape, she might have saved herself. But there had been no one more qualified available. No one would have stepped up to save them, and dozens more would have died.

There was no one qualified to defeat the Intriguer, either. Someone had to step up.

Even as I made my resolution, I was acutely aware that I could not do it alone. I needed all the help I could get, in any form—through unexpected allies, fortunate mishaps, or tiny signs that I might miss if I wasn't looking for them.

The two crying girls beside me didn't notice when a shadow passed over the window, and a matted head with slavering jaws dripping with blood peered into the room with its piercing yellow eye. For the first time, when I saw the wolf, I wasn't intimidated. I stared him down, communicating my thoughts through my gaze.

*Wait nearby. We need to talk.*

The eye gleamed, mildly surprised and calculating at the same time. Then the wolf licked his lips and opened his mouth in a silent laugh. He thudded off, leaving the sunshine to filter into the room once again.

Two minutes later, I was outside. I shivered in my nightgown as the wind whipped it around my legs. My slippers soaked up the snow. Cupping my hands around my nose, I breathed in and out through the filter, trying to give my throat some respite.

The wolf skulked near a boulder at the edge of the forest.

"I want you to train me," I said as soon as I was close enough for him to hear.

"Train you? For what?"

He swiped his tongue around his jaw, where there were still traces of blood. The sinew of some animal was in his teeth. Clearly, he no longer needed me to provide food.

"I want to defeat it."

The wolf cocked his head. "The Intriguer?"

"The Intriguer."

He regarded me for a few heartbeats, as if assessing my resolve. "I think we are beginning to understand each other." Pivoting, he padded away, flicking his tail for me to follow.

"We start now."

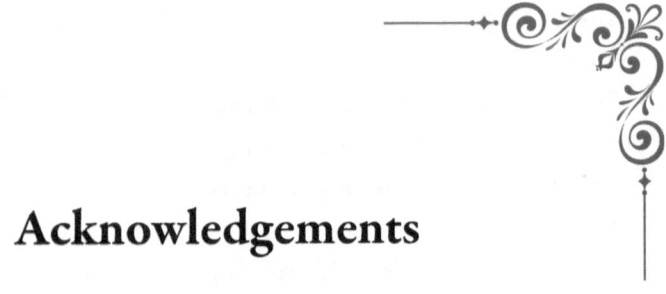

# Acknowledgements

Writing is my thing. It has been a true source of enjoyment for me since I was a kid. But there's a big difference between writing for myself and writing a story that can be understood and enjoyed by others. It's taken me over fourteen years since I started Chris's story to get to this point: my first published novel. But the book you hold wouldn't have come together in this way if it wasn't for a handful of key individuals.

My family members were my first supporters. Special thanks to my siblings for reading a bunch of early drafts and getting excited about them, even though they were far from polished.

Thanks to all my beta readers. Your feedback was incredibly helpful in figuring out what story elements worked or didn't work for the average reader.

Editors Clem Flanagan, Liz Gilbeau, and Katie Bucklein—you are truly awesome. Your feedback helped shape the flow and details of the story into a book I'm proud of, and your encouragement kept me going when nervousness and apathy threatened to paralyze me.

Rebecca Frank, I could not have imagined a more perfect cover than the one you created. I am so, so happy every time I look at it that it makes me want to cry.

I am incredibly thankful to you, reader, for taking a risk and investing in a self-published book. I hope you enjoyed it. I've been on this writing journey for a long time, and I know how Chris's story ends, but for you, it's just beginning. I hope you'll continue to follow The Forged Flower Saga as it unfolds. You might want to brace yourself for the next book. There will be dragons.

Finally, a big thank you to my husband, Corey. Even though you're not into reading (and will probably never see this), you are into supporting my dreams, which means everything to me. Love you.

# Don't miss out!

Visit the website below and you can sign up to receive emails whenever Coriana Hope publishes a new book. There's no charge and no obligation.

https://books2read.com/r/B-A-DQIR-IRRUB

**BOOKS 2 READ**

Connecting independent readers to independent writers.

# **About the Author**

Coriana Hope is just an engineer running reckless with a keyboard, typing up stories instead of equations. She grew up in rural West Virginia, where her favorite pastimes were exploring nature and reading novels. Currently, Coriana lives in Pennsylvania with her husband and pets, including a trio of cats, a fluffy white pupper, and a lovely corn snake named Dorito.

Read more at https://corianahope.wordpress.com/.